W9-AEJ-418

# FISH HAVE NO FEET

Also by Jón Kalman Stefánsson in English translation

*Heaven and Hell* (2010)
*The Sorrow of Angels* (2013)
*The Heart of Man* (2015)

*Jón Kalman Stefánsson*

# FISH HAVE NO FEET
## *A Family History*

*Translated from the Icelandic by*
*Philip Roughton*

**MACLEHOSE PRESS**
QUERCUS · LONDON

First published in the Icelandic language as *Fiskarnir hafa enga fætur* in 2013
First published in Great Britain in 2016 by

MacLehose Press
An imprint of Quercus Editions Limited
Carmelite House
50 Victoria Embankment
London EC4Y 0DZ

An Hachette UK company

Copyright © Jón Kalman Stefánsson, 2013
English translation copyright © 2016 by Philip Roughton
Edited by Andrea P. A. Belloli
Co-funded by the Creative Europe Programme

Icelandic
LITERATURE
CENTER
MIDSTÖÐ ÍSLENSKRA BÓKMENNTA

Co-funded by the
Creative Europe Programme
of the European Union

The moral right of Jón Kalman Stefánsson to be
identified as the author of this work has been
asserted in accordance with the Copyright,
Designs and Patents Act, 1988.

Philip Roughton asserts his moral right to be identified as
the translator of the work.

All rights reserved. No part of this publication
may be reproduced or transmitted in any form
or by any means, electronic or mechanical,
including photocopy, recording, or any
information storage and retrieval system,
without permission in writing from the publisher.

A CIP catalogue record for this book is available
from the British Library.

ISBN (TPB) 978 0 85705 441 8
ISBN (E-book) 978 0 85705 440 1

This book is a work of fiction. Names, characters,
businesses, organisations, places and events are
either the product of the author's imagination
or are used fictitiously. Any resemblance to
actual persons, living or dead, events or
locales is entirely coincidental.

10 9 8 7 6 5 4 3

Designed and typeset in Minion by Libanus Press, Marlborough
Printed and bound in Great Britain by Clays Ltd, St Ives plc

# Fish Have No Feet

— A FAMILY HISTORY —

# Prelude

Not even the sun could stop it, certainly not beautiful words like *rainbow* and *love*; they were useless, it was best to toss them in the bin – it all began with death.

We have so much: God, prayers, music, technology, science, new discoveries every day, more sophisticated mobile phones, more powerful telescopes, but then someone dies and you're left with nothing, you grope for God and grab hold of disappointment, grab hold of his coffee cup, the brush with her hairs still caught in it, hold on to it like a consolation, like magic, like tears, like that which never returns. What is there to say? Probably nothing, life is incomprehensible, it's unfair, but we live it anyway, can't avoid it, know no other way, life is the only certainty, that treasure, that worthless junk. After life there may be nothing. Yet it all began with death.

No, that can't be right, because death is the end, the thing that silences us, takes the pencil from us in mid-sentence, turns off the computer, makes the sun vanish, the sky burn, death is futility incarnate, we must absolutely not permit it to begin, it isn't allowed. Death is a fallacy of God's, it's what was created when God, perhaps in despair, fused cruelty and regret when it looked as if His Patience game of creation wasn't going to work. But in every death, there's a new life –

# Keflavík

*"Keflavík doesn't exist"*,
from "ICELAND"

*In Keflavík there are three cardinal directions:
the wind, the sea and eternity*

*Valueless, and nowhere*
*has the sky been measured to be*
*further from the earth*

I mean no disrespect, but Ari is the only person who could have dragged me back here, across the expanse of black lava that ground to a painful halt hundreds of years ago, naked in places, but elsewhere moss has softened and soothed it, clothed it in silence and serenity; you drive out of Reykjavík past the long aluminium smelter and into the lava, which at first is an old scream, and then moss-covered silence.

The sky is overcast, dark clouds have suffocated December's reluctant light, and the lava is like night on both sides of Reykjanes Highway. The kindled streetlamps line the highway with their steadfast light that keeps watch over you and robs you of stars and scenery, light that blocks your vision. I drive through greyness and memories, through lava and uncertain feelings, those who leave never return, yet I'm returning, not hesitantly but at 110 kilometres per hour, to Keflavík.

Keflavík, which doesn't exist.

I don't know if it has to do with that cheeky line, with the truth of the poem it's from, but going to Keflavík is always like driving out of the world and into non-existence. Yet it's a mere twenty-minute drive from the long aluminium smelter and the vapid vegetation surrounding it until the first buildings of Njarðvík rise out of the lava, cloaked in damp greyness and absurdity. This strange marvel, that life should exist here, never ceases to baffle me and Ari; that people live here, that there are quite a few buildings – there's something about it all that defies common sense, historical reasoning. Don't get me wrong, Njarðvík's buildings and houses shouldn't surprise me – I've been prepared for them. A little over halfway to Keflavík, Stapi comes into view on my right, the village that lived off the military but now dozes, half-sunk in the lava beneath Stapi, the big cliff after which the village is named, jutting into the unsettled sea like a giant fist or scream. A few kilometres further on, a large sign appears, a name that flashes slowly, like a heavy heartbeat, above the rushing vehicles:

*REYKJANESBÆR*

Flashes like a warning to passers-by, their last chance to turn back, the world ends here.

Reykjanesbær, the humdrum alias for three villages whose old names were Njarðvík, Keflavík, Hafnir.

Ten thousand people. And a quota-less sea.[1]

1 In 1984, Iceland adopted an individual, transferable fishing quota system. To begin with, fishing quotas were allotted either to communities or ships (fishing companies). Due to the presence of the U.S. military base and the economic stimulus it provided for the residents of Keflavík, the town was allotted a much smaller quota than many others (fishing being viewed as less necessary for Keflavík's economic survival). Occasionally, the owners of fishing companies would sell their quotas for large profits, sometimes to companies in other parts of the country, and so a town could lose its quota (its industry being based on the fishing companies headquartered there), and therefore the fish swimming in its seas. Hence references in this novel to a "quota-less sea". The residents of Keflavík had either lost their quota (it having been sold) or never had a viable one, and thus could not take full advantage of the sea's resources – the sea outside the town was therefore not "fish-less" but, rather, "quota-less".

I don't turn back, drive past the warning sign, drive out of the world, and am soon confronted with things that are difficult to understand; first of all the giant hangar on the old Base, for the longest time Iceland's biggest building, constructed by the American military, its size a confirmation of that country's military superiority – then the houses of Njarðvík rise from the lava, and beyond them lies Keflavík, the town where Ari and I spent important years of our lives, a place with three cardinal directions. Iceland is a harsh land, it says somewhere, "and barely habitable in bad years". Surely there's no truer statement: the mountains are foul-tempered, their slopes are deadly, the wind can be merciless, the chill breezes exasperating. A harsh land, and the Icelanders were nearly wiped out twice by hardship, disease, volcanic eruptions, and Keflavík is undoubtedly the most dubious place in the entire country. Compared to Keflavík, both Biskupstungur and the Skagafjörður countryside seem almost paradisical, reflecting the tenderness of lands much further south. If the fishing failed, there was little else to save us; brackish, gale-force winds pounded the population, life-giving rainwater vanished along with hope into the lava, and nowhere has the sky been measured to be further from the earth than here. "Valueless," says the eighteenth-century *Land Register* by Árni Magnússon and Páll Vídalín, the first comprehensive description of Keflavík, written with the impartiality of scientists.[2] They had no time for poetry, emotion, condemnation; these were superseded by perspicacity and candour: "No ships linger here; the landings are poor. No

2   *Land Register* (Icelandic: *Jarðabók*): The famous manuscript collector Árni Magnússon (1663–1730) and the lawman Páll Vídalín (1667–1727) conducted a land survey of Iceland in 1702–12 at the request of the Danish king, resulting in the creation of a census (1703) and the *Land Register* (1714).

meadows for grazing, the outer pastures in better shape but the water supply as poor as can be summer and winter. The path to the church long and very often impassable in winter. Nowhere in the entire country do folk dwell as close to death."

Ari and I left Keflavík in the late 1980s, boarded a bus with the things that mattered to us – clothing, memories, books, record albums – and never looked back. The bus driver, a respectable old man with silvery-grey hair, endowed with a good-natured serenity, slipped a tape into the cassette player at the start of the journey and turned the volume up, having become partially deaf, and all the way to Reykjavík, Wham! blasted over us like a cruel punishment. We made our way slowly out of Keflavík, past the harbour, alongside the Base with its fighter jets and six thousand Americans, all of whom are gone now, having left several years ago, taking with them their weapons and death, employment and hamburgers, radio station and dance clubs, leaving nothing but abandoned buildings and unemployment.

The bus drove through Njarðvík and out onto Reykjanes Highway, at that time a narrow, slow road, at least an hour's drive to Reykjavík, the driver played Wham!'s "Wake Me Up Before You Go-Go" three times along the way, his good-natured serenity having been transformed into ruthlessness.

"I'm pleased to be visiting the blackest place in the country," said the President of Iceland during his visit to Keflavík in September 1944, three months after the founding of the Icelandic Republic, the first words spoken by our President on his one and only official visit to Keflavík. The blackest place – how was it possible for anyone to live here before the arrival of the military, the era of mechanisation?

Easy answer – it simply wasn't possible.

"Nowhere in all of Iceland do people live as close to death."
The unrelenting wind seems to be able to blow from two directions at once, gusts bearing salt and sand took turns lashing us, the sky so distant that our prayers only ever made it halfway there, then dropped like dead birds or changed into hail, the drinking water as salty as the sea. This place isn't fit for habitation; everything is against it: common sense, the wind, the lava. Still, we've lived here all these years, all these centuries, stubborn as the lava, silent within history as the moss that grows over rock and changes it into soil, someone should stuff us, pin medals on us, write a book about us.

Us?

Of course, Ari and I aren't from here – wherever we might have come from – not really; we moved here when we were twelve, and then left, were gone, ten years later, after completing our obligatory schooling, working in construction, saltfish- and stockfish-production in Keflavík and Sandgerði, three years salting and wind-drying fish, completed high school, came here as children, left as something else. We're not from here at all, but why does my heart pound as the car approaches Njarðvík, the village that will always look like a warm-up act for Keflavík, like the band no-one's heard of, and which has nothing in it worth mentioning but the Stapi community centre? A new residential area has grown up where once a desolate chain of hills extended in the direction of the Base, mostly large, single-family residences, some of them towering over the road like lives that people forgot to live. Below the houses are stretches of low hedges and rows of spindly trees staked tightly as if to prevent them from fleeing.

The car crawls across the invisible line separating Njarðvík and Keflavík. My heart is pounding, that ridiculous muscle, mysterious rocket, the abode of eternal childhood, and I come to London Circle, the town's first roundabout, the next being New York Circle. Feeling a bit embarrassed by this attempt on the part of Keflavík's residents to raise themselves up or escape their own history, I exit the second roundabout and park by one of Keflavík's countless fast-food vans. From there I have a good view over the harbour, its gaping vacuity and hopelessness, as if a god had lost and then forgotten it. Three old fishermen stand at the end of the pier where they have a better view of the sea, their hands dangling at their sides, empty, unoccupied, and watch the only fishing boat that will dock today. I take my binoculars from the car, raise them to my eyes, there's a hint of pain or anxiety in the fishermen's faces – as if they've gone down to the pier to check whether their lost years have been caught in the nets.

### *This sorrow, this crushed heart, these seagulls and Jonni's Thunderburgers*

Ari texted Iceland and me goodbye nearly two years ago: "It's sometimes hard to breathe in small communities, the stuffiness can be stifling, I'm leaving before I suffocate." An excellent reason to leave. To be able to love Iceland, you've got to get away sometimes.

The stuffiness of a small community can be oppressive, and if you don't get enough oxygen, you think less, or on a smaller scale; your world view becomes more egocentric and thereby more ignoble. Ari is right, our society suffers from stuffiness, although the mountains ought to be able to teach us to think, rising high, as they do, into the air to meet the sky, there to seek oxygen and new perspectives, while we waste away between tussocks. Don't get me wrong – the tussocks are important, they're sleeping dogs, the country's thoughts, the silence that we miss. The tussocks are Iceland, Ari says frequently, yet again in an e-mail a week ago, adding, "My nostalgia for tussocks is doing me in. The Danes have neither tussocks nor mountains, which is unforgivable of them." Nothing further; just the date and time, then a smiley emoticon. His way of letting me know that he was on his way; he would never say such things outright. Ari's maternal ancestors were on the sentimental side, but from around the age of six, he was raised by a stony man from Strandir and an emotionally confused Easterner. Such a combination could never turn out well; it was bound to be cursed by sorrow, numberless hard times, restless nights. And indeed it was, as will be obvious from what follows, in a number of different ways. It can't be avoided; once you start writing, you've got to tell the whole story – that's the first commandment, the foundation stone. That's why I knew that the date and time meant that Ari was on his way home; he would land at Miðnesheiði on that day, at that time, and I replied immediately, using an expression from our younger days, when the world looked completely different, Then we'll drink the spoils of Duty Free together; where will you be staying? The answer was unexpected: The Flight Hotel in Keflavík.

Ari's secret code regarding his homecoming was obvious, perhaps, not requiring an expert to decipher it, although his parting words of two years before ("It's sometimes hard to breathe in a small community") might not have been as easy for others to interpret as for me, because their real meaning went something like this: "Sorrow is driving me hence, it is crushing my heart, devastating it. What is a person with a ruined heart? I'm leaving this place to save myself."

Sorrow.

Or, what snapped so abruptly, so unexpectedly, so frightfully, in his life, and hers, and their three children's. Or, what seemed to snap abruptly and unexpectedly. His arm swept like a scream across the kitchen table, and nothing was ever the same again. *Nothing*. It's a difficult word.

Ari drove himself away. Or, life drove him away, daily life, what remained unresolved, what he'd avoided dealing with, along with the tiny details that accumulate without us noticing them, too preoccupied, I guess, too careless, too cowardly, perhaps a bit of all of these. First his arm swept like a scream across the kitchen table, then, a little later, came the emptiness that regret – *flower* and *dagger* in the same word – filled slowly but surely.

Now he's coming back, his heart crushed, after two years in Denmark, which, strictly speaking, can't always be considered a foreign country.

I'm still standing above the harbour in Keflavík, watching the day's only boat sail in with its catch. The old fishermen have shoved their hands in their pockets, they've started chatting, and what I thought I saw in their faces has vanished like a misunderstanding; they laugh, several gulls follow the boat but indifferently somehow, as if they've also lost faith in seamanship and Keflavík's fishing industry, circling above the ship as if just for show. Raising my binoculars, I look at the gulls, whose expressions look almost sheepish, which is probably nonsense, gulls don't have expressions, except for the one associated with greed and a fear of death – they're probably libertarians, Ari might add. I'm startled by a car horn honking suddenly close by; five cars, two S.U.V.s, a

20

big pickup and two family cars are waiting to place their orders at the hot-dog-and-hamburger van, which has *Jonni's Thunderburgers!* written in Icelandic on a big, shiny aluminium sign on its roof and, beneath that, in English, or perhaps American, in the same-size lettering. Habit, I suppose; the effect of fifty years of proximity to the American military. Glancing towards the cars, I find myself raising the binoculars to my eyes. One of the car's drivers honks his horn again, perhaps out of boredom, perhaps to protest life, the situation here in Suðurnes, the unemployment, the hopeless-ness, the fishing quota gone, the military gone, perhaps honks out of impatience for an aluminium smelter in Helguvík or the American waste-disposal facility that Mayor Sigurjón is trying to have built here, honks out of impatience for security, for happi-ness, honks because his sex drive has dwindled, or, in contrast, refuses to dwindle; or honks simply because he's impatient for his order, it's undoubtedly tough to wait hungrily for one of Jonni's Thunderburgers. Unless he's honking at me because I'm standing here looking at the harbour, looking at this monument of a better time when the harbour had a role, was the heart of the town, was its purpose, the confirmation of its importance, as well as an unbreakable connection with the country's history and essence, as well as a valuable counterweight to the military, the impact it had on the lives and behaviour of the residents of Keflavík. I return to my car, know that folk here distrust people without cars, who frequently turn out to be Communists and destitute drunks. I look over my shoulder, the seagulls are gone, where they were is now a darkening sky, the day has begun to sink into the sea that has kept Keflavík and the surrounding area alive, a prerequisite for and preserver of life, sinks into the sea along with the winter sun glowing red with fatigue, sinks with seagulls, the honking of

21

car horns, Jonni's Thunderburgers, sinks into the generous sea, to all the fish that swim there safe from the people of Keflavík, most of whose ships were sold off after the quota was lost, it's nearly a quota-less town, justice and equality having long since abandoned it, the blackest place in the country, we look out of the kitchen or living-room windows, mutter, There's the sea, so it's that big is it?, before drawing the curtains, for who wants to have something that vast reminding them of better days, days of activity, when it was easy to walk tall, reminding them of having consented in silence to the sea's fish stocks being converted into the bank accounts of fishing moguls and their descendants, to the gaping cod, the gleaming herring, becoming their blood, to the sea being privatised – we draw the curtains quick as a flash because it's tough to have a sea teeming with fish right there before our eyes but to be prevented from fishing, to have a fish-processing company but nothing to process.

I can't see the seagulls or the old fishermen; they vanished along with the day, perhaps sank into the sea with the sun, the seagulls, the honking of car horns. I point my binoculars at the sky, where hopefully there's no quota system, through the darkening air, eastwards, whence Ari's plane will come. Pilot, fly carefully with this cargo, with this sorrow, with this crushed heart.

### Ten tips to stop crying

Seen from above, from the perspective of the gods, the mountains are neither threatening nor dizzyingly beautiful, but are violet herbs, and the winter's snow has changed them into ice-cream blossoms, into ancient roses given to the sky above Iceland, and to the plane where Ari sits in window seat 19A, his damaged heart beating with an intensity of which he feels ashamed, his heart that has been beating that way since the clouds suddenly parted to reveal Iceland, with its ancient roses, glaciers and the black coast of the south. Ari rubs his chest as if to calm his heart, that little creature that can treat us so badly, shuts his eyes to get a grip on the feeling that's assaulting him, frenzied memories, unbearable regret, something he does not understand. The woman next to him, short and plump, squinting behind thick spectacles, nearly finished with her second crisp packet of the journey, grabs another handful, speaks non-stop to the man in the aisle seat, a bruiser with wide lips and stout hands, paws, shovels that rub his knees. The bruiser has hardly said anything, grunted a few times, has eaten nothing, just rubbed his knees, sometimes vigorously, as if to calm himself through the woman's blabbing. He would kill her if the flight were much longer, Ari thought about halfway through it, over the Faeroe Islands; eighteen green rocks out in the middle of the Atlantic. Otherwise, he paid no attention to the two of them, tried to ignore them, but the smell of crisps assailed him every time the woman grabbed a fresh handful. Ari had stuck headphones over his ears as soon as the plane had climbed above the clouds and birds, burning fuel in its struggle against the heavy pull of the earth's gravity, the force that holds us to its surface and the Moon in its place, an invisible force we feel every second of our lives, asleep and awake, which is the way it is with all the major forces in this world of extremes and disappointments, beauty and mundanity: love, jealousy, hatred, inspiration, greed, ambition, compassion. They're invisible, don't show up on the most sensitive of meters and are thus always underestimated, never mentioned in reports or minutes of meetings. The forces that drive us onwards, that scatter and unite us. "Don't know if I saw you if I would kiss

23

you or kill you," sang Bob Dylan as the flatness of Denmark disappeared from view to be replaced by the ocean, which is never still and is no less filled with extremes than human beings. Then clouds blocked the view. Sometimes, we seek out pain. Regret. And plunge into our wounds. We've lost our vitality, and it seems increasingly complicated to exist, as if life is becoming ever harder to deal with. We take tranquillisers, stimulants, sedatives in order to endure everyday existence. The years pass, our purpose in life is ambiguous, our understanding vague, we put on weight, our nerves grow dull and worn, we're eternally plagued by dissatisfaction, unfulfilled desire. We yearn for a solution, yearn for clarity, but don't have the time, don't have the composure, don't have the stamina to search for it and, instead, gratefully gulp down easy solutions, fast food, hasty sex; whatever promises a quick fix – we live in an era of speed. Self-help manuals promise a better life, a richer existence; ten tips to stop drinking, gaining weight, missing someone, being afraid, ten tips for living, rarely more than ten, we're barely able to handle more, ten like our fingers, like the Commandments. Ten tips for living. I shouldn't be listening to this fucking song, he thought, above clouds and ocean, above eighteen green rocks, but he did anyway, four times, five times, whether he would kiss her or kill her when he saw her next. Explore the wound, it says in *Ten Tips for Healing a Broken Heart*, that's the way to overcome it. Ari is familiar with this book, was its editor at the company that published it in Denmark, the book sold 160,000 copies in the first five months, there are a lot of broken hearts – the papers here in Iceland jumped on this news and, in the typical Icelandic manner of exaggerating an Icelander's achievement, proclaimed, *Icelandic publisher scores a victory on the Danish book market!*

I'm inside the wound, he thinks, discreetly brushing crisp crumbs off his thighs and listening to Dylan's heartbreak. That's the way of the world: the young Dylan sang with cutting fervour about revolution, new times, about changes, but now, all these decades later, he sings almost exclusively about broken hearts, regret, about agonising uncertainty. Perhaps it's easier to change the world than to mend broken hearts, easier to invoke new times than to cope with loneliness.

Ari's life was always supposed to have been a journey among mountains, a road to the stars, to maturity, but here he is, nearly fifty years old, with a huge interest in religion, music, books, the ability to calculate the volume of a sphere, a good knowledge of history and the history of football, yet in fact he knows nothing; he doesn't feel at home anywhere, is disorientated as if lost, is plagued by regret and longing for his grown children and the woman he lived with for more than twenty years, and yet, despite missing them almost more than he can bear, he hasn't found the strength to return home, as if something is both holding him back and feeding his overwhelming longing. Holding him back – until he received an unexpected e-mail from his father, Jakob. Unexpected due to its content but also because their relationship, never close, had been nonexistent over the previous two years. The e-mail consisted of two sentences:

"Well, my boy, that's about it, time to kick the bucket, damned cancer. Look out for a package from me. :-)"

Ari didn't take this too seriously. It wasn't the first time his father had written that way, saying that his death was imminent – and who puts a smiley emoticon at the end of such an announcement, if it's really true? Yet he knew that something was going on, not least because just a few weeks earlier, he'd received a letter from his stepmother – something far more unexpected, almost as unexpected as being spoken to by the Moon in broad daylight. The letter, which Ari had yet to read to the end, seemed unusually frank, and was accompanied by a newspaper clipping, an article written by Sigríður Egilsdóttir – Sigga – a woman here whom Ari and I had known quite well. Ari started to read the letter but then decided almost immediately not to give it or the article another thought for the time being, decided to save it for later, like so many other things, to set it aside and let the passing days bury it, let it fall into oblivion. His stepmother and father had separated a long time ago, she apparently hadn't seen him for over a year but had heard a few things that caused concern, just so Ari was aware. He'd thought automatically, It's the drink, Dad's on the bottle again, I'm not going after him for that, not a chance, and he sunk back into his work, putting the final touches on *Ten Tips for Grasping the Meaning of Life*. Then the e-mail turned up, clearly out of the ordinary, so he rang his father, but there was no answer. This startled him, undeniably; no answer, what does that mean? A minute later, a text from his father appeared in his inbox: "Everything's fine – wait for the package." Which arrived two days later in the post, that is, the old-style mail, which is still delivered as quickly as you like on two legs in cities and towns, like a friendly memory of bygone times – a little package for Ari. Inside were two envelopes; opening one, Ari pulled out a photograph of his parents, obviously an old photo because Ari's mother died more than forty years ago. She died and changed into absence. Changed into a black hole. Changed into a wound that was never mentioned: a wound that is never mentioned, never nursed, becomes, over time, like a deep-seated, incurable ulcer.

His parents are sitting close together. He has his arm around her, she is leaning into him, they're both smiling and looking straight at the camera. For some reason Ari had never seen this photo before, or perhaps had never got to see it, and it surprised him. But it wasn't a joyful surprise; much more like a blow, a shock. All he could do was stare at the photo, at that bygone moment. Numbly. It made him feel awful without understanding why. And then it dawned on him: they actually looked happy. He couldn't recall them ever sharing a happy moment. It was him, Ari, and his mother. The two of them, and then his father, Jakob. That's how it was in his memory. His father – had he ever been so young, so smiling, so affectionate?

Second question: Why is he sending Ari this photo now and, on top of that, linking it to his own possible death? Third question: Why is it only now that Ari gets to see the photo, forty-four years after *her* death?

The package had been waiting for Ari when he'd come home from work at the publishing company where he'd been employed as an editor for more than a year, under the direction of an old friend of ours; he'd come home late, towards dinnertime, he never hurried back to his three-bedroom flat in Østerbro, why should he do so, anyway, nothing awaited him there but the three strings of his instrument: loneliness, regret, longing. He'd torn open the package, opened one of the envelopes, and everything inside him was turned on its head. He sat and stared at the photo as the evening darkened outside and lit the neighbours' televisions, lit the lamps above their reading chairs. He thought of nothing, nothing solid, he couldn't, his thoughts and feelings darted about uncontrollably inside him, crashed into each other causing showers of sparks. He was relieved to be far away from his father as he looked at the photo, relieved that there was an entire ocean between them.

27

They'd probably never looked at photos of her together, never dared to; the idea would never have crossed their minds.

He just stared.

As if in a trance.

A car screamed in the night, the wail of a siren cut through the darkening sky.

At first he stared almost exclusively at his mother, her smile, her eyes, blue-grey, big, gleaming as if, just then, they'd attracted all the light of the world, sun and stars, moonlight and auroras, eyes that had vanished long ago, that had been erased, extinguished, didn't exist, any more than she herself existed, her thoughts, facial expressions, that mischievous twinkle, her embrace, how can something so big vanish without the world tipping over, without the earth wobbling on its axis and losing its grip on the Moon? Ari managed to forget, or rule out, the fact that his father was also in the photo until an ambulance siren, a siren resembling a cry of despair, ripped through the night and sundered his thoughts, and then he saw his father, then he remembered him. Ari saw that they were happy – perhaps precisely because they were together. He listened as the ambulance's invocation faded away and felt his spiteful jealousy of his father well up and fill the entire world. He stared at his father and felt only hatred, pure, crystalline hatred. Looked him in the eye and thought, I hope you die.

His downstairs neighbour laughed.

By means of this photo, it was as if Ari's father had stolen his mother from him. As if he'd sent the photo to say, Look, we were happy, look at how she's leaning against my shoulder, look at how she's smiling, look, the only thing we needed was each other, and soon I'm going to die and then I'll go to her, look, it's just the two of us, she and I. Look, you're not in the photo, you're not part of the happiness. You're outside it. She's mine.

Getting to his feet, Ari downed half a bottle of whisky.

Great, he thought, so mature. And drank.

Didn't show up for work the next day, that's O.K., *Ten Tips for Grasping the Meaning of Life* was at the printer's, he deserved a day off. Awoke hung over. Looked at the photo as he ate breakfast, feeling much better, the hatred gone, only shame remaining. And perhaps a little jealousy, or a touch more than a little, it lurked somewhere inside him, he couldn't help himself. Now, though, he could rejoice in their happiness, knowing that hard times would assault them: daily life, disappointment, alcohol, impetuousness, and then her illness, death's murky message.

It wasn't until that morning's first cup of coffee that Ari remembered the other envelope in the package, quickly tore it open and cursed with astonishment when he pulled out a framed certificate of recognition awarded to his paternal grandfather Oddur. A pale yellow, stylishly penned document in a gilded frame, the certificate had always hung in a place of honour in the living room, first in the Safamýri neighbourhood of Reykjavík, then in the three places where his father had lived in Keflavík, in recognition of Oddur Jónsson, ship-owner and captain. It had hung in its place of honour, the first thing visitors saw, the glass well polished, yet was never discussed except when his father was drunk, after sitting in the living room for a long time, alone, drinking, listening to Megas and Johnny Cash.[3] He would call out to Ari, invite him in a tender but slurred drinker's voice to have a seat, put on his

3   Megas: The pseudonym of Magnús Þór Jónsson (b. 1945), a well-known and at one time controversial Icelandic writer and musician, considered the father of Icelandic punk.

specs and read him the text. His voice often trembled, as if he were suffering emotional turmoil, as Ari stared at the floor. For some reason this document was the only thing that Jakob had left of his father, and it was undoubtedly the first thing he would have saved had his flat been on fire. Yet now he has posted it to Ari in Denmark. With no explanation. "Be prepared to receive a package."

Looking from the certificate to the photo and back again, Ari drank coffee, cup after cup; outside his window the big city roared; he went on the Internet, booked a flight home, one way, picked up the phone, called our friend the publisher, told him he was going home to Iceland for good, repeated that difficult word *home*, emphasised it. Then he started packing, and now he was on a plane, high above the ocean and clouds. He pulls his bag out from under his seat, takes out the certificate, looks at the text, which he knows by heart, has known since childhood, and recites it silently:

*IN RECOGNITION OF ODDUR JÓNSSON, SHIP-OWNER AND CAPTAIN.*
*ON THIS OUR FIRST OFFICIAL CELEBRATION . . .*

Just then, the woman beside him plunges her hand into the half-empty packet of crisps, the smell gushes up, Ari looks out of the window, sees the clouds part, the plane has begun its descent, abandoned the upper reaches, the vestibule of Heaven, and Iceland appears with its ancient roses. Ari stops reading, shuts his eyes and is no longer sitting in an airplane but on a green bus, nearly forty years ago, a bus crawling slowly westwards, leaving a long plume of dust in its wake, long before the days of paved roads, crawls along, the gear box grating regularly as the bus struggles up hills, its driver's jaws clenched as if he himself were making the effort, a half-dead cigarette between his lips, and then Baula mountain rises on the right, the angels' scenic overlook from where they have a panoramic view of the west of Iceland, measure joy and laughter and death and report the news to Heaven. Ari and I are sitting near the front of the bus, have fought motion sickness for four hours, our eyes have drunk in the springs, multi-coloured hayfields and meadows of withered grass, but when the bus finally runs like a green celebration, a green exclamation, down the slope of Brattabrekka and the farmland below greets our eyes, Mount Bátsfell in the middle, our hearts beat so eagerly that our eyes tremble.

They are trembling like that now, as he opens them again in window seat 19A, and the ancient roses, the white glaciers and the dynamic black coastline appear; he opens his eyes and it's as if his heart crashes in his chest. He struggles for breath, emotion overwhelms him, he drops the certificate on the floor, reaches for the book in the seat pocket in front of him only to put it back again, presses the call button only to apologise, he blinks, looks out though he can barely see anything, his sight blurred by salty tears. When he more or less regains his composure, the woman leans over to pick up the certificate and hands it to him, stroking the back of Ari's hand as she does so, her fingers greasy from the crisps, and says in a low voice, in English, Those who feel no pain or emotion in life have cold hearts and have never lived – which is why you must be grateful for your tears.

*Honour and glory*

*In recognition of Oddur Jónsson,*
*ship-owner and captain*

On this our first official celebration of Sailors' Day here in Neskaupstaður, we are delighted to have the opportunity to declare our admiration and gratitude for your thirty years of vigorous struggle and initiative in our fjord's fishing industry. On this festive occasion, we are united in the wish that the banner you raised and bore so splendidly may forever inspire members of our profession to achieve great deeds that will never fade from memory, you, the honour and glory of Norðfjörður and its residents, indeed the entire profession of Icelandic fishermen.

NESKAUPSTAÐUR, JUNE 7, 1944
FISHERMEN'S COUNCIL OF NESKAUPSTAÐUR

# Norðfjörður

— PAST —

Norðfjörður is short, almost as short as a hesitation, surrounded by mountains just over a thousand metres high, some with razor-sharp crests and passes shaped like screams. In the past, no-one could get here in the winter due to the snow and storms except for death and, now and then, an exhausted postman. The valley lying inland from the fjord is long and lovely, green as the kingdom of Heaven in summer, with murmuring brooks, the buzzing of flies, the music of heath-birds, and is called Snædalur, "Snow Valley", because so much snow can accumulate there that houses and lives vanish. The fjord itself is as short as a hesitation, as something that has barely begun, and is sheltered by the tremendous power of Nípa, the mountain that halts storms and calms the world: the nights can be so silent and still that the fjord fills with angels, the air with the gentle rustle of angels' wings. Then it's as if no-one will ever die again.

Norðfjörður is one of three fjords that penetrate the coast at Norðfjörður Bay, and there was nothing to suggest, far back in the past, that a village would rise here, let alone a town with fifteen hundred inhabitants. The town stands on a stony spot with loose soil, cut extensively by the mountain's streams, and in the winter avalanches fall and bury houses built in the wrong places, perhaps too high up on the mountain's flanks, with their white death. Towards the end of the nineteenth century, the place had around thirty houses sheltering just under a hundred people who lived by fishing, a few sheep, perhaps a cow, and a merchant who foresaw a rather meagre existence for himself. In 1898, the great naturalist Bjarni Sæmundsson did research for the Danish governor on fishing in the Eastfjords and wrote a detailed report that he published in the journal *Andvari* the following year.[4] His report states that conditions in Norðfjörður were highly favourable for fishing "both because of its short length, which renders it unnecessary to row great distances for good catches unless the destination is the open ocean, and also because it is both well sheltered from rough seas and rich in fish, thanks to the promontory of Horn, which extends so far northwards". Following the publication of this report, the settlement grew quickly in both population and size, and just a few years later had become a village with a vigorous fishing industry. The history of the village of Nes, later the town of Neskaupstaður, the fate of the people who lived and died there, their kisses and stinging rebukes, their embraces and unquenchable tears, and, at the same time, Ari's entire history, owe their existence to four lines by Bjarni the naturalist published in the journal *Andvari*. Life grows out of words, but death dwells in silence. This is why we must continue to write, to narrate, to mutter verses and curses, and thereby hold death at bay for a while.

## *It began with a stormy night and death – and then she goes to him*

Oddur grew up on the shore of the village of Nes, among ancient mountains and passes shaped like threats. Like most houses in the

4   Bjarni Sæmundsson (1867–1940) was an Icelandic naturalist and teacher who wrote the first textbooks in Icelandic on the natural sciences; they remained in use well beyond his death. He is also renowned for his studies in ichthyology, including descriptions of fish species in Icelandic waters.

village, his parents' place stood a stone's throw from the water's edge with only a narrow path separating them and, below it, the sheds where the fishermen stored their equipment, and sometimes saltfish. The sheds were so near the sea that in bad weather, hazy light, they seemed to be transformed into boats. Oddur grew up on the shore of the village of Nes but was born in Vinavík, "Bay of Friends", which is just a tad to the south and was named by a woman in the early tenth century who witnessed two friends, both in love with her, fight to the death on the sandy beach, wrecked by drink, jealousy and the poison that trickles incessantly from it. The name Vinavík she chose either out of guilt, for having, by her existence, done the two men in, or purely to stave off bad luck. Oddur's forefathers had lived for many generations in Vinavík, which is exposed to the sea and defenceless against the fury of the elements, but from there it is only a short hop to generous fishing banks, besides which, it has a lovely, gentle-natured sandy beach, horseshoe-shaped, a bit like a beautiful sigh of the sea. His mother, Ingiríður, was from Norðfjörður, and her childhood home tugged at her constantly until she managed to convince her husband Jón to move, uproot himself from the bay of his forefathers. They brought with them a considerable quantity of timber to use to build a house, procured from an English ship that had run aground on a skerry just off the coast during a storm, only two of the crewmembers survived and made it with enormous difficulty to a farm at the tip of Reyðarfjörður, pushing their way through snow, cold, howling wind, without any idea of where they were, where they were heading, driven by the wind, it determined their course, made it by the skin of their teeth to the farm. Injured, battered by the elements, they remained there for a few weeks while regaining most of their strength, enough to make it possible to put them aboard another English ship, although it turned out, some time later, that one of the two had impregnated an unmarried milkmaid in her thirties, a woman who'd had a hard life, one of those people against whom fate seems to hold a grudge, yet who finally, through her relations with the Englishman, came to know the ephemeral bliss of sex and gave birth to a healthy baby boy nine months later. He turned out to be a first-rate fellow, his mother's sun and moon. Did this mean that the man's shipmates had to drown in order for a new life to be born, in order for the unfortunate milkmaid to experience bliss; is that how fate works?

The ship itself had remained surprisingly intact on the skerry. The storm might have managed to drown close to twenty sailors, but it hadn't managed to bash the ship to bits; it hung off the skerry, which had torn a huge hole in its keel, and at the next low tide, Jón was able to begin harvesting its timber at his ease, taking frequent breaks, and to stack it tidily against the old turf farm-house in Vinavík, having resolved to use it to build a new home. Which he then did, not in the bay of his forefathers, as planned, but up north in Norðfjörður. His brother-in-law joined forces with his sister and together they convinced Jón that better opportunities existed in Norðfjörður, and now, unexpectedly, he'd happened upon the timber to build himself a house on a patch of land offered to him by his brother-in-law. Jón agreed, barely resisting, perhaps because he wasn't entirely free of superstition, and something told him that the stranding of the English ship was a message from destiny, a sign that now everything would change and a new chapter would begin. It was thus this shipwreck, the drowning of all those sailors, that caused the wheel of destiny to turn, which it continues to do as the woman in the airplane hands Ari the certificate of recognition, honour and glory, a full century later. A stormy night and death are thus the beginning, the cause, the reason why we bring you this story. The English sailors had to encounter a storm far from home, had to run aground on a skerry that tore open the keel of their ship, making it easier for the sea to snatch them away, one after another, It was so dark that I couldn't see them, said the sailor to the unmarried milkmaid, whispering in the dark while everyone was asleep, wincing from his injuries and memories, she came to him with her misfortune, convinced of her ugliness but having good hands, healing hands, and he told her everything. Naturally she understood little, knowing only a few words in English, but she understood his tears, the melancholy in his voice. Later she had the feeling that he'd been telling her about the shipwreck: I couldn't see them, but I could hear them. In the darkness they were transformed into a cry snatched away by the sea.

But it was first-rate timber.

Jón preferred to transport it by land, even though it would take much more time to traverse mountain passes, steep, stony paths, but the old sayings, which Jón always heeded, specified that timber from sunken ships or from wrecks whose crews had drowned should not return to sea and could absolutely not, under any circumstances, be used to build boats or ships; such a thing would surely augur ill; any ship built of such timber would be doomed, at the earliest opportunity the drowned sailors would drag it down to the bottom of the sea. This was why it was out of the question to transport the timber by water. Which Jón did in the end, however, bending, as so often before, to the will of his wife and shuttling the timber northwards in several trips. They loaded the boat with as much timber as they thought it could hold and put to sea when there was little risk of storms, she at the helm, he so terrified of bad luck and curses, that the sea floor would angrily demand its due, that he just sat there, rigid, utterly useless, until they approached the sparsely populated village of Nes, when he tore himself free of his fear and took the helm. There aren't many men in this world of ours who dare to admit their fears. The house was built, a nice solid house, a few metres above the shore. The window in Oddur's room and that of his two brothers faced the sea, and he fell asleep every evening to the sound of the waves ceaselessly lapping the shore and awoke every morning to the same music. The sea spoke to him, composed its lullabies in the evening to rock him to sleep, woke him with its cheerful babble in the mornings, it's easier to be happy if you live by the sea. Oddur always spoke of the sea as if it were a friend and soulmate, built his first boat when he was four years old, sixteen centimetres long, got his mother to carve a little man, tied him to the mast, a nail, and launched the ship from its landing place. You're a born sailor, his mother often told him, as if she were awarding him a medal. It was no surprise when he and his childhood friend, Tryggvi, who lived nearby, a comely and energetic but dreamy boy, made plans to start their own fishing company, just ten years old, borrowing a dinghy and receiving permission to dawdle near the shore – No further out, said the adults; clear instructions. But human speech dulls quickly at sea, and parents' orders lose their potency when you're on a boat, sailing the waves.

They soon ignored the prohibition, the instructions, the sea called to them, enticed them, and they rowed further out, where the fishing was better, encountering waves that rose from greater depths, saw how they could suddenly darken, saw something in them that looked like death and were frightened, yet they continued to row further out, they couldn't help it, were likely spellbound.

44

Their daring grew in proportion to their experience, and, by the following summer, they considered themselves fully fledged sailors. One time that autumn, however, they rowed so far out that they were shocked to see how far they were from land, feeling almost as if it had rejected them, while all around them the waves darkened, grew. It seemed unlikely that they would ever make it back. They glanced at each other as if to say goodbye, as if life were over, having barely begun. For a long time they sat as if glued to their seats, staring, with lumps in their throats, fear like knives in their hearts, both wanted to give in and weep, weep for never seeing their parents or siblings again, for being just eleven years old, for how life is capable of so much cruelty, and Tryggvi gave in, he wept, or rather whimpered, being either weaker than his friend or having more capacity for remorse, feeling its sting more sharply, before Oddur said, trying to make his voice deeper than it really was, We're rowing back to shore. And that's what they did. Managed to row all the way back, nearly exhausting themselves, dragged themselves onto the shore, wanting so much to go straight home, drink hot chocolate, crawl into bed, be hugged, but that was out of the question, they'd made a good haul of fish and immediately began to gut them, soon took to whistling as if nothing untoward had occurred. Their legs may have been trembling a bit, but they cleaned their catch, and Tryggvi's sister, Margrét, came down to the beach and helped them, as usual, so deft and precise with a knife, a year older than them, that Oddur had trouble keeping his eyes off her, as if he'd never seen her before, hadn't been aware of her briskness, had never given a thought to her bearing, how she raised her head every now and then, and for some reason he began thinking of wings. They'd cleaned fish together for two summers, it was autumn, yet it was only now that he truly saw her. It may have been his experience at sea, the death in the waves, the colour of the end, that changed him; his newly acquired experience had made him a man; was this why he now saw Margrét for the first time? He found it so difficult to take his eyes off her that his attention wandered and he cut his left arm, drawing blood. A deep cut. First the blood tinged his knife, and then the fish he was standing over. Oddur put down his knife and watched the blood flow for a short time, perhaps thinking, So that's how I look inside, but then he looked straight at Margrét. They gazed into each other's eyes, the blood flowed, it was September, the jagged mountains had turned white over-night, though the snow was so shallow that it could not blunt the sharp crests, the black spite. You two finish cleaning the catch, said Oddur finally, I need to get home to Mother, he added, before walking slowly away, composed yet upset with himself for having said "to Mother", there was no dignity in it, as the blood continued to drip from his arm, though that was at least something. Margrét watched until he was out of sight, then reached down for a fish, straightened up, looked at her brother and announced, He's going to be my husband. But we're only eleven, said Tryggvi, angrily, in fact, as if to remind her that, despite everything, they were just children. That may be, she said, but I'm almost twelve, to which Tryggvi had no answer, naturally, so he went back to cleaning fish but with a feeling of sadness, as if he'd just been deprived of his childhood.

The following spring, she was sent to Canada.

Her maternal aunt, who had moved there fifteen years earlier, had died, leaving a husband and four small children, the eldest seven years old, and Margrét is sent in haste to look after them, herself

46

only twelve – and only returns eight years later. She travels east aboard the coastal ship from Reykjavík. Her family meets her at the shore, Oddur standing a stone's throw away. They'd exchanged no letters, or even goodbyes, though Tryggvi had mentioned him in his numerous letters, as if inadvertently, as asides, and had felt rather self-important delivering reports about her to Oddur, most often when they were at sea, at first just the two of them in a little boat, but this changed when they were seventeen and Oddur was put in charge of a 14-ton boat, thereby becoming the youngest skipper in the Eastfjords; Tryggvi gave him news of Margrét, often as if he were talking to himself, to empty air, and Oddur never asked him anything, said nothing, not even, Oh, is that so – as if he had no interest whatsoever. Yet there he waits, at the shore, a stone's throw from her family, whom she greets with profound joy tinged with sadness because of how much time has passed, how much has changed, she sees that her parents have aged, realises in an instant, as if in pain, that she will lose them. She turns to look at Oddur, as if by chance – Is that Oddur? she asks as if distracted, and only Tryggvi notices that the tiny muscles around her eyes are quivering slightly. That's him, says Tryggvi, you should go and say hello. She smiles. She has a rather small mouth, an unusual smile, bright but sensual, innocent yet gullible, and with a barely detectable trace of gloom, or melancholy. That smile was branded on the hearts of several young men out west in Canada, nestled deep within them and transformed into longing which stayed with some of them for the rest of their lives. She walks over to Oddur, wearing her smile and a foreign dress, her light brown hair brushed back as if to emphasise her fine, high fore-head, she goes to him, he awaits her and has to clench his fists. She sees this and feels a fire light within her, its warmth streaming through her and into her eyes. Then Oddur has to clench his fists even tighter, feeling powerless, defeated, he clenches both his fists, it's his declaration of love, she knows that this gesture is his love poem to her.

## *A short essay on the force that destroys life, makes deserts habitable*

This is the force that holds the planets in place, that causes the universe to expand and black holes to form. Human will is nearly powerless against this force when it makes its presence known. It deprives us of our intellect, our rationality, deprives us of our integrity, our caution, our dignity, but in the end, if we're lucky, it bestows on us dizzying joy, indescribable hope, even happiness. In its presence, every hour seems transformed into poetry, a brazen concerto. It is God's answer to death, when the Lord failed to save humanity from the darkness of death and instead bequeathed it this peculiar light, this flame that has warmed people's hands ever since and burned them to the ground, transformed slums into stairways to Heaven, palaces into desolate ruins, joy into solitude. We call it love; that was the only word we could think of.

Ever since then, the history of humanity, of all humankind, has, both overtly and covertly, revolved around finding it, revelling in it, hating it, missing it, fleeing it, which is hopeless, however, it is flight that makes us bitter, desperate, that turns us into rotten drunks, eternal fugitives, suicides. God's answer to death. The flame that warms hands, burns life to ashes, a gift that was cast over the world in days of yore. Delicate and insolent. Never asks your address, where you are in the world, asks for neither justice nor injustice, has no interest in your position, respect, victories or humiliations, they're all the same to love, it has no consideration for anyone, you're not safe anywhere, you're vulnerable, nothing can protect you, not common sense, religion, the philosophy of the past three centuries, not years of experience, the massive walls of a nuclear bunker or the oblivion of drunkenness, no-one is immune, it slips as easily into a sixteen-year-old girl with a heart that bounds like a stag as into a ninety-year-old with a heart like an old rhinoceros. A meteor, a cello string, transforms the best into the worst, the worst into the best, without even asking if you're married, if you're happy, whether you exist in a beautiful and enviable balance; it can elbow its way into you like a boor, a lout – a solar flare that destroys your life, makes deserts habitable.

*It's midnight, the fo'c'sle is open,*
*and someone goes down into it*

Oddur's clenched fists were his love poem, his heartfelt ode, proof that he was powerless there on the shore, that all his renowned – despite his young age – ruggedness and strength, will and character, did him little good, perhaps none at all. Margrét understood that. They said hello calmly, exchanged a few words, you've come back, yes, I've come back, how was Canada, vast and far from the sea, and you can speak American, yes, but I missed the sea, that I can understand, so you've become a skipper, yes, I have indeed, and maybe a boat-owner?, well, I own a few of its planks, What kind of boat is it, she asks, even though she already knows. Tryggvi had described it in minute detail in his letters, he himself being the first crewman that Oddur hired, a decked boat, *Sleipnir SU 382*, 14.37 tons, double-masted, with a pilothouse. A good boat, replies Oddur. They are silent for a few seconds, she

49

knows that her family is waiting, watching, it's spring, the time of year that fills people with anxiety, the time of increasing light, when the soil revives and becomes so swollen with life that people sense it in their sleep, in the commotion of daily life; the irresistible, swelling, impudent force of life. There is a gentle seaward breeze and a scent of the wilderness, and they are silent. Finally he says, putting effort into making his voice sound ordinary, as if what he is going to say is of no importance, The boat is moored at Konráð Pier. Oh is it indeed, says she, before walking off to join her family without a word of farewell, calmly, goes home, Oh, how everything has changed, she says, as she walks through the house, the little wooden house, not realising that it's only she who has changed. The day passes. He disappears behind the mountains, and evening arrives with a tiny trace of darkness, little more than a suspicion, at most the air appears just a bit darker above the mountains, towards the head of Snædalur Valley. Night falls, and she looks forward to falling asleep in her old bed, it's waiting for her like a trusted old friend, I can hardly wait to sleep in it, she says, before bidding everyone goodnight, goodnight and sleep tight and away with all evil spirits, that's how people have always bidden each other goodnight in this house, one should always look for ways to make the world a better place. She lies on the bed, sighs, has finally returned home, yet as soon as she is satisfied that everyone else in the house is sleeping, she gets up, puts her American dress back on, takes time to put her hair up again – and goes out. Into the glow of spring; it's midnight. Silence, and the stillness deepens the world. She walks past sleeping houses, sleeping lives, walks out onto Konráð Pier, down to the boat, *Sleipnir SU 382*, 14.37 tons, the fo'c'sle hatch is open, she climbs down the ladder, I've never seen such a dress before, he says. I know. Or hair put up like that. I know, it's the fashion in the West. They hesitate, stand there silently, she lowers her eyes but he can't control his own, they're an embarrassment, won't obey him, are drawn to her, and it must be told like it is, that she is more beautiful than everything he's ever seen or thought, he can't think of anything, at that moment, that compares to her, and he should probably do something about it, display his manhood, his virility, yet he does nothing, as if wrestling with something greater than himself, it's unbearable, he clenches his fists again, delivering his love poem unawares. She sees it, she says, If I let down my hair, you'll know that I'm naked beneath my dress, and then you'll know that I love you. He manages a nod. Waits, without moving a muscle. Then she lets down her hair.

*Now life can begin, it can get going,*
*with all its baggage*

Question: What travels faster than the speed of light?
Answer: Time itself.

It whizzes like an arrow straight through us. First the sharp point penetrates the flesh, organs and bones, that's life, followed shortly afterwards by the feathers, that's death.

Faster than the speed of light. It's raining and ten years have passed. You blink and you're older, the darkness of death hangs over the mountains. Time passes so swiftly, yet sometimes so slowly that we nearly suffocate. We're both the tortoise and the hare, come in both first and last, it's impossible to make heads or tails of it. So, we simply say: She slipped out of her dress.

Stepped out of it. Or at least that's how Oddur remembered it,

51

the sea hero, the boat-owner, the honour and glory of the Icelandic fisherman's profession. She stepped out of her dress, completely naked, impossible to find more complete nakedness than what confronted him, her breasts a bit small but fully voluptuous, as far as he could tell, like two sighs, two kisses, shining white and likely capable of stopping world wars, changing the course of history – they stopped his heart, changed its rhythm, it stood stock-still for several moments, became a silent planet in his chest. But he finally caught his breath and then took a step towards her, laid one hand, big and calloused, carefully over her breast, felt the nipple in his palm, she sighed, and everything could begin. It began. Six hours later, it was a new day, a cool midmorning, still and silent, and the mountains were hymns, even their sharp edges, black knives that sunder the air a thousand metres up, menace the sky, menace the angels in their flight, even they were something magnificent that rose towards Heaven. They stood on the deck of *Sleipnir,* which reeked of fish and sailing, after a nearly sleepless night, her long auburn hair tousled as if happiness itself had mussed it, holding each other, satisfied yet still hungry, eager for more flesh, smelling of each other and wanting more, breaths, shoulders, knees, breasts, penis, buttocks, toes, juices, semen, yet stood there completely still, so young that it was as if time could not touch them. The night had passed and they'd barely uttered a word, barely a sentence since she'd said what she'd said about nakedness, hair, love you, had hardly spoken at all, apart from, now and then, whispering each other's name and sometimes weeping, yes, even he, Oddur, had wept a little and in doing so made her even happier, almost delirious with happiness, made her even wilder for him, for his flesh, breath, hair, penis, eyes. She'd licked away those few tears of his, nearly paralysed with happiness, but then whispered in turn, Don't move, yes, move, no, yes, move now and faster faster *faster*! They stood on deck that morning of life, the mountains were hymns, and everything was as we've described it because they were so young and quivering with life, because they'd barely slept, because their bodies had become glued together by sweat, lust, happiness, because they'd wept. This is why they were so beautiful, and timeless, this is why the mountains changed into hymns, into precious poetry, and he held her in his arms and she held him in her arms and said softly, daring to say it, delicately yet without hesitation or shyness, as she leaned her head against his shoulder, Oddur, my love, I look so forward to life –

Now life can begin, it can get going, with all its baggage, we'll see what happens.

# Interlude

*Life is heavy luggage*

Remember this with me, that a man requires two
things to be able to bear this load, to stand tall,
more or less, to maintain the twinkle in his eye,
the briskness of his heart, the music of his blood:
a strong back and tears

# Keflavík

— PRESENT —

*Everything opened up when seven partridges*
*took off and white wings cut through the darkness*
*above our heads*

*Embrace* must be the most beautiful word in the language. To use both arms to touch another person, encircle another person, unite with that person, momentarily, two people become one in the heavy currents of life, beneath an open, perhaps godless sky. At some point in life, we all need to be embraced, sometimes sorely, an embrace can console us, releasing tears, or be a refuge when something inside us has snapped. We yearn to be embraced simply because we're human and the heart is a sensitive muscle.

Naturally, I wanted to welcome Ari, embrace him, transform myself into the most beautiful word in the language and embrace this soulmate of mine, my spiritual twin, embrace his sadness and his regret, but something held me back. I'm still standing above the desolate harbour, a monument to better times, an open wound in the town's side. Two ten-story blocks of flats stand east of the harbour, on the high bank, towering over their surroundings, reaching up into the relentless wind, built for old sailors, to help soften the evenings of their lives, so that they and their wives could sit in the comfort of their living rooms, look out over the ocean and the bustling harbour, and thereby, at the same moment, drink in life and memories. A beautiful thought, almost poetic, but no

61

sooner were the two buildings, the two towers, ready, no sooner were the old sailors sitting at their living-room windows, with thermos flasks full of steaming coffee, bowls filled with sugar cubes next to their cups, their skin cracked by salt and memories, than the district's fishing quota was sold, the fishing boats went elsewhere, and the harbour emptied. I check the time on my phone; one thing that Ari and I have in common, among many others, is that we never wear watches, finding them uncomfortable on our wrists, like being handcuffed by time. It's nearly 3.00 p.m., the plane will land soon, and when the short woman's slightly greasy fingers brush the back of Ari's hand and she says this about tears, that he should be thankful for them, which is undoubtedly correct, without them we would be lost, would turn to stone from the inside out, our hearts transformed into icicles, our kisses into ice cubes, the smell of Jonni's hamburger van hits my nostrils, and I realise that I haven't eaten since the morning.

I walk over to the van and the fellow at the window leans forward to hear better, waving his hand in the direction of his radio, as if to silence it while I'm placing my order. My stomach growling, I order a hamburger, Put enough of everything on it, I say, and don't skimp on the sauce. In that case, my good man, I'm giving you the "Quota Swindle", says the fellow cheerfully as he slaps his palms on the menu, which I hadn't noticed, printed on an aluminium plaque beneath the window. The menu is in fact placed so low that you have to bend over to read it; above it is a very long text on the quota system in the fishing industry, in both Icelandic and English, blunt lines giving a clear picture of how the system was "driven through Parliament in a few short days in the autumn of 1983":

*The bill granted the Fisheries Minister unconditional authority to dole out the riches of the sea, the fish that belonged to all the people of Iceland, to whomever he pleased. The quota was not supposed to belong to anyone, but it ended up doing so, creating "quota-kings" who soon started speculating with the quota, selling uncaught fish for enormous sums and forming a new class of capitalists (sea-barons) who bought up others' quotas over the years, eventually taking control of Iceland's fishing industry. They lord it over the districts, drive them to ruin if it suits their economic interests; they've bullied the government and controlled the Independent Party and, finally, bought the Morgunblaðið daily several years ago in order to spread their propaganda. All of this happened right in front of our eyes, and we let it happen. Instead of rising up, we cowered. Instead of protesting, we let ourselves be trampled on.*

So there's still life left in the people of Suðurnes, I think, smiling broadly. I start scanning the menu, but the fellow is so quick to serve me that I barely manage to read its first entries, the "top four":

The Rabble: Regular cheeseburger, 80-gram patty.
Sea-baron (he who devours everything): Double cheeseburger, each patty 100 grams.
Quota Swindle: Big burger with everything.
Keflavík Quota: Hamburger bun without a patty.

The fellow's strong arms have clearly lifted heavier things than hamburgers throughout his life, he's probably over sixty, his sturdy-looking face weathered by salt and wind, the face of a fisherman. Well, my good man, he says, as he hands me the Quota Swindle. Then I remember him. It may be that expression of his, "my good man", that springs him free in my memory, the way he says it, the way his lips pucker, making it unclear whether he is thinking of spitting or smiling – it's none other than Jonni the helmsman on *Drangey*, Jonni the gabber, the workhorse, a sailor from the age of fourteen who'd experienced all the sea's moods, a sought-after helmsman with the sea in his veins, knowing the way fish think, as well as how to maintain discipline among the crew, bending the worst of the riff-raff to his will like small boys. Jonni the workhorse. Jonni the helmsman.

Now Jonni Thunderburger.

He knows how to make good burgers. The Quota Swindle is perfect fast food, world-class. I wolf it down, then get my water bottle from the car, take a drink, and as I do so, a plane appears in the eastern sky, a dimple above the white peaks in the distance, all the mountains are in the distance here in Keflavík and have little influence on the town's residents. I grab my binoculars. There's Ari, in the blue sky, above the scorched lava looking black and utterly lifeless, although here and there green patches can be seen, spots of green grass: the lava's dreams. Ari's coming home, having given up on exile, on escape, on the search for a new life, after living in Copenhagen for nearly two years, working for an old friend of ours in publishing, was a managing editor of poetry books, to maintain his own mental health, as he put it, although his chief task was in fact the editing of a series of self-help manuals: *Ten Tips*; ten tips to avoid everything that afflicts us these days. Ten tips – all the books have the same subtitle, *Beauty and Hope*, to lend them weight, of course, and two white wings.

Beauty and hope, I whisper, lowering the binoculars – while in my head seven white ptarmigan fly up into a darkening October sky more than thirty years ago.

Ari and I were, as so often before, out west in Dalir, and we had got hold of an old Russian shotgun to hunt ptarmigan up on the mountain above the farm. Ari was using the Russian gun, which kicked terribly; his shoulder ached and the middle finger of his firing hand had begun to swell after three shots and four dead ptarmigan. We'd watched as they were tossed a bit by the shot, and then they lay motionless in the snow, their wings useless in death; everything is useless in death: wings, beauty, strength, memories, cruelty, courage – everything. That's why death is the worst, it destroys everything, four ptarmigan that were tossed by the force of the shot, then nothing, while the others flew up into the air, and it was downright beautiful, impossible to deny it, more beautiful to see them taking off than lying dead, their lives spilled into the void that seems at times to envelop our existence. Four ptarmigan wasn't a great catch, in fact, it was a laughable performance; around the same time, our peers in the countryside, farmers' sons, had been shooting twenty to thirty a day, four was an utter disgrace, so we kept at it but silently, because of all those things I've mentioned: the destructive power of death, the essence of life, the wing beats of the ones that escaped. What's more, a swollen finger, sore shoulder, pain at every shot. High up the mountainside, with a fine view, which faded quickly that short October day, over the surrounding countryside and out to the vastness of Breiðafjörður with its islands jutting like the teeth of a gigantic creature on the horizon, we found ourselves in perfect range of seven ptarmigan squatting beneath a fence, up against one of the posts, they didn't move at our approach, as if the fence had granted them asylum, but where in this world can asylum be found in the face of someone with a gun? Ari aimed the heavy Russian single-shot weapon – hesitantly, reluctantly, perhaps because of its powerful recoil, or because death deprives us of flight, makes wings and kisses useless. Finally he pulled the trigger, and the shot ripped through the October silence. The fence post jerked at the force of the shot, but seven ptarmigan took off undamaged and white into the darkening sky, like hope for a better world, undamaged hope; which is better, killing ptarmigan or watching them take off, as white as things we find beautiful? Our entrenched hunting instinct as opposed to our desire for beauty; isn't it to be expected that people feel torn when we don't have any real idea, any idea at all, who we are, or rather, how we want to be, eternally pulled between opposites, whether to dwell in the gunshot or in what takes off undamaged – or are we perhaps both the hunter and the hunted? They took off undamaged into the October sky, which grew dim, night was coming, the sky darkened around us and around seven white ptarmigan, their wings cut through the darkness, had a purpose, their flight had a purpose, we both felt it so strongly that it almost hurt. Ari removed the cartridge from the gun, let it fall on the snow, red and steaming hot down into the whiteness. Then we made a decision, because now everything seemed clear as the darkness deepened and erased the view before us; for a little more than two years we'd worked in fish factories in Keflavík and Sandgerði, and for three autumns in the slaughterhouse in Búðardalur, simply because we didn't know what life was for, why our hearts beat, didn't know why we were alive. Education, yes, old friends from Reykjavík were already more than halfway through high school, but what were we supposed to do with education if we didn't know what life was for, because how were we supposed to be of use to the world, why had some people died and left us if we lived without having fire in our hearts, a clear goal, if we were alive simply because we weren't dead? Weren't we born into this damaged, violent and beautiful world in order to try to improve it as best we could? We felt we were, somehow, yet without understanding it, and thus lived in a kind of limbo, in the hesitant moment before the jump. Now all was revealed, now we understood; when seven ptarmigan took off into the darkening sky and white wings cut through the darkness above our heads, it became clear that Ari and I should be writing, as some of our relatives had done, some well, others less so, none of them particularly successful people, and Ari knew he wanted to publish books, as well, ones that mattered, had something to say, were a flight that cut through darkness. Are we the hunter or the hunted – "What prevents us from cracking," Ari had written in the preface to the selected poems of a relative of ours a few years earlier, "from tearing apart, turning into misfortune, a dripping wound or base cruelty, is literature, music: the arts. Both a pardon and a justification for our existence, both a search and a provocation, an accusation and a scream, and the reason why we manage, despite irreconcilable contradictions within each person, to stay alive without going mad, without being torn apart, turning into a wound, a misfortune, a gun. The reason why we can, in spite of everything, forgive ourselves for being human."

The gulls have returned, hovering irresolutely above the harbour, one of them emits a wail, sorrow that so much is gone, that everything has changed, that the world we were born into is in a certain sense gone long before we die. I glance over at the blocks of flats, those exclamation points, and think I see curtains moving, the seagulls' sorrow has perhaps moved someone. *Behind Covered*

*Windows* is the title of a book of poems written by an unruly aunt of mine and Ari's, she's long gone, so many of those who mattered are dead, deleted by death, which changes meaning into meaninglessness. Ari is a good editor, is ruthless in cleaning up authors' texts, improving their work, though he deletes little of his own, tosses nothing out, doesn't delete phone numbers even when people die, his mobile is full of dead people's numbers, some long dead, even quite a long time before the advent of the mobile. He even has the phone number of his childhood home in Safamýri, 30183, a short number from the time when phone numbers were shorter, which makes us imagine that life was somehow simpler back then, but nothing is simple – ever – when humans are involved. Is Ari hoping, contrary to all logic, to all the laws of nature, that one day he'll get a call from one of those numbers, a long-dead relative making contact, perhaps his maternal aunt shaking her head over Icelanders' greed and self-centredness, his great-uncle, the poet, reciting a new poem, composed about a world that we know as nothing but darkness and silence, or even his mother, his very childhood home, the open wound, the regret, the lava tube deep in his living flesh? Absurd? Dubious? Yes, and probably totally unhealthy to have your phone full of dead people's numbers, numbers that only the past can answer, suggesting that a person who does so has unre-solved psychological issues, refuses to face up to reality, doesn't dare to, is an out-and-out escapee from life, a denier of the laws of nature; such things never end well.

But what do we really know about the laws of nature?

Just how deep is the cosmos, and why do some people's dreams reach beyond the outermost planets of our solar system, deep into what surpasses our understanding? Why do the majority of humankind believe in sacred texts that clash with the principles of rationalism, of scientific proof; according to rationalism, you have to be either a child or a simpleton to believe in the existence of God, but what has more consolatory power than belief in God?

Is that the reason why most of us can live quite unconfounded by the wild contradictions within us, the gunshot and the flight, the hunter and the hunted: because we are able to believe so effortlessly in the absurd, even base our culture, our very existence, on irrational stories? If that's the case, why shouldn't Ari have those old numbers in his phone, those doorways to longing, or doorways to nothing; who knows, maybe something important would be lost if Ari deleted the numbers? What do we know of the world, whether a ptarmigan that takes off into a darkening late afternoon in October is merely a breeding member of the grouse family, with a brain the size of a pea, or whether it is the beautiful essence of hope; whether it's what cuts through the darkness with its flight, whether the seagulls above the harbour are ravenous scavengers or a sad lament for bygone times – how can anyone who knows a thing or two about humanity, its history, culture, nature, inner world, ignore the absurd?

# Interlude

*Each day with you*
*is as Heaven, is as*
*the stuff of gods' dreams*

It begins so drearily, without dignity. Without a shred of dignity. And far too drearily to be able to use it in a tragedy or a hit song.

But first: There's little justice in the fact that love, with its passion, its silent intimacy, doesn't always survive as long as a person but pales with the years, cools, loses its individuality.

How can that be?

How can the unique, the incredible, become, in a relatively short period of time, perhaps just a few years, the ordinary, a drab Tuesday; how is it possible to make it through life relatively undamaged when so much wears out – when passions fade, kisses cool, and so little goes in the direction we chose? Why do we live in a world of imperfection, where marriages fail because love, that first, second and third wonder of the world, has changed into a drab Tuesday, into routine, sterile security? Why do people like Ari and Þóra, his wife, intelligent and educated people, stop, after having lived together for a good twenty years, had three children, a beautiful townhouse, no looming, obvious problems, financial stability, or as stable as possible in an unstable country like Iceland, where the economy appears always to be in the hands of predators, stifling economic interests, no visible difficulties, alcoholism, depression, infidelity, they seem happy, why do they suddenly stop living together, their lives ripped apart as if a bomb had dropped on them, a meteorite from the unfathomable darkness of space?

Why?

It's hard to say. Because with you, life is a sweet dance, a long kiss, your kisses never grow cold, the gleam in your eyes eternally lights my way through the storms of life, and my heart, that ridiculous muscle, that childish sage, that sigh, jumps every time I see you. Every single day with you. Deep inside us, we all carry the dream of an unassailable love that nothing can break in two, a dream that is nourished and amplified by the flood of pop songs and films in which the kisses are deeper, in which their heat sets the ordinary on fire, causes it to flare up, be transformed into a fairy tale. Has the gist of those countless pop songs, films and love poems unintentionally become the benchmark of our lives, towering mountains that might tumble down on top of us years later, with their shadows, disappointments, perilous boulders? Crash down over our lives, which can be so burdensome at times, so remote from the happiness of pop songs, the warmth of emotion, without the flames that make the world hold its breath. Is that why people have affairs, to rekindle the flame, the spark of life, as if the affair were an act of war against the ordinary, the years that pile up – unless that flame were to become a burning wound, a destructive fire?

It all begins so drearily. Without dignity, without a shred of dignity. Too drearily for it to be used in a tragedy, a hit song. It's a quiet Tuesday, no wind, a neighbour walking the dog, an old pop song on the radio, and then there's an explosion at the breakfast table. Ari asks Þóra, Do you really have to make so much noise when you chew? His voice is calm, but then he sweeps his breakfast, a bowl of muesli with soured milk, a glass of water and his coffee cup onto the hard floor. His gesture is a scream.

He doesn't wait for an answer, since it's hardly a question, more like a provocation, a shout at life, a fist shaken at drab Tuesdays, all those damned Tuesdays that so unexpectedly, so terribly, seem to be sitting before him with the beautiful face of Þóra, with whom he's lived for more than twenty years and had a life and three children with, a triple purpose, a life along with its most precious moments, a treasure chest; something abruptly and mercilessly changed all of those jewels into grey stones. He doesn't wait for an answer, just sweeps everything off the breakfast table, it's a scream, not a question. Then he's outside. Stands outside the townhouse, enveloped in a kind of buzz, fleeing from her, despite the fact that her embrace is the one in which he's often sought refuge, the bosom into which he's cried, the ears that preserve most of his secrets, preserve his clearest words, preserve his pain, the sorrow of his childhood, and he knows nothing more beautiful than her dark hair in the wind, her slightly husky voice and keen grey eyes that possess a hidden sensitivity, Are you going to leave me someday? she'd asked when life, for some reason or other, had rendered her helpless, and that fragility had come into her voice, into her eyes, so fragile, in fact, that an unexpected movement, a dog's bark, the sudden acceleration of a motorcycle, could have torn apart the sky above her. Never, he said, are you mad?, your name is carved into my heart with the knife of eternity.

Eternity carved your name into my heart.

We can say things with all the conviction in the world, yet end up betraying. Human beings are weak, and the ceaseless petty annoyances of daily life drain their strength, deprive them of their dignity in the face of existence, and then an arm sweeps across a table like a scream.

At first, Þóra was aghast, then stunned, then furious. The lower lip of Gréta, the younger daughter, trembled, as it always does when she tries to hold back tears; the older sister, Hekla, was still sleeping, while the son, Sturla, was thankfully at his girlfriend's. Swept everything off the table, and then was outside. Grabs his leather jacket, gets into the car, has backed out of the drive, is on his way out of their road without fully realising it, or not at all. Drives away, is gone. Three and a half hours later, books into a hotel in Hólmavík, had driven there without stopping, at high speed, much faster than was sensible, it was dangerously slippery at Brattabrekka Slope and in the Arnkötludalur Valley, but he couldn't have cared less, didn't slow down even when the car skidded on the curves, played Fauré's *Requiem* and felt as if he were on his way to his own funeral and was going to be late. He lies in his hotel room in Hólmavík for two days and nights. Outside his window is the sea. There it is, the sea, with its blue, grey, black waves, its blue and murky depths, but it doesn't matter. The sea may indeed be vast, and it may be larger than language and everything else that human beings have made, but even so, the sea has nothing to say. Ari thought it would offer consolation, wisdom, rest; that all the waves, the depths of the sea, its ever-shifting essence, could tell him something, guide him. The sea probably understands its fish, and even, in its own way, feels for drowned souls, but it likely has neither understanding of nor interest in our wounds, in lives that have been turned upside down. Or can something as big as the sea, let alone something bigger, comprehend a man's anguish, or imagine that something as small and ephemeral as a person possesses sufficient sensitivity and depth to be filled with anguish and end up on a dark path?

*

76

Ari had asked for a room facing the sea, I'm giving you our best room, said the woman, the hotel's owner, who also runs a pizza place and the village café, owns a share in a small fishing boat and is the director of the Ghost Centre, You've got to fill your days somehow, she said. Ari had asked about the village, about life there, asked out of instinctive politeness yet barely heard his own questions, almost as if he were absent from his own life, asked out of this habit he'd developed to act politely towards others and give them the feeling that they were interesting, intriguing, not bland Tuesdays, and then she told him, without hesitation, all the ins and outs of her own life, as if she needed to do so, it was a ten- or fifteen-minute summary. The hotel had few guests during the winter, it was rather quiet in the pizzeria and café, yet there was always lots to do whenever an exciting football match was on, especially a Premier League one; the Ghost Centre gets irregular visits from school groups and tourists that venture here in winter, so far from the south-west corner of the country, but it was the fishing boat that brought in the most money. Brandur goes to sea in almost any weather and is a damned good fisherman, and we process his catches together, no, Brandur and I aren't married, his wife, Alexandra, who's Polish, works at the Co-op, is terribly beautiful, you should shop there, invent a reason to see her. There are two men up north in Trékyllisvík, one of them married, been married for thirty years, who drive over here every week, separately, it's a two-hour drive each way in winter, just to shop where she works. Brandur is a champ, we would all like to marry him – wretched me, on the other hand, got rid of my husband three years ago, Lassi was more interested in studying the chemical composition of *brennivín* and beer than doing anything with me. You men can be strange! Over the years, he found it more

77

exciting to lose himself in Internet pornography than to take me to bed. What do you do with a man who's a useless lover and companion? You dump him!

Dump him. Of course, absolutely right, before your life becomes contemptible, before it becomes a miserable defeat, which must be a kind of mortal sin. But what do you do with a life that isn't contemptible at all, isn't useless, but which has suddenly, completely unexpectedly, come to a dead end?

Ari lies in his room, hardly goes out at all, quickly gives up trying to make contact with the sea, has little interest in going to the Co-op to see Alexandra, even though Sjöfn, the hotel owner, urged him to do so; We don't have an art gallery, she said, as if apologising, but we do have Alexandra.

Two days and nights.

An arm that became a scream.

Bland Tuesdays.

He lies in bed, on the floor, in the shower, under the stream of warm water, sees Gréta's trembling lower lip every time he shuts his eyes and tries to sleep, can't sleep, can't do a thing, is paralysed, knows that he should let them know where he is, forgot to take his mobile but could at least ask to use Sjöfn's computer, check his e-mail, try to answer the questions from his children that are probably waiting for him there; where are you, Daddy, why did you leave, Daddy, what has happened, is everything alright, when are you coming back? Some questions cut to the quick. But all he does is lie in his room, understands nothing, knows nothing, except that something's finished, that something important has been destroyed. He just lies there and stares at the ceiling, when did he stop loving Þóra, can love simply vanish like that, ebb away, trickle so slowly that you don't notice until it's gone, when every-thing collapses? Has he stopped loving her? He lies there with his eyes closed, thinks about Þóra, thinks about other women he's known, he thinks about Katrín who manages the ad agency he works with, she never seems to have a bland Tuesday, she's got a beautiful back, there's something special about her smile, he thinks about her breathing, she moves and he thinks about freedom.

The sea churns outside the hotel, resembling something very large, but that doesn't help at all. October can be dark and heavy, and the hotel's windows are narrow. He lies on his back. Þóra seems to have turned into a Tuesday, into a tube of toothpaste squeezed flat in the middle, the racket from a neighbour's T.V., noisy chewing at the breakfast table. He lies on his stomach. Gréta's lower lip trembles. He listens to the useless sea, to his useless heart, which throbs, which beats, which rises and falls to her name carved into it by eternity. How do you erase what eternity has written?

# Keflavík

## — PRESENT —

*Regret is the heaviest stone:*
*a February evening just over thirty years ago,*
*an old voice reciting a long poem, a pen full*
*of cod and two rust-brown lines of mucus*

It's only after Ari has taken the items from his trolley and the cashier in the Duty Free shop has begun to scan them that he, how shall we say it, awakes from the timeless – or rather, temporally disorientated – condition in which he found himself as soon as he walked into the airport; he awakes and sees the items on the counter yet does nothing, lets the cashier scan them all and then fills two carrier bags. A litre of Scottish malt whisky, a bottle of red wine and quite a lot of sweets: M&Ms, jellies, Belgian and other chocolates, liquorice, all the sweets he'd been in the habit of buying in Duty Free before, when the world was in its place, when nothing had exploded, been torn into so many pieces that it looked unlikely to be reassembled. When his three children were young and so looked forward to his return after short trips abroad; not like they were now, independent individuals, the younger girl in high school, the older studying geology at university and the boy in Spain studying Spanish, immersing himself in a language that Ari doesn't understand. He pays, takes the carrier bags. Sometimes it's as if we're trying to slow time with our behaviour, our thoughts, deny the facts that everything has changed and will continue to change, especially the things that matter, and that with each step we come closer to vanishing ourselves. The constellations move with the darkness and their secrets between them, the earth beneath our feet hurtles through black space at a speed of more than a hundred thousand kilometres per hour, but we constantly try to suppress the feeling, the certainty, the fact, that humanity is ephemeral, our lives birds' songs, seagulls' cries, then silence. What is Ari supposed to do with all those sweets he bought as if the world were the same as it was ten to fifteen years ago? He sees his seatmates from the plane, the woman with the crisps and her words about the importance of tears together with the silent giant, take their bags from the conveyor belt, they wave, the giant, whose name is Adam, raises one paw a bit, as if shyly, just enough to show his palm, while she, Helena, raises her right arm and waves energetically and cheerfully, her fingers reach the giant's forehead, she's barely 150 centimetres tall. This trip to Iceland is their belated honeymoon, they were married just over a year ago but haven't been able to get away until now, have booked a winter excursion up Eyjafjallajökull, the volcano that fused their lives when it erupted in the spring and summer of 2010, and, in doing so, saved her from an unhappy marriage, him from an unhappy life. Helena had said what she did about tears, their importance, as she brushed her fingers, greasy from the crisps, across the back of Ari's hand, and then went on talking. Apologised for Adam's silence and apathy, He has a profound fear of flying, which is not unusual, she said, nothing to be ashamed of; on the contrary, it's both logical and rational to feel fear in airplanes, humans don't have wings, can't fly, and therefore it's unnatural for him to float around in the air, it goes against our many thousands of years of experience. Experience "which lies like ancient caves deep within us".

84

She's an astrophysicist, in her spare time a poet, he's an ex-bodyguard of criminals, bankers and politicians; sometimes, unfortunately, there's little to differentiate them – money and power can irreparably damage morality. By chance, they found themselves in the same hotel in Istanbul during the eruption of Eyjafjallajökull, they both needed to get to London immediately, Helena for an important conference at which she was going to present the findings of the research team she was leading, something about time, what it was, whether there was any force that could make it change course and, if so, what type of force, Adam to be present during the final hours in the life of his father, who was nearing death following an automobile accident. They ended up sitting next to each other on the train, struck up a conversation and since then haven't been able to take their eyes off each other. Their story and their happiness began with a volcanic eruption and death. She was forty, he was twenty-nine. Helena promised to send Ari her latest book of poems, and an account of their trip to Iceland.

They're long since gone now, likely having boarded the bus outside, while Ari stands there unmoving, watching as the baggage carousel goes round and round with his two suitcases, the carrier bags in his hands, full of bygone times, dangling heavily. Hanging on to what's gone can be so burdensome. Ari watches his suitcases go round on the carousel and something stirs in his memory.

It's an old voice, speaking of memories and stones.

Memories are heavy stones that I drag behind me, said an old man who worked with me and Ari processing stockfish and salt-fish down south in Sandgerði more than thirty years ago, sometimes walking hunched over as if into a strong wind, even if he were just moving from one task to another in the fish-processing plant, walking into an invisible headwind with his hands behind his back, as if they were instinctively seeking shelter from time itself, which was making them weaker, clenching them more tightly; You walk slowly, I said to him once, with the tactlessness of youth, but Kristján didn't take offence, just smiled and said, in that husky voice of his, Memories are heavy stones that I drag behind me. Is it heavy to remember? asked Ari. No, only what you regret or long to forget – regret is the heaviest stone.

Ari numbly watches his suitcases make yet another circle as the low, persistent hum of the baggage carousel turns gradually into the voice of old Kristján, who had worked in fish factories since he was a child, knew their ins and outs, was a valued employee in his younger years, a quick worker, skilled, as tough as stone, untiring, quiet, uncomplaining; his only vice was an excessive interest in poetry, especially that of Einar Benediktsson,[5] quoting it at the least likely moments, always finding a reason to mention Einar, whether people were talking about fish or Sandgerði's pastor, about the weather or politicians, sometimes reciting entire poems – some of which are rather long – with a peculiar blend of monotony and empathy. Yet there was no reason to reproach him for this, even if he could be damned obnoxious, because the poetry didn't detract from Kristján's productivity; it was almost as if he worked even faster if he was reciting. But time changes all of us; it hurtles along while slowing us down, and Kristján had begun to

5    Einar Benediktsson (1864–1940), the renowned Icelandic poet, publisher and lawyer. Popularly known as "Einar Ben", he wrote in a bombastic, neo-Romantic style.

decline noticeably beneath the weight of years. By the time Ari and I met him, he'd become so slow that Máni, the co-owner of the Drangey fish factory along with Kári, skipper of the eponymous boat, a 200-ton, productive fishing vessel, was the only person who was willing to hire him. In fact Kári found old Kristján's presence a tremendous nuisance and made his irritation clear to everyone, including the old man, once giving Kristján a stern tongue-lashing, as he, Ari and I bent over a tub half-full of wet cod that we were cleaning and gutting, saying that it had been a total waste of company money to hire him, in addition to being a misguided act of charity; Kristján should have had the sense to rest his old bones instead of getting in people's way and making a fool of himself, annoying everyone. Kristján opened his mouth to answer, intending perhaps to evoke Einar Ben in his own defence, but had the good sense to say nothing; Kári had an impulsive, turbulent temper and wouldn't have taken it well if Kristján had recited a poem over the cod. The old man just laughed, looking down as he did so, making him look uncomfortably like a beaten dog.

Those of us who worked at Drangey never doubted Máni's decisions, just thought, Máni knows what he's doing, which helped us tolerate Kristján's poetic jabber and slow work habits. What we didn't know was that Máni had rejected Kristján at the start of the fishing season. Had patted him on the back, said, No, no, I've no work for you, and added, That's fine. Which meant, You should stop bothering working folk. Over the next few days, Máni heard reports of the old man's Via Dolorosa from one fish factory to the next, large and small, in both Sandgerði and Garður, where he was sent packing again and again. In some places the employees even refused to speak to him; it looked as if he'd had it. That he who'd once been such a highly regarded worker that the fishing companies vied for him no longer belonged to life, was outside it, was superfluous, despite all his experience, his knowledge, his old, expert hands. He should just keep out of everyone's way. One day while driving his van, Máni came upon Kristján walking away from the last factory with yet another "no" on his shoulders, so bowed over that it was almost as if he'd changed into a silent sob, that old toughie. Cursing softly, Máni slowed the van to a crawl, rolled down the window and stuck his head out into the wind, wearing his chequered cap that never blew off no matter how the wind raged, shifted the chewing tobacco in his mouth to make it easier to talk, looked down at Kristján, down at that sadness, that hopelessness, said, Right, come to the factory tomorrow, eight o'clock, before flooring the gas pedal and tearing off in the van to avoid having to hear the old man's thanks.

Kristján showed up every day that winter at 7.50 or 7.55 a.m. and threw himself vigorously into his work to ingratiate himself with Máni but often worked sporadically as if trying to free himself from the burden of age and hide his sluggishness. No matter how hard he tried, how hard he pushed, he rarely got half as much done as the rest of us. Einar Benediktsson's poetry no longer enhanced his productivity. Kristján's passion for Einar had become ingrained like calluses created by life's hardships yet intensified the older and slower he became, as if poetry's superhuman power might lend him the strength that time had taken from him. Which in a way was true, because his old eyes sparkled and looked young again whenever he recited Einar's poems. Even worse was that he tended to forget both his work and his surroundings, he who'd never tolerated loitering, to whom loafing was anathema, all it took was for something to remind him of Einar's poetry, perhaps something someone said, and he forgot everything else, started, began rocking back and forth as if to warm up, and then the lines began flowing unstoppably, one verse, two, even an entire poem.

What drives us to remember?

Ari stands there with a carrier bag full of bygone years in each hand, numbly watching his suitcases going round and round on the baggage carousel, whose hum had become the voice of old Kristján reciting "Starkaður's Soliloquy" just over thirty years ago;[6] might Ari have recalled the bitter line "Where is the dwelling of our ephemeral bliss?" Did this line spring to mind, set the wheel of memory in motion and stop it on a February evening at the start of the '80s?

Kári's boat had returned just before dinner weighed down with fish, which meant that we'd probably have to work until midnight. The three of us, Ari, Kristján and I, were last in the production line, taking the fish after they'd gone through the splitting machine, which spit them into a tub of water just over 2 metres long with a conveyor belt that delivered the fish wet, clean and cold to Ari and me, who arranged them in the tub. Kristján was in charge of the salting but sometimes couldn't keep up, at which point he'd start salting unevenly as a reflex, forcing Ari and me to grab handfuls of salt to strew hurriedly over the fish he'd missed before moving on to the next layer. Máni had just reopened the holding area,

---

6  "Starkaður's Soliloquy" (Icelandic: "Einræður Starkaðar"): A poem by the Icelandic poet Einar Benediktsson (see above), first published in his poetry collection *Vogar* (1921). The lines cited here by Kristján are I:24 ("Hvar á okkar skammlífa sæla heima?") and (on p.90) I:25-6 ("Hvíti faðmur – var hjarta mitt kalt. / Því hljóðnaði ástanna nafn mér á vörum?").

pulled open the large hatch and poured in a full lorry-load of cod, the last one, the dark evening white with swirling snow, brisk with frost, our fingers stiff from the cold in our unlined rubber gloves, the water left running to prevent it from freezing inside the hoses, time passed so slowly that it nearly stopped, the number of fish in the big container never seemed to decrease no matter how many were taken, the faces of the workers at the processing table little more than torpid. Goddamit, it's cold, I said, and cursed Máni, who stood for a long moment in the wide opening, surveying the catch, seemingly in no hurry, insensitive to the wind and cold, his hands bare and his jacket barely zipped halfway, as always, and the cold north wind, the evening and the snowfall were sucked inside. Every bit of me's cold, I said, Yes, said Ari, even my heart. Then it was as if old Kristján woke up; starting, he raised his salting spade, held it up like an exclamation mark, like an announcement. "White embrace," he said. We knew immediately what was coming and cursed the cold and the evening and the fish and motionless time and his damned poetry, because now our work would be interrupted. "White embrace – was my heart cold? / Why did the name of my loves fall silent on my lips?"

Then Kristján recited the entire poem.

Nothing could stop him, a power far stronger than he himself propelled the verses onto his lips, Ari and I were familiar with the pattern by now, whether he was holding a spade, a knife, a rope, a bunch of cod heads, was in the middle of some process or other, up in the break room used by the younger workers, which he preferred to the little room downstairs where the women took their breaks with Máni, in a dense fog of tobacco smoke. The words streamed out of him and the only power that could stop him in his tracks was Máni, but Máni was outside in the evening, in the snow's white embrace, having finally shut the hatch, which meant that nothing could save Ari and me from the grip of Kristján's poetry. As the conveyor belt drew the split fish out of the water and gradually filled the leaning container beneath it, Kristján recited "Soliloquy", standing there with his legs spread wide, as if to keep his balance in the exuberant current of words, leaning forward slightly, and soon rust-brown drops appeared in his nostrils, swelled and dribbled slowly, turning into two snuff-coloured streaks that quivered in time with the verses' metre – just over thirty years later, Ari walks down the corridor towards the Customs office and the exit gate, with two carrier bags and two suitcases on a trolley and Kristján's slightly husky voice in his head. His head full of poetry, an old voice, a February evening, a holding area full of cod and two rust-brown streaks of mucus that quiver in time with the verses.

*You need to undress;*
*remarks on guilt and damned leftists*

Where does the guilt come from? The pangs of conscience that many people seem to have floating around inside them, the feeling that we've done wrong or failed in some way, failed ourselves, our loved ones, the world, life, the feeling that we've acted fraudulently and sooner or later will be punished for it? Why do our hearts thump in alarm, beat harder, when we unexpectedly encounter a police car, catch a glimpse of a policeman – where does this guilt come from? Is it Original sin, the cruel Christian theory that we bear in our blood the sins of our earliest ancestors? Nothing but eternity matches up to God's terrible implacability. A suspicion of guilt that we imbibe with our mother's milk and that blends with our blood; in any case, Ari isn't at all surprised when a tall Customs officer steps forward and puts his hand up and, in doing so, silences old Kristján inside Ari's head; the heavy verses tear apart and everything vanishes: the February evening with its white embrace of snow, the bitter cold, the fish factory in Sandgerði, the holding area full of cod, the whirring sound of the heading machine, the noise of the splitting machine, the old man with his spade upheld.

The Customs officer steps forward, raises his heavy arm, everything inside Ari's head vanishes, he hears nothing but his own heartbeat.

Sorry, but you can't take the trolley with you, says the Customs officer apologetically, as if he is embarrassed, tapping the trolley lightly, with its two suitcases and two carrier bags, weighed down by a vanished world. Ari looks around, he's apparently the only passenger left, hadn't realised, standing there so long by the baggage carousel, watching his suitcases travel in their purpose-less circles, that Duty Free had emptied. Sorry, says Ari, looking at the Customs officer and suddenly finding him familiar, even uncomfortably familiar, though he suppresses the feeling immedi-ately and reaches over to pick up his bags, if he can manage to carry what has vanished so poignantly, but the Customs officer places his other hand over the bags and asks, or says, still apolo-getically, as if he finds this difficult or embarrassing, Do you mind if we take a little look inside your bags and these suitcases of yours, before glancing at his colleague, who has suddenly appeared behind him. A knot of anxiety the size of a fist forms in the pit of Ari's stomach; he clears his throat, shrugs his shoulders, pulls out his phone to check the time, sees that he has two unread messages. Without a word, the second Customs officer grabs the two carrier bags, lifts them easily, he's a young man, isn't wrestling with a bygone era, Follow me into this side room, says the older officer, adding, softly, if you don't mind. Ari mutters something and then a third officer, a young woman, comes over and takes one of the suitcases, the one that Ari had hastily opened at the baggage carousel, just enough to slip in the three magazines that he'd purchased in Kastrup Airport, the music magazine *Rolling Stone*, the science magazine *Astronomy* and an American magazine whose contents seemed to fall between the erotic and the pornographic; Ari had chosen it in something of an agitated mood, or perhaps in a trance, suddenly finding himself standing in front of a rack of magazines and D.V.D.s having to do with sex, the primal instinct that we hide and trumpet simultaneously, admit and deny, which is perhaps why there is little that is as distorted or misrepresented in the human world as the sexual instinct, whence, nonetheless, all life springs.

To his relief, the woman leaves the room after depositing his suitcase on a long table, shuts the door behind her, and then it's just three of them standing over Ari's suitcase and carrier bags, he himself and the two Customs officers, who, quickly and agilely, begin emptying them, placing everything tidily to the side; the younger officer flips quickly through the manuscript of Ari's book on the poet Jóhann Sigurjónsson,[7] the draft of the book that Ari had dreamed of writing for so long, more than twenty years, yet had always hesitated, never daring to do it, without knowing why, perhaps fearing to fail in this dream of his youth, fearing that he wouldn't be able to lift that stone, but that he finally began writing during his exile in Copenhagen, hardly telling a soul, almost

7   Jóhann Sigurjónsson (1880–1919), an Icelandic poet and dramatist, best known for his play *Fjalla-Eyvindur*, about a renowned Icelandic outlaw.

writing in secret, which makes it truly distressing when the Customs officer appears to read a line or two here and there, and when he moves his lips, it feels to Ari as if he's reading into his very core. The officer puts down the manuscript, disinterested, flips through the books in the suitcase and the three magazines, shakes them, Ari looks down as he flips quickly through the erotic one, which, at that moment, seems for some reason to be more pornographic than anything else. The younger officer exhales, or perhaps snorts, at the magazine, which he puts down on the long table, well off to the side, front cover facing up; a scantily clad girl stares straight up at Ari, and the provocativeness that had filled her eyes in Copenhagen is gone, replaced by a mixture of sadness and emptiness, as if the photographer had said something horrible about her life just before snapping the photo. Ari suddenly realises, it hits him like a blow right between the eyes, that she's probably no more than eighteen, or about the same age as his younger daughter. Her mouth is drawn, her grey eyes sad, perhaps because no-one wants to embrace her anymore, whisper beautiful, comforting words to her when the nights are bleak, when life is sharp knives. The two officers stand there as if lost in thought over the empty suitcase, the empty carrier bags, which lie crumpled together, near the magazine, like two dead eyes. One of the officers, the tall one, who reminds Ari uncomfortably of someone he ought to recognise from the past, opens Ari's carry-on and empties it: two books, one a short novel by Roberto Bolaño, *By Night in Chile*, the other a collection of poems by Hannes Pétursson,[8] a notepad, mostly filled with ideas for Ari's book about Jóhann Sigurjónsson but also with lines that resemble verse or

8    Roberto Bolaño (1953–2003) was an acclaimed Chilean writer; Hannes Pétursson (b. 1931) is an acclaimed Icelandic poet.

flashes of a novel, lines that had come as if out of the blue, to Ari's great terror, since he hadn't written a novel in twenty years, his iPod, the photograph of his parents and, finally, the certificate of recognition honouring Oddur. The Customs officer flips almost curiously through the notepad, so curiously that it borders on indiscretion, and then lifts up the framed certificate and appears almost startled. He stands there, head bowed, reading the text as Ari watches, notices the wrinkles radiating from the officer's eyes, either from insomnia or from smiling, though the corners of his mouth turn down slightly; life can be difficult, even for those wearing the uniforms of authority, of control, his substantial belly pushes his white Customs-uniform shirt out, perhaps the corners of his mouth point downwards because of the extra kilos, at least twenty, likely closer to thirty, weight that he has to carry wherever he goes, lie beneath at night, 365 days of the year, the corners of people's mouths have drooped for much less. His eyes are peculiar, appearing light grey at first, before Ari notices their greenness, as if faint rays of light shine deep within them – and Ari realises as soon as the Customs officer takes his eyes off the certificate, realises so abruptly that he starts slightly, while simultaneously feeling bad for not having recognised him earlier, because how can you possibly forget your cousin, especially this cousin, how can you possibly forget those light grey eyes with their green rays, how can you possibly forget, and is it possible to forgive such forgetfulness? The Customs officer's lips part in a smile, or a smirk, as Ari shouts, Dammit, is that you, Ásmundur!?

Afraid so, man, says his cousin Ásmundur, acknowledging his identity with a grin, which transforms his entire face; the charming, brazen self-confidence, blended with indifference, everything that Ari and I, and so many others, had admired for decades, becomes apparent in his face. What the devil, says Ari, without knowing for certain whether he's startled or simply happy. Something along those lines, agrees Ásmundur; I thought you didn't recognise me. You've changed a bit, says Ari, apologetically. Ásmundur strokes his belly reflexively, his hand moving out over its bulge; a little over thirty years are embodied in that movement.

Ásmundur: I see you've brought none other than Grandpa's certificate with you.

Ari: Yes, Dad sent it to me recently. I live, or rather was living, in Copenhagen.

Ásmundur: I know. Naturally, we're all very concerned about your father, but he's the same as always, gets upset whenever someone tries to show him a bit of concern. It's good to have you back. We've read and heard about your success. The whole family is very proud – we're proud of you!

Ari: Success – give me a break!

Ásmundur: You were in the papers.

True, says Ari, suddenly sad that this cousin of his, our old leader, role model, hero, equates success with being mentioned in the papers now and then, that that's the way he measures life, or fulfilment in life. Ari is suddenly filled with an indescribable sadness about life, that it treats us as it does, that he and Ásmundur should have to meet here, after thirty years, under these conditions, in these roles, and that Ásmundur hasn't made more of himself, we always thought that he would conquer the world in his own way, we never dreamed that he would wind up a Customs officer at Keflavík Airport, at least 15 kilos overweight. He looks down so that Ásmundur won't see the disappointment in his eyes, it must be obvious, But what do I know of his life, Ari thinks, maybe he's happy, and isn't that a greater victory, finding happiness and keeping it, than most people can boast of; isn't it the only victory that matters? Glancing away, he sees the magazine, and his anxiety returns, the persistent feeling of having somehow done something wrong. He looks at the girl. She's unforgivably young. What is her name, what did she dream of becoming when she was seven, eight, ten, a ballerina, a princess, an artist, a shop-keeper, maybe, certainly not a woman who sits naked in front of a cold camera lens so that strangers, boys and men, from the age of fifteen up, boys and great-grandfathers, can masturbate over her. What might be her name, is she good, scared, tattered, damaged?

Ásmundur clears his throat. Not loudly, yet it sounds like a gunshot, startling Ari. The other Customs officer, not much more than thirty, lean, muscular, his dark hair combed back, screws up his eyes. I'm afraid, says Ásmundur with embarrassment, his forehead having reddened, that we'll have to do a more thorough search. His colleague nods, puffing out his chest, as if expecting a confrontation.

Ari: Thorough?

Ásmundur: I'm afraid so. Terrible to have to put my cousin through this.

Ari: How thorough?

Ásmundur: Either you do your job or you piss off home and don't show your face again.

Ari: How thorough?

Well, says Ásmundur, suddenly laying his hand on his big belly, as if to remind himself and Ari of the thirty years that have passed in both of their lives, and of how so much has changed, more than they can handle. You see, he says, pausing, but then his colleague comes to his aid, looks Ari in the eye and says calmly but firmly, You need to undress.

Undress? Take off my clothes?

They both nod.

Everything?

Ásmundur: Unfortunately we were tipped off.

Tipped off, repeats Ari, his voice breaking.

A very precise one, says Ásmundur.

Ari: Tipped off, how, I mean, about what?

The younger officer, curtly: About how there's more to you than meets the eye.

How can Ari deny that there's more to him than what's apparent on the surface, that he's occasionally failed in life, failed his loved ones, those who matter the most, and himself at the same time, failed the dreams of his youth, failed his mother, her memory, and his paternal grandmother, Margrét? And how can Ásmundur deny that Ari carries some serious guilt – they haven't seen each other for thirty years, haven't exchanged a single word. Ari, who published two collections of poetry and two novels, as if intending to fly the flag of both branches of his family and improve and expand the world through literary creation, but who gave up after having barely started and hid his capitulation behind publishing other people's books. His last two years had been devoted almost exclusively to editing the *Ten Tips* books, books about quick fixes, books that try to convince people it's possible to repair life in simple, speedy ways – mustn't such a man have something to hide?

Ásmundur is saying something about doing one's duty, about receiving a tip, that Ari's taking his time leaving the baggage claim area hadn't looked too good either, and then he says something about dogs, that there aren't any available at the moment or wouldn't be any use anyway, Ari is uncertain, he's numb, can't feel a thing. He starts undressing slowly, almost mechanically, taking off his jacket, lightweight pullover, dark-coloured jeans, and his feeling of vulnerability increases, grows with the removal of each garment. Ásmundur looks away as Ari undresses, hides his light grey eyes with their mysterious green streaks, or rays, which gave them so much magic power thirty years ago, forty years ago, almost as if he'd seen worlds that others didn't know existed and could escape the constraints of daily life at will, as if the sky was brighter above him than above anyone else; Ásmundur looks away and past Ari, as if he's looking off into the wild blue yonder, while his colleague stands there with his legs spread, his hands behind his back and his eyes never wavering from Ari, who has removed everything but his underwear. He grabs the elastic band, lets go, glances at the door as if afraid that the woman will come back in, looks at the younger man, perhaps for confirmation, whether he really has to take everything off, the young man seems to understand, nods curtly, with determination. Ari grabs the elastic again and thinks, involuntarily, Some people find authority and uniforms sexually exciting. In a flash, he remembers a German novel that begins in Italy; the protagonist, a young man, has, by chance or misunderstanding, ended up in a police car in the middle of the night, is sitting in the back seat, his hands cuffed behind his back, wearing thin pyjama bottoms, opposite a beautiful young policewoman in leather boots, and even though he tries to resist, his dick starts hardening until he has a full erection, which is obvious through the thin pyjamas. Ari is still holding the elastic, feels his nervousness travel down his spine, what if he gets an erection, even just a partial one; that scene, the young man opposite the policewoman, always affected him, good Lord, what a disgrace that would be! He pulls down his underpants, feels disembodied and stares straight ahead, not daring to look down to check whether his dick has hardened. Ásmundur's colleague watches him, as does the girl on the magazine cover, who now has a lustful, slightly sarcastic look on her face, and Ari is completely naked. Stripped of everything, deprived of everything, his personality, his rights, his arms dangle awkwardly at his sides, not knowing what to do with themselves, as if they're strangers, belong to someone else, and now they're both looking at him, Ásmundur and his younger colleague. Directly into his face, fixing their gazes there, unflinchingly, as if they're trying with all their might not to look down at Ari's dick, it's so shameful to look at another man's dick, almost as if you're declaring an interest in it. But perhaps they're trying so hard to avoid looking down because the unthinkable has happened, the exciting memory of the German novel has caused a bit of warm blood to flow into his dick, making it stiff, hard, swollen. Ari bows his head slightly, looks down, aside, as if in contemplation, as if in sadness, and is inexpressibly relieved to see that his dick hasn't hardened and enlarged but contracted, as if in fear. He's suddenly filled with a ridiculous desire to say, apologetically, It's unusually small at the moment.

They've positioned a table reminiscent of those in the primary school in Keflavík in the centre of the room, and on top of it a lectern at which they ask Ari to stand, as if he were going to give a talk, maybe admit his guilt. The younger officer pats the lectern lightly and his glance, which was stern, even threatening, has softened. Ásmundur clears his throat, stands behind and to one side of Ari, who looks back at him and flinches when he sees that Ásmundur has slipped a disposable glove onto his right hand, while his left holds a tin of ointment. It's best, old boy, says Ásmundur, looking down at the tin as if addressing it, if you lean forward on the lectern; then you'll be more relaxed. So this is a lectern, says Ari, completely naked.

Ásmundur: A gift from the Keflavík Kiwanis Club. We usually use it at our meetings – saves money. To be able to use it both here and at our meetings, I mean.

There's enough damned squandering in Icelandic society, snaps the younger man, as if he'd lost his temper.

Ásmundur, in a low, even a reproachful voice: Sævar!

Sævar: You've got to tell it like it is – damned leftists are ruining this country!

Ari and Ásmundur both look at the young officer, apparently called Sævar. What leftists, Ari asks, longing to cover his genitals with his hands but knowing that he wouldn't feel at ease doing so, instead putting his hands behind his back but realising he would have been better off not doing so; it's almost as if he's pushing his genitals towards Sævar, who looks from Ari to Ásmundur and back, almost as if he feels sorry for their inability to see things clearly. Well, who's been running this country the past few years, he says, before running his eyes down Ari's body, who lets his arms drop, dangle. It was other folks who brought us to financial ruin before they took over, the darlings, says Ásmundur from behind Ari, harshness in his voice, and so energetically, in fact, that there was nothing left for your blessed leftists to ruin, except for our debts! My leftists, says Sævar, Mine, he repeats, and then snorts twice, Those bastards are no more mine than . . . than the balls on this here cousin of yours, and Sævar gestures towards Ari, as if he could possibly have meant someone else. The only thing these leftists know how to do is argue, read poems and tax the rest of us to Hell!

Ásmundur: Sævar...

Sævar: Probably just to publish more of those damned poems!

For some reason he points again at Ari, in the direction of his genitals, as if they have something to do with the publishing of books of poetry, but then he stops, takes a step forward and slaps the lectern.

Ásmundur: Goddammit, Sævar, I should be paid double for having to listen to your crap!

Sævar: Someone has to point these things out, tell them as they are, otherwise everything'll go to Hell; where do you stand, he asks Ari, curtly. I, says Ari hesitantly, I just . . . I would rather just put my clothes back on. Sævar stares hard at him, as if wanting to say, You're not getting off so easily, but then it's as if Ásmundur regains his senses. I'm afraid, he says, that we have to complete our search, no getting round it, the tip we received was clear, as Sævar said, and though I'd never believe you capable of doing anything wrong, cousin, everyone's got to do their job, no matter how repugnant it is, you understand what we need to do? Ari has turned round to look at Ásmundur, and feels as if his genitals have changed into a billboard hanging from him. He wants to ask more about this tip, and about the dogs, not having followed what Ásmundur said about them, whether their sense of smell couldn't prevent . . . such an inspection, but he says nothing, just nods.

Ásmundur: As I said, it's better that you bend over the lectern, it'll relax your muscles; you know what I mean. It'll be over before you know it, and we won't mention it again. Ásmundur looks down at the tin of ointment, Ari takes a step towards the lectern, leans forward, spreads his legs automatically, Sævar positions himself in front of him, perhaps as a kind of consolation or, conversely, to prevent Ari from resisting. Behind him, he hears Ásmundur fiddling with something, preparing himself; instinctively, he looks aside but is suddenly seized by the ice-cold fear that Ásmundur has pulled down his own trousers, yet he doesn't dare to turn his head to look, though he does glimpse Ásmundur's silhouette directly behind him. Ari's gaze searches frantically for some sort of anchor, yet finds nothing before landing on the magazine, the girl's face. There's an uncomfortable blend of bitterness and irony in the corners of her mouth, as if she wants to say, as Ásmundur's bulky, probing index finger slides up into Ari's rectum, Now you get to know what it's like to be a woman in a man's world.

# Interlude

*Dark hair, green dress,*
*and from now on I can love other men than you*

At some point, this thought assails us all: Why have I lived? Why am I living? Because if we never ask, never doubt, and pass our days and nights thoughtlessly, or dash through them so quickly that little stays with us but the newest mobile phone, the most popular song, it's not unlikely that sooner or later, we'll run into a wall. It's not unlikely that doubt, our questions, will explode from within us like bombs and throw everything out of whack, make everything change, distort, and things that you've hardly noticed, things that at most have been dull irritations in your daily life, loud chewing at the breakfast table, a tube of toothpaste squeezed in the middle, will suddenly become so overwhelming that your arm changes into a senseless scream that sweeps all life off the table.

And then, two days and nights at Hotel Hólmavík.

Ice-blue Húnaflói Bay fills all the fjords and inlets, the fish swim silently through the deep, their blood cold, and know almost nothing about life. Brandur takes his small fishing boat out to sea, the muffled sound of the diesel engine accompanies him into the vast bay, the north wind brings news of eternal winter and scrapes the bare coastal slopes, Brandur sinks his fishing lines into the sea, it's deeper than human life but has a less vulnerable core, he listens to the diesel engine murmur its oily song, listens to the radio or a C.D. of the Heimur male choir, sips coffee, smokes his pipe, back at home in Hólmavík, Sjöfn is at the hotel, waiting for him with her filleting knife, her unhappiness, her desire for a man, while his wife, Alexandra, is at the Co-op, with her black hair and infectious laugh, Brandur lets his eyelids droop, chews on his pipe, two farmers in Trékyllisvík drive a hundred kilometres in risky weather, dangerous conditions, just to buy a sandwich, warm food, a litre of milk, two beers from the liquor section, just to sense her presence, see her, just to hear her say her own name.

Ari stops at the Co-op on his way south, yet not on his way home; we won't use that dangerous word *home* right now, maybe never. He stops for a time at the Co-op, a box-like building at the edge of the village, resembling a warehouse more than anything else, not much to be proud of, there are far too many ugly buildings in Iceland, as if we still haven't realised that buildings are part of the landscape and that a dreary building makes the environment in which we live, and thus our existence, even drabber. Within this warehouse sits Alexandra, who stands up twice as Ari is rummaging through the shelves, and he sees that Sjöfn hasn't exaggerated her beauty and radiance, or her magnetism; She looks like music, thinks Ari involuntarily as he pays for two apples and a yoghurt drink. Alexandra smiles at him, her smile reaches up to her brown eyes beneath her dark hair, and his heart skips a beat, idiotically, as if he were a teenage boy, a young man, exposed, defenceless, not a man well into his forties with a life in ruins, having crashed two days and nights ago, a mysterious atomic bomb that caused every single building to disintegrate, he continues to live among the ruins, but the radiation is spreading through his blood. Maybe she's grumpy in the morning, thinks Ari as he heads to his car, the sky has grown darker, and then the day's first snowflakes begin to fall. Maybe she's unfair, egotistical, preoccupied with her own beauty and listens to horrible music, he mutters to himself, repeats it like a mantra, as if to break free from Hólmavík, he'd seen a little house on the slope for sale or rent, overlooking the sea. Those who are able to look out over the sea day and night must undoubtedly feel less unhappy. The idea to settle down here preoccupied him for a while, to live here as if on the margin of life, let the torn ground beneath his feet heal and even write his book about Jóhann Sigurjónsson, which he had for so long, ever since he was twenty or so, dreamed of writing. A mad idea, of course, yet not devoid of a certain attraction, which swelled excessively whenever Alexandra looked at him.

He starts the car, drives away, drives into the snowfall, cursing Brandur, who owns a fishing boat, a life at sea, who is married to that woman, is undoubtedly blessed, can undoubtedly smoke his pipe without worrying about cancer, his pipe gives him nothing but tranquillity, contemplation, certainly not cancer, certainly not a painful death in a hospital, morphine in his veins, stripped of his dignity, nothing left of him but pain.

He drives into the snowfall, which soon becomes delightfully dense, the wind awakes and adds blowing snow to the falling snow, the entire world, the air, earth, sky, turns totally white, as if he has driven deep into the thoughts of angels. He crawls along at 30 kilometres per hour in his Kia Jeep, listening to Bach at high volume, both hands on the steering wheel, leaning forward, driving so slowly that the hope kindles within him that he'll never make it to his destination, will die of exposure within the thoughts of angels. He'd checked his e-mail on Sjöfn's computer, she'd put up her hair, was wearing a green dress that looked good on her, and there was something about her that said, Aw, stay a little longer, I'll anoint your wounds, gently, and perhaps you'll anoint mine, I think that both of our lives veered far too close to loneliness, were even shaped by that terrible word, I can hardly offer you happiness, or contentedness, even less liberation, just a bit of company for now, oblivion in my embrace, I have a shoulder for you to cry on, I have fingertips to anoint your wounds. Everything about her expressed this, offered this, and for several seconds he longed to have the chance to let down her red hair, take off her dress, caress her beautiful hips, and it must've been apparent in his eyes, because she'd smiled as if it was, because her eyes warmed – but he only asked if he could use her computer. Waiting for him were twelve unread e-mails. Eight having to do with work, printers' bids on two books, a draft cover design, a message from one of his authors, who'd got good reviews for his book in Denmark: "Here are the links, wouldn't it be good to put them on the homepage, as well as send them to the newspapers?" A message from a literary agent urging him to buy a novel that would astonish the world; he'd already sold it in twelve languages, a story of murder, mental illness, alcoholism, sex and love, a perfect cocktail, a book that touches readers' nerves, the only problem being that the author is unknown and nearly sixty, it's tough to sell such an old rookie.

And then five messages from the people who mattered.

Gréta: Daddy, where are you? Why did you leave? When are you coming back? Aren't you coming back??? Daddy, I'm scared!

Hekla: Dear Dad, I don't understand why you left. Did you and Mom have a fight, I mean, are you unhappy? Has something happened? Mom won't tell us anything, but I can see that she feels awful, obviously. I'm terribly worried; yesterday Gréta cried herself to sleep. I might well have done the same. Where are you? Why don't you ring? It's so hard not knowing anything.

Sturla: Dad, what's happened!? Gréta told me that you suddenly shouted something, swept everything off the kitchen table and rushed out. I, we, all thought that you two were happy, Dad, I pretty much based my life on that certainty. I feel as though everything has fallen apart. My fingers are trembling as I write this. What happened, Dad? Have you betrayed each other, I mean, cheated on each other, I wouldn't believe it if you did!? Or? It's as if someone's put a blender inside my head, I can't think clearly. Dad, call!!!

Þóra: I know that the kids have sent you e-mails, you should ring them. That's the least you can do. There's a lot that I want to say, I just don't know where to start. I don't know, I just don't know anything, except that I feel like I've been beaten. I don't think that anything can be as it was. You've managed to ruin something great. You – no, I can't, I won't write more now, because I might say something really bad.

Sixteen hours later, another message from her, sent at 4.13 a.m. I didn't go to work, and I can't sleep. I took two sleeping pills, but they didn't help at all. I see everything clearly now. In my last e-mail I said that I didn't want to write any more, was afraid of losing control and writing a lot of things without really thinking about them first. You know I'm not one for doing that. But I read the messages on your phone. Did you forget it in your moment of madness, or did you leave it behind on purpose so that it could tell me what you didn't dare to say? Our world collapsed, I don't think it's possible to express it more clearly, when I read your messages to Katrín, the last four, and her replies. Any one of them would have been sufficient to destroy our world. Remember, the world we had, and that I thought we'd built on trust, affection and tenacity. We. First we two, then the children as well. That world, you managed to destroy it. I don't want to say any more about those messages, don't know what I might say, either, I'd probably end up puking, as I did after I read them. I lay on the bathroom floor and puked like I was dying. I thought I was dying, I felt that I was, and I probably did die, I think you've managed to kill me, congratulations. I'm sure you remember what was in the messages, both yours and hers. I recalled that you sometimes talked about her, I mean, made a point to mention her. I really want to say a lot of hideous, monstrous things, but I won't. I'm not going to try to describe my disappointment, my anguish and my sorrow at what you've clearly done. Did you run off so suddenly because I disgusted you? "Do you really have to make so much noise when you chew?" you asked, with an ugly frown on your face. Do I disgust you? Am I so terribly inferior to her? Or was it simply cowardice that got the best of you – were you trying to save yourself by running away?

No, you don't need to reply, and anyway, I'm not interested in your replies. They belong to another life, the one that died in the bathroom as I was puking. From now on, you can expect nothing but coldness from me. That will be my revenge. You can forget about your phone. I took a hammer and smashed it to smithereens, all those bloody words and betrayals. It was a stupid gesture, I know, but fun. Tonight I couldn't sleep; you can see that I'm writing this at night. The bed still smells of you, of course. I loved you so much, so incredibly much that it almost hurt sometimes. I wandered around our flat, not knowing what to do, cry or scream, scratch my eyes out, live or die – but then, like some sort of sick joke, I grabbed the book of poems by the Polish poet that you gave me for my birthday last year. Did you realise what sort of gift it was, what was in it? Sometimes it's as if everything is predetermined and organised down to the smallest detail by some (how much I want to say "fucking"!) power, completely invisible, someone or something that knows what's going to happen and guides our behaviour accordingly. A power that made you buy this book for me, made me reach for it when everything had collapsed and I felt utterly lost. In the book there's a short poem called "Goodbye", it's as if it was written for me. Do you remember it? Here it is, and you can take it as my goodbye to you:

Your words
tore the sky to shreds
destroyed the forest
the squirrels
your kisses.
In my body there are fifty million cells
from now on their purpose will be different
from now on they will think differently
from now on they will divide in unexpected ways –
from now on I can love other men than you.

Some people believe, Ari among them, in fact, that the poem surpasses the other literary arts in every way: in its depth, potency, bitterness, beauty, as well as its ability to unsettle us; that by its nature, the poem is more closely related to music than to words. In ancient texts, poetry is sometimes called the language of the heart or blood, even the lost language of the gods, but here we find ourselves on a rather slippery slope, or thin ice. At the start of his publishing career, Ari often referred to those ancient texts, even saying that poetry was the language of the gods, but he soon learned to avoid this idea, that some poets took such notions too literally, let them go to their heads and became even more difficult to deal with. He quickly learned that poetry and its authors are two very different things, and that the former generally surpasses the latter, sometimes to a great degree; poetry is important, the author is not. Ari published numerous books of poetry and a half-dozen collections of translations before the world screamed, became an arm sweeping everything off the table, and naturally lost money on all of them. But it's fine with me, he often said, if I lose money publishing wisdom and beauty, pain and love. These are beautiful words from the mouth of a publisher, and publishing wisdom and beauty may indeed be a noble cause, but no-one can make a living on publishing at a loss. There's nothing as important as poetry, yes, yes, maybe so, but there within the snowstorm, the blowing snow, at 30 kilometres per hour inside the thoughts of angels, their dreams, that cursed Polish poem echoes in his head, sometimes overwhelming the broad, deep music of Bach, and Þóra's voice echoes along with it, mild but a bit husky, a quality that could make her voice irresistible, a bit like a cello, although this same quality could also make her voice as biting as a saw, and the entire way, from Hólmavík south over the heaths, through countryside invisible in the snowstorm, her voice blazes up over and over again, declaiming, murmuring, reciting the poem and its final verse, *from now on I can love other men than you*, sawing his life slowly but surely in two, and then quartering it, cutting it up, sawing his life into pieces, the coherence of his existence, the saw at once blunt and razor-sharp, all day and through the night as well, because it becomes so dark towards evening that he drives into a snowdrift at the side of the road at the foot of Brattabrekka Slope, a few kilometres from the farm where he'd spent his summers as a boy and teenager, gathered memories full of sunshine, scented tussocks, green grass, tranquil skies, deep into a drift, and there he sleeps, wrapped in a blanket that

114

he always keeps in his car, curled up in a ball, in the cold, sleeps lightly, fitfully, tries to remember his text messages to Katrín, the four that he sent about a fortnight ago, and her replies, remembers when he sent them, the hesitation, the excitement, but can't remember the words no matter how hard he tries, sent a few days after they'd gone to a bar together at the end of a long working day, drunk numerous beers and several shots, and he doesn't remember how it began, but suddenly they were kissing, he who hadn't kissed a woman other than Þóra in twenty-five years, a quarter of a century, and it was so strange to feel Katrín's tongue in his mouth, he remembers thinking about freedom, about flight, remembers that she pressed herself against him, tightly, eagerly, ardently, passionately, and that he pressed back, remembers how their excited, brazen hands searched, but then her mobile had rung, it was Pétur, her husband, who'd already sent her several texts, Where are you?, he asked, and that stopped them. But it didn't stop Ari from sending his own texts a few days later, he simply had to send them, couldn't restrain himself, and she'd answered immediately, in the same tone, not bluntly but enigmatically, if he remembers correctly, stupid, reckless, deceitful text messages, deceitful kisses, deceitful hands, is there really nothing more to him than this; doesn't he have the strength to live with integrity, couldn't he bear the petty annoyances of daily life, did he let the blandness of Tuesdays diminish him, bend him to its will? Katrín is beautiful, and yes, she's sexy, and yes, he allows himself to dream of her, sometimes brazen dreams, fantasies, but it's one thing to think, another to act – the gap between them, isn't that what betrayal is, and did he then have to betray everything, his children, Þóra, their life together, happiness? – in order to realise this: that the name Þóra remains etched on his heart?

Throughout that night, the mountains tumble down on his life, he's buried beneath a landslide of despair, accusations, his children's questions, but at dawn he manages to dig himself out from under those mountains, that landslide, dig himself out of the snowdrift, a snowplough pulls the Jeep out, the plough's driver says something but Ari hears only scattered words, the saw inside his own head, Þóra's voice; the line of Polish poetry, *from now on I can love other men than you*, slices the man's words apart, it was most likely something about road conditions, the persistent snowfall, the blowing snow, Ari drives off, sees the snowplough driver shake his head, drives into the thoughts of angels, into the dreams of those who are as white as happiness, Or is it perhaps hell that's white, mutters Ari, makes his way slowly southwards, gets stuck twice on Brattabrekka, takes two hours to drive it, a stretch that only takes fifteen minutes to drive in good conditions, and the line of poetry continues to saw apart the coherence of his existence, as well as what holds his heart in place on the left side of his body, the things called veins and suchlike, saws those apart as well, and when he finally shoots out of the Hvalfjörður Tunnel, having inadvertently accelerated, as if to escape the voice, the poem, shoots out of the tunnel at a hundred kilometres per hour, and there's no snow falling at Mount Esja, hardly any blowing snow, and Reykjavík appears in its entirety, her voice and the line of poetry have finished sawing the conduits of his heart to pieces, which is why Ari drives into the city with his heart hanging freely within him, roaming about his body like a moon that's lost its mother planet – floats about in solitude, and futility.

# Keflavík

— PRESENT —

*Death is in a black Mercedes-Benz down south in Berlin,*
*someone's gait threatens*
*the mathematical equations, but then the air*
*spits out white seagulls*

It's a rainy late afternoon in Keflavík. The absence of snow and
the rain make this December even darker, and there isn't another
passenger in sight when Ari enters the arrivals hall; all the travel-
lers have gone, he sees the last bus pull away from the airport. The
land outside appears depressed.

It hadn't exactly been painful. Ásmundur had smeared a substantial quantity of ointment on his finger, had placed his left hand
on Ari's left buttock, stuck his long, broad finger into Ari's rectum
and probed, gently but very thoroughly, as if searching for something he longed for, for something we miss, but found nothing,
and there was a soft, slimy sound as he pulled his finger out. Ari
had thought, dejectedly, in fact on the verge of tears, I hope that
I wiped myself well enough when I went to the toilet at Kastrup.
It didn't hurt, though Ari's anus itched, so much so that he slips
between the postcard stands outside the 10-11 shop in the arrivals
hall and starts scratching himself vigorously, looking at the same
time at the colourful postcards, pictures of the pearls of Icelandic
nature, along with a few of horses. Then he takes out his phone,
puts on his spectacles and checks his text messages, hoping that

they're from his daughters, hi, welcome back, dear Daddy, something along those lines, something sweet, something that says, You matter to me. But it's unlikely that the messages are from them, he hadn't let them know about his sudden return, would have had to explain, explain the story of his father, their grandfather, that he appeared to be at death's door, wanted first to find out exactly how serious it was, whether it was in fact serious, didn't want to cause them unnecessary worry, they're both sensitive to such things, especially Gréta, who loses sleep if something happens to those who matter to her, if the world takes a turn for the worse, she wasted away and missed school the first few months after his separation from Þóra – Ari knows that he will never forgive himself for this fact.

No, the messages aren't from his daughters, the first one is from me, asking whether we can meet tonight, drink the spoils of Duty Free – the second is from Þóra. He stares at the screen. He stares at her name, at the photo of her in the lefthand corner, she's leaning against a wall and smiling at him, she was able to smile like that at him almost three years ago, my God, so those times really existed when she smiled like that at him, when it was he who called forth that smile; how did he manage to ruin his life, to misunderstand everything, how did it ever occur to him that he could live without her or that he wanted to at all? What a bloody idiot. For his days quickly bound him to a pole and began firing at him relentlessly with four rifles: regret, longing, self-loathing, despair. He stares at her photo, at her name, at the words below it: "Your father let me know that . . ."

There's no room for any more. He has to press the screen to see the rest. Are they words that point towards happiness, towards reconciliation, or are they just another hail of bullets from the four rifles; how many more bullets can his heart endure? He places his thumb on the screen, presses lightly, but looks up when the text appears, looks at the postcards. On all of them, the weather is fine: calm, clear skies. So that's Iceland: nothing but pearls of nature, calm weather, blue skies and docile horses.

We probably never tell the whole truth. Sometimes not at all, and we always leave things unsaid, to make life more manageable and prevent unhappiness. Perhaps more often out of self-delusion, to make ourselves appear more beautiful, perhaps more often out of cowardice. We turn silence into a lie, turn it into betrayal. Rarely tell the whole truth and, because of this, never possess integrity. Is it because we don't dare to face ourselves, the world as we've created it? Does human life consist merely of escape and illusion? Ari looks at the postcards, phone in hand, its screen light off, the words sunk in darkness – the postcards don't show the real Iceland but rather our fantasy of Iceland; they don't show the wind, the temperament of the weather, its capriciousness, don't show the dampness, the horses drenched and dripping in the rain, don't show the squalls, the sleet, the grey days, and absolutely don't show Keflavík. Keflavík isn't Iceland, isn't part of the fantasy. The postcards show us the illusion, and the things we don't dare look in the eye.

Not exactly painful. After taking off the glove, Ásmundur had introduced Ari to his colleague Sævar, who had just put away the lectern, looking angry or nervous: My cousin, formerly a poet, now a publisher, Ásmundur had said, grinning vaguely, and Ari didn't know whether he was tormenting Sævar, who had just cursed poets and poetry and connected them with the destructive left or, in the way he used the word *formerly*, making insinuations about Ari. In any case, he caught a hint of criticism in Ásmundur's words, or assumed it, and abruptly remembered, almost as if a window had opened in his memory, a short letter that Ásmundur's mother, Elín, had sent him some fifteen years earlier, after he'd stated in an interview focused entirely on Ari as a publisher his ambition to publish poetry of literary merit, not least translations, world literature – it would be his contribution to Iceland, Icelandic culture, the Icelandic people; we could hardly call ourselves a literary nation if we didn't translate works like *The Magic Mountain* by Thomas Mann, or poems by Fernando Pessoa. Towards the end of the interview the journalist had asked him, What about your own writing, you've already published two collections of poetry and two novels, all of your books have got excellent reviews, one of your novels was translated into four languages, you don't see a role for yourself there? No, he'd replied, with a smile, as people smile at innocent and slightly naïve childhood dreams . . . no, there are other authors so much better than I, who have so much more talent. My role would never be as valuable as theirs in this regard – I've set my own writing aside.

Then came the short letter from Elín Oddsdóttir. An entirely unexpected letter. Ari had neither seen nor spoken to her in ten years, no more or less than to anyone else on his father's side of the family, apart from his father, whom he saw three or four times a year, both of them scrupulously silent about things that mattered, discussing only superficial topics: the weather, politics, football. "It really hurt me," she wrote, "to read your remarks on your own writing in the interview. You should know that I, like most of the family, to say nothing of your father, am proud to have a relative in the publishing business, especially one with such a sublime goal and such burning ambition – it would have made my mother, your grandmother, very happy. But she would also have greatly lamented your comments about your writing. You probably don't know how important it was for us to see one of our own in this particular field of endeavour. It made us feel almost as if everything had a meaning, not least the difficulties, that everything had turned out as it was supposed to have done, that – no, I don't want to; I don't feel like talking about it. You must have some inkling of these things, and are therefore bound to understand my pain, as well as the reason why I'm sending you this little letter. That said, I apologise for it – it's probably annoying for an educated man, such a terribly good writer, I must add, forgive my intrusiveness, to receive such an awkward missive from his old, ignorant aunt. I remember that my brother Þórður hated the distance there always seems to be between seeing and expressing. Between sensing and writing. Of course, it's untrue that I remember it; it was Mother who sometimes spoke of it, and my sister Anna as well. (I know that she also regrets your remarks in the interview, but she doesn't want to bother you. I've always been the intrusive one, or the one who never learned how to behave.) I've never understood very well until now, when I see my thoughts changing and becoming awkward before my eyes. Or, well, cheeky. But I hope that what is of importance in them comes across. Forgive my nonsense, but I'm getting older, maybe not terribly old, yet enough for me to start to suspect, or understand, that the time will come when it's too late to say anything. It's not too late for me to send you greetings, nephew. We will of course continue to buy the books that you publish, though I don't understand them all."

Of course he didn't remember the letter by heart – far from it, in fact; only the tone, perhaps a few words, but he would re-read it later in his hotel room, two hours later, after the taxi driver had taken him to the Flight Hotel in Keflavík, take it out of a thick yellow folder full of letters, clippings, photos, poems and verses, the folder that he always carried with him, dragging it behind him like the stones that old Kristján had talked about, but which he hadn't opened in many years – as if afraid to do so. This word of Ásmundur's, *formerly*, didn't have the same reproachful tone that he'd sensed in the letter when he'd first read it – read it and promptly set it aside, like so many other things, set aside, suppressed, like an old ghost, like an accusation, like a misunderstanding, constantly suppressing, constantly denying, constantly – until something broke. Until it broke. Until he destroyed – everything. And his days tied him swiftly to the post and the four rifles began to fire. Formerly a poet, Ásmundur had said, and Sævar had looked askance at them, as if Ásmundur and Ari were ganging up on him, as if what had just happened, Ari completely naked on the lectern with his cousin's finger in his rectum, hadn't happened at all. Have you started writing again, asked Ásmundur as he helped Ari re-pack his belongings, pretending not to notice when Ari pushed the erotic magazine under the other two and vowed to himself to throw it away when he got to his hotel, or rather, take a walk and toss it in a rubbish bin, Have you started writing again, asked Ásmundur, picking up the manuscript, reading the title, *There Is Much that the Darkness Knows: The Rootless Days of Jóhann Sigurjónsson*, and the enthusiasm in his voice made Ari uncomfortable. Nah, said Ari, I always wanted to write about Jóhann, I just did this in my spare time; how's your mother, he asked quickly, as always, to shift the topic of conversation away from himself, too quickly, far too quickly, remembering this as soon as he asks, while the words are still in his mouth, yet he remembers too late to stop the cruel question, and thinks,

124

when he sees Ásmundur's expression, It would have been more honourable of me to punch him in the face.

How's your mother – Elín, who'd died three years earlier, run over while on holiday abroad, in Berlin. The car was going at full speed and Elín, with one foot in the road, was thrown more than 3 metres on impact. The car drove off; its driver, perhaps drunk, high, seemed not to have noticed anything, a black, newish Mercedes-Benz, drove home, went to bed, awoke to the world once more and had no idea that he'd killed an elderly woman from Iceland, a woman who'd grown up on the east coast, in Norðfjörður, and whose older brother, Þórður, liked to smell her hair in the mornings, and embrace her small, warm body, liked to tickle her because her laughter was "like silver, like merry sunbeams". She'd been loved and mourned, had died a few minutes after the accident, though *accident* might not be the right word, it looked more like an attack, an execution, How awful I must look, she muttered to her husband, who knelt beside her, who'd thrown himself down beside her, who cried, he cried, that big, powerful, sturdy skipper, his face like a weatherbeaten cliff, cried when she said this, when he saw her, and then she said nothing more in this world.

How could he possibly have forgotten?!

He noticed Ásmundur's expression and was quick to say, almost terrified, said it sincerely, Forgive me.

You've been gone too long, was all that Ásmundur said, as he handed Ari the manuscript.

Ari looks at the postcards, mobile in hand, Þóra's words waiting behind the darkness of the screen, it's a Samsung phone. Looks at the postcards and thinks, They show us our dreams. He thinks, sadly, Sometimes our dreams are nothing more than illusion, escape, proof that we don't dare to acknowledge the world as it is, don't dare to face the world and ourselves in it. He thinks, Was Ásmundur alluding to this when I asked if we should meet up during my stay in Keflavík? – Do you think it's safe, he'd asked, do you think we can bear it?

Did he mean: Because then we might need to talk about what we fled from, might need to face who we were thirty years ago, and explain who we are today – it's unlikely that the explanations will be comfortable. In fact, the likelihood of that is small.

Is everything alright?

The voice startles Ari so much that he drops his mobile on the floor, the back pops off, the battery pops out, and Þóra's words sink even deeper into the darkness. One of the cashiers in the 10–11 shop had moved one of the postcard stands, Ari having stood there for maybe five minutes, motionless, and who does that among postcards meant for tourists, unless something is wrong, unless the person is ill, is having a crisis, heart failure, is crying, has something suspicious in mind, is maybe a pervert, who knows, he might have been standing there masturbating over the pictures, knowing that there were two women in the shop?

This woman, who turned out to be a girl of around twenty, had pulled the stand carefully away from the other two, and said, Hello, can I help you?, but corrected herself immediately, because what if this was a pervert, not someone in distress, in anguish, but a pervert like the ones you read about in the papers, on the Internet, and he stood there with his dick like a little devil in his hand and replied, What?, Yes, you certainly can help me! So she hastily corrected herself, and asked, Is everything alright?, pulling the stand aside as she said it, while the other cashier, also a young girl, waited, phone in hand, ready to ring for help. But the pervert turned out to be just a middle-aged man, lost in the difficult landscape of memories. He picks up his mobile, reassembles it, mutters, Sorry, and the girl apologises as well, to have startled him like that, but he'd stood there motionless for so long, they could see nothing but his feet and didn't know what to think; No, the other one says, you just never know, and Ari smiles apologetically at the girls, their faces bright with youth, one with two rings in her lower lip, the other with pink hair, both a bit plump, it wouldn't hurt the one who'd moved the postcard stand to lose 40 or even 50 kilos, such a burden for so young a person, to have to drag around 50 extra kilograms every day of her life, as if she were forever, every second of her young life, condemned to hard labour. People eat too much, exercise too little, they gain weight and fatten beyond measure, the poor earth, to have to revolve with all of us on board, doesn't it say something about our culture, that it's degenerate, that we live in times tinged by death, thinks Ari, but promptly feels ashamed of thinking such a thing, they're just two lovely kids, and the one with the rings in her lower lip has gone to get him a trolley to make it easier for him to move his bags out into the rainy late afternoon, and he thinks, as if excusing himself, It's the culture's fault, not yours, you're victims of the times. And out he steps.

The taxi driver, a woman of roughly his age, gets out of the car and is so quick to put his heavy cases in the boot that he hardly has a chance to think of helping her. He catches a whiff of her discreet, pleasant perfume and says, Keflavík, Flight Hotel. That's not far, she replies cheerfully, It seems far to me, he mutters as he gets into the car, and then he clicks on the text messages from Þóra, retrieves the words from the darkness: "Your father told me you were coming. Did they do a thorough search? Sorry, I couldn't help tipping them off, letting them know that there's more to you than meets the eye, and that they had good reason to search you thoroughly. Did they? And did they find anything? Did they find what you've hidden from everyone, especially from yourself – did they find your infidelity?"

Ari puts his mobile in his jacket pocket. Fastens his seatbelt.

The taxi has hardly pulled away before the driver's phone rings; Do you mind if I answer, she asks softly, regarding Ari in the rear-view mirror, big brown eyes, Not at all, he says. She's wearing a headset, allowing her to converse without being distracted, both hands on the steering wheel. She speaks to the person at the other end, it's someone she cares for; she says "my love" twice in the space of a short conversation, both times with affection.

My love, big brown eyes. Now Ari recognises her, thirty years on, She's greeted me like a message from the past, he thinks, unable to remember her name, although he remembers her face – how he remembers it! Naturally, she's aged, time passes through everything – people, animals, houses, fence posts, rocks – just at different speeds; slowly through rocks, quickly through fence posts and people, yet more slowly through some lives, hers being one. Isn't she far too good-looking to be driving a taxi? Thirty years ago. It was the era of The Smiths, Dire Straits, Egó, books of poems by Einar Már, Brezhnev had just died though his coldness still held sway, and "Hello" by Lionel Richie was the slow-dance song at school proms.[9] Ari and I were classmates of hers in high school; she'd been nearly invisible the first two years, just a conscientious girl with large spectacles, but that changed one autumn day during our third year, when she turned up at school utterly

9    Egó was an Icelandic band founded in 1981 by the singer Bubbi Morthens; Einar Már Guðmundsson (b. 1954) is a well-known Icelandic writer.

transformed, wearing a short skirt, a green V-neck jumper, perky breasts, long, loose, blonde hair, moving with confidence, walking like someone who's won a great victory, and her slender body turned out to possess an enchanting softness, a mysterious flexibility. Thus passed that autumn, thus passed that winter, and she knocked a lot of things off balance. All that winter her maths teacher had difficulty concentrating, a married man in his thirties, simple problems started becoming too complicated for him, as if her presence, her short skirt and her mysterious flexibility invalidated the laws of mathematics. In the fall she was elected Beauty Queen of Keflavík and then came in third place in the Miss Iceland pageant. Ari still remembers his surprise, even his anger, at how she hadn't been crowned Beauty of Iceland and sent around the world to invalidate all the laws of mathematics everywhere, completely perturb the sciences, challenge the limits of languages – Ari and I often tried to write poetry about her but with drab results. He contemplates her profile, she smiles, her teeth are white and straight, she laughs softly and says, likely for the fourth time, My love. Probably, Ari thinks as he looks out over low-lying Miðnesheiði, the flat, sparse land, brownish in the rain, probably the judges refused to believe that such beauty could come from Keflavík, the blackest place in the country: that would have called for a re-evaluation of everything.

He looks at her again, can't help himself, nor should we ever deny ourselves the chance to look at anything beautiful, that's obvious, life is too short and uncertain for us to look away. She speaks in a manner that only happy people possess. Could it be happiness that keeps her so beautiful, so attractive, slowing the destructive power of time?

Ari notices that they're approaching a roundabout with exits in four directions, one onto the heath, towards Sandgerði, and he makes a sudden, undoubtedly foolish decision; Could you, he asks, make a short detour? I would like to have a quick look at Sandgerði. She nods, smiles at him in the mirror, but is obviously surprised – who would want to make a detour to see Sandgerði, let alone in December, let alone on a late afternoon over which the rain is falling like melancholy, falling like a merciless sentence on Miðnesheiði, which extends flat and nearly barren, the expanse of land that God created at the end, at the very last moment, having completed everything else, exhausted all His ideas, a land created in a moment of insipidness and fatigue. It's why God never looks down here, why the sky has nowhere been measured to be further from the earth than here. Ari knows what she's thinking, that he must be from Sandgerði, it's the only explanation, sees it in the slight furrow between her eyes, and for several seconds they look inquisitive, trying to determine if she recognises Ari, a man from Sandgerði, close to her in age, but then she turns onto the heath, towards Sandgerði, moving closer to God's insipidness, it's clear that she doesn't remember him. Of course not, in her eyes Ari and I were like all the nobodies, invisible, while she wore a miniskirt and threatened the laws of mathematics. She says, My love.

Do I really want to see Sandgerði again, he thinks, surprised by his decision, or am I simply putting off going to my hotel room, being alone there, having to ring Dad, having to open the folder with the letters, the fragments of poems, photos, clippings?, knowing that he'll do so, knowing that he must do so, and read the letter from Elín; do I just want to continue living in hesitation, avoid dealing with myself, dealing with life, dealing with my failures? Dear God, is that the reason why I immerse myself in Jóhann's

130

life and poetry; not to live the dream of my youth but quite the opposite – so that I don't have to deal with it? The dream that cut through the darkness with its white wings. "Did they find what you've hidden from everyone, especially from yourself – did they find your infidelity?"

He looks out over the dun-coloured heath, saddened by his thoughts, shattered by the fact that his book on the life of Jóhann, which was now nearly ready and had been a consolation during difficult times, a deep-seated happiness born of his conviction that he was finally going all out, putting every cell, every drop of blood, into doing something by which he would stand or fall; but now, suddenly, and perhaps because of Þóra's text messages, because of Ásmundur, because of the heath's mercilessness, of how the rain falls, it appears tragically obvious that his book about the poet's life has nothing to do with the dream of his youth but rather the opposite: it's yet another betrayal, or an escape from the promise made on a mountainside out west in Dalir as the darkness closed in on the white wings of the ptarmigan, which flew away undamaged, cut through the darkness with their lives and flight. Sitting in the back of a taxi, heading deeper into Miðnesheiði, in the direction of Sandgerði, to meet the past, he asks himself, How or why have I lived, then? Where's the fire? He thinks, Ásmundur was right, maybe it isn't a good idea to meet, face ourselves as we were thirty years ago. He glances at the rear-view mirror, wants to see her eyes, wants to look in the direction of happiness, in the direction of what causes people aged around fifty to say, over and over, My love, but she's focused on her driving, on talking on the phone, on saying, My love, and then Ari notices the card dangling from the mirror, slowly revolving, one side has a message from God, that He loves you as much today as yesterday, A bold claim, he thinks, the card revolves and on the other side is an advertisement from the Suðurnes Estate Agency, as if there were a direct link between the two things, as if God and the Estate Agency are two sides of the same coin, "The Suðurnes Estate Agency will find you a home!"

They drive over the heath, down to Sandgerði. Ari asks her to park by the sculpture above the town, or village, *town* is somehow too large a word for Sandgerði. And then he's out in the rain.

Late afternoon. Looking out over the houses. He sees the ocean; he sees its vastness and the rain pounding it. He thinks of nothing, he closes his eyes, listens to the rain pounding his forehead – and it's as if the sky is knocking on a door. Because his memories respond inside him, they wake and jostle forward with such zeal, almost fury, that his head swims, he feels nauseous, has to lean on the sculpture, rest his forehead against the cold iron. Then it passes. Having recovered, Ari breathes calmly; he thinks clearly, and he's merely cold. Awful weather. December, yet raining, 7 degrees centigrade, where's the snow that illuminates the darkness, where's the cold that fetches stars for us from the depths of space?

He gets back in the car, where memories await, they fill the back seat, leaving hardly any room for him. He peers at the metre, thinks, Do I have to pay for them, too?, before saying softly, Well, let's go on to Keflavík, and she nods, she who we should have sent around the world and, by doing so, forced the scientific community to doubt mathematical equations. She turns the car around, gently, accelerates, gently, as if wanting to protect him, as if he's fragile cargo, turns on the C.D. player, asks, Do you mind?, and he doesn't mind and immediately recognises the hazy, slightly dark but dreamy tones of the Irish group Clannad, yet another messenger from the past. They head back over Miðnesheiði, and he looks out over the emptiness, over the low heath that once was daily life for me and Ari, having gone there for the first time in January 1980, in such a powerless Trabant, owned by Drangey, that it had trouble crossing the heath in a strong headwind, and was soon exchanged for a nine-man Toyota, when the fishing season started and a larger workforce was required than could fit in a Trabant. We drove six days a week at dawn from Keflavík to Sandgerði, drove home for lunch, home towards evening and often back again after dinner.

Ari straightens up in his seat, trying to remember where Drangey's drying racks had stood, the racks that we filled slowly with cod, heads and bodies, during the winter. Old Kristján was generally spared trips to the racks; the work there was far too cold for such an old man, and on the few occasions when he came along, when the weather was bearable, he made everything worse, in such a mad rush to grab the split fish or head-bundles from the tubs, scrabbling for them without thinking; everything got so tangled that it took us ages to untangle it again. The heads were strung in the mornings, so early that the sky still seemed frozen by the night, our minds sluggish, our bodies exhausted from the work of the previous evening, the diesel forklift on the go until our coffee break at 9.30 a.m., tidying up after the processing, piling up the heads, taking down the saltfish tubs, and the cold air inside grew so dense with diesel smoke that soot covered the top layer of the saltfish stacks, lying there like black thoughts. When we'd finished stringing the heads, threading six to eight onto each cord according to their size, sticking the needle beneath the gills and out through the eye, we started on the saithe that sometimes awaited us, if it had been caught in large quantities, in a big heap to one side of the holding area, looking a bit like a huge pile of devil's curses. We scraped the scales off every last fish, tied them together two by two, yawned, cursed, exchanged lewd remarks and jokes, someone told a story, another smoked in silence, Kristján muttered lines of verse by Einar Ben in the hope that they would give him the strength to keep pace with us, in the hope that they were a shield against time's weapons. Then we'd drive up to the heath, up to the racks, the heath that God was ashamed of but that has its own special beauty, which it reveals to few people and hid carefully from us, sitting on the bed of the truck, huddled behind the cab, inefficiently sheltered from the wind made that much more bitter by the speed of the truck. Máni leaned over the steering wheel, munching tobacco, and we drove out of the village in rain, sleet, snow, blowing snow, damp, a yellow sun in a brisk north wind, beneath a frost-polished, distant sky, everyone wearing orange coveralls from 66°NORTH, no other colour was available, there was only one style, only one colour, the world might have been a bit simpler but not our hearts, which never have just one colour or a simple cut. The thick fabric quickly became stiff and unyielding in the cold, almost as if it were angry with us, but we emptied the tubs as quickly as we could, hung the fish on the beams, as much as each one was strong enough to hold, two of us pulling the fish from the tubs, cursing the tangles, not least the head-bundles, which could become so terribly enmeshed that it was as if the Devil himself had chased us onto that heath in order to torment us, Máni honked the horn if he felt things were going too slowly, while those of us standing at the sides of the truck bed and hanging fish on the racks' top beams rose orange into the weather, cursing the cold, the bunches of heads, the saithe, time that passed so slowly that it seemed to have forgotten us, left us behind in that eternal toil, with horrendously tangled bunches, the piercing wind and the cold that cut the sky in two. On the way back we set two of the tubs on end, sat inside them, wonderfully sheltered, rested, nodded off, laughed, joked around and looked forward to something: the next Saturday night, the chance to sleep in on Sunday morning, to drive across this same heath in a Saab convertible, blasting music: Dire Straits, Deep Purple, Led Zeppelin, Pink Floyd. We sat inside the tubs, threw the remaining scraps out of the back of the truck, at which point the gulls would suddenly appear, white as angels, greedy as imps, appearing so abruptly it was as if the air had woven them in a flash or spit them out so that the scraps wouldn't go to waste in this harsh land. On the hard heath, which hoarded its beautiful days for us, the summer days when the moss was fragrant beneath a gentle sky, the flies buzzed, the potatoes grew in long rows, the crowberries darkened, the redshank was a shrill note in the blue sky, and we took down the stockfish, emptied the racks, mended them, sang; when it was fun to be alive, but said, Fucking hell when the American fighter jets roared off just a few kilometres away and burst into the sky.

Time creates distance, and the drying racks are long gone, Ari and I dismantled them, along with Máni and two others, in the late '80s, soon after the Leifur Eiriksson Air Terminal was built, that elegant building, a modern terminal, the pride of the country, and, given where it was built, the drying racks suddenly were positioned close to the main thoroughfare, in plain view of the new road driven by every traveller. Ari and I had returned to work at the fish factory temporarily, taking a break from university, Ari to save money for the printing of his first book of poetry, and I joining him, uncertain about where my life was headed, where it

135

should go. We returned to the saltfish and stockfish of Drangey and unintentionally ended up dismantling the drying racks in midwinter, after the office of the President of Iceland asked Máni, rather brusquely, to take them down and move them further onto the heath, out of sight of the road. They were eyesores; preferably do it yesterday, the President and Iceland were expecting distinguished guests shortly, and it was unnecessary for their first sight of Iceland to be old stockfish racks loaded with fish, it would be an insult to unaccustomed eyes. Just ask them to look in the other direction, said Máni, before hanging up the phone. Yet he didn't turn away from the phone but leaned back, popped his dentures off his lower gum, sprinkled tobacco over the bare flesh, put the dentures back in, making it far less boring to wait; the Ministry of Fisheries rang half an hour later. Máni picked up the receiver, listened, said nothing, made no reply, and then hung up, and fifteen minutes later we drove away from the factory, he and Bjöggi, the skipper's son, in the cab, as Ari and Þorlákur and I hunkered down in the questionable shelter of the truck's bed, the north wind blew its knives over the heath and made life unnecessarily difficult.

The job took three days. Plus more than half a night – we took down the last posts just a few hours before the distinguished guests landed at the airport, with their sensitive eyes, as we worked non-stop the final day, from 8.30 in the morning until 4.00 the next morning, using the truck's headlights to see by; we had to wade through the snowdrifts beneath the racks, and it was so cold and we were so tired that we were on the verge of punching each other. Þorlákur cursed the most, had the choicest words, the most volatile temper, having come from Strandir up north, like most of the folk who worked for Máni; it was almost as if what drove him were his impatience and foul language, which had their regular outlets in fights on weekends, at dances at the various community centres of Suðurnes. By Monday he was already waiting impatiently for the next weekend, his face occasionally scratched, his knuckles bruised, brooding spitefully if he'd lost, which rarely happened, he being both strong and quick, unhesitating and violent. Thirty-seven wins, three defeats. It took us three days and half a night to dismantle drying racks that had held hundreds of tons of stockfish over the course of thirty years, all because of some goddam fucking foreigners who'd probably never pissed in the salt sea; no-one's too good to see drying racks laden with fish, in fact, they'd be better off looking only at them, that is to say, if they want to understand Icelanders, because these and other drying racks were the foundation of the Icelandic economy and supported all those elegant assholes in Reykjavík, with their elegant farts and their elegant shit, with their perfumed pussies, Dammit how I'm gonna pound the living shit out of some fucking Reykjavík douchebag this weekend, hissed Þorlákur that night, our fingers so numb in our gloves that we could no longer feel them, and preferably some goddam university prick with a university degree in place of a cock, I'll tear him to shreds and fuck his girlfriend so hard that she'll never look at him again, fucking pussies, the whole lot of them!

Þorlákur, muttered Ari to himself in the back seat of the taxi, how the hell did I manage to forget him?

They approach Keflavík. Pass the new cemetery outside the town, amid tussocks, in an open field and strangely distant from the town, almost as if the inhabitants of Keflavík were trying to forget death. Christmas lights have been strung on most of the

137

crosses, they glow dimly in the rain, like a hazy message from death. The new factory in Helguvík, the pride of Mayor Sigurjón, towers over the cemetery, towers over the dead, and, not far away, at a distance of several hundred metres, stands the Suðurnes Waste Disposal Facility, conceivably built close by to emphasise humanity's eternal life, that people will, like rubbish, gain a new life after death.

The taxi drives past the outskirts of Keflavík, narrow terraced houses, quite a long row, the majority of the houses poorly maintained, their paint faded, the cement crumbling in many places, the curtains dirty and worn, these houses are like old, exhausted people on their way to the cemetery for their own funerals. The car turns down Vesturgata. Clannad continues to sing. Turns down Hafnargata and suddenly Ari is afraid of life. He's afraid of everything that he's forgotten, suppressed, because what's the point of living if you forget most things, people, events; doesn't this suggest that human life is disposable? As if to stress how wrong it is to forget, a life-size image of Þorlákur appears before him in the window of the Suðurnes Estate Agency, easily recognisable despite everything the years have done to him, despite the extra kilos, standing there cockily, legs spread wide, smiling, his chin raised and thrust forward, his fists clenched as if ready for a fight. The words above the photo – REALTOR OF THE YEAR – form a sort of halo over his head, and, beneath his feet, in equally large letters: ÞORLÁKUR FIGHTS FOR YOU!

Ari looks away.

Are his memories lying in wait for him? Has fate, Þóra or even Ásmundur arranged things so that he can no longer escape from remembering?

Remembering that life was supposed to be a white flight that cuts through the darkness.

The car crawls up Hafnargata, crawls slowly, it can't go any faster, an enormous white van dawdles in front of them, and there's the New Cinema, where we saw *Close Encounters of the Third Kind, Mad Max* and several Danish porn films that were shown to full houses on the third Thursday of each month in winter, the film usually skipping in the old projector and often losing focus, like the even older projectionist when he tried, fumbling and gesticulating to the whistles and shouts of the young people, to focus the image, focus our perception of sex. A bit further up the road was the shop where we bought sweets before going to the cinema, considerably less expensive than the cinema's own concession stands, but now it's gone, replaced by a bar. The bar's name is difficult to read on the broken neon sign, its light flickering as if attempting to break free, until it finally does and the name shines out into the short, dark winter day, a name that pummels Ari like a baseball bat, like a massive fence post. He thinks, Dammit, he thinks, No, this is ridiculous, and hears the taxi driver, as if from an incredible distance, she's perhaps noticed where he's looking, seen his reaction, and says, as if apologetically, Yes, it's a peculiar name for a bar, but the wife of Biggi, the bar's owner, died a few months before the place opened. The bar was supposed to be called the Sports Bar or something like that, but Biggi abruptly changed his mind, wanting to name the place after his wife, which didn't work, because her name was Sólveig, and what kind of bar is called Sólveig?, besides the fact that her mother begged Biggi not to, simply couldn't imagine a bar in Hafnargata flashing the name of her daughter for all to see, given the outrageous drunkenness the place sometimes witnessed, so he finally decided on this name, which is to say the month and year when they first kissed, it's kind of romantic, don't you think?, but here's the Flight Hotel, she says, glancing over her shoulder at Ari, motionless beneath the burden of memories – the sign flickering a couple of hundred metres below, sending its name out into the dark afternoon, slinging that bygone time into the world's face:

*JANUARY 1976*

# Keflavík

*—1976—*

*Is Keflavík a beautiful prayer*
*or a bright embrace?*

Ari moves to Keflavík in the dark.

He's twelve years old, and it's so dark on Reykjanesbraut Highway that the car's headlights barely cut through the darkness – it's January. The longest month of the year, two times longer than the others, with heavier darkness, deeper nights than the other eleven combined. It takes them little more than an hour to drive from Reykjavík to Keflavík, from the block of flats in Safamýri to the small single-family residence in Keflavík, from the block of flats where Ari grew up, after being carried into it aged one week, on Christmas Eve, by the woman who is gone, who vanished despite being the sky above him, the force that moves the planets, makes the summer come, fetched pastries from the bakery, and knew how to blow big bubble-gum bubbles. "The only sky that didn't fail / just died."

It takes them a little more than an hour to tear themselves away from the flat she'd bought, together with Ari's father, Jakob, who's driving with both hands on the wheel, looking as if he fears the darkness will snatch it from him. Her books and records, literature and classical music, have long since gone into storage in the basement, almost as if her things were a hindrance to the new life that Jakob acquired along with Ari's stepmother. Now the storage room is empty; Ari went there yesterday and it was empty, everything gone, her books and records, along with the freezer, the car tyres, the tools, just bare walls, grey and coarsely finished, and a naked light bulb hanging from the ceiling, as if after an execution.

The car, a Russian Moskvitch, crawls towards Keflavík, and the January darkness is so dense that the car can just barely reach a speed of 50 kilometres per hour, his father and stepmother don't say a word the entire trip, just stare motionless into the oncoming headlights. Life, it says somewhere, is a ray of light that scratches the darkness, and then disappears. Still, it's good to be part of the darkness of the back seat and merge with the hum of the engine, the murmur of the tyres, a bit like being invisible, as if no-one can reach you; I hope, he thinks, that this trip never ends. But time has no regard for people's dreams; rather, it penetrates everything and eventually turns life into death. Not even the darkness can save him now. The car might be moving slowly, but it does make progress, it manages, and Ari hears his father sigh softly, as if relieved, as the Moskvitch drives into the lights of Njarðvík. Not a peep out of the stepmother, she never gives anything away, but it does seem as if her lean, sturdy-looking body relaxes a little. They drive through Njarðvík and then into Keflavík itself, down Hafnargata, which the American military paved many years ago, transforming the road of a thousand lakes, as it was called, full of potholes and bumps, into silky-smooth modernity. Drive past the Skúli Million freezing plant, which would later burn to the ground, along with its owners' debts, and on whose ashes the Flight Hotel would be built. The hotel where Ari – fully grown, just returned from Copenhagen – is going to stay.

*

144

He gets out of the taxi, the driver takes both suitcases from the boot, her body still has that mysterious flexibility, he sees that she can still threaten mathematical equations, bewilder sciences. Closing the boot, she says, with an indecipherable smile, hard to tell whether it's shy, veiled, occult or simply mocking, I remember you – you're the poet.

They move into the small, three-bedroom, single-family residence. A master bedroom, a room for Ari, the third intended for a child that would never be born, and that became over time a monument to what we would never have, a vault where the regret succeeding happiness is stored. They move from the capital to Keflavík, out to the end of the world, to the place that doesn't exist, because the stepmother's family, her parents, brother and three sisters, have lived there for several years, and because the stepmother wants to get a job. She can't stand it in the Safamýri block of flats, her working hours are irregular, having to face the books and records of Ari's mother every time she goes down to the basement to get something from the freezer, can't stand drinking coffee any longer, listening to the blather and coffee-slurping of the other housewives, waiting for something that never happens, her hands starting to shrivel from idleness, Anyone who doesn't work withers and dies, she said. This is why they move to Keflavík. Carry everything out of the flat and empty the storage room, Ari asked about his mother's books and records but received no reply.

His father didn't oppose the move, it was all the same to him where he lived, and besides, two of his sisters live in Keflavík, Elín, married to an enterprising and respected ship's captain, and Ólöf, who didn't marry anywhere near as well – her husband works at the Base, for the Yanks. She and her husband are both prominent members of the Keflavík Pentecostal Church, where Jesus Christ is the answer, and for years have been the shield against the prejudices that assault the Church and its members. Ólöf is an editor of the journal of the Pentecostal Church, which is published four times a year, an unwavering soldier of the Lord, and has been so for fifteen years, unwavering apart from those four or five times that she misstepped, fell for Satan's enticements. It always starts the same way, when the Evil One surrounds her with darkness, conjures up painful memories, deprives her of sleep, until even her prayers no longer provide refuge and comfort. As if she's trapped in the dark, within painful memories. She manages to hide her suffering from her family and brothers and sisters in the congregation, has succeeded in doing so for a long time; but then a day comes when perhaps she decides to go for a walk, get some air, get her blood circulating, and before she realises it she's standing in front of the state liquor monopoly, then finds herself unexpectedly inside the shop, already having asked for something, hardly knowing what – and, equally unexpectedly, has returned home and begun emptying the bags, white wine, vodka, schnapps. Takes her first sip straight from the bottle, and God in Heaven, how good it is, how relaxing it is, how soothing. Goes into the living room, closes the curtains, sits in the best chair, puts some music on, American country music, Dolly Parton, John Denver, Patsy Cline, with a glass and a bottle of wine in front of her, lights a cigarette, she who never smokes, didn't even realise that she'd bought cigarettes, yet there they are, so it's best to smoke them, and life is good again, the darkness is gone, the memories aren't painful any longer, and the alcohol flows like whispering solace through her veins.

The alcohol: See? I won't ever betray you. I'll wait patiently, won't ever get angry even when you reject and denigrate me for a long time. I'll wait patiently and welcome you with open arms when you return. When everything has failed you, it's I who console you, I who help you to forget, it's I who set the world straight and allow you to see everything in the best light. Why do you need the world when you have me?

Ólöf is the first to stay in the small house's spare room, and on the second day, in fact. They haven't even settled in properly, found places for everything. But Ólöf needs a place to recover, has been drinking for days, eventually sent her children to Elín, her sister, and then locked the door and drew all of the curtains. A while later, her husband, Ágúst, came home from work at the Base to find the door locked, and he had no key on him. Ágúst pounded on the doors and windows, pleading, softly at first, then shouting, I'm here, love, let me in! I'm here, love, steadfastly waiting, I'm out here with the Lord, let us back into your life and together we'll drive this evil spirit from you! Together we'll cut the forked, poisonous tongue out of his mouth!

Without replying, Ólöf appeared suddenly at the living-room window, waved at him cheerfully as he stamped his feet to keep out the cold, Let me cast out Satan from your body, screamed Ágúst when he saw her, don't listen to his forked tongue, get down on your knees, do as I do, see, he shouted, and knelt in the cold, on the pavement outside, his knees sunk into the snow and he began to pray, his powerful, persuasive voice resounding like church bells, like a heavenly trumpet, the neighbours' faces appeared in nearby windows, some grinning, because hardly anything ever happens in Keflavík, it's just work, just fish and the Yanks and the wind, and it's refreshing to have a diversion, to watch this idiot from the Pentecostal Church shouting and kneeling outside his house, his wife completely smashed inside – how holy these two are! Then it began snowing hard on Ágúst, as if the sky intended to silence him.

The alcohol: Don't let him fool you, all he can think about is separating us, and then you'll just start hurting again. He doesn't understand you, and you'll be afraid again, you'll start remembering everything that torments and persecutes you. You did well to go to the living-room window, wave a bit more convincingly, wave cheerfully, then he'll think that everything is as fine as can be, and leave us alone.

Ólöf stayed in the spare room for a week while recovering, getting over the alcohol, getting a grip, gathering the courage to face the world once more.

It's good to have you here in Keflavík, says the other sister, Elín, Ásmundur's mother, to Ari's stepmother, and it's a very long time before death sets a black Mercedes-Benz in motion down south in Berlin. She's married to Eiríkur, the ship's captain, a big, powerful man. Oddur was especially happy about this son-in-law of his but sometimes acted as if Ágúst didn't exist, as if he were a misunderstanding, at best, and insisted that Ágúst made his daughter unhappy and depressed; What woman wouldn't be, he said, married to a man who worked for the Yanks, making him soft, and who blathered on and on about God? Every now and then during the last years of his life, Oddur stayed with Elín and Eiríkur, and persuaded Eiríkur to take the man of God to sea with him, as an extra deckhand, the sea and honest work would undoubtedly put some real life into him and tear him away from the triviality of the Base. Eiríkur, of course, didn't put much stock in this but didn't resist; impossible to put the old man off for long. It was easy as far as Ágúst was concerned, being as he was so eager to please Ólöf's family; it was difficult being held in such low esteem by them, besides his having been born and raised in Keflavík and dreaming as a child about the sailor's life, about great deeds at sea, but ending up getting a good job working for the Yanks at a young age, and of course it was stupid to turn your back on a comfortable, secure job, where you could be confident of being paid, every single króna, on payday, the same could never be said of the fish factories, which regularly experienced setbacks and had to postpone payment for weeks at a time. What is a person who isn't paid his wages? He's a person in trouble. A family in trouble. And he's a person without freedom, a person who's yoked to those who have money.

Eiríkur took Ágúst aboard one dark February day; the sea was heavy, rough, and at the beginning of the fishing trip all of Ágúst's energy went into vomiting. There are few worse things in this world than seasickness, than being seasick far out at sea, it's worse than dying; a seasick man would welcome death like a miracle-working friend. Ágúst sat, or rather half-lay, in his own mess, without a thought for this world, without caring whether he smeared vomit on his clothes, that hugely tidy man, whether he slobbered, looked weak in front of the others, the only thing he could think about was getting to the toilet in time to throw up. Yet as horrible as he felt, he couldn't help but notice how misguided the crew was, how distant from God, he felt almost as if the Lord had forsaken the ship, as if it had been sailing all those years without His blessing. Little by little it sank in, through the numbness and misery, that seasickness was merely one of the Devil's devious weapons, designed to humiliate him and make him lose faith in God. He thought, I'm a soldier of the Lord, and I will not be bowed! And he was resurrected from seasickness. The ship sailed further out to sea, the waves became dark mountains, the ship rocked, it pitched, but Ágúst tottered about, his legs as soft as bread soaked in water, the ship's pitching tossed him to and fro, occasionally casting him at the feet of a crewman like a bit of rubbish, down into the fish offal, vomiting, powerless with seasickness, but he kept getting to his feet again and started talking about God, about His bright and splendorous army. Jesus Christ was the answer, he said, and described the glistening path to Heaven to the crew.

Eiríkur paid no heed to his brother-in-law, having decided to ignore him, as well as figuring that seasickness would do him in, but as they sailed further out to sea and Eiríkur began to see and understand, little by little, and completely against his will, why Ólöf had married this man, who was too polite, too sentimental, in fact, and far too well dressed, and who had worked for the Yanks since he was a teenager. Eiríkur knew all about seasickness; he'd seen even the most robust of men laid low by it, acting as if they were at death's door, vomiting, whimpering, completely wrecked. He witnessed Ágúst's tireless struggle against seasickness, saw that he wouldn't be bowed, saw, to his surprise, Ágúst's will of iron.

The crew were amused by this saint, as they called Ágúst, whose mouth ran constantly about God and Jesus, as if he knew them both personally, as if they had coffee with him every morning, thus constantly arming Ágúst with the latest news from eternity and the heavenly light. It was the greatest diversion, it was even fun to watch him fight to keep from vomiting before he concluded one of his speeches, to wait to see who was mightier, the word of God or his vomiting. Their fishing trip, however, was protracted; although they made slow progress in the heavy seas, in return they fished in spades when they finally reached the fishing bank, but then it grew tiring, because Ágúst wouldn't stop, he was everywhere, you couldn't turn around without him being there, with his jabbering, the latest news of the Lord and the flames of Hell, the latter clearly awaiting all of them if they didn't mend their ways, as if anyone had time to think about the Lord, Jesus and the Devil while they were raking in fish, you think about such things during Christmas mass, or when someone kicks the bucket, otherwise you have enough on your plate already, and there isn't a spare moment to think about something as distant and vague during an enormously busy fishing trip, Aw, stop now, said someone. Stop, he retorted, yes, the Enemy wants me to stop, he's always promising beautiful things if only I stop, even for a moment, Rest, he says, you deserve it, he offers you sweets, one and then another and then a third, until finally you can't make it through the day without sweets, and then he's won. You tell me to stop, but you don't know his tricks, you don't know what an expert he is at disguising himself.

Eventually, it became extremely annoying. Twice they tossed a good saithe at him, but it had no effect. By the time they headed back, their morale was stretched rather thin; some of the fishermen needed to sit on their hands, restrain themselves, wanting to stick him in a tub of fish guts, toss him overboard, anything to shut him up. Yet there was one who could make out the voice of the Lord in Ágúst's jabbering, namely the youngest deckhand, a lad of around eighteen, not yet hardened, vulnerable, his young life plagued by difficulties; his father was a drunk and a boor, and his girlfriend cheated on and humiliated him. At first he grinned like the others at Ágúst's exhortations, but eventually something stirred within him, at first vaguely and hesitantly, but then it was as if his veins became filled with light, his heart with song, and he clung to Ágúst's words as fervently as a man drowning in churning waters grabs the life preserver tossed to him. He promised Ágúst that he would attend the next church meeting, and could hardly wait to go. As they approached Keflavík, the waves had subsided so much that Ágúst was able to go up on the bridge, where he saw Eiríkur standing spread-legged at the wheel, looking towards their town, and it was all so beautiful; the sky of course was leaden, almost black, but the lights of the town where both of them had been born drew closer like a bright embrace, and Ágúst's heart swelled with joy. Looking over at Eiríkur, he realised that he liked this big, tough man who had come so far in life; he'd been born into a poor family and grown up in poverty but had fought his way up with commitment, determination and discipline. We're like brothers, Eiríkur, said Ágúst, his voice trembling with emotion, with a love of life, with his love of the town that approached them like a radiant exultation. Yes, here we stand, you and I, like brothers, and our town comes to greet us like a beautiful prayer.

Eiríkur looked below, where one of the crew was walking resolutely to starboard to throw the boat's Bible overboard. Then he looked towards Keflavík for a long moment, silently, and Ágúst looked in the same direction, also without a word; they stood there, the two brothers-in-law, side by side, legs spread, and it was a good moment. Finally, Eiríkur said, very slowly, as if it were important that Ágúst not miss a word, I've never understood what Ólöf sees in you, and to be honest, I've never held you in any regard. And I've never liked you. But now I understand how she feels. I've seen that you possess toughness and strength, and no-one can take those things away from you. You're your own man. Which makes it possible to respect you. But you should be aware that I don't like you any more now than I did before. You joined us for one fishing trip, and I've never seen a crew of mine so agitated – and I gather that you've screwed up poor Óli's mind so much that he's spouting some rubbish about attending a meeting with that congregation of yours. You should be ashamed of yourself, confusing such young, unhardened men, it's disgraceful, and unforgivable, and let me tell you, Ágúst, that if you weren't married to Ólöf, I would toss you into the sea without a second thought.

The boat approached Keflavík. Keflavík is a bright embrace in the darkness.

*She's a string vibrating between*
*God and man; drinking a great deal of coffee*
*and Jóhannes Nordal, the director of the Central Bank,*
*is on T.V.*

The families of the stepmother and Jakob come together for evening coffee after places have been found for nearly everything, which
didn't take long, the stepmother works briskly, never taking a break
from a task until it's finished. Ólöf is still occupying the spare room,
she's sitting on the sofa when folk begin to arrive, grey, distracted,
miserable following her binge, two of the stepmother's three sisters
settled on the sofa beside her, they smell like fish, all work in the
Haförn freezing plant, where Ari's stepmother will also start work
after the weekend, it being Friday evening now. Their father is
short and stocky, and his skin is so weathered that he most resembles a lump of peat as he stands next to one of the windows along
with Eiríkur and an exhausted Ágúst. Eiríkur and the old lump of
peat appear to get along excellently in their mutual silence, while
Ágúst wrings his hands behind his back as his heart staggers in his
chest like a wounded bird, trying to broach some topic of conversation and turning now and then to look at Ólöf on the sofa, terrified
of losing her completely someday, terrified that someday she'll be
sucked for ever into the hell of alcohol, that she isn't strong enough
inside, this spirited woman whom he's loved so passionately ever

since he first saw her walking down Tjarnargata, eighteen years old in her freezing-plant coverall, this industrious woman with so many talents but also enormously fragile inside, and wounds that have never healed. He stands across from the two taciturn men, who seem so strong even in silence, but he needs to squeeze his hands together with all his strength in order not to lose control and burst into tears, thereby making a fool of himself. He can't imagine life without her. Life without her would be no life at all. He knows nothing more beautiful than when she stares into the blue as if enraptured, or stands up in front of the congregation of the Pentecostal Church and bears witness to God and the radiant Jesus Christ; at such moments she can become so eloquent and persuasive that she seems like a string vibrating between God and humanity. It's no wonder that Satan should lie eternally in wait for her, tireless in setting his traps. Ágúst wrings his hands, I've got to say something, he thinks, I've got to start talking, otherwise I'll snap. He looks over at the two men, opens his mouth and says, Well, boys, it's a new year and the prospects aren't great, no, and downright bleak as far as the job market's concerned. Layoffs left and right in the construction business, precious little work in the freezing plants since fishing season hasn't started yet, and anyway, the trawlers are sailing to other countries with their catches instead of landing here and creating jobs. Yes, boys, what do you think of that? And Jóhannes Nordal, director of the Central Bank, just said on T.V., I saw and heard it as I was getting ready to come over here, not that you have to get ready in any particular way because you should always meet others in the way that God chose to create you, isn't that right, boys, he says, and curses himself for continuing to address them as "boys", it's a stupid term to use for these two men, and Eiríkur says nothing, keeps his mouth tightly shut beneath his cap as the old man shoves his hand calmly into his pocket, without taking his eyes off Ágúst, pulls out his worn tobacco horn, inhales snuff into both nostrils, one of his eyes is completely motionless and icy. Anyway, continues Ágúst, as Jóhannes said on T.V., the economy is in such a sorry state that it would not only be out of the question to give people wage increases but would be downright irresponsible; he said that there was absolutely no leeway now, for the first time, it was necessary to stand together, face the difficulties assailing us, withstand them. We need to think as a nation, not as individuals. Sure, it's a nice thing for him to say, very mature, he being an intelligent man. But he said nothing, boys, about how he and other bank directors received wage increases two months ago amounting to half the monthly salary of an industrial worker, even though these good gentlemen weren't anywhere near being out on the street – what do you have to say about that, boys? And the same music's being played by the *Morgunblaðið*, the voice of the Independent Party and thereby the country's financial powers-that-be, that workers must act responsibly because it would be dangerously irresponsible, indeed unforgivable, to demand wage increases, because inflation would spiral out of control, that ugly monster they use to silence the rabble. Yes, what do you say about that, boys?

Damn, that word again.

I always forget that you're not a conservative, says Eiríkur; do they know at the Base that they have a communist working for them?

I work for the Yanks to have job security, and so that the conservatives can't get hold of me with their cunning tricks down here below the fence. It's obvious that the quality of life here would be worse if we didn't have the Yanks; it would be a downright lie and falsehood to deny it, they've literally kept us going at times, and come to our rescue when we've bitten off more than we could chew, as we always seem to be doing – who'll come to our rescue if the military leaves?

Eiríkur: You're a strange communist. I'll never understand how you can work for them.

Ágúst: I'm no communist. I'm just a human being. What do you say, boys, do we always have to bow down to the moneymen? Isn't it always us who have to bear the burden while they go home with their pockets stuffed with money?

Eiríkur: I think I'll just cut myself a slice of this sandwich loaf – as long as I have my boat, and my fish, I'll manage. I can hardly imagine that those gentlemen will ever be powerful enough to take away my boat and my fish!

Ágúst: They're always stronger than we think.

We're in a tight spot, says the stepmother's father, his voice hoarse and stern as if coming from his chest rather than his mouth. He looks out of the window, it's snowing, he has nothing more to say.

Nor is much being said in the living room, as if the snow outside and the dark evening are breathing silence over everyone, but they drink a great deal of coffee, which, for centuries, has made the silence and scarcity of people bearable in Iceland. Finally, Elín, with her affability and frankness, manages to get the mother of the sisters and Ari's stepmother, who, like her husband, is short, but very slender, hardly more than a vertical line, no wider than her spinal column, to talk about Strandir, where they're from, about the fjords behind countless mountains and heaths, and then the three sisters come to life; What I miss most, says one of them from the sofa, is being able to get good seal meat, because nothing tastes better than freshly caught seal pup, at which the other laughs loudly and abruptly, almost as if she'd spat out a stone – the laughter carries up to Ari's room, where he's sitting on the floor, his back against the radiator, staring at an adjustable shelf filled with his books, mostly Tarzan and Enid Blyton, shy around his cousins, who are sitting on the bed and two chairs; he hardly knows them. The books were the first thing that he pulled out of the boxes, their world had been a refuge and a joy to him for many years, but now, in his cousins' company, he has the uncomfortable feeling that they're thought of as childish, which makes him enormously sad, as if he were losing a friend, as if the light of the world were beginning to fade. He sits up against the radiator, it's snowing outside. He expects to be beaten on the first day of school that coming Monday. And feels anxious, of course, although violence is something that passes; the humiliation is worse – for instance, he fears having his trousers pulled down, and then his underpants, being teased for having a small penis, that he'll even be peed on, after which he'll be scolded for smelling bad when he comes home. Ari would have preferred that they all left the room, he preferred to be alone with his books, to disappear into one of them and never return. He says nothing. It's good to say nothing, you're generally safe in silence. He tries replying to his cousins in monosyllables, thereby hiding the stutter that had almost stopped plaguing him back in Reykjavík but which had returned, having slipped into the back seat of the Moskvitch as they drove into Keflavík. He chooses his words with precision, which makes him speak slowly, as if he were wise, and tries to find innocent words, but the stutter is sneaky and slips itself into unsuspecting ones. His cousins eye him curiously, watch him struggle to articulate simple words, and he hates himself for blushing, feels his face flush, feels sweat on his back, and thinks, How will it be when I go to school on Monday? He sits with his back against the lukewarm radiator and doesn't look forward to life.

Long evening.

It seems as if it will never end, as if the darkness has taken it hostage, yet it does end eventually. The others get ready to leave, the adults stiff from sitting and drinking coffee, but Ólöf stays behind, can't face going home immediately, isn't quite ready to deal with daily life, Ágúst goes out to the car with his daughters, his head is bowed, he sweeps the snow mechanically off the roof and windows barehanded, and his hands shake as he tries to open the car door; shake so much that he drops his keys. He bends down to pick them up, but no matter how hard he tries, he's unable to get the key into the lock, actually doesn't understand why he locked the car, looks down at his hands, they tremble, they shake, as if they don't belong to him anymore. He gives up, leans his arm on the roof of the American car, his forehead against the window, stands there unmoving. Dad, says the younger daughter, sounding frightened, also having begun to shiver, it's cold, a January frost covers the entire world. Just a second, girls, says Ágúst, his voice muffled, I've probably just drunk too much coffee. It starts snowing again, placidly, large flakes come floating down from the darkness, as if the sky were dreaming, and Ágúst's arms soon turn white, he resembles an angel that God has abandoned or forgotten on earth, in its blackest place, and the younger girl has begun sobbing quietly. Don't cry, Rúna, whispers the elder sister, not here, but then she starts crying too, just as Eiríkur comes striding out of the house, he hasn't put on his overcoat, only has his suit jacket on despite the world being very cold. Eiríkur pats the elder girl's shoulder, quickly strokes the cheek of the younger girl, who thinks, involuntarily, Goodness, what big, warm hands he has. When the boat's taking on water, says Eiríkur, without looking at anyone in particular, a bit as if he's addressing the falling snow, the only thing to do is stand together. This is much worse than seasickness, says Ágúst, so faintly that he can barely be heard. You've got to give her time, my man, says Eiríkur, you've got to give everything time, and the skipper pats Ágúst on the back, perhaps not amicably, but he does pat him on the back, and his hand says, There, there. Then he takes the car key, opens the door, starts the car, holds the door open for Ágúst, says, I still think that you should find a decent job. He stands there, spread-legged, in the middle of the road, watching as they drive off, Ágúst sees him in the rear-view mirror, sees him as something that can't be blown away, that stands fast even as the world pitches to and fro.

In the house, meanwhile, Ásmundur, Elín and Eiríkur's eldest son, fourteen years old, big for his age, unexpectedly pulls Ari aside and says, Be ready outside at 8.00 tomorrow morning, dress warmly, it'll be cold as hell, don't tell anyone.

Tell anyone what?

That I'm coming tomorrow morning, and that you're coming with me.

What are we going to do, and why so early?

It's better that you don't know, replies Ásmundur, resting his hand on Ari's shoulder and looking right at him, and for the first time, Ari notices the green rays of light that lie deep in Ásmundur's eyes, so deep that they're almost invisible, as if they're normally hibernating but begin to shine when conditions are right, lending his eyes an enchanting, irresistible hue. Ari would do anything to please him. I'll be ready, he says, straightening up, as if to accept a medal, I'll be ready, he says, without a hint of his stutter, and Ásmundur smiles slightly, pats Ari on the shoulder, and Ari is torn between eagerness and anxiety. Eagerness to get to do something with Ásmundur, anxiety at the idea that perhaps the violence won't wait for school on Monday but will begin tomorrow morning. Then comes night. Comes with its bag full of January darkness and stars that twinkle like distant memories in the sky, comes with dreams that it doles out justly and unjustly. Then comes the January night, which can be so deep, so murky, that whoever wakes within it and looks outside is convinced that the sun will never rise again into this world of darkness and stars.

*What do you do with sharp knives in*
*Keflavík – the Yankee ship and then . . .*

You really shouldn't keep people waiting.

At 7.50 a.m., Ari and I are standing outside the house, and a bit later Ásmundur appears, comes walking down the curving road, almost as if he owns the world, as if everything is modelled after him, his facial features, his gait and aspects of his character, which are reminiscent of Þórður, his maternal uncle, it's nothing less than magnificent to get to walk along with him. The morning is dark, except when the clouds part to reveal a nearly full moon that illuminates the snow and the sleeping houses and the sea glimpsed between them like a black empire. A cousin of ours lives here, says Ásmundur as we pass a small, wooden, two-storey house. He's great, says Ásmundur, once played in a band, on bass, and knows the guys who were in Hljómar, you two have heard of Hljómar, haven't you, and Rúnni Júll and Gunni Þórðar?[10] Ásmundur asks, his tone leaving us no choice but to nod yes while duly committing the names to memory, the names of those most treasured

10  Hljómar (also known as Thor's Hammer): A renowned Icelandic rock group from Keflavík, active 1963–9. Hljómar's bassist was Rúnar Júlíusson (Rúnni Júll; 1945–2008), its guitarist, Gunnar Þórðarson (Gunni Þórðar).

sons of Keflavík. Our cousin, says Ásmundur, works at the Base like Ágúst, though of course it's not a real job; Dad says that it turns the most manly of men into wimps within a few short years, since the Yanks suck the marrow out of us Suðurnes folk, though this cousin is O.K. all the same, a truly great guy, but pop these in your pockets, he says as we approach the Community Cinema, one of Keflavík's two cinemas, its interior a smaller version of the University Cinema in Reykjavík, and hands us each a box cutter, They cut bloody well, he adds, tossing back his head whenever his hair falls over his eyes, he's so superior that it's a miracle he should even want to speak to us. All the same, we don't feel entirely comfortable, there in the morning darkness, darkness that keeps being transformed into half-light by the moon, causing the shadows to deepen and a kind of menace to settle in the atmosphere. Ari looks at me, Umm, I say, great knives, but, umm, what are we supposed to do with them, I mean, where are we going? Ásmundur says nothing, he just keeps going, we follow, anxious, both a head shorter than Ásmundur, who comes to a halt at the street corner, waves his right hand as if to make an important announcement, or even to offer us the world, Hafnargata, he says, and we can hear the sea just below us. Hafnargata, we echo. New Cinema, says Ásmundur, waving his arm again just as Hafnargata angles uphill, you can watch Danish porn movies there every third Thursday, I still haven't managed to sneak in, they're supposed to be amazing. One of my friends managed to sneak in last fall, in September, those movies show everything, I mean, *everything*, and he had a hard-on until Christmas.

We walk along in the darkness, the ocean roars to our left, the moon peeks out every now and then and transforms everything, we have razor-sharp knives in our pockets, we're this close to getting into a Danish porn film, we're with none other than Ásmundur, who might as well own the world, Ari feeling as if he could accept having moved here behind the world, behind lava and nearly barren land. We walk tall and think about that term – *hard-on*. Have never heard it before but have a sneaking suspicion regarding its significance, and that it's worthwhile to have such a thing, or feel it, or however it works. At the very least, we're certain it's important to know what it is, which means that we obviously have to go and find it in the library after the weekend, preferably first thing Monday, look it up in the dictionary and try to figure out whether, and then how, we can get one of these hard-ons, or figure out how it works, anyway. But now isn't the time to think about words, how they work, Ásmundur has stopped walking, he turns around and now we'll know, now's the time, now we're about to find out why we've come out into this cold, dark morning, with its uncertain patches of moonlight. We're standing outside Keflavík's post office, our hearts beating fast, to our right anxiety, to our left eager anticipation – what do you do with sharp knives in Keflavík?

Yesterday afternoon, towards evening, a Yankee ship sailed into the harbour. It moored at the long quay, loaded to the brim with cargo intended for the defence forces, reducing, with its size, the boats and ships of the Keflavík fleet to drab banality. Ásmundur leads us via a shortcut to where we can, unseen, spy on the harbour, the hub of Keflavík, packed with fishing boats, hardly any out at sea, the fishing season hasn't begun yet, secretly spy on the Yankee ship, which is of course an Icelandic ship but takes the name 'Yankee ship' when it's sailing on behalf of the American forces. Ásmundur points out its immense size, its holds jam-packed with cargo for the American military and all the people

163

living on the Base, nearly six thousand, including approximately a thousand children and teenagers, a huge ship is certainly useful to all the people trapped there on the heath, barren and so desolate that it's as if they're being punished – because, just to remind you, the area is enclosed by a high fence topped with triple barbed wire woven out of tin, monotony and boredom. Look, says Ásmundur, pointing at what matters most of all, the reason we're here, this particular morning, with razor-sharp box cutters in our pockets, points at the lorries lined up along the quay by the dozens, the queue goes from the ship's hull far up into the harbour, they're waiting for the cargo to be hauled up from the holds. The lorries' engines are all running, smoke ascends from their exhaust pipes, is dispersed on the wind, the fumes hit our nostrils as we stand there hidden on the hill, some of the lorry drivers wait inside their lorries, others stand in small groups, sheltered, shuffling their feet in the cold, waiting for things to begin. With a sweep of his arm, Ásmundur checks the time on his confirmation watch, wearing time itself like an ornament on his wrist. Fifteen minutes until they start, he says; let's go and meet the others.

Remember: this is during the years when there were four cardinal directions in Keflavík, not three – not the wind, the sea and eternity but the wind, the sea, eternity . . . and the American military. The military that had been stationed continually in Iceland for twenty-five years, not counting the actual war years, because after the war there was a five-year period, from 1946 to 1951, when Iceland was military-free, no Americans here in the pastures of Njarðvík, no profits, no work, no gunshots in the rain, no fighter jets flying over the houses – and when everything took a step backwards. But for twenty-five years, there were six or seven thousand

164

Americans, who needed food, needed sweets, household products, socks, hats, toys, magazines, newspapers, needed a bit of home, where there was plenty, in order to get by here, to survive at the end of the world, to return home sane, for the most part, after being trapped on a barren heath where boredom is the most dangerous enemy, and this is why the huge Yankee ships docked regularly at the long quay in Keflavík harbour, and did so for years. For the longest time their arrival was a grand event for Keflavík's inhabitants; it was almost as if spaceships landed with goods from a distant galaxy. In the '50s and '60s, young people would crowd onto the quay, their pockets full of the money they made processing fish, and buy music from the crews, both 33- and 45-rpm records, music that you couldn't buy anywhere else in Iceland, not even in Reykjavík, except perhaps a year later, which is half a lifetime when you're a teenager, when life is at a boiling point, when you're a firework in time. Thus, the arrival of these ships in Keflavík was awaited with great impatience; they crossed the ocean filled with everything that made our lives richer, and the sailors who bought the records in America to sell to the teenagers on the quay in Keflavík unknowingly became pioneers of a new era.

But those days are past, the Yankee ships are no longer spaceships from the planet Music, they no longer sail across the sea to change the lives of teenagers in Keflavík, now you can buy the latest records at the Hljómalind record shop on the corner of Tjarnargata and Hafnargata streets, the owner was once the lead singer in Hljómar, says Ásmundur, as we move away from the harbour and approach a large group of teenagers; there seem to be around twenty of them, though it's difficult to judge in the morning's half-light, and they seem so agitated that the fear- and anxiety-knots in my and Ari's stomachs start tightening. When we're closer, we see that one of them is lying in the road, the others are laughing, two or three are shouting and their raw cries make the morning a worse place; it appears not to be a boy lying in the road at the feet of a tall, strong-looking teenager but rather a girl, it must be, because someone shouts, Tear off her fucking pants, GÓ, and another yells, Yeah, dammit, man, then we'll get to see a pussy!

Certain ideas apparently come easier to males than others. Around twenty boys form a circle around the teenager, who holds the writhing girl's body down with one foot, and they begin stamping their own feet rhythmically, forcefully, on the asphalt, chanting as quietly as they can, Pussy – pussy – pussy! With such fervour, so rhythmically, that the roof of Hell must be reverberating. Ari and I are standing just outside the circle, listening to the rhythmic trampling, the rising and falling chant, we no longer see the girl nor this GÓ, and are near tears in our exasperation at having agreed to follow Ásmundur here, not to be in bed with a Tarzan book, Tarzan who would shove these kids aside and toss that GÓ off the girl like an empty sack and save her. We're dying to run away, disappear, but we don't dare, we can't, there's something holding us there, hopefully the desire to help this girl, though we don't lift a finger, hopefully not curiosity to see what happens next, hopefully not the hypnotic power of the chanting and stamping feet, the hypnotic power of the cruelty, hopefully not, but humans are questionable creatures, and history records an uncomfortably large number of cases of respectable people freely and willingly participating in despicable acts, attacks on innocents, their smiles mutating into sneers in their lust for cruelty. Demons lurk within us, behind our warm blood lies great savagery, and only beauty can save the world.

166

Ásmundur check his watch, appears to mutter something to himself, and then makes his way through the group, determined, impatient, they give way before him, move aside, opening a path to the boy whom they call GÓ and the girl lying beneath his strong foot; she has fallen silent but hasn't given up, just knows that she's fighting a superior force. She had yelled, I'll kill you all, you fucking idiots, murder you, before lying there silent and motionless. I'll kill you all, presumably meaning that group of around twenty boys, which would be mass murder, impossible to take such a threat seriously, it's ridiculous, and they laughed to see her lying there, puny and miserable beneath that pillar, GÓ, that superpower, GÓ, who looked down on her as the group stamped and chanted that word, urging GÓ to rip off her clothing, allowing them to see what's forbidden, what some of them had started to think about, dream about, what was beginning to drive them mad, looking down at her lying there motionless yet staring up at them defiantly. Then Ásmundur checks his watch, disrupts the hypnotic trance, and the importunate rhythm crumbles, the shouts and the trampling dissolve into individual, uncoordinated sounds, and it's almost as if each and every one of them hears his own voice and is filled with insecurity, and perhaps shame, it's hard feeling like you've suddenly been separated from the pack. Ásmundur's voice, slightly irritated, rends the air: Stop this fucking nonsense, the first lorry will be leaving in five minutes! This GÓ looks at him, calmly, and then removes his foot nonchalantly from the girl, who immediately springs to her feet – she is rather small in stature, with dark, short hair; her wide, flint-coloured eyes are like a scream. Time to choose teams, then, says GÓ, and he spits.

GÓ.

Guðmundur Óskarsson. Fifteen years old, the leader, captain, the most talented goalkeeper that Keflavík has ever produced, twice goalkeeper for teams in the Masters' League, has had a girlfriend, smoked, got drunk, it's as if he can do everything, he's got in to see the Danish porn films many times, no-one has snuck onto the Base more often than him, he knows many of the soldiers by name, can speak American, has played basketball on the Base, those who get to stand near him automatically become more beautiful, better, stronger. GÓ – it's a nickname he came up with himself, from English: *Call me GO*. GO. As in: ready, set, go. "Go!" – with an exclamation point.

GÓ looks at the girl, into her raging eyes, into the scream, he grins, opens his mouth to say something, but Ásmundur cuts him off, announcing, almost coldly, The girl's on my team, thereby taking her under his wing. GÓ shrugs, GÓ spits, GÓ gestures to a few of the boys to follow him, GÓ says, Fine, he leaves but turns around and says, I'll tear her fucking pants off if she gets in my way.

### (*In parentheses*)

No-one knows which events deserve to be told, which events rise, shining or murky, out of time, ardent or placid. The scale of events is always relative, and always variable.

Ari and I may not be on the front page of our lives, there at the intersection of Hafnargata and Vatnsnesvegur, early on a Saturday morning, but those hours in the morning darkness are extremely vivid in Ari's mind as he stands at the window of his room at the Flight Hotel, looking out at the same intersection, one of his suitcases open on the bed, he's taken out photos of his three children and positioned them on the desk. The yellow folder, with letters, poems, a few photos, lies open on top of the minibar. He stands at the window almost forty years later, looking out at the intersection where we're getting into position: I, Ari, Ásmundur, the girl and a few boys. Ari recalls that it soon began to snow. He leans his forehead against the windowpane. The American military is long gone from the heath, the inhabitants of Keflavík have lost their entire fishing quota, they're no longer fishermen, the harbour is empty, like parentheses around nothing, and, a short time ago, Ásmundur stuck his index finger into Ari's rectum.

Those that can foresee the future, and say what they see, are always taken for madmen.

### . . . the action begins

It starts snowing on that Saturday morning, it snows on the tension, the tickling tension, the unbearable tension. Ari and I swallow, lick our lips, crouching behind a concrete wall a short distance from the street corner, listening for the sound of the first lorry to turn from the harbour onto Vatnsnesvegur, panting from the effort, grinding its gears, a heavy load on its bed, cargo for those who live just a few kilometres from us, on the barren heath, six thousand Americans enclosed by a high fence topped with triple barbed wire, triple boredom, just a few kilometres that are, all the same, an immense distance. We see excitement and concentration on the faces of Ásmundur and the girl, whose name is Sigga. Sigga, she said curtly to me, Ari and Ásmundur after we knelt behind the fence in a desolate yard containing one stunted, salt-burned fir tree, wrapped so tightly in Christmas lights that it resembled despair. Sigga, she says, and Ari and I mumble our names while Ásmundur just nods, as if to confirm that it's O.K. to be called Sigga. Three boys on the other side of the road, hidden behind a brown American Chevrolet, three others in the yard next door, it's Ásmundur's team, the rest went with GÓ, who distributed them along Hafnargata, while he himself is just a bit beyond the intersection of Faxabraut and Hafnargata, choosing a spot where the vehicles headed to the Base pick up speed and the drivers feel safe, it's the most difficult place to jump onto the lorries, not like our corner, where the lorries slow down so drastically in the turn that they nearly stop, but GÓ doesn't want it to be easy, he waits until a lorry has crossed the intersection, has picked up speed, has shifted into second gear, and then he runs and jumps up onto the bed, jumping gracefully, as only he can jump, soars majestically, like a big cat, with agility, power and perfect timing, GÓ who's never lost a lorry he's jumped onto, has never missed a jump, anywhere, not here, not between the goalposts, he blocks every shot, it's as if nothing could ever escape him, as if he could grab everything he chose to grab in this life, yet he didn't manage to jump away from the misfortune that would snatch him many years later.

We hear the first lorry turn up Vatnsnesvegur, the gears grind, its engine gasps for breath in the silence and tranquillity of the falling snow, then it bursts into motion and casts its weight forward, Sigga starts cursing softly to help herself relax, she clearly knows an immense number of curse words, and finally Ásmundur explains to Ari and me precisely what's expected of us. At a signal from him, for everything must follow rules, be subject to discipline, we are to climb onto the bed of the lorry, It's not without its risks, he says in a low voice, frankly, especially when it's icy and slippery, like now; things have gone badly for some when it's been like this. What's more, certain drivers have it in for us and try

170

everything they can to stop us, spinning their wheels and zigzag-ging and abruptly changing speed, sticking their heads out the window and shouting threats, which is O.K., but some slam on the brakes and come storming out, and in that case, it's better if you run as if the school principal were after you, it's not much fun getting caught by such guys. The main thing is to keep a good grip on the sides or tailgate, or on the edges if they don't have sides, otherwise an unexpected jolt may make you lose your grip, and in these icy conditions you'll slip right under the tyres, where you'll be crushed, turned into a bloody pulp, it's happened before, boys have died doing this. This isn't child's play. Don't worry, think only of getting up onto the bed, get a good grip, shore yourselves up, and then it'll be time to take out your knives, absolutely not before then, you'll be completely useless on the bed if you lose your knives. Take them out, make a good cut in one of the boxes, and empty it of everything you can. You won't have any time to choose which box, or to stop and start on another – just empty the ones you cut open, even if they're filled with nappies, it doesn't matter, because we can sell anything that comes from the Yanks. Four other guys will be running alongside to pick up the stuff, O.K.?

We nod, we smile, we say, O.K. Though it's not fucking O.K., in fact it's not O.K. at all. But we nod, and then the first lorry of the morning drives up, with a blue, convex hood, no headlights, as if to camouflage itself, and it sighs into the turn; We'll take the next one, whispers Ásmundur, this one is GÓ's.

Then it stops snowing, and when the sound of the engine fades into the distance, we peek over the wall and see several shadows suddenly sprint out, some appear to pop up out of the earth, others come out from under parked cars, a group of boys who become shadows in the dim light, the semi-darkness; the lorry approaches the intersection of Faxabraut and Hafnargata, unwittingly begins to slow, noticing the shadows too late, or at least not until they've nearly reached the lorry, we hear the driver step on the gas, he pushes the engine, it's as if a giant beast has let loose with a sudden, fearful cry, and then the shadows are up on the truck's bed, and shortly afterwards things begin raining down from it, some of which are caught, some of which land in the road and are collected there; It's our turn soon, says Ásmundur, taking out his box cutter, testing its blade.

Ari and I jump onto the fourth lorry, having already run after another, gathering what Ásmundur and another boy have torn from the boxes, seeing how to do it, anxiety grips us, but we're afraid of the driver's reaction, afraid of meeting the same fate as Ásmundur, who had to put up with a stern warning from the lorry driver, who had slowed, stuck his head halfway out of the cab, shouted, not angrily, rather as if he were sad, as if what we were doing was a personal affront, as if we were disappointing him, You should be ashamed of yourselves, boys, this is downright humiliating, don't you have any self-respect, don't you know what the Yanks say about us, calling us savages, Eskimos, parasites, are you really so determined to prove them true, how do you think I feel driving up to the Base with sliced-up boxes and seeing them shake their heads, it's downright degrading that you shouldn't have more self-respect; what does it mean to be an Icelander, he shouted finally, or seemed to shout, as if we could reply, we thought he should loosen up a bit, and suddenly he seemed to agree with us because he stopped shouting, settled back into the cab. Only to reappear shortly afterwards and look straight at Ásmundur, who was frenziedly emptying a box two metres away from him; Listen, boy, aren't you the son of Elín from Norðfjörður, the grandson of

Margrét, I know that face, you're the spitting image of Þórður, don't you see that you're disgracing your family – how can the police allow this to happen?! He said nothing more. Pulled his head back in, slammed the door, hit the gas; Damned bastard ruined my fun, cursed Ásmundur when he returned, You two take the next one, he said to me and Ari, silencing Sigga with a gesture when she shot up like a gust of wind and asked, What about me?

Ari and I are lucky with our lorry. The driver turns so carefully up Hafnargata that it's almost as if he's transporting something extremely fragile, we run up to the lorry, our legs wobbly with excitement and nerves, but steady ourselves as we draw closer, the blood starts throbbing in our veins, we jump and grab the sides, find ourselves on the bed, pull out our knives, but then Ari notices the driver's eyes in the wing mirror, hesitates with his hand in his pocket, stiffens, feels a tightening in his chest, but the driver just smiles, or grins, sticks a cigarette in his mouth, lights it, rolls down the window, sticks his elbow out and drives slowly up Hafnargata, acting as if he hasn't noticed us, how we cut big holes in the boxes, stick our hands in greedily, grabbing at their contents, something rustles, we pull it out to find it's a packet of M&M's, that treasure that can only be got abroad or in Duty Free, Fucking hell, we hiccup with excitement, cut the box open wider and start tossing out the packets, shovel them down to the boys, who catch them with excited shouts, and then Sigga is up on the bed with us, when she was supposed to be running alongside, The fuck if I'm missing out on this, she says, cutting quick as a flash into a box, ripping into it and then tossing the rustling packets into the road.

Then it's finished.

After approximately ten lorries.

173

It's nearly 10.00 a.m., the sky has brightened above Keflavík, a hesitant, fragile light, apologetic in the realm of darkness. A few people are out and about, a police car as well, which means, of course, that it's time to stop. Some of the drivers cursed us, tried to shake us off, shouted reproaches, and one stopped his lorry in the middle of Hafnargata, got out, tried to grab Sigga, who was gathering things up in the road, but she got away, jumping with a giggle between yards, fast and agile; when the driver gave up and turned back, panting and cursing, there were no fewer than six boys on the bed of his lorry, finished cutting open countless boxes and strewing their contents all over the road, making it look as if there'd been an explosion: tinned food, luncheon meat, biscuits, frozen chickens, teddy bears. The driver, a short, stocky man, went back to his lorry, said not a word to the six boys, pulled himself cumbersomely up into the cab, drove off slowly, up Hafnargata, up to the Base, behind the other lorries, many carrying tattered boxes, crawled up the slope, through Grænás Gate, where an Icelandic policeman and an American M.P. stood guard and watched the lorries crawl past, like great wounded beasts, the soldier stood outside, his legs spread wide and his face stern, while the policeman stood in the doorway, leaning against the doorpost, smoking and wearing an indecipherable expression.

We carry the loot, a substantial haul, some having to make two trips, into the yard of the Independent Party's headquarters, several blocks from Hafnargata. It's a safe distance away, and the yard is enclosed; there, GÓ divides up the booty.

Long afterwards, Sigga would describe this incident in a series of articles entitled *Who Owns Iceland?*, written during her time as editor of *Víkurfréttir*, a weekly distributed to every home in

Suðurnes and read cover-to-cover. In these articles, which cost her her job, she was sacked the day after she published the third and final one, a few months before the economy collapsed, she delved into, among other things, how the Icelanders took fantastic advantage of the military base, directly and indirectly, by every conceivable means. At the end of the last article she told of this custom of Keflavík's teenagers to rob lorries loaded with cargo from the Yankee ships, sometimes by jumping onto them when they were parked at the weighing station and sometimes, as we'd done, ambushing them in Hafnargata. "Often," she wrote, "we carried our booty to a secure location in the yard of the Independent Party's headquarters and divided it up there – in a far-from-comradely fashion. It's safe to say, of course without our having realised it, that there was something poignantly symbolic about choosing that particular location, the yard of the political party that, more than any other, directly or indirectly, and unfortunately without regard for justice and honesty, has divided Iceland's wealth among its own members ever since we gained independence from the Danes."

But these sharp-edged musings are far from Sigga's mind this Saturday morning. Everything is gathered, everything is divided, everyone gets their share, portioned out "far-from-comradely" – GÓ is considerably more "equal" than others, and his gang takes the things that will be easiest to sell. Remember, says someone, with a blend of regret and lust in his voice, that time we found the porn magazines? Yes, sighs another, sixteen copies of *Hustler*, damn, man!

And then everyone goes home.

With their booty. Their treasure.

Some sneakily, hiding it in their rooms, or in a safe corner in the garage, others without needing to hide anything, cheering their families up with rare American products, sliced ham, tinned food, biscuits. Ari and I get a bag of M&M's, a few packets of biscuits and a box of some sort of sugary breakfast cereal. None of these things could be got in Iceland, not even in Reykjavík; it was as if we'd taken a trip abroad that Saturday morning. This is how it is to live in Keflavík, says Ari as we walk home, although Ari always had difficulties using that big, troublesome word *home* to mean the small single-family residence; we walk past Keflavík Municipal Park, where the trees are engaged in a continual struggle against the wind and the salt it carries, and grow so slowly that a thirty-year-old fir tree just reaches the shoulder of a twelve-year-old boy. Yes, I agree, it's just like this.

# Norðfjörður

— PAST —

*The world has been composed*
*– the poem is an hour old*

Without my brother Tryggvi, this wouldn't have happened, says Margrét, a few weeks after she stood on the foreshore and received Oddur's love poem – two clenched fists. They're in his fishing shed, lying naked on a heap of his fishing lines, staring up at the ceiling, smoking. Margrét had felt the lines chafing her back when he was inside her, as if he wanted to rub his life deep into her, the salt in the ropes, their fishy smell, the movement of his hand, the toil at sea, the freedom that he feels deep inside as they set sail and the sea merges with the horizon, all of this was in the lines, and towards the end, when he was about to explode, the wild pleasure that distorted his features and made him seem somehow so wide open, as if she could see into his core, he bore down so hard on her that it was almost as if he wanted to press the lines into her back, making everything one: the sea, the freedom, her. Afterwards they lie there panting, soaked with sweat, he reaches for a sail and spreads it over them, as if they're saltfish, and they have a smoke and she says this about Tryggvi, that without him they wouldn't be here, she might even still be in Canada. Oddur smokes, feels his heartbeat slow, and also how the world that had been torn apart is coming back together, realigning itself, getting back on track, everything returning to its place. Yes, he says, Tryggvi, yes, that may be

179

right, yes, that's probably true, but he reads too much, that's a fact. She laughs softly, Why do you say that? Especially poems, they tend to eat into his concentration, it wouldn't surprise me if that was why he tends to be outspoken about things that shouldn't be mentioned in front of others, feelings and other things that are nobody's business, a lot of people don't appreciate such talk. She laughs again, You're, says she, you're, but she can't continue, he cuts her off with a kiss, it's nice to taste his lips, feel their warmth, now with the added tang of tobacco, it's so nice that she bites him.

Without Tryggvi, this wouldn't be happening, they wouldn't be lying there all sweaty, deeply satisfied, happy, naked, like saltfish beneath a sail, and later, much later, when it will be too late to change, turn back, stop the disappointment, death, she'll sometimes think, having written it at least twice in letters to her brother, In a sense, you made all of this happen. Without you, without your letters, what you wrote or, even more, what you left unsaid, between the lines; for the unsaid slips more swiftly into our hearts, where it's quicker to begin making changes, while it's easier to resist what's said and written, and silence it. We can silence words but not hints. In all the letters you sent me in Canada, Oddur was like a hint between the lines; it was there that I sensed his strength, and his greatness – you made me mad with longing for him! Without those letters I would probably have settled in Canada, which is a much gentler country than our strange island, and never returned. There were young men pursuing me, you knew that – some of them promised me happiness, one promised to bring me the sun and the moon, as well as the stars and bliss, if I said yes to him. Hardly trifles! A tremendously handsome boy with a strong jawline; I remember it well. In the end, he went into politics and became an M.P., or maybe a governor, I don't remember which. Became a politician, no less. Those who promise so much, even the sky itself, are in all likelihood either poets or politicians. The former because they sincerely believe that words can change the world, the latter because they know deep down that words can easily bring you power and popularity. They aren't as innately naïve as poets, and therefore don't truly believe that they can reach to the sky with words; what's most important to them is to use words in a way that will bring them what they're seeking. I sometimes wonder if I would have been happy in his big house. He must live large. Does one feel happier in a big house; would one be happier than in cramped conditions? Oh, I don't know, no-one really knows about such things. Don't misunderstand me, dear brother, I don't regret my life, yes, the sorrow, everyone regrets that, but I had my shining moments, they keep me company in old age. Of course you were right, all things considered, to hide Oddur, your friend Oddur, between the lines and, in doing so, spirit me back here.

Where should one stop in a story; how many stories should one tell, and what becomes of the lives that we ignore, leave behind in silence, do we condemn them to a kind of death? It's never possible to say everything, the world doesn't have the patience for it, but little of what's said here, what has been said here, and what will be said, life and death, sorrow and smiles, would have happened without Tryggvi, without him we would be at the very bottom of silence, we would be silence itself, would be nothing, not even death, because what never comes is nothing, it never even manages to die. But time – it takes one small step, it's November, just over a year later, and Þórður is born. The eldest child. He who would turn out to be as beautiful as a poem, as robust as a savage, it's night, around 1.00 a.m., after four days of storms, the wind had screamed in the mountains, screamed itself through a heavy, frenzied, dense snowstorm, sweeping it, whipping it in every direction, out of the question to be outdoors, except to go astray, be buried in snow, become a toy of the wind howling over the houses, which tore at the sea like some sort of power, God or something, truly meaning ill, which is of course nonsense, there was nothing abnormal about it, no thought behind it, just an unfavourable low-pressure system surrounding Iceland. People stayed indoors, which is what we do in such storms, life is precious to us, which may not be significant, but it's all we've got, apart from a few farmers and farmhands who had to crawl out to the sheep sheds to feed the sheep, crawl to avoid being blown away, disappearing and being lost – not to be found before the storms abate, dead, buried in snow – crawled, waddled and relied on their own strength, stamina, luck, the loving-kindness of the Lord, who hopefully was somewhere far above the storms. Perhaps God could not see the earth through all the snow, falling and blowing in furious gusts, blinding, relentless, because one farmhand was driven astray, a boy of just twenty, and lost his way and his life, the wind took it, and the snow, but he isn't part of this story, we have no room for him, and so leave him behind in the silence. And the snow. The storm subsides around 1.00 a.m., they both awake to the silence, Tryggvi and Oddur, each in his own house, they can't be kept inside so go out, needing to dig their way to the surface and emerge at the same time, see each other as shapeless heaps in the snow; the village houses appear to be halfway, or entirely, buried. The fury has abated, the howling wind, that wild, transparent giant, invisible, the violent energy, gone without a trace, incredibly, and the world is left dazed. Calm and stars. And a full moon! So there's the moon, it was hiding behind the storm, all the snow and wet, high above the clouds, safe and sound in outer space, waiting patiently for the right moment, and now pours its light over the silent countryside. The snow-covered mountains, cloaked in pale white, a corpselike light, are a silent threat, a tranquil beauty. The two friends stand side by side, they hadn't exchanged greetings, just walked towards each other and nodded. A thousand stars twinkle in the black sky, the white moonlight sparkles on the heavy snow and transforms it into a treasure chest, the sea is black, and the calm deepens the tranquillity following the storm – there's no room for words, they're unnecessary, too clumsy, superfluous. There they stand, Oddur and Tryggvi. For quite some time. Just looking, taking everything in. Until Tryggvi finally opens his mouth and says softly, even cautiously, as if in the presence of something fragile: God composes magnificent poems. He appears to want to add something, which would be totally his style, the desire to put the world into words is a persistent buzz inside him, but nothing comes. The world has been composed, the poem is barely an hour old, now is the time to shut up and read it. He closes his mouth.

God composes magnificent poems.

He's not entirely wrong, thinks Oddur, and never forgot it, that moment, to emerge from the snow into still air, stars, moon-light, after a relentless tempest, cooped up inside; the tranquillity penetrated him, his heart, penetrated it, and then Tryggvi's sentence – is that perhaps why Oddur remembers this moment, always, never forgot it, remembers it as solace, proof that the world can be beautiful, do we really need, despite everything, to rely so desperately on words?

Silence, says Tryggvi finally.

Yes, says Oddur.

Tryggvi: Silence.

Oddur: Yes, yes.

Tryggvi: I think I can hear eternity.

Oddur: Hear what?

Tryggvi: Eternity – just try and listen, don't breathe, close your eyes and listen, see, like this, and then eternity will come to you like contentedness with no beginning.

Don't go and spoil everything, says Oddur, and starts looking around.

But I hear it, and I want you to hear it too, a sentient being mustn't miss out on such a magical moment. Eternity is like a giant, silent church organ.

You shouldn't read so many poems, because sometimes it's as if someone has put shit in your brain.

Can't you hear how deep the silence is, and . . .

Yes, yes, but . . .

. . . if you listen a bit more carefully . . .

. . . but it's much deeper at Grettir and Helena's, says Oddur, nodding in the direction of the elderly couple's house, or towards where it ought to be standing, a bit further back and above the village, except that now there's not a trace of a house there, only snow, a huge quantity of snow. Bloody hell, says Tryggvi.

They fetch snow shovels.

And take half an hour shovelling their way back up towards the house, a five-minute trip when the world is decent, but the snow is horrendous in places, besides the fact that the temperature has dropped rapidly, it's now minus six or seven, maybe eight, and the snow has crusted over, a 3-centimetre shell that gives way at each step and makes everything more difficult, heavier, This is how it is to walk in Hell, mutters Tryggvi when they reach the house, except that here of course there's no house, just snow, white fury that has fallen silent, is still, motionless, welcoming the moonlight and making so many things beautiful. They look around, they look up at the mountain, Nípa, which rises so steeply there, on its way to the sky and stars, and aim in the direction of a crag that juts out of the mountainside like an insolent forehead. They start digging.

Are quick to dig down to the house, and then beat on the roof with the blades of their shovels to announce their presence, we're here, on our way, don't worry, and they make for the door, dig a good tunnel. Meanwhile, Tryggvi jabbers away, which can be a bit tiring, but Oddur knows his friend and doesn't let it annoy him. Most people struggle with some sort of weakness; one person is stingy, another drinks too much, a third is terribly vain, which must be one of the Deadly Sins, one thinks too much about sex, another can't control his temper, and Tryggvi talks too much, that's his vice. You've got to accept it, endure it, which Oddur does, because Tryggvi has so many positive qualities that you couldn't imagine being without him; he's an optimist, extremely fair-minded, can't abide injustice, a true socialist, few are as industrious, labours tirelessly, is capable and resilient, it's a downright pleasure to work alongside him, everything always goes so smoothly, never a hitch, so it makes sense to put up with that dreadful vice dwelling in his vocal cords. In Icelandic, said Tryggvi once when Oddur couldn't help but criticise Tryggvi's loquacity, which had begun to get seriously on his nerves, everyone has a right to silence – In Icelandic, there are more than seven hundred thousand words, began Tryggvi, but Oddur interrupted him, slashing through whatever he was going to say: Do you really need to use all of them today? Oddur was forced to admit, though solely to himself, absolutely not in Tryggvi's hearing, and preferably not in Margrét's either, so little separates them that sometimes when he's speaking to her, it feels like he's speaking to Tryggvi, and vice versa; he does admit, to himself, though grudgingly, that Tryggvi has a tendency to say remarkable things, even in a way that catches you off guard, perhaps causes you to start looking differently at things around you, such as this business about God composing magnificent poems. The trick was just to let his rushing current of words transform itself into a low hum, a background noise, because no-one gets annoyed at the hum of a boat's engine, the buzzing of flies, the whine of the wind; now they've managed to dig down to the door, which opens, and there stand the old couple, Grettir and Helena, Tryggvi shuts up for the time being, so there's no need to worry about that anymore.

The elderly couple stands at the door, You two are true lights and the pride of all humanity, says Helena, kissing each of them on the forehead, as if blessing them. It's not much fun being buried so deep in the snow and unable to go anywhere, the house transformed into a coffin, and above the coffin lid nothing but awful silence. The couple climb up and out unassisted, We may be old and nearly useless, says she, but we still have legs that obey us, more or less. They ascend to fresh air and moonlight, to reassure themselves that the world is in its place and hasn't blown away. All four of them look out at the fjord, which is unusually calm, it should still have the storm in it and be breathing heavily, perhaps the moonlight has calmed the sea, hushed it, the moonlight that sparkles on its surface, transforming it into a song, into something upraised and lifted to the sky. Now is when you curse old age, says

Grettir, when you're no longer fit enough to go to sea, it wouldn't be bad to sail with you in such incredible moonlight. Grettir puts his arms around Helena, who gives him a nearly toothless smile; he reaches into his coat and pulls out a flask, Have a drink, fellows, let's drink deeply, and may benevolent spirits bless you, to have remembered two old folks like us down there in the silence. They all take a swig, and it's astonishing how liquor can be so good, particularly when it appears unexpectedly, like now, just after you've woken up, so to speak, and are therefore more alive to everything. Come on, we're going to sea, says Oddur, Yes, it's time to sail into the moonlight, says Tryggvi. You sail on the sea, the moon hangs fixed in the sky, the elderly couple hears Oddur say, as the young men walk away, walk briskly through the tiresome snow, eager to put to sea as soon as possible, preferably before everyone else wakes up, which won't be anytime soon, it being barely past 2.00 a.m., It's impossible to look out over the sea and not sail somewhere, such a thing can only make you miserable. They look back twice, wave, Good lads, she says, gathering her husband into her arms, two old bodies, old lives, that hold each other close. Do you remember, he says, when we were that young? Yes, I remember, my dear! But suddenly we're so old, when did it happen, sometimes it's as if time creeps up on you in your sleep, when did we stop being young? To me, you're always the same mischievous boy inside, she says, and he laughs and they watch the young men disappear from view, she sees them for longer than he does, has better eyes.

I want to be like them, says Tryggvi as they turn around a second time to wave and see the old couple still standing there, she taller, beautifully plain-looking, with her coarse, plump face, thickset arms, radiant blue eyes, he so much slenderer, having never looked very strong, but the years have whittled him down, if they continue in the same way, he'll be transformed into an axe- or shovel-blade.

Do you want to be old, hunched, so helpless that you need to be dug out of the snow?

No, just old beneath the moon and stars and still loving my wife so ardently that I simply must embrace her, and desiring nothing more passionately than to live with her a thousand years more, still loving her lips and eyes, that's how I want to be, old and happy in the moonlight.

One day, says Oddur, I'll be forced to cut you into pieces, for bait. That wouldn't surprise me, replies Tryggvi. Then they sail out onto the sea. Or rather, into the moonlight; there are more worlds than we can count, and none of them is the right one.

### *May you be blessed with happiness;*
### *concerning the many sides of life*

Time knows neither discretion nor tact; it takes one step and you're older, just like the mountains and the grass. One step and they're both dead, Grettir and Helena, their lives will no longer be part of these pages; where does justice come from, and why is there not more of it? They both went in early summer, in June, "when it's easier to dig a grave", a week apart, he first, having been in much worse shape, while there hadn't seemed to be anything noticeably wrong with her, she buried her husband, her beloved companion of sixty years, carried herself with dignity, went home after the funeral and cleaned the house, dusted every little item, picked things up, turned them between her fingers or her hands, depending on their size, almost as if she were recalling their

188

histories, the life that had surrounded them, took her time, even allowed herself to sit down and shed a few tears every so often, although weeping was nearly as bad as loafing. The tidying took four days, the house had never been so clean, and finally she had a bath, very slowly, so slowly that it was as if she were also recalling the history of her own body, and yes, she shed a few tears then as well, What a great crybaby I've become over the years, she thought, before drying her face and blowing her nose. She concluded by writing two short letters to her two children, one living in Canada, the other in Reykjavík. The first letter consisted of ten lines, the other, twelve, by accident, with a swarm of misspellings and the handwriting little more than a scrawl, a scribble, to her shame, it was Grettir who'd always seen to their correspondence, "but now he's dead, and therefore can't write to you. I've cleaned and dusted everything, I also had a bath and made everything neat and tidy, and now I'm going to go to him. It will be the longest journey that I will ever take, yet all I need to do is lie down and close my eyes and wait. It was nice to be alive. Kisses to you. May good fortune bless you as it blessed Grettir and me."

One step and they've both vanished in snow so deep that the brothers-in-law Oddur and Tryggvi wouldn't have been able to dig them out despite having the finest shovels and all the days of their lives to do so. Nothing that could be called extraordinary ever occurred in their lives, they merely worked with fish and sheep, knew the names of the mountains around them and several of the streams, and could tell from the behaviour of birds whether a sudden drop in temperature was imminent; apart from that, they'd had little to offer, were easily forgotten, yet managed to achieve what most people only dream of, to be happy in their own way for a full sixty years, how do we measure a person's greatness?

189

A mere two steps, and Oddur and Margrét find themselves with two children.

He'd built a house for them a little way up the slope, not too high, absolutely not where avalanches could get them, the white death, but high enough to have a good view out over the fjord and to the bay, the sea itself. She'd helped a bit with the construction when she could, when she had time away from the children, the younger, Hulda, suffered sometimes from stomachaches, and an eye had to be kept on Þórður, Hulda's brother, who was lively and inventive – many dangers lurk in the world for a frolicsome child – but it was too difficult to watch Oddur build their house and contribute nothing, her arms literally ached with restlessness, which is why she often turned up, grabbed a tool and gained a reputation for being cold towards her children, for showing little concern for them, women turn into targets whenever they try to step outside the cramped space assigned to them. But hold on a second, time has just taken another step, it's forbidden to stand still, to deal slowly and carefully with our happiness and our youth, the house is ready, they move in and their third child is born. A girl, her name is Ólöf, she would live much later on in Keflavík and end up in darkness, despite sometimes being a string vibrating between God and men. You have a child and your life is divided, it just happens, into before and after, you're forced to bid farewell to your former life, and your love is distributed, it's no longer focused exclusively, with its unfathomable power, on one person. Everything changes, looks different, some people can bear it, others less so, others not at all, but for the longest time Margrét and Oddur don't notice anything, so occupied are they with the children, their childhood, their helplessness, these are the years when the world simultaneously shrinks considerably and expands infinitely. Everything revolves around the children. The major events of history aren't the construction of the Pyramids, Napoleon's triumphs, the expansion of the British Empire, but the first word, the first attempt to stand, perhaps there is nothing greater than watching a life grow. In Þórður, Oddur gains a friend; We'll go to sea together someday, he says, and he walks the boy through the house and imitates the motion of the waves with his arms, accustoming him to it. Then comes the older girl, Hulda, followed by Ólöf. Oddur would plunge into the sea for both of them, without any hesitation; they're his princesses, he likes to pretend he's a horse, gallop with them to Reykjavík and foreign countries where one can buy dresses that would leave everyone speechless here among the mountains of the Eastfjords. Oddur returns from a fishing trip and gives Þórður a beautiful conch shell. If you put a conch to your ear you can hear the sea, hear its breathing, catch the sea's thoughts. Of course, Oddur doesn't say a word about breathing or thoughts, that comes later, from Tryggvi, a strong link between the uncle and his nephew, Oddur simply hands Þórður the conch, says, Listen, and the six-year-old boy puts the conch to his ear. Do you hear the sea? asks his dad. Yup! That means you're a sailor, declares Oddur, and Margrét has to look away to hide her smile when she sees the pride in Þórður's face. The girls receive shells, they're beautiful, they can be transformed into many things, they're like an open palm.

An open palm, Napoleon's triumphs, the first attempt to stand – for some reason, as time passes Margrét begins to feel vaguely despondent about daily life. Yet she lacks for nothing, her children are fairly healthy, Oddur is a hard worker, and the family is thriving, she's able to work now and then processing fish, whenever she can break away from her commitments at home and join the rest of the world; why does she have this feeling, then, as if she's unhappy with life? What sort of mother feels sadness when her children are healthy? I can't wait to start living, she'd said softly, not bashfully, to Oddur after their night together on *Sleipnir*, and the world opened itself to them, brought forth its treasures, because the two of them were quivering with life. Seven years have passed, she still loves Oddur, but daily life can be shaped in such a way that we occasionally need to remind ourselves of what's important, so as not to lose sight of it, which is perhaps why she sometimes goes down to the pier when she sees *Sleipnir* sailing in and gazes at Oddur, in among the other sailors; at such times, she sees and remembers his beauty, his strength and infectious self-confidence, that immoveable force that is so good to encounter given the precariousness of life.

"May you be blessed with happiness as it has blessed us."

Can happiness be luck, a lottery win, or does it come, on the contrary, only to those who have worked for it, with their diligence and way of looking at things? Life, writes Margrét in her diary, is nothing but a senseless beast if happiness is just luck. During the first years of her marriage, she writes regularly in her diary, the entries always beginning with descriptions of the weather, not because it's good to begin with what's obvious, but because weather has done so much to shape life in Iceland for more than a thousand years, because it is what determines whether Oddur will return from the sea or not. Following the weather come descriptions of the previous day, the small details that hold up the dome of the world, "Þórður made up a little story about a mountain that wished to become a sea, and asked me to write it down . . . Hulda was very inquisitive yesterday: Why can't we see

God, doesn't He live with the pastor? Why do you have these things on you, but not Daddy, she asked, poking at my breasts . . . Why do you have to wipe Grandpa's bottom, didn't he ever learn to do it himself?"

Has Grandpa never learned to wipe his bottom – meaning Jón, Oddur's father. They take him into their home when Hulda is three years old, time hasn't shown him much consideration, his health failed far too early, then he had a stroke, darkness bled into his brain and extinguished many of its lights, he became virtually helpless, became someone other than himself. He lies like an old rag in the front bedroom and occasionally emits loud, monotonous groans, as if out of boredom, or perhaps pain, for hours at a time, a groan that penetrates walls and Margrét's nervous system. Around this time, Ólöf is born, and some days become such heavy stones for Margrét that she can barely lift them. Winters are particularly arduous, from February to April, which is when Oddur, like most of the Norðfjörður fishermen, sails south to Hornafjörður, whence they head out to sea, leaving her on her own for weeks at a time with the three children and Jón. But what of it; throughout the centuries, women have had to carry the family on their shoulders; why not her as well? Still, they're burdensome weeks. Months. Some nights she lies awake, fatigued, listening to the rumble in the mountains when an avalanche falls somewhere, is never certain whether one will fall above her, rush down the mountainside, or perhaps inside her. She lies awake and listens to Jón groan. When she can manage it, and when he's alert enough, she reads to him – when he's aware of what's going on around him and is not in a haze, trapped in the pain, the humiliation, the forgetfulness. She reads Icelandic folktales, books on Icelandic history and culture, Jón Trausti,

193

*Grettir's Saga*,[11] and he listens, his eyes abnormally large in his haggard face, large and dark, as if night has settled within them, night without hope, without stars. Sometimes he tries to hit her, beat her, when she cleans him up, feeds him, and calls her ugly names, but she dodges the words easily, as well as his groping hands. One night, having just finished nursing and putting little Ólöf, just over a year old, to bed, Margrét still breastfeeds her, doesn't dare quit, she hears a peculiar noise coming from the front bedroom, finds the old man curled up in a ball, whimpering hopelessly because he's unable to die, had tried to strangle himself in the night, ordered his withered hands to encircle his neck, tighten and not let go until he was dead, Don't worry, he'd told his hands, as if he were speaking to two autonomous beings, I'm sure you'll die soon afterwards and then you'll find rest, like me.

But life always has many sides, many more than we can ever count, or understand. There are days, even several in a row, when his head is clear, when he's grateful to be staying with them, calls Margrét his light, and laughs joyously when the children play in his room. He takes particular delight in Þórður, they're drawn to each other and the boy is often in his grandpa's room, playing quietly with fantastical creatures of wood and bone that Tryggvi has carved for him, thus creating nice moments, rays of light that disperse the darkness, and they're connected, the old man with his roots in the nineteenth century and the child with his in the twentieth. The days grow brighter, spring is just around the corner,

11  Jón Trausti (pen name of Guðmundur Magnússon, 1873–1918): An Icelandic writer popular in the early twentieth century, known for his four-volume cycle *Heiðarbýlið* (*The Mountain Cot*). *Grettir's Saga* (Icelandic: *Grettis saga Ásmundarssónar*) is a medieval Icelandic saga describing the life and adventures of the outlaw Grettir Ásmundarsson.

the sun climbs ever higher in the sky, this eye of God that strews
the light of life over us and expunges the winter darkness. But
then a new side of life appears; there's a flash, a strike, that we
don't understand. It's April, light expands the world, and Margrét
is dozing in bed with Ólöf at her breast when a cry tears through
the silence, blows it to pieces, a cry filled with anguish, with mad
terror. Margrét reacts without thinking, sets Ólöf down on the
bed, crosswise, against the wall, with a pillow to protect her, all in
one motion, rushes to the front bedroom, barely giving herself
time to cover her breasts, heavy with milk. Old Jón had somehow
managed to sit up in bed and put his arms around Þórður, had
longed for the contact, to hold what is precious, hold what is
young and far from death, embrace him, cuddle him, but then
something struck, something that we don't understand; when
Þórður wanted to keep playing, Jón tightened his grip and refused
to let go. He didn't feel like letting go, or forgot to do so, or didn't
realise that he needed to let go, or absolutely didn't want to let go
and find himself alone with his old age, the humiliation and time,
so dreadfully heavy. At first Þórður had tried gently to break free,
you do everything gently when you're around Grandpa, he's so
delicate, fragile; he's a wafer-thin being trapped in time and can
break so easily, which is why Þórður was so gentle, but the gaunt
arms just tightened harder around him, and with unexpected
strength. Þórður could see the bones beneath the taut skin, could
see the knuckles and bones in his grandpa's hands, and felt frightened, and then absolutely terrified when his grandpa squeezed
him even tighter: he's squirming, kicking and punching when
Margrét enters the room, but Jón is staring into space with his big,
dark eyes, as if he isn't there, or is trying to remember why he has
his arms around this little boy, trying to remember who this is

wriggling in his grasp, and then why, his toothless mouth a gaping hole in his face, like a dark cave. Mum, says Þórður, his voice breaking as she enters the room, Mum, he pleads, reaching out to her, and it takes everything Margrét has not to lose control and assault the old man. There, there, she says, trying to sound calm in order to reassure Þórður, but is astonished at the strength in the old man's bony arms as she begins to free her son. Jón doesn't respond at all to Margrét's demand to let the boy go, doesn't change expression, there are only those big dark eyes, that gaping mouth, that opening into darkness and a terrible smell. It's so difficult to free the boy – the old man's arms simply won't be budged – that she loses her composure, feels frightened, desperate, frees Þórður with force, tears him away violently and rushes him to the kitchen.

No need to be afraid of your grandfather, says Margrét, as she sits with Þórður on her lap in the kitchen, stroking his blond head, trying to alleviate his fears, your grandfather's just ill from . . . old age, and he . . . That's not my grandfather, says Þórður, the words extraordinarily clear and harsh between sobs; it's something that's come to take me away. I'm never going in there again.

Unfortunately, he keeps his word, much to Jón's chagrin. Yet Jón appears not to remember the incident, has begun to forget most things, and over the next several days calls for Þórður, asks whether he's going to come and play on the floor in his room, it would be so delightful, but Þórður never comes, and Margrét invents excuses, explanations, in order not to sadden the old man. Must I always be alone, then? asks Jón, after calling in vain for his grandson yet again, and he weeps in the painful way that old people weep, because life is departing, the light is fading, most of his friends are dead, energy and health dwindle, until there's nothing left, really, but memories and tears, plenty of tears, bucketsful, as if they could fix anything, bring back anything that's gone, bucketsful of tears, and only death can wipe them dry.

Which is what it does. A little less than a week later, Jón breaks his silence with a scream, as if from joy or terror, and calls for Margrét, who sighs, she's standing over the laundry, wipes her hands on her apron, goes to his room and Jón dies as she enters. It's as if he'd waited for her, held death back with his dwindling strength, because it's so awful to die alone; as she steps into the room, he takes his last breaths, disappears into the darkness. She stands over him, her hands swollen from the laundry, rests them on her lower back, she's seven months pregnant, so tired that she can't even feel sad. Is just relieved. Leans against the doorjamb, sees him die, vanish into the incomprehensibleness that awaits us all, and thinks, without being able to stop herself, Oh, what a relief. Now I can have a nap in this room sometimes.

Aren't these the most difficult years?

Three young children and a problematic, decrepit old man at home, Oddur away for weeks at a time in the heart of winter, down south in Hornafjörður; it's February, March, well into April. The fourth child is born. Just over a month before its due date. Some people are in such a hurry; it's urgent, out of the way, out of the way, I've got to get on with life today. Jón's corpse is still in the front bedroom, it'll be a day or two until the funeral, depending on when Oddur returns, they're expecting him, he was far out at sea when his father died, when he uttered his cry of joy or terror, far out at sea, hauling in fish and freedom. A day or two. Of course it's very inconvenient to die when the ground is still frozen, when there's so much snow, it's hard work digging a grave, preparing the body's final home in the earth's darkness. Margrét's water breaks, unexpectedly, she's scrubbing the floor, on all fours, she's baking for the funeral feast, she's mending the children's clothing so that she won't feel ashamed. Her water breaks. Hulda is at home and runs as fast as her five-year-old feet can carry her, to get help, it's urgent, life and death, and neighbour women arrive ahead of the doctor, women who've experienced it all, both life and death, actually the doctor needs to do nothing, they've prepared everything, and Margrét gives birth to a little boy, he comes silently into the world, peacefully, He'll be a quiet child, thinks Margrét, sweaty, exhausted, but happy, the other three began immediately to scream and cry, as if life were suffering, but this little boy isn't going to make any noise, maybe he'll turn out to be a philosopher, always thinking, therefore having no time to make noise, she's going to christen him Jón. She's allowed to hold him a little, or have him lie at her breast, he's allowed to lie there, so peaceful, beautiful, his face unusually pure, too pure for this life, he'd grown well in her womb, and died there, never got to look at the world with those blue eyes of his, never got to say Mummy with his small mouth – did he die because she felt relieved at the death of old Jón, is that the price she has to pay, her punishment?

# Keflavík

— PRESENT —

*What do we really know*
*about the world – several*
*real pop songs played*

A December evening in Keflavík.

I took my suitcase to my and Ari's cousin-once-removed, who
lives in a small, two-storey wooden house in Keflavík's oldest
neighbourhood, alone with his two cats – he'd tried keeping a
hamster but the cats ate it, and then got himself a cheerful parakeet but the cats did it in, frightened it to death. Obviously they
couldn't stand its singing, our cousin told me after I put the suitcase on the little table in the room I'd been given to stay in, as
he distractedly ran his hand over the bird cage that he couldn't
bring himself to get rid of; the cats stood in the doorway and didn't
take their yellow eyes off me, cursing the fact that it would be
much more complicated to do away with me than the hamster and
that damned bird. They're good company, said the cousin, as if
to excuse the cats' behaviour and the cruelty in their yellow eyes.
He'd filled the refrigerator with all sorts of food, besides buying
three six-packs of beer, to all of which I was invited to help myself,
and then we had coffee in the living room, along with marble
cake from the bakery; he asked about Ari, and Þóra, I could never
understand why they separated, he said with a gloomy sigh. It's

cosy in his living room; an imposing old floor clock fills one corner. You don't see them very often these days, those big old clocks, which is such a shame; it ticked so gently that I got the feeling that I would never need to hurry again. Two bulky bookshelves overflowing with genealogies and historical texts accentuate the room's peacefulness, but you've got to move cautiously, watch your head; eighteen big model airplanes hang from thin wires, nearly 2 metres above the floor, which is well above the head of this cousin, and fill the space with their silent flight – American fighter planes from the first designs until the present day. I avoided answering questions about Ari's life; what was I supposed to say anyway, what should I try to explain?, and instead asked my cousin about the models, which lit a spark within him. He forgot everything else, his coffee cooled, turned into cold darkness in his rosy cup, as he spoke passionately, even lovingly, about the heroic exploits of each aircraft, in what wars they flew and were given their chance to shine. That's how he worded it, "were given their chance to shine", and became names, legends, in the military and among those who've discovered the beauty in model aircraft. I noticed the evening outside, that it had fallen over this peculiar town situated behind the world, far from everything that we know, even though an international airport sprawls on the heath just above it, suffocating the old pastures beneath its tarmac. Evening had come, painted the windowpanes dark with its brush, lit the tall streetlamps that stand close together almost as if they're afraid of the dark and want to put an absolute end to it. I bade our cousin goodnight, left him in the small living room, in the centre of it, with cold coffee in his rosy cup, time itself in the floor clock, and eighteen fighter jets and bombers in silent flight above him.

*

I walk through his yard, the shortest path down to Hafnargata, where I turn right, in the direction of the hotel. It's a dark December evening, but the electric lights shine brightly above me. The lighting is so powerful that there's probably no darkness anywhere in Keflavík, except in a back yard or two, and within two cats in an old two-storey wooden house. When I reach the New Cinema, the sky suddenly darkens, the wind picks up, and a hailstorm is unleashed. I run up Hafnargata, past the January 1976 bar, run the remaining 300 metres to the Flight Hotel. The four flags outside the hotel, Icelandic, Norwegian, American and that of the European Union, flap this way and that in a desperate attempt to escape, the hail pours down like a punishment from Heaven, hard, tiny fists that lash me and the cars in the car park. I sprint the final few metres.

The hotel appears empty, and the hailstorm ends almost as soon as I open the door. Deep silence greets me and I realise that I'm hungry, that I haven't eaten – apart from a slice of marble cake at my cousin's – since I devoured my Quota Swindle burger above the harbour, as the gulls hovered irresolutely in the sky, which looks a bit turbid. Rarely does the sky sparkle above Keflavík, except perhaps on rare days of calm, when everything is so silent in the early morning it's as if someone has died; otherwise the wind always seems able to swirl something up to dirty the sky, limit visibility: dry soil, dust, sea foam, disappointments, unemployment. The flapping of the flags can be heard quite well here inside, but otherwise, the silence is so deep that I hear the soft ticking of the eight clocks above the long, convex reception desk, counting the seconds in Tokyo, Sydney, New York, London, Cairo, Moscow, Singapore and Keflavík. Each clock ticks to its own time, in clear sight of all who walk through the door, as if to remind people that every second something happens in the world completely untouched by our lives, to remind us that we have so little influence, that we take such shallow steps.

My heart is beating faster than normal; I feel slightly ill at ease, the silence and the ticking of the clocks agitate me, it isn't always easy to remember time, to hear it ticking above your head, it's almost like hearing death's footsteps approaching from a distance. We probably shouldn't think too much about time, it unsettles so much, weighs down our steps, reminds us that life passes more quickly than we can understand, sometimes in less than an instant. You're young, and then you're something other than young: nearly thirty-three years ago, I stood on this precise spot, or very close to it, together with Ari, but then it was outside the freezer room of Skúli Million, having just shut the heavy door behind Ásmundur and Gunnhildur; we stood straight-backed like sentries, like an honour guard of life, of our impulses.

Thirty-three years.

I inhale deeply as if to catch a whiff of fish and fish processing, of a bygone time, of a building that burned to ashes about thirty years ago, just a few weeks after the quota system was introduced and Keflavík was deprived of its fish; burned to ashes along with its owner's debts and people's livelihoods. The sheet-metal-clad wooden structure that had for decades been one of the most powerful freezing plants in Keflavík. I inhale deeply to catch a whiff of the plant and the winter when Ari and I were tempered by our cold toil in fish offal, men's curses, women's lewd chatter. It did nothing to assuage the tumult of my emotions when our cousin informed me that the hotel manager was none other than Sigga, Sigríður Egilsdóttir, my and Ari's old friend, whom we first met on a January morning in 1976 as she lay in the road with GÓ's foot pinning her down, Sigga whom we hadn't seen since the late 1980s, when we'd worked in Drangey for a few weeks, dismantling drying racks to earn the money we needed to print a book of poems. We hadn't seen her for twenty-five years but occasionally heard about her, besides enthusiastically reading her fiery, occasionally saucy articles in *Víkurfréttir*, which reached their zenith in a series entitled *Who Owns Iceland?* That series cost her her job, and since then we'd heard nothing more about her. She'd ended up here in Keflavík as the manager of a four-star hotel – that wildcat! Who could have predicted it, and how must she look; as slender, as quivering with energy, with restlessness, with something we never managed to identify?

He who sinks into memories and bygone times tends to forget where he is – I'm no longer alone in reception. Sensing something, I look up from my memories and meet the eyes of a hotel employee standing behind the convex desk, perhaps having stood there for some time, silent, huge, nearly 2 metres tall, with enormous shoulders, as if created to bear something extremely heavy: bags of cement, our disappointments, the weight of the world. His strong but expressionless face turns almost hostile when I ask, perhaps a touch testily, startled at suddenly finding this giant staring at me, Where are you hiding Sigga, I mean, Sigríður, the hotel manager – I'm an old friend of hers!

The man places his paws on the reception desk, as if to give some idea of his strength; She's not here, he says, his voice like the roar of a powerful diesel engine, a big S.U.V. Then he directs me into the dining room. There I find Ari, sitting at a table by a window facing Hafnargata, with a book in front of him, he reads a few lines, then looks up and out of the window, as if comparing the book's text with the world outside.

\*

He's reading Dante, *The Divine Comedy*, three books that describe Dante's journey through Hell, then purgatory and then up to Paradise. Ari is in the middle of Hell, It's hardly possible to go much deeper in literature than that, I say, sitting down at the table and taking a sip of the beer that Ari has ordered for me, a dark Kaldi, I take two big swallows, it's nice to feel the beer spread round my stomach and then to wait for its mild intoxicating effect – Life isn't so bad, I say. True, Ari agrees, as he closes the book, closes Dante, closes Hell, closes the poetry, which seems sometimes to have no boundaries and thus goes on for ever, longer, deeper, higher, in search of what we don't know yet still desire.

There are few people in the dining room, a mere four souls besides us. An American couple well into middle age, both exceptionally fleshy, and two men of indefinite age; Norwegians, says Ari, both looking bleary-eyed, as if bored with existence, as if bored with being Norwegian, to have those enormous oil resources, the only country in the world without debt, as if bored with wealth, abundance, security.

Ari: They're here as guests of Mayor Sigurjón, he's turning sixty in a few days and is throwing a party – these are old classmates of his from when he studied administration and marketing at university in Tennessee.

Norwegians, I say; they're interesting. You get the impression that they're all prudent, religious, honest, healthy, since they're always skiing, and, besides that, they award the Nobel Peace Prize – a bit as if peace itself resides in Norway. Yet the most famous Norwegian artist of all time is a half-mad painter who made unforgettable pictures that quiver with darkness, restlessness, erotic tension, yes, quiver with everything that you don't generally connect with Norwegians.

Ari: I took a taxi here from the airport, though not directly, because, like an idiot, I asked the driver to go first to Sandgerði, which was an interesting detour, and you'll never guess who was at the wheel, even if you tried all evening! Anyway, I noticed the Norwegian flag as we drove up to the hotel and brought it up, The Norwegian flag, I said, and asked whether Norwegian tourists actually came to Keflavík to squander their wealth. Then she, the taxi driver, who was a woman, see, started telling me about a blog that's apparently become the subject of heated discussion here in Keflavík, with some people being enthusiastic about it and others wanting to shut it down. Well, in the blog's last update there was an article about Norwegian visitors; I just had to read it, she said. Which I did, after going up to my room, and the article stated that the Norwegians weren't here solely as birthday-party guests and old classmates but also, and perhaps most importantly, as employees of the American company that Sigurjón is trying to bring here, along with its prospects for employment. As far as I could make out, the Norwegians were a kind of cross between image consultants and marketing specialists.

Image consultants and marketing specialists, I mutter; is that a demonic or a heavenly combination?

It probably wouldn't be difficult to find them a place in Dante's Hell, says Ari with a smile, patting the book, and then I recognise it: it's the old Danish translation that Tryggvi, Ari's maternal great-uncle, bought from a travelling salesman nearly a hundred years ago; it was read and reread by him and then by Þórður, Ari's paternal uncle, numerous notes written in the margins by both of them, reactions to the text, reflections on life; some of the comments touch Ari just as deeply as the text itself, that seven-hundred-year-old poem. I'm on the verge of mentioning this: that he's reading this old Danish translation instead of a new translation that's closer to us in time and mind set, because most translations seem to age more quickly than their original texts; that's one of the mysteries of literature, despite the translations' importance and quality, it's almost as if they're bound more closely to their own time periods than the original works. I'm unable to ask why he's not reading one of the new translations because the waiter arrives at our table with a menu, and to my surprise it's the same man who showed me into the dining room, who'd looked at me so grimly in reception and placed his paws on the desk when I asked about Sigga, as if to make me aware of his strength, even threaten me with it, or perhaps silence me. Now he's a different person entirely, smiles warmly, and his roaring voice has become pleasant. He smiles as he runs efficiently yet amicably over the menu with us, though his professional, courteous attitude nearly fails to dampen down the titanic force apparently exuded by his body. Why isn't he somewhere saving the world with those arms of his, with those huge shoulders, I say in a low voice after he leaves, having taken our order for grilled plaice with artichokes for our starters and lamb for our mains, "from the heaths of the North, where the mountains breathe the sky", as the menu put it.

Ari: I think you watch too many Hollywood films in which the hero saves the world with his courage and his muscles. The era of physical force is in the past. Cunning reaches further than a spear. But what I wanted to say was that Sigurjón has put a lot of effort into bringing this American company to Keflavík; if it sets up shop here, it would be a real coup. But it's a delicate matter, a difficult deal to seal, because the company specialises in the disposal of industrial waste in the U.S. and is interested in buying the waste-disposal facility here in Helguvík. It would be a huge deal for Keflavík, solve all its problems in one night. And wouldn't that be apt? For fifty years we profited enormously from the Americans and their military, and now we could profit enormously from their waste.

It seems pretty damned far-fetched to me, I say, shaking my head; no-one is dying to dispose of industrial waste, let alone that of other nations! And why should an American company have Norwegians in its employ?

Ari: That's obvious: because everyone trusts Norwegians. They are, as you yourself said, so scrupulous. They award the Nobel Peace Prize, are the wealthiest nation in the world, yet are modest and unobtrusive. It's nearly hopeless trying to pin something bad on them. But of course it's far-fetched, you're absolutely right! Economic interests are the driving force behind the world's societies, which is why simple solutions appear far-fetched, or even naïve. We're destroying the earth with our lifestyles, that fact confronts us every single day, yet we do little to change it, as if we couldn't care less about those who will come after us. We do little, doubtless because we feel too well: those who have it good have little interest in fighting to change the world. Those who wish to control our existence know this full well – the unseen, the owners of big industry, of retail chains, or whoever they might be. Their goal is to maintain the status quo. Or, if you prefer, to maintain the laws of the absurd.

The laws of the absurd, repeats Ari, before beginning, as if it were an aspect of the absurd, the far-fetched, to tell me about his reunion with Ásmundur, about the finger that slipped into his rectum in search of faithlessness, and I don't know which I found more unbelievable, the description of Ásmundur as a middle-aged customs officer with a huge paunch, no longer tall, strong, sparkling and magnificent, but rather, far from all those things, or that Ari had to undress completely, bend over a lectern on top of a desk from an elementary school in Keflavík so that his cousin, the selfsame Ásmundur, could slip his index finger into his rectum. The only thing I could say, and in a rather crestfallen tone at that, as if the world's absurdity had disarmed me, was: I would have thought they performed their searches differently. Ari smiles, and his face is suffused with the expression I know so well from the old days, an indefinable expression that says, What do we really know about the world?

Yes, what do we know?

Despite all this, there is something of a bright side, which helps to set the world to rights: the food is absolutely delicious, and the Argentinean red wine that the waiter recommended made it even better; we are fulsome in our praise when the giant asks how we like it, and he smiles happily, like a large child. Nor is there any reason for us to spare our compliments; Ari and I are seriously impressed by the quality of the food – by the fact that such a skilled cook, such an excellent restaurant, should be hidden here in Keflavík; it would never occur to anyone to associate this black place with the culinary arts, this slice of the country where Icelanders have starved the most and suffered the most ever since the country was first settled. The quality of the food is so high that we're astonished that there aren't more people here in this unfortunate place looking for answers, something to rely on, than just Ari and me, the American couple that have begun to spoon-feed each other their pudding – the man is wearing Bermuda shorts, the veins on his broad calves are swollen and meander down them like creeks about to overflow their banks – and the two Norwegians, so gaunt and bowed that they resemble large knives. Anywhere else, this place would be reviewed in the papers; anywhere else, you'd need to book well in advance. Obviously, no-one expects a top-flight restaurant here in Keflavík, and the locals don't show themselves, perhaps preferring one of the town's countless hamburger- and hot-dog vans. The hotel's chef can hardly compete in popularity with Jonni Thunderburger.

Ari and I finish our bottle of wine and order whiskys; the selection is exemplary, and evening has fallen over the town, has slowed its residents with its darkness, at least the cars drive more slowly than before up and down the streets, almost gingerly, as if something were in danger of being broken: the evening, the glow of the streetlamps, life. We look out of the window, at the houses lined up diagonally across from the hotel. That's where Glóðin was, I say. Ari says, Yes, that's where it was.

Glóðin – The Embers – which for the longest time was the only restaurant on Suðurnes, always full of people, and which even became fairly well known after one of the Reykjavík newspapers reviewed it, the *Morgunblaðið* or the *Dagblaðið*, or maybe it was the *Helgarpósturinn*; though the reporter's attention was drawn mainly to the large signed photograph of four American astronauts that hung over one of the booths. The astronauts had come to Iceland in the early '80s to train for a Moon expedition that never happened; Ari and I saw them twice on our way to work at Drangey, they appeared to be wandering aimlessly back and forth across Miðnesheiði, as if they were searching, with little hope, for something extremely precious, for what the world was missing. The desolate heath, its solitude, was supposed to prepare the astronauts for the landscape of the Moon, and the discomforting and painful feelings that a person must feel when they stand on its surface, alone in the ominous silence of space, looking out

at the earth, our blue abode, as excruciating loneliness seeps
through their airtight spacesuit.

For some reason the astronauts preferred Glóðin to the
Officers' Club on the Base, where the food was better and the wine
selection considerably more varied. The menu at Glóðin offered
chicken and chips, lamb with caramelised potatoes, fried cod with
onions and chips, and three rather lame varieties of red wine. No
beer, of course; it was a few years before beer would be permitted
in Iceland, but there was plenty of vodka; the astronauts polished
off one or two bottles each night. They looked rather drunk in the
photograph that hung for years above their table, a huge portrait,
probably 70 by 80 centimetres. The locals always wanted to be
seated beneath the photograph, to get to sit in the same seats as the
famous astronauts, men who'd been closer to Heaven than the rest
of us could dream of ever being. Space heroes, friends of the stars.
They looked jovial in the portrait, as if they were laughing, even,
and two of them appeared to have yelled something the moment
the photographer snapped the picture. Extremely jovial, and one
of the astronauts had scribbled at the bottom of the photo:

*Glóðin is great, simply fabulous –*
*it should be on the Moon!*

The American couple stood up, both tottering from either their
drinks or their weight, the woman giggles like a girl while the
man lays his stout arm on the shoulders of the giant waiter, as if
wanting to rest his weight momentarily on those shoulders, gain
a moment's respite from himself, or else check how much weight
they're able to bear, whether it would be possible to rest the world
on them, and then he says, loudly enough for us to hear it clearly,

that he knows this town, that he'd been a soldier and was stationed at one point at the Base, up on the damned heath that God wouldn't recognise as His own, And hardly the Devil either, he adds, then says nothing for a moment, as if to digest his own words better, before continuing, still with his arm on the waiter's shoulder, Damn it all, it was in the '70s, I was a fucking M.P., man, he shouts suddenly, from 1975 to 1978, fucking hell! Ari and I exchange a quick glance, both remembering, at the same moment, that Saturday morning in January 1976, maybe he'd been the guard standing at Grænás Gate, stern-faced, as the lorries crawled past like huge, wounded beasts. Very interesting, says the waiter, very interesting indeed, staring hard at the American, as if trying to imagine the young, skinny soldier somewhere within that massive body.

Ari: Time takes us in strange directions – most of them unexpected.

The evening continues to darken.

The Norwegians have gone up to their rooms, one of them carrying a black briefcase. He held it almost as if he were holding our fates in his hand; those who govern the world don't go around shouting anymore, they avoid the front pages of newspapers, and they're behind all the scenes, we're barely aware of their existence, they're transformed into air, vague shadows, if we gang up against them.

The waiter clears the Norwegians' table, every movement displays his powerful physique, he's unable to hide it, Ari watches him, his eyes are distant, there's too much sadness in them, they weren't like that before, yes, of course they always had a bit of sadness in them, regret but also joy, those eyes could easily and effortlessly become two excited puppies. I miss those puppies.

One of the Norwegians reappears in the dining room and says a few words to the waiter, who nods and goes into the kitchen, the Norwegian remains standing among the tables, his long arms dangling at his sides, his head hanging; he looks branded by loneliness, gaunt, uncomfortably resembling a long knife – he suddenly, unexpectedly, reminds me of what we fear. Shortly afterwards, the waiter returns with a whisky bottle, Laphroaig, a Scotch whisky with a dense, smoky taste, hands it to the Norwegian, who thanks him. I watch him leave and am about to mention this business about the knife and fear, but Ari begins reading from *The Divine Comedy*, muttering a few lines to himself in Danish, as if they'll help him understand the world better. Then he closes the book and says thoughtfully, as if taken aback by his own statement, Yes, greed is probably the worst vice; it's humankind's black hole. It devours everything, leaving only misery and emptiness, hopelessness and ennui.

Are you describing the world of liberalism? I ask, emptying my glass of whisky. Still just as unable to stand it?

I was just thinking about the last update on that blog – I read it on my phone while I was waiting for you; it says that greed is humankind's black hole. That whoever wishes to rule the world must above all convince us that we always need more. Convince us that we deserve to have more today than yesterday. The recipe for power, enormous influence, is to make us insatiable. Change us into addicts.

And everything will end in darkness?

With one more victory for materialism at least, says Ari, unexpectedly and almost as if he's happy, and then he looks out at the cars crawling on their endless circuit up and down Hafnargata family cars and S.U.V.s. A huge white van, nearly the size of our

214

lorry when Ari and I worked here for Skúli Million, crawls by, the driver has rolled down his window, stuck out his bare elbow, his music cranked up so loud that we can hear it clearly here in the hotel, and we immediately recognise the song – the band is Brimkló, doing their bittersweet song "I'll Never Forget You" from their top-selling 1979 album *Real Pop Songs*. The velvety voice of Björgvín Halldórsson fills the big van, resounds over Hafnargata, slips through the windowpane to us: "Please hold my hand / wherever I go."[12]

Good old pop.

The song hits us like past times, penetrates us like an arrow, its tip cloven by regret and poison, regret and accusation. One more shipment from the past, as if someone had sent the lorry with this music just to scatter our thoughts, silence us, set our memories in motion in the hope that they would make us forget the present, forget humankind's black hole, forget our blunders, forget and stop rooting up doubt, nagging questions. Real pop songs: "Please hold my hand / wherever I go / because I'll never forget you."

12 Brimkló was an Icelandic pop and country-and-western band, founded in 1972. Its lead singer, Björgvin Halldórsson, also known as Bó, or Bó Hall, born in Hafnarfjörður in 1951, has been a prominent fixture on the Icelandic music scene throughout his career. *Real Pop Songs* (Icelandic: *Sannar dægurvísur*): "I'll Never Forget You" (Icelandic: "Ég mun aldrei gleyma þér"; lyrics, Jón Sigurðsson, music Marty Robbins).

# Norðfjörður

— PAST —

*Shoot me to the Moon!*
*But first, maths homework;*
*a woman in the Eastfjords turns into*
*a living mummy*

Margrét is standing outside the house, leaning against it, looks out to sea, looks at the colours on the mountains. It's been two years since the old man died and the boy was born dead. The two girls are indoors, playing together on the floor, with shells, sheep bones and dolls, chattering away; it's nice to listen to them and the day is calm, so calm that Þórður was allowed to go to sea with his father, the two of them walked with Tryggvi down to his boat, I'll need you to take command of *Sleipnir* sometimes, said Tryggvi to Þórður in the kitchen before setting off, because every time your dad drinks coffee he can't think of anything but coffee, and I need you to steer the boat in the meantime!

Margrét goes out regularly to look at the sky, checking to see if the weather looks likely to change, there are no real indications of it doing so, but it's late October and it wouldn't take long for it to change from tranquil and peaceful to purely evil. It's hard knowing that Þórður is far out at sea, he's only nine and the sea is horrendously big. Þórður was so excited that he barely said good-bye to her, she had to grab hold of him to kiss him on the cheek, Lots of kisses, Mum, he'd said impatiently, trying to wriggle out of

219

her embrace, his eyes on the two men, Oddur and Tryggvi, who stood there, legs spread wide, waiting, like something invincible, like something he wanted to become. She, like a dunce, held him too long, knew it, sensed it, but it felt as if she were losing him. As if they were taking her boy from her, his fragility, his dreaminess, which is why she held him too long.

Two years had passed since the pure-faced little boy was laid in the ground he never got to know, never got to run on, to smell, to feel how soft and pliable it could be in the summer, how hard and cruel in the winter, was laid down into it along with his grand-father, one who'd lived too long, another who hadn't lived at all.

Oddur had come home a few hours after the birth of his son, had come home to bury his father, but found himself also having to say goodbye to his child, who didn't get the chance to exist. Margrét was lying in bed when he arrived, she couldn't get up, couldn't eat, couldn't speak, couldn't think, couldn't cry, could only hate the world, but then Oddur arrived and he might not have said much, nor does he know many words, but he said what was so good to hear: We'll get through this together. And held her in his arms. It might have been the most beautiful thing he'd ever done or said, and because of it, she was finally able to cry.

When she goes in after lingering outdoors for quite some time, the serene sky managing to breathe some stillness into her heart, the girls have stopped chattering, they're sitting close together, having gone and got Þórður's conch, and are listening to it, their faces pictures of concentration. Margrét smiles, creeps about so as not to disturb them, Do you hear the sea? Ólöf, the younger one, asks her sister; No, replies Hulda. Me neither, says Ólöf, and the disappointment in her voice is so poignant that Margrét turns to look over at her. It's probably just boys who hear the sea, says Hulda, which is why Daddy gave Þórður a conch, and not us.

Ólöf: Daddy's always at sea.

Hulda: Yes.

Ólöf: And soon Þórður too.

Hulda: Yes, soon. When he gets even bigger.

Ólöf: Not us?

Hulda: No.

Ólöf: No matter how big we grow?

Hulda: Don't be so silly. We're girls.

Ólöf : So we won't get to spend as much time with Daddy and Þórður.

Hulda: No.

Ólöf: It isn't fair! I don't want it to be like that!

We're girls, repeats Hulda, and her voice takes on the tone of an adult when she adds, Later you'll marry someone, and he'll take care of you.

But I want to take care of myself.

I know. Me too.

And I want to have a conch to hear the sea.

You'll get shells, says Hulda, without the slightest touch of maturity left in her voice, and Ólöf starts crying, and says with a sniffle, I want a conch from Daddy, too; I want to have a daddy like Þórður does, too.

Hulda: But you have the same daddy – it's our daddy.

*No*, screams Ólöf, and she jumps up, tosses the conch aside and runs outside.

*

Margrét knows that she should run after her, comfort her, calm her and soothe the wound that so suddenly and unexpectedly opened inside Ólöf, her infant, but she's unable to do it, stands there powerless in the kitchen, as if paralysed.

Time crawls along. We grow older, life gradually abandons us, we lose it, everything disappears. Life is one chance, we get one chance to be happy, how can we make the most of it?

Moments of happiness.

Somewhere she writes in her diary: I have to train myself to enjoy them more and longer, and use them as nourishment in my fatigue; then I'll complain less to myself.

Moments of happiness.

When Margrét helps Þórður with his homework assignments in Icelandic: Describe a day without rain in Norðfjörður. Assignment in Danish: Translate into Danish: Once there was an old woman who had an only daughter. Math problem: 4½ m cost 9 kr. 30 aur. How much do 7½ m cost?

Þórður is a diligent pupil, enthusiastic, sometimes acting as if he wants to learn and understand everything in the world, asking his father question after question about fishing, translating news-paper headlines into Danish, always earning the highest marks in his class, and for two years he begins each day by composing a verse on how the day will go, and composes another verse each evening describing how it went. Margrét is so proud of him that she has to work hard not to be too obvious about it.

She also has to work hard so that fatigue or depression, the darkness that lurks deep within her and refuses to let go, doesn't alter her behaviour, distort her mood. Distort the moments of happiness – they have another child, Gunnar Tryggvi, a beautiful boy, bright eyes, My godsend, she sometimes sings: *Godsend and bird of happiness / come cuddle up with me.* What to say about this; these are hard times. Heavy weather, a gloomy outlook for society, a difficult struggle by workers against the hegemony of economic interests, she and Oddur attend protest meetings at which he is greeted with particular enthusiasm, as a skipper, an owner of a productive fishing vessel. She's unable to attend as often as she would like, no decent woman leaves a baby behind to attend a political meeting, and then something starts irritating Gunnar, he awakes often in the night, and then Ólöf also falls ill, lies in bed for days with a high fever, cries at night, and Margrét watches over them. Over Ólöf. Over Gunnar. Watches over them and is with them, week after week. As we do, we watch over our children, protect them, that's our purpose, it's why we're here.

The outside world recedes, the life of the village, the struggles of the people, and the world of her family tightens its grip, as if no longer allowing her to take part. What is more precious than our children; aren't they themselves the meaning, the beauty, the source of everything?

Constant fatigue, however, doesn't seem to have much regard for beautiful words like *meaning* and *love* – sometimes beautiful words are no help whatsoever – instead, they gradually settle over her like delicate wrappings, envelop her, tighten around her, tighten and change her slowly but surely into a living mummy.

A living mummy, she writes; I should let the papers know about this, of course! Even the ones in Reykjavík would publish the news: "Living mummy in Norðfjörður!" Maybe I would be sent to famous museums abroad, and thus get to see the world. Oh, if only someone would shoot me to the Moon, where I could sleep in peace. I would give a great deal for such a thing to happen!

*

Shoot me to the Moon: there are long periods, weeks, even months, when the fatigue never leaves her; envelops her, imprisons her, turns her into a mummy, she dreams of being shot to the Moon just to be able to sleep, take a break, her fatigue turns into grains of sand in her blood and the days stretch her nerves between them, transform them into a vibrating string plucked by the hours, the same vapid song about fatigue, sleeplessness, numbness. Without sleep and rest we're ruined, fatigue distorts our entire existence, it changes insignificant, everyday events into shipments from Hell.

*(In parentheses – a tiny bit about my and Ari's*
*maternal grandmother, who was as fair as the moon,*
*her hair like the dawn,*
*her breasts two roe-deer calves)*

Our grandfather was a sailor, but later he would paint houses, first in Reykjavík and then in the Norwegian town of Stavanger; Ari has written a book about it. A down-to-earth, hard-working man, though at one point, Grandma's beauty seemed almost to turn him into a poet; he wrote her a long letter when he was working in the herring industry in the east, seven weeks away from home, his homesickness for her and their two daughters was almost too much to bear. He envisioned them every time he shut his eyes, they smiled at him in his dreams, he could hear their laughter, he could see the basement flat they'd rented. Her hair like the dawn. He wrote her a long letter, from far out at sea, on bouncing waves, had to steady himself to be able to write, a long letter, overflowing with passionate expressions, he even wrote her a poem, it was about her hair (like the dawn), her breasts, smile, ears, the first and only poem he ever wrote in his sixty-seven years of living. Posted it as soon as he came ashore, proud but a bit bashful about the poem. He knew nothing, suspected nothing, understood nothing.

Didn't know that she who was as beautiful as the moon, as mysterious as an August night, could tolerate neither responsibility nor crushing fatigue, the two of them wove themselves together and became the face of a demon that haunted her in her sleep, greeted her when she awoke; she bent, she broke, she cracked, she ran up the stairs of the basement in the Old West Side of Reykjavík, away from her three-month-old daughter who cried, who screamed in her cot, away from her elder daughter, Ari's mother, then eighteen months old, full of colds and coughing, snot dripping continuously from her nose, refusing to eat, knocking the spoon from her mother's hand, who screamed and stamped her feet, they both screamed, howled, all three, the youngest from fatigue, colic, the elder daughter from indisposition and fear of her mother's reactions, me and Ari's grandmother, who screamed because what should have been the best thing in the world, the point of it all, the source of beauty and innocence, your child, your children, had turned her life into something like being stuck in Hell. Surely life was never supposed to be like this, constant struggle and chronic exhaustion, insomnia, a husband who was away at sea and understood nothing, noticed nothing, the fairy tale having vanished, evaporated, she screamed in fear of the diabolical visions inside her, the diabolical voices that whispered to her to hurt her children, to beat them into silence, she screamed at the life that turned out to be little but thorns – screamed and fled up the stairs, out into the street, into the freedom of alcohol, the freedom of surrender. Never to return. The letter from Grandfather arrived the following day. They'd phoned him, he'd hurried home, south to Reykjavík, and the first thing he saw when he walked into the basement flat was the unopened letter, and in the envelope that stupid poem – which she would never read.

*September or April?*
*It doesn't matter, the important thing*
*is not to slip*
*on the ice and drop*
*the boy who twitters like a shorebird*

It would never occur to Margrét to run away from her children, her home, responsibility, fatigue; where was she supposed to run, anyway?, the village of Nes has nothing to compare with the streets of Reykjavík, with its countless houses, clubs, cafés. The village of Nes is just a handful of streets, wooden houses, fishing sheds, fish, sea, the mountain overhead, as steep as life, there is nowhere to hide, to vanish into another existence.

Gunnar is a good-natured child who sleeps peacefully the first few months, but then something starts to bother him and he awakes in the night, crying, five times, six, seven times, cries almost as if it hurts to be alive, as if he wants to return to the place whence he came, as if he were asking his mother to help him return. Thus do the months crawl by, like a wounded beast, like a crushed worm, numbing part of the brain, turning it into a frozen tundra where Gunnar's cries echo, sounding most like the screeching of birds long after he himself has been soothed and is asleep once more. During the most difficult months, Oddur sleeps in the front bedroom when he's not down in Hornafjörður for the fishing season; there's no way that he can captain a boat on little sleep, he's responsible for his crew, for assuring both their safety and their productivity, that they have decent hauls, he has a responsibility to their families, to the village, fish is everything to us, it's our alpha and our omega, without fish the economy of the young, sovereign Icelandic nation would collapse, and then we could very likely forget about ever gaining full independence from Denmark. Oddur has got to hold his own, and she gets up promptly when Gunnar awakes crying, tries to comfort him and stop his sobbing before it cuts into Oddur's sleep and wakes him.

Gunnar turns five months, six months, seven months, eight months old, and each month is just more than four weeks, each week is seven days, each day is twenty-four hours, it's a long time, a road that has to be travelled, a road that seems to extend to infinity. But it's even worse when Gunnar is peaceful and happy and twitters like a shorebird, when everything is so beautiful, a miniature version of the Garden of Eden, then she tolerates nothing, then her head feels as if it's being cloven in two. The days come, they go, and she has to make an effort not to scream, not to ruin something, Oddur touches her but she withdraws, stiffens, closes off her body, yields only once, twice, three times during those months, he won't leave her alone, like a persistent fly, one more attempt and she opens up, lets him in, opens her body, just to be left in peace, to be rid of him. Lies stock-still throughout, her legs spread wide, staring at the ceiling, at its timbers, fights against sleep, which presses her hard, but it's impossible to sleep with him lying on her like that, with all of his weight, he pants something in her ear, he's saying something, but she doesn't catch his words, If Oddur were to drown, she thinks, maybe I could get a bit more sleep. It's such a comforting thought that she loses herself in it momentarily, and Oddur has to repeat what he said. Huh, she says, sluggishly, Don't you want to tidy yourself up, he says for the third or fourth time, surprised, perhaps startled, as if shaken by an unpleasant feeling, and then she realises that he's no longer on top of her but lying next to her, she with her legs still spread and her dress pulled up. She reaches down, places her fingers between her legs and they become sticky with his semen.

And Gunnar cries. He cries and he cries and he wakes, he wakes all the time and is inconsolable and he cries, why does he need to cry so much, and how much pressure can a person's skull withstand?

One day, the solution came to her!

He was crying but has finally calmed down and gone back to sleep, yet the crying continues to resound in her head, so clearly that she needs to bend over to convince herself that the child is sleeping, peacefully, quietly – and then the solution comes to her! One of the girls is saying something, but she curtly waves her away, does so to save the girl, in fact, feels as if she's no longer in control of herself, that she's about to explode, her skull can't take any more, her veins protrude, her eyes bulge. The solution is clear – so obvious, in fact, that she's absolutely flabbergasted that she hadn't seen it earlier. Calmly and deliberately, she bends over, picks Gunnar up, pauses to consider whether she should take along the rag doll that Tryggvi gave the boy but decides not to, and goes outside, cautiously, because it's slippery, notices it immediately but is slightly surprised, having forgotten what season it was, having forgotten that there are different seasons, tries to recall, as she inches her way down the slope, extremely carefully so as not to drop the child, whether it's September or April but finally gives up, since it doesn't matter, the important thing is not to slip and fall on the ice. She looks so forward to being able to sleep sometime soon. Gunnar has stopped crying, likely knowing what awaits him, and looking forward to it, like her. She makes it down to the shore without falling and realises that she's forgotten to put on her shoes, that she's barefoot, and, in fact, isn't wearing a coat either; it's incredible, what would people say if they got wind of that, yet it's alright because she doesn't feel the cold. So it's probably April, yes, probably, she vaguely recalls that Oddur has left for the fishing season, gone south to Hornafjörður, yes, April, and summer is on its way, That's great, she thinks, looking down at Gunnar, who looks up at her in return, but there's no meaning in the glance, nor does she feel anything, the thread connecting them has obviously been cut, that's how things are taken care of and it will certainly be great for them both to take a little rest, he in the sea, it will rock him and calm his tears, and she in her bed. She smiles, can't help doing so, but then something touches her elbow, the left one, and someone says, Mum. Yet she's the only one there, so it must mean her, and for that reason she turns and looks and there stands Þórður, nine years old, with a slightly bewildered look in his eyes, and barely dressed as well; Just look at you, dressed like that in this cold weather, she says, too tired to be angry, but then she asks, Is everything alright, because he continues to look at her so peculiarly, is he ill, perhaps? Let's go home, Mum, he says, and then it's almost as if there's a slight break in the clouds, as if understanding, awareness, stirs within her. She looks down at Gunnar, sees the waves lapping at her feet, the hem of her night-dress, which lifts regularly over her knees, and then she feels the bitter cold and starts crying. Silently. She allows Þórður to lead her home, to lay her down in bed, she barely notices it when he places her ice-cold feet against his belly, that little belly, incredible how he's able to accommodate such enormous cold, she wants to say something, perhaps ask about Gunnar, ask where he is, but at

229

that moment something big enters the house and bends over her, something big and soft, and it's sleep and she drifts off, I'm falling asleep, she thinks happily, feels herself sinking fast and so deeply that she's not certain she'll ever come up again.

*The night is night, and you shall see the world as*
*as I see it, as I want it to be*

It's undoubtedly necessary for everyone to step outside their routine and do something irresponsible, exist without responsibility; carelessness can alleviate fatigue, correct life's magnetic deviations: he who never steps off the path gradually ceases to hear his own thoughts.

Oddur and Tryggvi sail out to sea aboard a small motorboat that Tryggvi has acquired and uses to fish just off the coast, when he has the time, and in so doing makes a bit of money. They don't need to go too far, and it's good to stay in sight of the village, the houses lined up along the coast like big seabirds unable to fly.

It's good to drink.

Everything becomes easier for a time, you can hear your own thoughts, feel lighter. Oddur looks towards the land, which has been transformed into a deep, dark shadow; it's November, around midnight, very nearly calm, no stars, no moon to lift the heavy darkness off the land. He looks towards the land, which has been transformed into darkness, has become darkness, and says, You're young, and then you become something other than young. You know that a little more than a month ago, Margrét wandered down to the shore barefoot and wearing only a nightdress, with Gunnar in her arms, in snow and frost, and waded into the sea up to her hips?

230

Tryggvi: Yes, I know.

Oddur: What sort of nonsense was that? It was so cold that the child could have become seriously ill, yes, and she as well. When I asked for an explanation, she told me she'd been incredibly tired and needed some fresh air! That's no explanation; that's just bollocks. Who hasn't been tired?

Tryggvi: You . . .

Oddur: You know that people talk about her.

Tryggvi: People are always talking.

Oddur: Dammit, you know what I mean.

Tryggvi: You should hug her more often, she's like Mum, she's . . . special. I think she needs more from life than we do, and that makes her, I don't know – sensitive to shock. And what happened with little Jón hit her hard, perhaps harder than the rest of us can understand; yes, you should hug her more often.

As if I haven't tried, says Oddur, staring out into the darkness, because sometimes it's easier to look in the direction where there's nothing to see. They say nothing, drink, drink a lot, both look into the darkness. I'm not so sure, Tryggvi says finally. No, replies Oddur, I don't understand it either.

Tryggvi: I'm not so sure we seriously try to understand other people – do we really give it our full attention? Don't we actually do the opposite, and constantly try, all our lives, to make others see the world as we see it? Isn't that our great misfortune?

Oddur: I don't know. I just know that it isn't normal for a mother to rush out into the cold half-dressed, with an infant in her arms, and wade into the sea. I just don't get it. I'm not sure that you're supposed to get it. On the other hand, I know that we're drunk, and therefore something should be happening; we should be fooling around and singing, wrestling, telling stories,

231

looking at beautiful girls and cracking lewd jokes; you know, clearing our heads.

Tryggvi: Normal, what's normal, can you tell me that? Thou shalt have no other God, it says in the Bible. Or, in other words, thou shalt not see the world through anyone else's eyes but Mine. Thou shalt see the world as I see it, as I want it to be.

Oddur: You read too much, and that's why obvious things become so complicated in your mind. I shouldn't have to explain what's normal. It's something that you know, imbibe at your mother's breast, something that, I don't know, is just all around you as you grow up. You rely on it. It keeps everything in its place, and guarantees that we don't lose our grip on things. Naturally, you can say anything you want, tug and stretch and befuddle yourself, but that doesn't change the fact that when all is said and done, I know the difference between what's normal and what's not.

Tryggvi: Normal, that's exactly what I'm trying to say: thou shalt see the world as I want it to be. Haven't we all adopted this, how shall I put it . . . this aggression . . . this narrow-mindedness? Do we really try to understand others? Do we try, do we even care to understand those who are different, for example, those who stand out in some way – because it's probably much easier to condemn others rather than try to understand them. We make our lives easier by saying, This behaviour or this way of thinking isn't normal, I condemn it! As if our lives become easier by condemning others – have you noticed that we do this? Who doesn't want a more comfortable life? Who's entitled to judge what is normal, and isn't there aggression in the word *normal*? Is "normal" a sturdy cage surrounding all of us, perhaps? Surrounding our lives? A cage from which we can never escape? Except perhaps when we drink.

He takes a swig from the cask.

Oddur: Are you drinking the same thing as I am?

Maybe we never drink the same thing, says Tryggvi, before starting the engine, sailing off, piloting the boat further into the night, further out to sea. Tryggvi sails, sails a long way, mutters something, heavy lines of verse, he drinks.

Where are we headed? Oddur asks finally.

Tryggvi raises his right arm, gestures upwards, points at the Moon, which emerges gradually, tears off the clouds covering it, There, he says, we're headed to the Moon. Oddur curses. He knows this side of his friend, his solemn, theatrical side; soon he'll recite a verse about heartache and feelings. Sometimes Tryggvi seems unable to hold his drink. Oddur looks back towards the land, which can just be distinguished in the hazy moonlight; he's startled to see how far they've come, reaches for the motor, shuts it off, says, We don't have enough fuel, and silence settles over them out there at sea, it seeks them out and makes this night even deeper. Tryggvi says, You're right, you've got to have more fuel if you're going to sail to the Moon. You're a sensible man. It's good to sail with a sensible man. I mean, says Oddur, that if we're going to make it home on motor power, we can't go any further.

Tryggvi: Home? My abode is there.

He points at the Moon.

Oddur: No-one lives on the fucking Moon.

Tryggvi: For a long time I've felt as if I have no home. I've never understood that feeling. Mother spoke about the same thing, though never to us; she kept such thoughts for her diaries.

Oddur: That she also lived on the Moon?

Tryggvi: She kept a diary and sometimes wrote, following a terribly ordinary description of the weather, or noting that this or that person had come for coffee: I sometimes feel as if I have no home. Or: Why do I feel as if I don't belong anywhere? It wasn't easy for me to read such statements, and to discover that she might have been unhappy. But then you wake up thirty years old and feel the same thing yourself. The good thing is that now I understand why: because the Moon is my home. What am I doing here, if my place is there, why doesn't God give me wings so I can fly away, why doesn't He change me into an angel, one of those extraordinary combinations of bird and human being? I want to break free from the shackles of life. I want wings. If you weren't with me, I would sail to the Moon and never return.

Oddur: You don't have enough fuel.

Tryggvi: Where the fuel ends, poetry begins.

He jumps overboard.

# *Keflavík*

— 1980 —

## *Is Tito's heart failing?*

It's February and the heart of Tito, the dictator of Yugoslavia, seems to be failing, Ari reads about it on the front page of the *Morgunblaðið*; the top story is a fragile heart. Yugoslavia is a large country on the Balkan peninsula with about ten million inhabitants, but their fate is hanging by a fragile heart. Does that mean that the world cares after all, that life matters? Ari eats porridge. Tonight on television, the news presenter Bogi Ágústsson will be presenting a special report on Tito's heart, and on what will happen to Yugoslavia if it fails. The capital of Yugoslavia is called Belgrade.

It's morning. Cold and darkness blanket Keflavík and the little single-family residence, the sky is blanketed with stars, it's like a musical score, it's like what's beautiful and what we desire, but it's too cold to raise our heads, the cold bends us. Ari reads about Tito's heart and then browses the newspaper, reads a few lines here and there but continues on to the comics and sports pages, leafs through the newspaper like that six days a week – there's no paper on Monday – throughout the entire year, around three hundred times a year, runs through it each morning, drowsy, half-asleep, eating porridge, flips quickly through it, yet, despite rarely reading it carefully, apart from the sports and comics, its cultural and ideological worlds sift into him. He suddenly realises, as if waking from a long sleep, there at the kitchen table, as his porridge cools, as his father, Jakob, finishes his breakfast, pours himself a coffee, lights his pipe, crosses his legs, places his elbow on the edge of the table, replete with porridge, the coffee is good, the tobacco is good, he has a day of masonry ahead of him, his stepmother has gone to work, has to start at 7.00 a.m., she left them porridge and the silence between them, and Ari suddenly realises something, as if someone has swept aside an invisible curtain of illusion – and he sees the world as it actually is. Naked, no frills. Unexpectedly realises that his world view is right in front of him; it's printed in the newspaper's words and photos. He's read or leafed through the newspaper all those mornings for years, subconsciously taking in its version of the world. A world view that's a collection of well-established opinions, standardised images, everything that's come to be dominant and that we call prevailing thought, that we call facts. It's how the world is supposed to be, how it is; it's our understanding of it.

He leafs through the paper again and notices that the truth is masculine. Yet there's a photo of a woman on page 13, a grandmother in her sixties, living in Hvammstangi, who has knitted a pair of woollen socks and wishes to send them to Yugoslavia, to Tito, as if woollen socks could heal an ailing heart, or save Yugoslavia from its uncertain state. It's certainly a nice thought, sweet, but childish. Such is the woman's logic. On the other hand, Brezhnev, the leader of the Soviet Union, is going to meet Jimmy Carter, President of the United States, and on their agenda are the following: nuclear weapons, missiles, the Cold War, tank battalions and economic interests in Asia. Concern for others does not make the list, nor woollen socks. Ari leafs through the paper, reads the comics, where two women appear: one is a scrupulous housewife, the other is about to be saved by Tarzan; she's vulnerable, concern is always vulnerable. Towards the back of the paper is an interview with three young singers, who all sing about love. Brezhnev and Carter, two of the most powerful men on earth, don't have love on their agenda, which is obviously illogical; it must be a mistake, because there's nothing we care about more than love, and happiness. Why isn't happiness on the front page of the *Morgunblaðið*, why can't you send in classified ads asking for happiness, a bit of love, and preferably before the weekend: I long for happiness, can anyone help me, dear God how I long to be loved!

Jakob clears his throat, Ari looks up from the newspaper, his father is impatient to read it, they've both finished their porridge, now there's nothing but silence between them, and the paper is written and published by men, yet there's still space for women on pages 13 and 35, there's space for knitting and love. Ari pushes the newspaper, our edition of the world, over to his father. It's been four years since they moved to the south, driving their Moskvitch there from the block of flats in Safamýri, behind the world, to the blackest place in Iceland. His mother has never been spoken of in this house, Ari hasn't said her name out loud for many years, as if it too were dead, and he's never asked what became of her records and books that were kept in the storeroom in Safamýri, on the shelf above the freezer; he still remembers four book titles: *Quick Quick Said the Bird*, *Wood on the Fire*, *A Farewell to Arms*, *And Quiet Flows the Don*.[13] These titles had managed to impress

---

13   *Quick Quick Said the Bird* (*Fljótt fljótt sagði fuglinn*, 1968): A novel by the Icelandic writer Thor Vilhjálmsson (1925-2011). *Wood on the Fire* (*Sprek á eldinn*, 1961): A collection of poetry by the Icelandic poet Hannes Sigfússon. *A Farewell to Arms* (1929): The famous novel by the American writer Ernest Hemingway (1899-1961). *And Quiet Flows the Don* (1929-1940): An epic in four volumes by the Russian Nobel laureate Mikhail Aleksandrovich Sholokhov (1905-84).

themselves on his memory before the storeroom was emptied and they moved to the south. Over time, they'd begun to take on the appearance of important messages, messages that will break free of their fetters only after he reads the books; when he's ready to do so, when he has matured sufficiently. He tried to read *Quick Quick Said the Bird* shortly after we jumped onto the lorries in January 1976 but didn't understand a thing; it was as if there were no plot, no identifiable hero, no clear message from his mother, and he'd thought, I'll read it when I'm older; I need to grow up a bit more and read many hundreds of other books first.

He's never asked about her books and records, he doesn't need to, doesn't dare to, is afraid they've been thrown away. He looks at his father, whose face is impassive as he reads the paper, looks and knows that he'll never forgive his father if he has thrown away what belonged to her, even though *never* is a very long time. He looks at his father, through the silence separating them, and suddenly longs, almost uncontrollably, to say her name out loud, she who died when she was nearly thirty, leaving behind a baby, a home, possibilities, unread books, songs that she hadn't yet sung, cities that she hadn't yet visited. Her name lies on his tongue, light as a feather, heavy as lead, and he longs to sling it in the face of his father as a punishment, an invocation, a bridge, a tear, a fist, an act of despair.

Jakob reads about Tito's heart, it's there on the first page, the heart of authority, of a man, we're concerned about it, the heart of a woman knits woollen socks, the heart of a woman has a beautiful voice, it sings real pop songs. Ari watches as his father reads the paper. What if this were suddenly turned around: the paper written and published by women; would we then need to flip to page 13 to see our first photo of a man, what would we think then, would we even be the same afterwards? What would our essence be then, the true viewpoint, does it even exist, and are we little more than containers filled to the brim with prevailing opinions, established views – and consequently almost never perceive an independent thought in our lives, except in flashes that are immediately snuffed out, extinguished by standardised ideas in the news, advertisements, films, popular music; real pop songs?

It's a February morning, and Ari is troubled by the unpleasant suspicion, the persistent feeling, that he sees life, the world, through conclusions drawn by others, and that a mere fraction of his world view is self-determined. Almost as if it had been pre-programmed; but by whom?

He tries to explain this to me as we walk along in the freezing February morning, gesturing vigorously as he does so, he just can't find the words for that feeling, or suspicion, and he stamps his feet in frustration, feeling almost as if he needs to invent a new language. The stars twinkle in the black sky, lights shining above us at an infinite distance, like lights from a life we never get a chance to live.

As always, I'd stopped by his place on my way to work, waiting for a few seconds on the drive to his little house until he came out. His father had poured warm water over the lock on his Lada, was sitting behind the wheel and thinking, perhaps, when the car started on the third attempt, If we could only start happiness.

We walk towards Skúli Million, though not via the shortest route; we always go through the old quarter, feeling as if we're disappearing from the world for a time; the same path that we took with Ásmundur our first Saturday morning in Keflavík. Ari waves his arms, but it doesn't help him one bit in finding the words for

241

the great delusion. For the suspicion that we have so few autonomous thoughts – that our minds have far too few of the ptarmigan
that cut through the darkness of delusion with their white flight.

I looked at Dad, says Ari – no, of course he didn't say "I looked
at Dad," because there are two things that Ari can't say out loud:
"Dad" and the name of his mother. He says, "I looked at the old
man and thought, Who is he, in fact? Why don't I know anything
about him, why don't I have any idea what's going on inside him
in the morning when the two of us sit in the kitchen together,
eating porridge, with nothing between us but silence? And I
thought, involuntarily, Was this the life he'd dreamed of as a child
out east in Norðfjörður?

We walk through the old quarter. His father's Lada nearly grazes
us, red like a bleeding heart, but Jakob acts as if he doesn't know
us and drives slowly past the church, where the pastor is standing
on the steps, fiddling with the door, but it's going badly, as if the
frost has nailed the door shut and is refusing to let him in, as
if God has rejected him. He kicks the door. Violence has always
been an inseparable part of the history of the Church; cruelty,
abuse, hunger for power, mercilessness, yet the Church ought to
be our prayer to God, a consolation for humankind, an aspiration
to harmony here on earth: we have failed miserably.

He kicks the door again.

It's hard to be a man when everything is failing, when consolation becomes aggression, when a door refuses to open, when your
wife has stopped loving you, when she makes you coffee as she
does every morning but then declares, out of the blue, that she has
probably stopped loving you. Expresses it like that: probably
stopped. Which she said as she poured steaming-hot coffee into

his cup. Then started accusing him of having lost his passion, his youthful spark. At one point, she said, you thought everything was possible. That's how you spoke: as if everything were possible, and you spoke with such passion that I couldn't help but fall for you, I couldn't help but love you. You said that everyone had the same possibilities, but what made the difference was having the spark and keeping it alive. We both had a dream: you were going to bring the earth and people's lives closer to Heaven, and I dreamed of finding a rewarding job, studying the piano, learning French, whereas now I'm raising children, making you coffee, haven't been on the job market for ten years, my diploma like a past misunderstanding, and I feel as if I've been deleted from life. You think more about advancing your career in the Church and being a member of the right club here in Keflavík than about bringing this place closer to Heaven. You had a spark; that's why I loved you. That spark seems to have grown cold long ago; how can I continue to love you? How can I continue to live with you?

He kicks the door, it doesn't open any more than happiness does; he turns, looks out to sea, can't remember the last time he thought about happiness, he's had too much to do, and then it hits him, now, when it might be too late, that you lose what you don't think about, what you don't cultivate. He stands on the church steps, sees me and Ari, they're young, I should go to them and urge them not to lose what I've lost.

But he doesn't go anywhere, instead sits down, lights a cigarette, feels like getting drunk, Tito's heart beats weakly on the front page of the newspaper, we thread our way through the old quarter, past our cousin's house, the little wooden house that I would stay in many years later; he has started his car, the spare tyre is in its

243

place in the boot but lacks an inner tube, leaving him space for about twenty Budweiser beers inside it. He waves cheerfully and says hello, always seems happy, we reciprocate his greeting, we walk up Hafnargata, a Danish porno film is showing at the New Cinema next Thursday evening, two topless women adorn the poster, they're laughing, have hard nipples, we're dying to stop and stare at those tits, take a good long look at them, we're turned on out there in the cold, our erections point upwards, towards the sky, as if paying their respects to God, expressing their gratitude, shaped like sceptres.

### The Skúli Million freezing plant, Spanish Júlli and she whom we betray

Approximately fifty people work for Skúli Million, men and women, aged sixteen to seventy, an important workplace in Keflavík, fifty people and none of them have ever stayed in a hotel, or eaten at a fine restaurant, such things are the stuff of foreign countries, films, love stories, Reykjavík, and not of real life, which is fish and fish offal, fishing and a hubbub at the harbour.

Ari and I walk into Skúli Million, but it's actually not accurate to say that none of its fifty employees have ever stayed in a hotel, gone out to eat; these are exaggerations, because Júlli, for example, who operates the forklift, went to Spain last summer with his girlfriend, it was a memorable trip, though in fact he remembers very little of it. That was the summer of 1979, ten years before beer was legalised in Iceland, and there was no way to get beer unless it was smuggled from the Base or foreign ships, or else purchased at the airport if you were on your way overseas. No man could be thought of as real unless he guzzled at least three or four beers before boarding his flight and continuing to drink on the plane; he who could walk down the gangway in Spain on steady legs could hardly be considered a man among men. Júlli's no milksop – otherwise he wouldn't be operating the forklift; he crawled down the gangway on all fours, giggling, and hardly ever stood up for the three weeks he was there beneath the blazing sun, was drunk the entire time, even in his sleep, remembered almost nothing, was badly sunburned, plunged into debt, and his girlfriend left him, or rather, she didn't leave anything, he caught her in bed with some bloody Englishman, she who could barely speak a word of English and who tried, using this as her cover, to make him believe that it was just a misunderstanding. But Júlli isn't so stupid, nor was there any "misunderstanding" on his girlfriend's face when he entered their hotel room to find the Englishman taking her from behind, like a dog in heat. Júlli didn't say anything, just watched them, and saw, as if in a trance, her boobs swing as the Englishman pounded her buttocks; and the man found no reason to stop, or to slow down, despite Júlli standing there, gaping. Finally, however, Júlli came to his senses, hastily grabbed a shirt, trousers, a wad of bills and marched out of her life, with her shouting his name, begging, screaming that it was all a misunderstanding, A pretty damned horrible misunderstanding, thought he, strutted out of her life and slept outdoors the last two nights of the trip, it was then that he got so badly sunburned, lost the rest of his money in a brothel and was never called anything else that year but Spanish Júlli.

Skúli Million is run by three brothers, the sons of Skúli who built the freezing plant a quarter of a century ago, the first of all of Keflavík's residents to become a millionaire, for which he was called Skúli Million ever afterwards. He died in the late 1970s, well into his seventies, was seated at a chessboard playing black and had just two moves left for a checkmate, had demonstrated an outstanding command of the game, a brilliant match that now hangs, described in detail, on a wall at the company's offices, where chess is followed match by match, a shining example of Skúli's imagination and acuity at the game, only two moves left to checkmate his opponent, but instead he was checkmated by death. A great chess player, one of the founders of the Chess Club of Keflavík, had won many prizes over the years – and thus undeniably met with a dignified and beautiful end. His sons had his coffin painted to resemble a folding chessboard, transforming their father into an eternal chess piece, a knight or rook. It was truly memorable. But the truth isn't always as beautiful as the stories we tell; sometimes it lacks charm. The story persists, and refuses to go away, that Skúli Million didn't die playing chess but in the arms of a woman who unfortunately wasn't his wife, and, to be more precise, not in her arms but on top of her, *in flagrante*, hard at it, goes the story, which few people dare to tell in public, let alone write down – we'll undoubtedly be given a hard time for including it here, and won't be given a warm welcome the next time we go to Keflavík.

The woman was considerably younger, little more than twenty years old; Skúli was going at it and had just shouted, Oh fuck, I'm coming, when a strange expression came over his face and he abruptly stopped thrusting, just lay on top of her like a heavy sack. At first she poked at him, said, Skúli, cut it out, what's got into you, Skúli, hey, don't frighten me. But he didn't reply, couldn't reply, he'd been forced out of the match, checkmated by death. Then she started screaming, and shouting, her screams could be heard outside, two neighbouring housewives came running but were too late because Skúli Million lay lifeless on top of her, his right arm beneath her shoulder blade, having shoved it there at the moment that he'd shouted, Fuck, I'm coming, and started to ride her as if he were late for an important appointment, thrust his arm beneath her shoulder as if to get a better grip on her, leverage, and died that way. She couldn't extricate herself, death held her down, which is why she screamed, shouted, it's no fun being young and having a dead old man on top of you. Being trapped beneath death.

No-one seems to know which version is true: death at the chessboard or *in flagrante*, the appropriateness or the ridiculousness; the girl who was supposedly with him moved up north shortly afterwards, to Akureyri, where she found a good job, and has never returned. It's too late to ask her about Skúli Million's last living moment – but of course we can always let ourselves believe the chess story.

Ari and I see the description of the match when we go to pick up our pay cheques on Fridays, handed over by Ásrún, the wife of the youngest brother, who's called One Króna by the employees and who looks after the company's accounting and finances. Few people have anything good to say about him, whereas she, on the other hand, is sometimes called A Thousand Krónur – due to her sweetness and beauty. She's about forty and is therefore old in my eyes and Ari's, if not downright elderly, in rapid decline and already a grandmother, yet despite all that, she might well be the most beautiful woman we've ever seen. As fair as the most beautiful adjectives, gentle as a summer night, caring, happy to chat with the employees, even with me and Ari, boring nobodies, retarded, clumsy, often chastised, but she asks with interest what we want to do with our lives, says that we should educate ourselves, insists on it, says that she regrets how her children all quit school after completing their compulsory education. She speaks to us as if we matter in this life, as if we actually have something to contribute, and aren't just failures, mediocre, best relegated to oblivion.

One Króna and A Thousand Krónur – such was the difference between them in the eyes of their employees. The middle brother, on the other hand, is a well-liked, plump teddy bear, who had the title of foreman but preferred to hang out with the women, clown around, chat and pester them, no-one's quite as skilled at pestering, he's particularly talented in that field, but makes himself scarce if there are decisions to be made; on such occasions, he goes out to get some Prince Polo chocolate wafers, or hides in Ásrún's office. Anyway, it's the eldest brother who makes all the decisions and is responsible for the company's management, apart from financial matters, which he's barely involved with at all, is always at it, is the first to show up in the mornings and last to leave in the evenings, is slender, has straight teeth, never raises his voice yet always manages to be heard above the chatter and noise of the machinery. They call him The Iron when he's out of earshot, his drawn face stiff with concentration, appearing never to need any rest, never takes breaks, never sits down, is never sick, doesn't take days off, except for three weeks in July when he travels to Spain with his family, a trip that his wife organises, and there he lies in a lounge chair by the hotel swimming pool, smashed beneath the scorching sun, hardly moving a muscle, while his wife drinks Campari, reads romance novels, goes on sightseeing and shopping trips with other Icelanders.

One Króna makes the most of his brother's absence, sends employees to do repairs on his house, plays football with his children, waxes the family's cars, while Ari and I are assigned the task of painting the little single-family residence that he's had the company buy for his mistress, yet tried to hide from his wife by fiddling the books. The mistress, who is three or four years older than us, super-elegant, confident, with long dark hair, brown, almond-shaped eyes, doesn't speak a word to us during the fortnight it takes Ari and me to paint the house; in her brown eyes we don't exist, and we're not allowed to show up before 10.30 a.m. so that she can have a lie-in, but then we work like mad and only go down to the freezing plant on Fridays to pick up our cheques. It isn't easy to take our pay cheques from Ásrún's hands, to answer her sincere questions, having just finished painting the south wall of the little house and listening to the moans of her husband and his mistress inside. You aren't very talkative today, she says with a smile, having gathered her brown hair into a ponytail and looking almost girlish, we hardly dare to look at her, don't understand how it's possible to betray such a woman, to go in search of something else, we don't know what the world has to offer that would be more or better, her smile creates dimples and three faint creases that radiate from her eyes, the sun is shining, the weather is mild, she's wearing a skirt, a blouse, has already hit forty, perhaps, and had her first grandchild, yet is still very beautiful. You've been painting, she says, that's a nice change from fish; what were you painting, my dears, she asks, looking us in the face, with that bright smile, those dimples, with that affability in her tanned face, and what can we say, how should we answer, Yes, see, we were painting the house that your husband bought for his mistress, a nineteen-year-old girl, they were fucking on the living-room sofa while we were painting the south wall, we think it's extremely ugly of him because you're so kind and beautiful, despite the fact that you're forty years old and a grandmother, even, but unfortunately our dicks stiffened when we heard them and we desperately

249

wanted to peek in through the living-room window, we've never been with girls, see, to be honest we aren't sure how to go about it, so to speak, terrified of making laughingstocks of ourselves should the opportunity arise, should someone ever decide to have anything to do with us, which seems unlikely, at least not in this life, on this planet, not in this solar system, not in this galaxy, because, well, just look at us: boring, lame-ass nobodies!

She looks at us, crosses her right leg over her left, sexily, she's like a roe-deer or something majestic and proud, still smiling, fiddling with a lock of her brown hair, What were you painting?; we're too innocent or stupid or too idiotic to lie, and for that reason we say nothing, not a word, not a single thing, we just stand there like two cod, looking at her, with helpless expressions on our faces, of course, expressions that undoubtedly reveal what we mentioned here earlier, because her face changes, her smile fades, it dies, and with it her affability, her brightness and her girlishness, she ages quickly before our eyes, becomes old, bent, like something the world has betrayed. The following Friday the middle brother comes with our pay packets, he has a peculiar look in his eyes, hands us the pay packets without saying anything, we look at each other and learn that guilt can also gnaw at a person who hasn't done anything wrong.

*I can't recall having seen*
*anyone blush so beautifully, but why*
*is it so difficult to repair life?*

Just to be clear: it's still February, long before that summer day when we betray without culpability, betray a beautiful woman, watch her life crumble, the sun crack and the world turn into the darkness called treachery. It's February, and she doesn't know a thing about the mistress twenty years younger than she is in the little single-family residence, perhaps suspects something, an enigmatic entry in the ledger, her husband's elusive glance, an odour on him that she doesn't recognise, has some sort of premonition but pushes it aside, does so instinctively, as instinctively as someone who ends up in the sea starts swimming, as someone who finds herself in darkness lights a light; she suppresses the suspicion to keep the world from perishing. Life is unjust, which is why there isn't always a great difference between the survival instinct and cowardice. It's a February morning and Tito's heart is at risk, it beats weakly on the front page of the *Morgunblaðið*, and somewhere in Keflavík Jakob mixes concrete, he adds a little resin to the mix to bind it, to keep it from separating, to keep it from sliding down after it's been spread on a wall or used to fasten a weatherboard, so that it remains whole and thereby acquires a purpose. Needs just a small amount, hardly more than a capful in the concrete mixture, which is composed of numerous shovelsful of sand and cement, a certain amount of water, yet all it takes is one capful of resin for the mixture to remain bound together rather than slowly separate or crumble off the walls. After tossing the resin into the mixture, Jakob hesitates, watching the raw materials spin and combine, watching the resin disappear into the mixture. Why is it so easy to combine cement, sand and water into one, a whole, a unit, a purpose, all it takes is one capful, it isn't fair, because it seems so difficult to get life to hang together, this human life that you've got to drag around with you wherever you go, wherever you are. Jakob holds the tin of resin, feels like having a drink, perhaps thinks about Ari, about his son's expression as he read the newspaper over his porridge while he himself smoked

251

and pretended to look elsewhere. My son, my flesh and blood, my son. He'll never forget the joy he felt the first time he held him, looked into his clear blue eyes and thought, This is why we exist; for the first time, I understand life. Now, for the first time, I realise that everything had to go exactly as it went. Remembers that he thought, Here I stand, holding the very purpose of life. And also thought, So life is beautiful! But many years have passed since then.

About three thousand.

He smoked, pretended to look elsewhere but carefully observed Ari's face out of the corner of his eye, and thought, I have no idea what's going on inside him, I don't have the slightest idea what his expression means, have no idea how he feels, how he looks at life. He emptied his pipe and suddenly longed to cry, which would have been absurd, of course, shameful, terribly embarrassing for both of them, hastily refilled his pipe, acted as if he were impatient to read the paper, as if he could fucking care what was written there, it was absolutely ridiculous, of course, to be a subscriber to that fucking conservative paper, just as well that his parents didn't live to see it, but there's no other newspaper with better or more detailed sports reporting, and it's so good, even liberating, to read about sports, let yourself sink into numbers, results, accounts of matches, there's no doubt in sports, there's never a question of happiness or unhappiness, just victories or defeats. Ari pushed the paper over to him, across the kitchen table between them, across the Atlantic Ocean between them, the solar system that separates them. Shortly afterwards they were both out, and Jakob had driven past Ari, right by Keflavík Church, a lot of snow on the pavement, so Ari and I walked down the road and Jakob was forced to drive past very slowly, he'd had to slow on the icy road and turn in order to pass us, barely half a metre between us, but he didn't greet us, didn't honk his horn, didn't smile, didn't roll down his window, stick his head out and say, Hey, have a nice day, or something like that, a few words carrying a grain of positivity, affection, because words can so easily improve the world, life. Drove past without a word. Perhaps it was just as well that he didn't roll down the window and say have a nice day or something along those lines, because they both would have felt terribly awkward and apprehensive about seeing each other again that evening. Besides, he was busy tuning his radio to The Yank, that blessing to us residents of Keflavík, because sometimes you desperately need a peppy pop song, or just something other than fucking seriousness, the damned austerity of National Radio, the announcer's descriptions of the snow on Mount Esja, of the weather, the value of the Icelandic króna, the out-of-control pace of inflation, as if such things could help you in any way here in the early morning, at the cold, half-lit break of day, when you drive past your son, nearly brush him with your car, but neither father nor son waves, neither glances at the other; at such a time, you absolutely don't want to hear any more about inflation, the snow on Esja, the cessation of capelin fishing. Thank God for The Yank, thought Jakob when he finally managed to tune the radio properly, and the American announcer, located up on Miðnesheiði, in the realm of the wind, the kingdom of wet and cold, shouted something funny into the microphone, as if he'd been hired specifically to be lively, absolutely exuberant, at full throttle, perennially cheerful, infectiously jubilant, to balance out the depression, the unbearable boredom that the heath breathed over the soldiers winter, summer, spring and autumn, the cold wind, the storms, the rain that seemed to come from all directions at

253

once, or the blizzards that blew like white curses between the blocks of flats.

What's the difference between Miðnesheiði and Hell? – a riddle or question that the Americans pose to new arrivals, before replying smugly, Those in Hell are lucky enough to be dead! Thank God for The Yank and its exuberance, thought Jakob as the presenter laughed into the microphone and said that it sure would be nice to be dancing with a pretty girl; When wouldn't that be nice, thought Jakob, smiling and humming along to the song being played, "Knock on Wood" by Amii Stewart, an explosion of pure joy:

The way you love me is frightening
You better knock, knock on wood, baby.

Knock on wood, baby baby; that's something quite unlike inflation, the snow on Esja, the fishermen's anger over the capelin news, the heaviness of driving past your own son as if he were a stranger. Come on, give me pop music, give me the hit parade, come on, oh baby baby, and take the pain from my heart!

Jakob drove past the church and saw the pastor kick the door as if it had done him an injury, what complaints did he have, he who believes fully and faithfully in God, and therewith in the purpose of life, therewith in a beautiful life after death, therewith in love; what a luxury, what great good fortune, not to mention having such a cushy indoor job, all he had to do was quote a few passages from the Bible, practically everything was already scripted for him, never dirty, never has to work outdoors in the cold, in the biting wind, pounding rain, eternally within the comforts of home, yet kicks the church door; what does it take for people to feel a bit of gratitude?

Jakob sticks his tongue into the resin. He never makes mistakes in his job, is a sought-after mason, is painstaking, completes his projects perfectly, nothing falls apart, it's only in life that everything seems to go wrong. He sticks his tongue into the resin; if only you could get by with one drink per day and everything held together, if only joy would rise from the depths, and you could feel happy about being alive. Why, he thinks, pouring the concrete into the wheelbarrow, is it so difficult to repair life? If a car breaks down, you just open the bonnet and have a look at the engine. But what can you open and have a look at if your life breaks down?

If life breaks down, if Tito's heart fails. Ari and I have put on our coveralls and the work day is in full swing, it's so noisy in the processing room that we're unable to converse very much, and not at all about Tito's heart, let alone the disturbing discovery Ari made this morning, over his porridge, deep within the silence between father and son; the suspicion that we're containers filled to the brim with standardised ideas.

By the 9.30 coffee break, Spanish Júlli and Elli, called Kung-fu Elli, have come close to running over Ari with their forklifts three times as he stands there staring at the floor, intent on finding words for the suspicion that's buzzing inside him, scratching him on the inside, that won't leave him be, causing him to forget time and place, he stops noticing anything, forgets Júlli and Elli driving back and forth, as fast as they're allowed, and maybe a bit faster, with heavy tubs full of redfish on the forks, they drive out through the big door that's left open most of the morning, allowing the cold north wind to slip in unhindered, fetch tubs crammed with redfish from the lorries and dart back inside, practically flying, leaning on the horn, people have got to get out of the way, they have the right of way, no doubt whatsoever about that, they're the ones with the momentum, which is the combined weight and speed of the forklifts and redfish, and Ari is nearly run over three times, knocked onto his head, I manage to pull him out of the way at the last second. Júlli yells something at Ari, we make out words like *pisshead*, *commie* and *codfish*, but Elli doesn't yell, he just leans on his horn. Kung-fu Elli, known in Keflavík for having practised this Chinese martial art for years, eagerly works his forklift's forks as if in a frenzied fight with an invisible enemy.

Nearly run over three times. In Iceland, people who think, who try to get to the bottom of things, are most often considered to be in the way; we shout at them, economic interests run them over; nearly run over three times and, after the third time, given a thorough tongue-lashing by the eldest brother, The Iron, who prowls around the company with his grim expression, his drawn face, his chilling focus, gaunt, straight-backed, with dark, twinkling eyes, reminding me and Ari of the Indians in our old children's books: Lightfoot, Sitting Eagle, Flying Crow, who could prowl around without a sound, eyes sharp as a hawk's. Like them, nothing gets by The Iron – who is slacking, whose work isn't accurate enough, who takes overly long breaks; he sees everything but the negligence and self-indulgence of his brother's accounting, or else saw it too late, the company's debts already unmanageable by the time he realised. Fortunately, however, it all worked out in the end; Skúli Million burned down, because debts have always made first-rate fuel in Iceland – they just need to be substantial enough. Everything went up in flames: machinery, furniture, both forklifts, the framed chess match on the office wall, the employees' rubber boots, the coffeemaker and the biscuits in the cupboards. But hold on a second, because all of this happens in the distant future; right now it's February 1980, and during the 9.30 coffee break, Ari and I try to find seats near the radiator in order to suck a little heat into our cold bodies, lying low but watching, listening. It's hard to determine which gender tells the most dirty jokes, and there's a certain tension in the air, something quivering within the dense tobacco smoke, whose odour blends with that of fish guts. The machine operators, seven or eight fellows of around twenty, who bring fish to and from the women in the processing room, arrange the blocks in the big freezer, then tear them out and stack them in boxes when everything's ready for export, are imposing during breaks, sitting at the biggest table, exuding self-confidence and testosterone; they're the company's noblemen, Spanish Júlli and Kung-fu Elli might be the main bigwigs in the processing room, but they're reduced to squires next to the machine operators, who talk loudly, flinging questions in every direction: Gunni, did you get some from your old lady yesterday; Elli, do you use kung-fu when you're fucking Gréta; Elli, show us some kung-fu. Elli is always ready to show them; he stands up, raises his right leg as if it were an independent organ, unattached to his body, kicks the air, swings it around like a club; Fucking hell, screech the machine operators, are you that agile with your dick? The women, aged seventeen and over, laugh along with them, giggle, shake their heads, or tell them to shut up and hold their own in the clowning, holding nothing back: How are you, Gunnhildur; feeling good today; want to come sit on my lap? Gunnhildur, a woman of about thirty, with red hair, lights another cigarette, exhales, replies, No thanks, dear, my Siddi gave it to me last night, enough to fill me up for the next two days – ask me on Thursday.

Ari and I are next to the radiator, tempering ourselves within the storm of cold and dirty words, dozing and listening by turns,

257

no longer on tenterhooks about being targeted, as we were when we first started working here; One of you, one of the technicians had said to the women in the processing room, should take these two greenhorns under your wing; they're such babies that they've never had a shag, never smoked, never smashed anyone's head in, in short, never done anything starting with "s" – one of you should show a bit of compassion, take them out back during a break, and teach them a thing or two, it would be such a good deed that I'm sure you'd go straight to Heaven when the time comes. Ari and I sat next to the warm radiator and the entire break room looked at us, the technicians and the girls grinning, the women smiling, Júlli chuckling, Elli whinnying. They sure know how to blush, says one of the women, finally, her voice hoarse from Camel cigarettes; they're experts at it, she adds, lighting another cigarette. It's true, says her friend, I can't recall seeing anyone blush so beautifully.

Ari and I sat there like two convicts. It was as if our heads were on fire. Our brains buzzed and we could hear the synapses beginning to burn apart, slowly. Our backs were sweating, our underarms, faces, toes. We wanted to hide our discomfort by reaching for the coffee flask, refilling our cups, but our arms were shaking so much that we pulled them back immediately, to seek shelter under the table, like frightened animals. All eyes were on us. We longed to escape, let the floor swallow us up, stand up, run outside, clear our heads in the cold air before they became any hotter, before our brains burned out, and with them all our thoughts, all our memories, all the Pink Floyd songs, run outside to save our memories, escape from the shame, the humiliation – sometimes, however, flight doesn't solve anything but does the exact opposite: it adds to the humiliation, and the only thing we could do was to stay sitting there, against the radiator, our heads on fire, our vision and hearing blurred and obscured, and for a time it felt as if we were levitating and floating above them, we could see our fiery-red faces, our glowing-hot heads, the sweat on our foreheads. Our only consolation was the thought that this would pass; soon someone would bring up another topic, and, if not, then at least this coffee break would come to an end at some point. Our only redress, our sole consolation, our last thread of hope, was that things could hardly get any worse. But then Spanish Júlli stood up, excited and happy, as if he'd just remembered something hilarious, pointed at Ari and said, And that one stutters!

Well, alright, so it could get worse.

Which shouldn't have come as any surprise.

Because everything can always get worse, as long as there's another person involved.

At this revelation, this information, the room fell silent, all eyes were on Ari, as if waiting for him to say something to confirm it, do a sound check, we sensed the room's impatience, people's faces seemed to say, Come on, say something, let's hear you stutter, hurry up, man, coffee break doesn't last for ever, give us a little stutter, a little example; there are always distractions, new things, it doesn't hurt to try something new, because with each passing day our lives seem to spin ever deeper into repetition, God knows how it will end, so open that trap of yours and give us a little stutter, and who knows, if you do it well enough, maybe you can stutter something every coffee break, it'll be your time of day, you'll enjoy it, being in the spotlight.

If only he could sh . . . began one of the machine operators, but at that moment three things happened: one of his cronies, another machine operator, stood up, and a woman, probably Gunnhildur – we couldn't see or hear clearly – said something that seemed a bit sharp but to our advantage, because Júlli sat down, looking extremely sheepish, and the machine operator who'd stood up came over to Ari and me, sat down at the table and said, Well, cousin, you're always reading, I hear; do you have any coffee for me – I've finished mine. Ari and I couldn't utter a word, so grateful that we nearly burst into tears, but we pushed the coffee flask over to Ásmundur, because it was of course him who had stood up to come to our rescue, Ásmundur, the head of the machine operators, their leader; he said, Well, cousin, and said it so that everyone in the canteen could hear it, making it clear that if anyone had thought about messing with us afterwards, they'd have to get past Ásmundur first. Well, cousin, and then added the bit about reading – you're always reading – thereby conferring special status on Ari, the person who reads, he's always reading, which meant he's an eccentric genius, leading everyone to view us as unbearably nerdy and clumsy, all thumbs, yet with slightly more indulgent eyes: they can't help it, they're always reading.

# Norðfjörður

—PAST—

## If God is a woman, the Devil must be a man

It's at least 2.00, if not 3.00 a.m., and it's a dark night, as dark as a night can be. November, the sky seems to have opened, it pours stars and moonlight over us. At least 2.00, if not 3.00, and Oddur staggers off the boat, completely naked, makes his way with difficulty onto the pier, holding Tryggvi, fully dressed, in his arms.

Tryggvi had jumped overboard and begun swimming vigorously, heading towards the Moon, as Oddur watched his friend disappear into the distance, saw the ocean's waves lift him like an offering to the sky. He'd simply watched, no longer able to distinguish what was normal from what was far from normal, as if Tryggvi had invalidated every law of nature by jumping overboard, as if it were natural to swim in the ice-cold November sea and making for the Moon. Oddur had watched, and didn't snap out of it until he thought he noticed a change in Tryggvi, as if he'd grown numb, the cold sea having begun to cool his blood down to the temperature of death. He snapped out of it, sailed over to Tryggvi, hoisted him with difficulty into the boat, by now semiconscious, tore his clothing off him as if he were gutting a fish, massaged his freezing body, managed to pour some cognac down him, then stripped off all his own clothes, feeling it important, for

263

some reason, to strip naked, then put his clothes on Tryggvi and headed for shore, pushing the motor as much as he dared, because it was a race against death, which never gives up, doesn't recognise surrender, is untiring, never runs but always catches up with the fastest sprinters and most enduring long-distance runners in the end.

Oddur, too, is freezing, as he races away from the pier with Tryggvi in his arms; he intends to go straight home to Margrét but then glimpses a faint light out of the corner of his eye and instinctively changes direction, for we should always head towards the light. But no matter how fast he runs, the light never appears to move any closer. We who have done so much together, he pants, beginning to falter under the weight of Tryggvi, so fatigued that he blabbers incessantly without realising it, Do you remember when we were kids and you wanted us to hold hands, but I said, Are you nuts, and wouldn't hear of it, but I want you to know that sometimes I wanted it too, liked the idea, but never dared, forgive my cowardice, nothing is as worthless as cowardice, is that why you have to die now? asks Oddur, because he's exhausted, he can't take any more, the champion himself, the untiring dynamo, when he has truly come to the end of his rope he staggers beneath the weight, sits down on the cold ground with his friend in his arms, blabbering like an idiot, and the stars sparkle in the firmament. They're beautiful, yet there's nothing between them but cold, darkness and death.

But the brightest star has set off towards earth to fetch them. They must both die tonight, which may be O.K. It's a beautiful star, and it's almost as if someone is holding it; yet who could manage such a thing but God Himself, who else is powerful enough to travel around the world with a star for a lantern? Lord, says Oddur, my friend threw himself into the sea way out in the bay, intending to swim to the Moon. He says that it's his home, which is nonsense, of course; no-one lives on the Moon, he reads too much literature. It's a vice, confuses you. Don't take him; I really don't want to lose him just now.

**Those who read so much literature that they think they can swim to the Moon should be allowed to live longer. The world can't afford to lose such people.**

Says God to Oddur. But in a female voice!

Oddur is thunderstruck. God is a woman? Who's supposed to protect us now?

I'm not happy about God being a woman, he says, unable to help himself. He didn't intend to say that, but as soon as he does, he feels that he's denied God, that it's impossible to think about it any other way, and in His hearing, as well. Or Hers. Now his tongue will turn into a black stone, now he'll be put aboard the first boat down to Hell. But then the Devil must be a man; there must be some sort of justice.

Yes, the Devil is definitely a man, and as blind drunk as all of you, says the woman with the lantern, who turns out not to be God at all but rather a twenty-year-old called Áslaug, from Vatnsleysuströnd on Reykjanes, all the way at the opposite side of the country, she'd moved here in the summer in search of adventure but also to escape a neighbour boy, Gvendur, they'd been together twice, had found a place in a grassy cirque out on the end of Stapi, that huge cliff jutting into the sea, she mostly out of curiosity, and the desire that flares up sometimes and is almost impossible to control. Just be careful not to put it in me, she'd whispered, her voice trembling the first time, after they'd lain down and she'd hastily pulled up her skirt, excited and frightened, felt the heather poking and scratching her buttocks, and he whispered, Yes, one quivering, trembling Yes, and was careful, but the second time, he was savage, it was weeks later, You have to marry me, he said, on top of her, inside her, his face pale, as if all the blood had drained from it, his eyes strangely piercing, and unexpectedly, very uncomfortably, resembling his mother, who keeps watch over the district with her religious fervour and harsh temper, he who has always been her opposite – where she was harshness and obduracy, he was nothing but tenderness, but he was transformed there on top of her, unless it was his true nature finally shining through, thrusting himself so deeply into her, so violently, that it wasn't nice at all, it just hurt, as if his penis had become a club, and then, with that disconcerting resemblance to his mother, said, You have to marry me, or we'll burn in Hell! Stop, she said, Stop, she begged, and began struggling, trying to break free, terribly fright-ened, but her protests only seemed to fuel his fury and make him even wilder, You'll marry me – or you've got the Devil in you, he panted, his voice shrill, as he thrust even deeper, but she screamed and finally managed to kick him off her, at the very last moment, and he groaned or cried out as his semen shot onto the heather between her legs, she watched it drip over the bilberries like spittle. Mum was right, you've got the Devil in you, he said dismissively as he pulled up his trousers; that's why you seduced me. You're the one with the Devil in you, just look, she retorted, pointing at the semen in the heather: there are his eggs.

And then she fled to the east, had to change skies, escape from the oppressive slander that the mother and son started spreading about her, fled eastwards to the fish, lives in the house that the elderly couple Helena and Grettir had owned, rents a room there, awoke in the middle of the night to a strange dream that she forgot almost as soon as she opened her eyes. But she couldn't get back to sleep, no matter how much she tossed and turned, and finally she went out into the cold to pee. Squatted, watched the steaming urine form a meandering brooklet, when she caught a glimpse of something white walking towards her, something white and peculiarly big, Maybe it's death, come to fetch me, she thought, and felt her blood freeze with fear, she wanted to flee into the house, into her room, up into her bed, pull the cover over her head, yet nonetheless decided to go to meet it, knew that no-one could flee death if it was on its way to get you, that it's better in that case to meet it and try your luck against it, trust to your own strength, the benevolence of fate; from where did people like her derive their courage?

It turned out not to be death at all, just two sailors, one buck naked, both clearly smashed, and one of them, the one wearing clothes, had planned to swim to the Moon because he'd read too many poems and thus lost sight of normality. The naked one, Oddur, now she recognises him, he being a famous man here in the village, naked or clothed, is babbling something about God and the Devil, she only half-listens, he reeks of cognac and his drunken mouth won't stop running, she mutters an occasional response as she crouches next to the other one, the poems-man, instinctively strokes his beautiful face, softened by drink, the delicate corners of his mouth, strokes the kissable corners of his mouth, finally looks at Oddur and says, Go home to your wife, your nakedness belongs to her, says it so resolutely, and so directly, that it's as if his head has cleared; he stands up unsteadily and instinctively grabs his crotch, as if to assure himself that it's still where it should be, he can hardly feel anything and for that reason is indescribably relieved when his hand touches his genitals, what sort of shitty life would it be without them? Tryggvi, he says, or tries to say, but she cuts him off, Tryggvi, his name is Tryggvi, she says softly, as if to herself, then raises the lantern to illuminate his face better, and adds, Thank you for coming in the darkness and bringing him to me.

# Keflavík

— 1980 —

*"Warm and soft in the morning – for you"*

Folk who live in Keflavík can hardly be said to live in Iceland, and hardly in the world, either; they live elsewhere, behind everything, within the three cardinal directions. Except that there were, of course, four in those years, because the Yanks' fighter jets flew over our heads and the roofs of our houses, drowning out teachers, who have to wait to decline an adjective, say something about Snorri Sturluson, explain mathematical equations while the jets whizzed over, those cries in the blue air, everything must remain silent while the American military, the fourth cardinal direction, searches for the enemy that justifies its existence, that gives it strength, makes it a world power; those who pilot fighter jets must have enemies, they're their compasses, their mantras. The jets scream over the roofs of Keflavík, The blackest place, said the President of Iceland in 1944, those three words were his gift to us from the Republic when he made his first and so far only visit here and let these heavy words fall on us, like stone slabs, we're still lying beneath them, listening to the screams in the air, and no-one comes here unless they have pressing business, to profit off the back of the military, process fish, dock in the harbour, compete in basketball, fight at dances. Then, of course, the military left, the fourth cardinal direction, which is why we have just three, and in addition, we've been prohibited from catching fish, it's difficult to find a sensible explanation for that, something to do with economic interests, which often take precedence over common sense, justice, humanity, just ask Jonni Thunderburger, he's in his hamburger van above the empty harbour, and after the military left no-one comes here, absolutely no-one, it's as if we don't exist. Mayor Sigurjón might have a few tricks up his sleeve; perhaps that, among other things, is the reason behind the Norwegians at the hotel, those knives, not solely to attend a sixtieth birthday party or facilitate agreements with an American company but rather to get people to come and visit, fill the town with happy, wealthy tourists, we can envision it perfectly, we could put a big sign up just outside of town: Welcome to the Blackest Place in the Country! It would probably be better to follow it with a smiley face; some people, family folk, might take "blackest place" the wrong way and turn back. Tourists could have a coffee or a beer at the January 1976 bar, Ari and I would show them where we jumped onto the Yank lorries, or someone could re-enact the entire incident onstage; they could visit the childhood haunts of Rúnni Júll and Gunni Þórðar – who moved to Keflavík from Hólmavík when they were eight years old – and take photos of the empty harbour. Have one of Jonni's Quota Swindle burgers and take a look at the two blocks of flats, those exclamation marks above the harbour, the storage space for fishermen who are unable to go to sea, it would be great if one of the sailors would agree to go to his living-room window whenever tourists came to town; Jonni could give him a signal, send him a text message, and then he could stand there holding his coffee cup, looking out over the harbour, mournful, his face furrowed with wrinkles, a perfect photo opportunity: *The seaman discarded by economic interests.*

*

Wait a second, let's slow down a bit, we're not even close to that point, Jonni is still the helmsman of *Drangey* and Ari and I are so young that it's impossible to do more than throw up our hands, sixteen, seventeen years old, and the military hasn't left, far from it, it's grinding out profit all around it and it's still winter, February 1980, Tito's heart staggers through the world like an old moose, the Soviets have invaded Afghanistan, incredibly few people knew of the existence of that distant, mountainous land, the enormous power of the Red Army pitted against partisans on horseback, it isn't fair, but human beings are unlikely ever to have been fair, the desire for power, domination and wealth is situated deep within them, it's like a poisonous snake in a cave at the roots of their hearts. What can be done; or is there perhaps no hope for a better world?

The days pass, often identical to one another, Ari and his father eat the porridge that Ari's stepmother has prepared for them within the silence. Ari reaches for the newspaper when his father goes to the bathroom, turns quickly to page 42, wants to get a better look at the advertisement there, the picture of a very young woman in a sexy pose, her mouth half open, her lips moist, her eyes bewitching: "Warm and soft in the morning – for you." It's an advert for a bakery in Reykjavík; she's holding a freshly baked loaf of bread. Ari stares at the picture. Hot and supple, her half-open mouth – for you. Her cleavage is so apparent, she's wearing tight black trousers, his penis begins to stiffen, to rise, that ancient sceptre, it rises towards Heaven, to the glory of God. So that's the reason for women being in the world, their role, so that the sceptre, that symbol of power, a covenant between God and man, the bridge between Heaven and earth, can become erect? Show us, woman, your cleavage; put on a miniskirt, so that we can have erections and thereby come closer to God, so that we can raise our sceptres to Heaven, to His glory alone. Ari and I walk six days a week from the little single-family residence in Vitateigur up Hafnargata to Skúli Million, always the same route, confused, no idea what we want to be, which direction we want to go in, perhaps especially surprised about not being children anymore, just boys who have the chance to go to the countryside in the summer and forget themselves there among the tussocks, fall asleep in the barn nearly full of fragrant hay. Confused and sad about having lost our relationships with Tarzan, Enid Blyton, Tom Swift, and terribly distressed about having to make a decision about what we want to be, what direction we want to go in. Confused and distressed in the face of life. Not children. Not adults. Roaming between two worlds, not belonging anywhere. Confused. Yes. Distressed. Yes. And sad, yet still thinking about the bakery advertisement, about the girl so sexy and seductive, thinking about her cleavage. She's probably older than us, at least nineteen, twenty, beautiful, confident, and would never, ever, look at us, we're kids, lame-ass nobodies, she would waste neither a look nor a word on us, yet is so sexy and seductive: "for you".

Even we could be the "you".

Everyone could be the "you". There was no definition of "you" in the advertisement, no proviso or parentheses following "you", nothing to point out that it excluded us, who were pretty well nothing; she, on the contrary, looked sexy, beautiful, confident and available to everyone, including us, which is incredible, downright brilliant, but inconceivable, of course, absurdity itself, because we're nothing and she's clearly something far greater. I don't get it, says Ari, I don't understand the world, it's so absurd, the world is absurd, it's simply impossible to understand it. No,

274

I agree, you're probably right. We walk up Hafnargata, the cars crawl past like big, clumsy beasts, the wind blows, stirs up dust, dirt, sand, sea foam, and Ari and I walk into Skúli Million, two uncertain life-notes, broken chords, we put on our stiff, cold coveralls and go to the processing room, Spanish Júlli sits yawning and smoking on his forklift, he's tied a big boombox tightly to it, the only thing that he bought and didn't lose on his trip to Spain, and he yells when he sees us, yells across the room, so loudly that everyone hears, including the girls to whom we never dare to talk and who make us breathless whenever they say something to us; Hey, boys, did you have time for a wank this morning, and is it true that your dicks are so small that you have to use tweezers to hold them? He laughs, starts his forklift, cranks up his boombox, the work day has begun, Júlli peels out, diesel smoke fills the air, and fragments of The Captain and Tennille can be heard above the noise of the machinery, the throttling of the forklift, and Júlli sings along loudly to the hit song we all know, while others sing along though they can barely hear it, I can never get enough of you:

Do that to me one more time
Once is never enough with a man like you.
Do that to me one more time
I can never get enough of a man like you.


*You wouldn't even make the Top-100*
*list at the North Pole*

A world without music is like the sun without light, laughter without joy, a fish without water, a wingless bird. Like being condemned to live on the dark side of the Moon, with a view of darkness and

275

loneliness – which is why Ari bought a stereo system one day in February, when Tito's heart was so terribly fragile.

He'd been saving up to buy it since the autumn when we'd worked in a slaughterhouse out west in Búðardalur, a village that has the look of oblivion, though he'd had little remaining in his pocket from the fishing season, difficult to be so dizzyingly young, to be travelling at a thousand kilometres per hour through time, and simultaneously demonstrate sensibility and control in money matters; such a thing is undoubtedly contrary to the laws of life. Ari fell in love with a girl out west who had freckles and eyes that were like two pop songs, one composed by Lennon and the other by McCartney; we walked past her at least three times a day, her place was near the beginning of the production line, mainly on the platform where the carcasses were hung on hooks, while our first days were down in the holding pen, alongside the knocker, pushing lambs, sheep and rams in his direction. We often had to place our hands on the lambs' backs, as if to reassure them, and felt their tremors of fear under our palms. We looked into their eyes, especially if they had to wait, were given a chance to live a few more moments, though terrified, extend their lives before they vanished into the incomprehensible. We looked into the lambs' eyes, tried to calm them, let them know that we cared, while making sure not to let anyone else see, covertly stroked their heads during that short interval before death, as the knocker took a pinch of snuff, or had trouble killing an old ram, the gun didn't work properly on the ram's hard forehead, the bolt couldn't penetrate the skull, he needed to reach for the pistol that fired real bullets, take the time to load it, the ram bleated gloomily in the meantime, its forehead damaged, as we attempted to grant a terrified lamb a bit of companionship and warmth in its last living moments. Lambs' eyes are among the most beautiful things in existence; their purity calls to mind blue mornings before the world awakes, we saw the bolt from the stun gun burst its way into the bone between them – those weren't the most pleasant moments in life. The distance between extremes, between darkness and light, is often minimal in this world; because shortly after we experienced our best moments, when we walked past the girl whom Ari loved on our way to lunch, coffee breaks, or at the end of our shifts, walked the length of the production line, saw how lambs, sheep and a ram or two were separated from life, how they were skinned, their guts torn out, heads cut off, we saw that there was cruelty in the world, or else that was how life looked, plain and simple; that it's not as beautiful as music at all. We walked down the production line and naively hoped, or innocently hoped, that there was a Heaven for sheep, with eternally green pastures and no slaughterhouses; we saw dead lambs turned into sides of meat, yet Ari's heart pounded as we approached the girl who skinned the carcasses; with her curly hair, freckles like kisses and then those eyes, one of which was "Here, There and Everywhere", and the other "If I Fell", and it was enough, nothing else was necessary, the world had those eyes, and therefore was saved.

What bliss, what incredible luck to be alive at the same time as those eyes, and what's more, to be in the same place, out west in Dalir, a district that few people visit, and in Búðardalur, a village that even God hasn't heard of, where there's no church, no cemetery, the siblings death and eternity shun this village, angels never fly over it, yet those eyes shone there for a few weeks that autumn, those freckles that are like kisses could often be seen in the Co-op; what's front-page news, if not that? What's a headline story if not that girl with incredible eyes, freckles fairer than stars, she's an entire universe, or at least a galaxy. Ari and I were stunned by the negligence of the media, incomprehensible that the world's major newspapers didn't make a big deal out of this, the *New York Times* could have put those eyes on its front page, filled it with them, nothing but her eyes on the page, probably a great many things would have come of it, many people would have taken comfort, murderers would have thrown down their guns instead of firing them, fathers would not have hit their children. The following day, the paper could have published photos of her freckles, those kisses to the world, and rocket launchers would have turned into greenhouses, fathers' blows into tender caresses. But no such thing happened, and, to tell the truth, no-one seemed to notice her eyes, her freckles that resembled kisses, except for Ari and me, how apathetic can the world be? The fellows in the slaughterhouse, our mates, most of them farmers' sons, saw nothing but the tits of the other girls, their asses, although one of them finally mentioned her the evening of the closing dance, which was held on the first day of winter, after everything that needed killing that autumn was killed, and what a dance it was, God help us, wasn't that a dance!

None other than Geirmundur Valtýsson played at the dance, as lively as a wind-up toy,[14] we fellows in the slaughterhouse having long since ordered schnapps and vodka from the south, plenty of bottles, because now we were going to fucking drink and have fun, goddammit, because it's no small thing simply being alive, and just sixteen, seventeen, eighteen, nineteen years old. Ten or so of us meet early in the evening at a house that five of the fellows

14  Geirmundur Valtýsson (b. 1944): An Icelandic musician and farmer, often called "the king of swing".

had rented together, and there someone mentions the name of she who has eyes by Lennon and McCartney yet doesn't say a single word about them, that they should be on the front page of the world and save it with their beauty, no, just says her name, Sigrún, and that she has fucking tiny tits, like little lamb droppings that you'd hardly want to tweak, and that would barely give you a hard-on to look at.

Tits like lamb droppings.

You'd barely get a hard-on looking at them.

Ari downs some schnapps, which he'd mixed into low-alcohol beer; this blend allowed people to imagine they were drinking real beer in a foreign country.[15] He takes a big gulp, and then looks at me. He'd never thought of anything below Sigrún's lips, which curved slightly downwards, as if due to a very vague or very ancient melancholy, as if she retained some memory from the dawn of time. We'd never thought about her body: tits, hips, legs, ass; we just knew that all these things had to be there, but their role was to support her eyes, freckles, lips, carry them along throughout the world. We're no angels; no innocents. We were familiar with books like *Passion Tramp*, *Risque Stories*, *She Never Got Enough*,[16] and several times we stole dirty magazines, showing everything, from the bookshop in Keflavík. So we knew a thing or two, but Sigrún didn't belong to the world of dirty magazines or erotic novels; she was, as Ari wrote in one of

15 The ban on beer in Iceland was lifted in 1989, but prior to that time, vodka or schnapps were often mixed into a "near-beer" of 2-percent alcohol (known in Icelandic as "pilsner") for a stronger effect.

16 The first title, *Passion Tramp*, was the original title of a book in English by John Dexter (a pseudonym), translated into Icelandic in 1970 as *Götustelpan: Líkaminn var hennar bankabók* (*Street Girl: Her Body Was Her Bankbook*). The originals of the other two titles remain unclear.

his romantic frenzies: The eternal summer, a dream of the solar system, a breath of God.

Her tits were like lamb droppings.

Then off to the dance!

Up onstage, Geirmundur Valtýsson yells something about getting into the swing, feet pound the dance floor, some people actually try dancing, but most just toss themselves to and fro, drunk and revelling. Weatherbeaten farmers, creamy farmers' wives, sons and daughters, the youngest sixteen years old, the oldest well into their seventies. The dean of the elderly, Gaui from Brú, seventy-nine years old, had always said that he wanted to die drunk and dancing at a swinging country dance, not like some old bit of rubbish, hay blown by the wind, a calf dribbling diarrhoea, in an old folks' home. He never leaves the dance floor, his cotton shirt drenched with sweat, his face beaming, his toothless mouth one big smile, his teeth lingering in his half-full vodka glass on his table, They rattle so annoyingly in my mouth when I'm dancing, he says, sticking them in his glass before stepping out onto the dance floor, It'll sure be bloody nice to put them back in again, he adds, shaking with laughter, with joy, so euphoric that Geirmundur, with all his wound-up swing, is like a zombie in comparison. Sigrún, his niece, a dream of the solar system, dances with him a lot this night, wearing tight blue jeans, a white top, she's sweating as well, it's so hot, she dances so much, and then we notice her breasts, that they're not big at all, that, on the contrary, they're very small, and we notice her thighs as well, her ass, though we don't think that word – *ass* – far from it, but we see that it's wonderful, plump, it's like something we want to see unleashed, and it is transformed before our eyes, because when she shimmies on the dance floor, when she sways to the rhythm, quickly, with suppleness, and when she turns in circles, she becomes a comet slipping through the darkness of space with its fiery light.

Ari and I see all of this as we lean against a column at the community centre, wait there, loiter there, as Ari drinks in the courage to ask her to dance, she who'd smiled at us so often as we walked down the production line, she who'd spoken to us, twice sat down next to us in the canteen, right next to Ari, so close that he felt the warmth of her thigh, so close that he could hardly breathe from sheer bliss. She'd smiled at us at the dance, and once came over to us to say something, but before we could answer, an uncle or aunt dragged her onto the dance floor, where she instantly became a comet, illuminating the world's darkness. Ari drinks and waits for courage to arrive. Maybe, we say, it's more clever to wait until 3.00 a.m. and catch the last dance before the slow song, just think, slow dancing with her, Paradise is nothing but a piece of shit in comparison. Good idea, says Ari, and he takes a drink, gazes at her out on the dance floor, looks at old Gaui, who's begun to stagger from exhaustion and alcohol. It's 2.00, 2.30, 3.00, Aren't we having a fucking blast, screams Geirmundur from the stage, some of his band members appear to be so drunk that they no longer know what instrument they're playing, Yeaaaahhh, shrieks the dance floor in return, Gaui loudest of all, having perked himself up by sucking his teeth. His niece, the comet, Sigrún, is heard shouting, Yeeeeahhh, but suddenly she's no longer shining, suddenly she's dimmed, suddenly she's not a comet flashing through the world, but rather, a melancholy moon, at most. Maybe, I say, she's so sad because you haven't asked her to dance. We look at her, she places her hands on one of the tables, so beautiful, so pale, her freckles have never been so evident, she's without a doubt the most beautiful thing we've ever seen, and she's leaning on one of the tables, nearly seventeen, beads of sweat on her forehead, her eyes half closed, her shoulders sagging, She doesn't feel well, I say, No, we've got to do something, says Ari, I think she needs to throw up, I say. Dear God, he says, and repeats, almost desperately, We've got to do something! But we do nothing. We don't move, afraid of attracting attention, terrified that she'll push Ari away and hiss, contemptuously, Leave me alone, do you really think I want to see you, childish, stuttering, red-haired, the fuck if I'd have any interest in you, the fuck if you appear in my dreams, just go and shoot yourself, you're like a lame-ass pop song, you wouldn't even make the Top-100 list at the North Pole. This is why we hesitate. But not Kári, a man from Akranes, married to the sister of the farmer for whom Ari had worked in the summers, well over thirty, father of three, came out west to work in the slaughterhouse, wasn't far from Sigrún on the production line, lightning-quick with his hands, he doesn't hesitate, he comes to her rescue, he puts his arm around Sigrún's shoulders to protect her, comfort her, he says something to her, probably something about how fresh air could do her good, something sensible, spoken out of experience and a sense of responsibility, because we see Kári lead her out, clearing a path for her across the writhing dance floor, she unsteady, he with his head held high, she never would have made it without help, would have puked over the dancers, such a humiliation, Kári is a good person, the world would be worse off, far more difficult, without people like him. He leads her across the dance floor, cleaves the frenzied crowd, takes her outside into the fresh air and we follow, hesitantly, I'll walk her back in after she's recovered, says Ari, and then we're out in the frosty night air, the cold, and there are the stars, they're up in the firmament and make us think about eternity, about the music of the heavens, they're the light that cuts through the darkness, but Sigrún vomits as she leans on Kári's car. Ari and I slink stealthily over to the blue Land Rover belonging to the farmer with whom Ari spent every summer since 1975, we want to remain hidden, pretend not to notice her humiliation, we do it for her, to shield her, if there were only more people as respectful as us. We slip into the front seat, hear the echo of Kári's voice, hear the pounding beat coming from the community centre, the joyous rhythm of life, drinking and revelry. We turn on the car's cassette player, turn on Brimkló, it's Björgvin Halldórsson, BÓ himself, who sings real pop songs. Now she's finished throwing up, my God, how pale she is, God in Heaven, how beautiful she is, our hearts tremble, they're shaped like tears, Kári reaches into his car for something, probably a tissue so that she can wipe her face, pass it over that mouth of hers, which hides a vague, ancient sadness, no, he has a bottle, is going to give her water to perk her up, wait, no, it's a bottle of vodka, he hands it to her and she takes it willingly, that's weird, that she wants to drink more, it's disappointing, the night becomes a touch darker, she drinks with half-closed eyes, takes a big gulp, coughs, the drink sprays from her mouth, Kári laughs, so he's a prankster, strokes her hair, strokes her face, her freckles that are like kisses, her eyes that should have been put on the front page of the *New York Times* and allowed to change the world, transforming murderers into gardeners, and then Kári has begun kissing her, passionately, as if it's he and not Ari who loves her more ardently than anyone has ever loved on this earth, and she seems paralysed by joy in his arms, as he opens the back door with one hand and now they're in the car, in the back seat, the door shuts and shortly afterwards the car begins rocking. It's a Lada estate car, and it rocks, sways, undulates, and soon something white starts appearing regularly just above the seat backs, it's Kári's buttocks, peeking over the seats, as if on the lookout, checking whether anyone is watching, or else like two little kids bouncing happily up and down, they go faster and faster, appear and disappear in a flash, such happiness, such joy, so that's what she wanted, to let an old man fuck her, just as well that Ari didn't ask her to dance, she would have laughed at him, she would have humiliated Ari, who's just a lame pop song that wouldn't even make the Top-100 list at the end of the world. Brimkló on the cassette player, Björgvin Halldórsson singing, his voice as soft and beautiful as blue velvet:

Please hold my hand
wherever I go
because I'll never forget you.

# Norðfjörður

— PAST —

## There's very little pluck in
## drowned men

It's astounding, enormously so, that there are those who feel that
they fulfil the role, that they're worthy of the honour, of being
thought of as real men without having tested their mettle at sea.
We live on an island, quite a large one, of course, but its size doesn't
change the fact that the sea surrounds us completely, that it's
waiting, calling to us; some, of course, have to remain on land,
that's only natural, someone has to run the shops, build houses,
publish newspapers, teach children, care for the sick, that's
obvious, and some live so far inland, in such deep valleys, that for
them the sea hardly exists, which must be terribly painful. That
someone, a man, can go through this life without wanting to prove
himself at sea, test his strength against it, come to know himself
in the face of mountainous dark waves, in howling storms, when
the sky booms and thunders, as if Armageddon or the wrath of
God dwelled in the sky, and the boat, with all its tonnage, its
engine power, were a mere twig and human lives nothing at all –
that's a man who doesn't know who he is; he'll never be more than
half a man. Or, as Tryggvi says, To be at sea is to be alive.

It takes seriously severe weather to keep Oddur and *Sleipnir* on
land; if Oddur doesn't sail, it's undoubtedly suicidal to do so, and

it's no mean achievement to be invited to join his crew, it's almost like receiving a medal for courage and bravery. His crewmen have to put their all into their work, and have to have excellent reasons to remain at home if there's a fishing trip; in fact, they have to be dead, it's the only valid reason, or plausible excuse. Are you the one giving birth, or her? asked Oddur when one of the crew, the youngest, asked for permission to skip the next trip because his wife was expecting. Oddur himself sails even if he has such a burning fever that he's hallucinating. But one thing is beyond incredible, namely, that nowhere in the entire Eastfjords are such strict safety measures taken than by him, that iron man, as if he were, despite everything, something of a coward behind all the unbending toughness. No-one, for example, earns a place on his boat unless he's a good swimmer; there are life jackets to both starboard and port, but to top it all off, the very height of absurdity, is the fact that aboard *Sleipnir* there's a little dinghy, meant to serve as a lifeboat. To waste valuable space on a lifeboat – in the old days, when men were men, all they thought about was catching enough fish; they had no time for safety. If something happened – an accident, a dangerous swell, you just had to deal with it as best you could, show what sort of man you were, and if it wasn't enough, well then, your time was simply up; time to pack your belongings and leave. Things have changed, obviously; there's a clear difference between the champions of the past and of the present. Oddur, of course, could just order a sufficiently long fucking rope from down south, tie one end of it to *Sleipnir*, the other tightly to the pier, and then he could sail without fearing anything!

It was really quite funny.

Around thirty sailors are seated or standing, drinking, the

weather is rough, almost squally at times, it's no weather for sailing, and news spread of a bottle of French cognac in one of the fishing sheds, the sailors thronged the place, filled the shed, It's so crowded, says one of them, that there's hardly room to fart. Most of them smoke, take snuff, chew on hardfish, but every now and then the door is opened to the storm so that they aren't asphyxiated, parting the thick fog of tobacco smoke slightly and making the stench less heavy and suffocating. They sing, they tell stories. Tryggvi is first among them in both fields, possessing a beautiful baritone voice and great skill as a narrator, making every story come alive, building atmosphere, drawing such clear images of incidents that they seem to be taking place right in front of the men. He recounts the adventures of the old heroes, back when men were men, when they never gave in and would rather chew on stones than show signs of weakness, such as feelings, and it was after one such story that the bruiser Konráð made the remark about the rope and Oddur. Konráð the Bull – given his nickname because of his incredible strength, temper and ugliness – had tried to join Oddur's crew nine years before, when a place had come free: someone died, contracted tuberculosis and coughed his life out down south in Reykjavík, but someone else was picked instead of Konráð, someone who didn't have half of his strength. You're pretty funny, Konni, says Tryggvi, and are probably a much better entertainer than a sailor. Oddur, on the other hand, says nothing, sits there on a stool, staring into the distance as if he's bored; his face, darkened and marked by sun, weather and the sea, is expressionless.

Suddenly, there's silence in the shed, deep silence. The men don't realise it right away; it takes time for the silence to seep into some of them through their intoxication, make its way through the howling of the wind and the tobacco smoke, but when it comes, it fills the shed, becomes tangible, besieges them, and all they do is breathe, they hear only their own breathing and the storm raging outside, shaking the sky high up in the darkness and reverberating on the shed. The men look in turn at Konráð and the two friends, Tryggvi and Oddur, something's about to happen, it's absolutely clear, a memorable event is about to take place, damn it's good that we came down here to the shed, now Konráð's going to take revenge for being rejected nine years ago, in just a few moments his nine years of accumulated hatred are going to burst out, he's cursed the crew often enough over the years, nine years of bullish anger. Those nearest Konráð try to back away, take one or two steps, though it's nearly impossible because of the mob, Konráð pulls himself up to his full height, as if to remind himself and the others of his size, and slowly realises that he's said too much, has gone too far, and now there are only two possibilities, to retreat or to attack. He isn't entirely sure which is preferable, but then he notices a change in Oddur's expression, as if the bastard grinned, but hardly for more than a second, or even less, and then the same impassivity, but Konráð saw it, the grin, the sarcastic grin that cut him like a knife – now it was impossible to retreat. He says, It's easy to see why you chose that wanker Fúsi over me; I always thought it was because you wanted to get hold of his wife, Rúna, play with those big tits of hers, fucking giant tits, and I can understand that, who wouldn't want to find himself between her legs, when the whole time it was because you knew that your chicken-heartedness and paltriness would be obvious to everyone if I stood next to you. No wonder your wife has a few screws loose, she's simply gone mad with horniness and wants to feel a real man inside her. But don't you worry, I'll stop by your place at the next opportunity and promise to show her what it is to be fucked by a man. You can even watch and learn.

Now he'd gone too far. Way too far.

Isn't that precisely the measure of courage, daring to go too far? He grins.

Shows, in that way, that he isn't afraid of anything or anyone. Clenches his fists, which are practically giant-sized, like two big boulders, stares hard at Oddur, who's a head shorter, not nearly as broad-shouldered, clearly not as strong – is that why he does nothing? Because Oddur sits tight, perfectly calm. Then he pulls out a pocketknife, tests the blade on his cheek and then starts cleaning his fingernails. Slowly, and determinedly. Looks up once, directly at Konráð, boring into his skull with those grey eyes. That's Oddur's only reaction to the bruiser's vulgar insults, the attack on his good name and the defamatory words about his wife: to scrape the dirt from beneath his fingernails!

But slowly.

Unbearably slowly.

Every single man in the fishing shed is watching, all of them still and silent as stones. They don't take their eyes off Oddur's pocketknife, his hands; watch as if captivated, as if attending a religious rite. Finally, Konráð can no longer stand it, and shouts, in such a thundering voice that any normal person would have been frightened to death just to hear it, What is this? What kind of wimp are you, huh?! Oddur looks up, stops scraping for a moment, looks up, and then quietly resumes where he left off, and Konráð suddenly feels as if Oddur is not just scraping the dirt from under his nails but also scraping the courage and balance out of him, Konráð. Obviously, it's fucking bullshit, yet he feels that way anyway. Sure, he drank too much, yes, probably, there was also that goddam moonshine they drank when the French cognac was finished, fucking homebrew, and that's why he went too far. He looks at the knife beneath the skipper's fingernails and feels as if he's hearing the sound in his head as the blade scrapes out the dirt, and the storm, the noise and fury of the tempest, has receded to an unfathomable distance. The fifth nail, and Konráð feels discomfort in his stomach, the sixth, and the discomfort increases, the seventh, and the air inside the shed becomes unbearably heavy and revolting, he actually feels nauseous, the eighth and he has to get out, get some fresh air, bloody hell, the ninth, and Konráð shoves men out of his way, leaps to the door, makes it out into the storm, so quickly that the wind manages to throw him down and he's on all fours, vomiting and retching, while inside the shed Oddur folds up his pocketknife.

This is one of the stories that Jakob, Ari's father, hears often, and in various versions, as he's growing up there in the east, as well as later, after he's come south; both during his year on Vatnsleysuströnd, among the lava fields, and then in Reykjavík. Stories about Oddur, all sorts of stories, not always beautiful but with him invariably coming out on top. Jakob knows Konráð quite well, the giant, the bull, the bruiser; he often played with his two sons, and Jakob was always a bit frightened of him. Konráð was a violent person and became very dangerous when drinking, was a nightmare for the village policeman, tossed men aside like empty sacks, it took no fewer than three to four men of more than average size to control him, bring him down, but Oddur defeated him by cleaning his fingernails!

*

Oddur the victor. Skipper of a profitable fishing vessel, respected by young and old alike, endowed with unshakeable strength and stamina, sailed confidently in risky weather conditions, and the wilder the sea was, the higher and blacker the waves, the more fearless and happy Oddur seemed. Yet at the same time – and this was seen as a great contradiction – he was a pioneer in safety issues in the Eastfjords; no-one was more prudent in this area, with his lifeboat, life preservers, his demand that his crew be able to swim, himself an excellent swimmer, though he learned to swim later in life, in his twenties, and had the tendency, even in midwinter, to strip down while at sea and swim naked two to three times around his boat, the water perhaps so cold that the Devil himself couldn't have endured it for long, his men felt frozen just watching their skipper, and stood there shivering; You'll kill yourself doing that, they said, but he never even caught a cold from it. "I always enjoyed danger," he said many years later, in one of the interviews with "Old Sea-Heroes" that were published in the daily *The Will of the People* on Sailors' Day,[17] and claimed to feel at his best in bad weather, "when you were put to the test, had to prove what you were made of; it's just my nature, but to me it was utter stupidity not to take the most stringent safety precautions. I was responsible, not just for the boat and fishing equipment, as well as my own life, but also, first and foremost, for the lives and limbs of my crew. A ship's captain who doesn't put his crew's safety above all else shouldn't be allowed on board; he shouldn't captain a boat any bigger than would fit in a bathtub."

Utter stupidity. For the longest time, however, Oddur had been the most careless of men when it came to safety issues, but that

17  Sailors' Day (Icelandic: *Sjómannadagurinn*) is celebrated annually on June 1. It was first celebrated in Reykjavík in 1938.

changed gradually, due, naturally, to the sense of responsibility that kindles within you when you have children, and are suddenly the sun and moon, the earth itself beneath the feet of a little individual, their world collapses if you die; and it's nothing but the purest selfishness – a mortal sin, unforgivable – if you disregard their safety.

It was Margrét who made it happen.

What happens, she once asks Oddur, it's a tranquil winter morning, many years before Konráð the Bull pulls himself up to his full height in the fishing shed; the weather had been quite bad the day before and most of the night, heavy snow, but now everything is quiet, they awake long before the children, she in a spirited mood due to an exciting dream that she felt she ought to be ashamed of, yet that lingers as she lies there on her back; she can't help it, needs to open her mouth, part her lips, to contain herself, as she listens to Oddur's steady breathing. She breathes but doesn't manage, is unable, doesn't want to calm the rush of her blood, she gets up quietly, slips out, checks to make sure that the children are asleep, goes back in and wakes Oddur with her lips. They lie tightly together, so entwined it's as if they're one, she breathes him in, feels his arms around her; What if I didn't have these arms to hold me, she thinks – and then broaches a subject that she has often raised, and has just as often avoided. Now she's determined. Now she desires him so passionately that she can't stand the idea of losing him. Yet one must approach things in the right way, when the stakes are high; one must tailor one's words to the person listening. What happens, she asks, if one of your crew falls overboard in bad weather; well, for example, you? That doesn't happen, he says, or murmers, with a smile. You can't say such a thing, no-one can guarantee it; the sea is bigger than you. Oh, well then, I'm pulled back on board.

Margrét: But if there's a heavy swell and the waves sweep you away from the boat?

Oddur: That would certainly be unlucky.

Margrét: What do you mean, unlucky?

Oddur: You know as well as I do that being a sailor involves risk. We drown; that's the price we pay. You've just got to stand tall.

Margrét: It's hard for a drowned man to stand tall.

Oddur: A damned misfortune, that's for sure. But that's the sea – it gives, it takes, and it makes us men.

Margrét: Damned misfortune makes children lose their fathers, lose people to look up to, maybe even breaks up their families. Naturally, men who know how to swim have a far greater chance of being saved, especially if there's safety equipment on board. Surely it must be better to see your children again than to drown – and a drowned man doesn't catch many fish. In fact, there's very little pluck in drowned men. They're of no use to anyone. They don't fish, they don't get erections, they're made to leave the playing field, which is bad enough, but it's much worse if they could have saved themselves by being able to swim. Otherwise, it might well be that being cautious at sea, taking safety precautions, requires more courage than most men possess.

Oddur sits up in bed, looks angrily at his wife.

He curses.

And then learns to swim.

At first, it's unbearable. He feels like an idiot in the swimming pond that had been created at the mouth of the fjord, kicking and wriggling about like a fish on dry land, such a stinging humiliation, apparent to everyone, mainly women and children, both he and Tryggvi, whom Oddur had ordered to come with him; after the first lesson, they were so furious that they nearly came to blows. On three occasions, Tryggvi had to prevent Oddur from climbing out of the pond and attacking the fucking teacher, that arch-idiot Björgvin, the village postmaster. The two sworn brothers are the targets of derision and jest; they're called the two fish, the two mermaids, and more than once they find fish tails on their doorsteps when they leave their houses early in the morning, lying there like sarcastic grins. But Oddur is absolutely determined to learn how to swim, damn it all, to conquer it, the sarcastic nicknames, the fish tails, to cultivate it, and little by little the wonders of swimming open up to them; this Björgvin is a real master and an outstanding teacher, completely useless at sea but otherwise a genius, because it's an out-and-out miracle, bloody brilliant, to be able to float on water, even propel yourself through it. A year later, the entire crew of *Sleipnir* knows how to swim. The first boat in the Eastfjords with a crew of swimmers, all of whom are torn to shreds by ridicule. The crew that swam after fish instead of using fishing tackle. They're called mermen, seals, selkies, and what's more, they have life preservers on board – why don't they just stay on land since they're so terrified of the sea? To top it all off, there's the lifeboat, the dinghy, which is so outrageous that you can hardly make a joke about it. For Oddur, it becomes a matter of pride to stand out not only in seamanship but also on safety issues, and he is untiring in his advocacy of them. He gets hold of a copy of the booklet on safety at sea that Björgvin, swimming instructor and postmaster, publishes and distributes in the Eastfjords. This booklet had considerable influence, not least due to Oddur's account of when his great-grandfather drowned not far from shore: "My great-grandmother, my grandfather, and his siblings watched him struggle and sink. The weather was nice and calm. They watch, helpless and desperate, as he thrashes in the water, and then he sinks. Vanishes, doesn't come back up. Then the youngest child, the infant, asks, 'Why doesn't Daddy come back up?'"

The correct answer, says Oddur, though the article was undoubtedly written mainly by Margrét, such things coming far more naturally to her, was simply: "Because he can't swim."

"It's peculiar indeed," concluded the article, "that very few sailors seem to possess the courage to think about safety. Yet everyone knows that the sea will punish us cruelly if we don't take appropriate measures. No-one, of course, can stop death, but it's unnecessary to clear its path."

### It's March – the hands of death are as white as moonlight

One night, death rises from the sea and enters the village of Nes.

Oddur sleeps deeply next to Margrét, there are five children in the house, five universes, five-fold happiness, three girls, two boys: little Gunnar and Þórður, who will soon turn twelve and has begun to accompany his father to sea now and then, big for his age and with excellent sea legs. It's March; Oddur should be in Hornafjörður for the fishing season, but he has returned home for a few days to recover from a work accident, having stumbled over a knife that stuck in his thigh. The wound became infected, but he's recovering quickly; he'll leave soon, take back command of the boat from Tryggvi. Oddur sleeps heavily, but Margrét had awakened when little Gunnar climbed into bed with them after having a bad dream; lying between them, he was quickly soothed and went back to sleep. Margrét, on the other hand, finds it difficult to fall back to sleep, so she goes outside, washes her face, pees and then waits for some water to heat up, looking in the meantime out of the kitchen window. All is silent, the village, the mountains, the sea is heavy with tranquillity, and at first it's pitch-black, but then a faint glimmer of moonlight manages to seep through the clouds, allowing her to see the vague outline of whatever it is that emerges from the water and heads up the beach by the pier. Obscure at first, just a vague blob, which soon takes on form and becomes a tall, dark-coloured being, and Margrét is immediately convinced that it's death itself that has stepped like that from sea to shore in order to fetch someone from the village. She absolutely must stay awake to watch. It walks with slow, measured steps, as only those outside of time can do, and the air appears to yield to its passage. I'm dreaming, she thinks, but feels fear close around her as death comes up the slope and heads straight for their house.

She meets it in the hallway.

It is very tall, with a cold, austere glance, its pupils so black that the night itself brightens around them, and its hands are extremely large and very white, they're like moonlight; Why do they have to be like that, she thinks, moonlight is so beautiful, why can't it continue to be so? She stands in the hall, steadies herself, armed only with her life. Her children are sleeping inside. And Oddur. She says, You're not taking anyone here, not tonight, not tomorrow night or the next, not for a very long time.

I take what's mine, no living blood can stop me.

It's as if its voice is made of nothing. Without sound, without nuance, without cadence. Words that come from the abyss and are nothing but boundless sorrow, and it's as if all hope is gone, every blade of grass withered; she wished she could curl up in a

298

ball in a corner and shut her eyes. But she doesn't move, she looks death in the eye, looks deep into its eyes and sees that they're like two graves. Looks, doesn't flinch. Death raises one hand – she could never remember later whether it was the right one or the left, but its fingertips are bluish, its skin scarred and ancient, thickened with some sort of calluses, it raises its hand and lays its fingertips very lightly on her left breast, over her heart, which changes instantaneously from a warm muscle into an icy stone.

Then she wakes up.

In the hallway, shivering with cold, cowering on the floor, it's the middle of the night, and the moonlight streaming in through the window is like a cold hand.

## May, spring has arrived

"In the old days," it says in the daily *Vísir*, read like a heavy sentence by Margrét over coffee, "the sea ice was our bitter enemy, but in recent years, its place has been taken by tuberculosis. It is unstoppable, and more deadly than sea ice. It spreads throughout the country and leaves behind death and open wounds in the memories of those who survive but who have lost a loved one or loved ones. Tuberculosis spares no-one, neither innocent children nor the most vigorous of men."

Like a heavy sentence – just a few days after Margrét stopped death, she was diagnosed with tuberculosis, as if death had thrust the deadly disease into her breast with its cold fingers – yet it doesn't manage to fell her. She turns out to be one of the lucky few, life's reward for daring to block death's path. She recovers remarkably quickly; the disease doesn't penetrate too deeply, and, just over a year later, she's perfectly healthy. Or as healthy as a person who has blocked death's path can be, having looked into its eyes, those two black graves, and been touched by it. No life should have to endure the touch of death; is this why she occasionally has the feeling that something important, perhaps the very thread of equilibrium, has snapped in two, that it may be the price she has to pay for obstructing death, for having looked into its eyes and refused to look away?

Or is this simply the price she has to pay for her excessive imagination, and for having so little control over it?

She never tells Oddur about death's visit, whether it was a dream or not, that death's eyes are two graves, the bones in its large hands made of moonlight. Oddur has never had any patience with what goes against rationality, lies beyond its borders, what isn't possible to grasp with your hands, break with the power of your hands. A fear of superstition, ghosts and supernatural forces, and a belief in mysterious events, are signs of a nervous disorder caused on the one hand by an overactive imagination and on the other by a lack of self-control. This opinion of his is so strong and unwavering that ever since they began their relationship, she's always tried to suppress her restless imagination, sometimes to deny it altogether. But then she sees death emerge from the sea. She blocks its path, and everything changes. She blocks death's path, defeats tuberculosis and discovers how precious life is, that it's a rare spark. But she also starts asking herself, Where are my dreams, where did they go, dreams of bright happiness, laughter, dreams, dreams about knowledge, wisdom, poetry, education?

She probably just thinks too much. Broods excessively, makes too much of things and is consequently too quick to criticise things around her, sees only the negative. And forgets that every-one needs their own space. For example, men drink more than women; it's their way of coping – their fault, if you want to see it that way. But everyone has their faults, that's life, and other women don't let the drinking bother them; drinking is a part of life, but why is she sometimes cold and disagreeable when Oddur comes home drunk? Might it be because she feels almost as if she's losing him when he drinks, or that she may not be so important to him; does she fear that he's chasing other women, that they'll steal him away from her, steal the things that she still loves about him, despite everything? Every now and then she hears a rumour about Oddur and other women down at the drying lot, half-veiled in innuendo, ambiguous remarks. Might he drink more because she doesn't give him enough space, is too inflexible? Alcohol is a refuge. It isn't easy being the captain of a ship, to be responsible for others' lives and livelihoods, to show unwavering strength, to act as a role model, distinguish yourself from others, come home tired and find little rest among the children and stress of daily life; everyone needs to let off steam sometimes. He comes home drunk, sometimes without her having any idea where he's been. She's stuck at home, with the children, the cooking, the housework, but he comes and goes, freedom personified. That's how she thinks sometimes, negatively; she can't help it, is always finding fault, won't give him space, as if she resents his having it, he comes home drunk, even smashed after a binge, but never staggering, never gibbering, never helpless, as if he's always in control – and is sometimes downright cheerful. He'll play with the children, tease them, making everyone happy but her; she can't help but stiffen, no matter how she tries to remain composed – she becomes grumpy, he becomes funny. Oddur takes the children in his arms, tosses them in the air, turns them upside down, tells stories about the sea, its fury, its storms, but also its calm moments, When the world seems to expand, and we to expand along with it, as your uncle Tryggvi says. When can we go to sea with you? ask the girls, to which Oddur replies, becoming nearly, and involuntarily, poetic from the drink and his unexpected popularity, The sea is what makes us men, but the land is for you women. You keep it safe for us. We live with danger and it shapes us, or destroys us, it's our life, while you live in the security of the land, and keep watch over life. We meet on the shore.

Margrét hears this. She's in the kitchen, had been trying to read, but couldn't concentrate, upset with herself for being so stiff and grumpy, for feeling cold and angry towards Oddur, now when his attention is entirely on the children and she hears their raucous laughter and shrieks of joy. It's why she starts baking, unfortunately not to make them happy but to lose herself in work. She bakes and hears these things about men and women, the land and the sea, and something cracks inside her; before she knows it, she has reached for a plate and thrown it against the wall. As hard as she can. The plate shatters noisily.

Then there is silence.

We hear the sound of something breaking, see the consequences, see that what was a mere moment ago whole has become a mess. Nothing frightens us as much as messiness. What once had a specific use, and consequently a certain beauty, is now unuseable, has become a repulsive mess. And the power that created it is to be found in the jagged, irregular, menacing shards. Oddur and the children come into the kitchen, see the shattered plate, see Margrét standing there, her expression unreadable, a frenzied or fearful look in her eyes – Þórður sees fear, Hulda frenzy. Oddur sees the smashed plate. I'll sweep this up, Margrét says, trying to sound calm. You've got to learn to control yourself, says Oddur, his voice hardened by anger which boils over suddenly like an eruption from the depths, and she sees what confronts her in the shards: her own inadequacy. Those who are inadequate are always wrong.

She kneels down, sweeps up the mess, as he goes over to the wall and runs his hand over the shallow notch left in the wood. Margrét, he says, your dreaminess is wrecking your nerves. You let things bother you too much, confuse things that don't exist with things that do and, because of that, are less tolerant.

## A short essay on darkness and light

It hurts to be inadequate, and even more badly to be aware of it, to feel it, such awareness penetrates deeply and is no good for your vital organs, impairs their function, especially your heart and its interactions with your brain. She tolerates less.

She doesn't tolerate blocking death's path, being touched by it. She does of course recover from tuberculosis, but not from the touch, the cold remains behind and becomes darkness that rises and subsides within her, unpredictably, as if it has a will of its own, comes and goes when it pleases, winter or summer, birdsong or snowfall. Two or three times a year it fills her veins so completely that everything becomes too difficult, she can barely see to the housework or her job of spreading saltfish out to dry unless she makes an extreme effort. At its worst, she stays in bed, like some layabout, or as if she were old and infirm, incapable of anything, completely useless; it would be no great loss, and probably best for everyone, just to be rid of her. The children have to do the

303

housework, do the cooking for their father, what sort of mother and wife can't even look after her own home; that's what Oddur has to put up with. No wonder he likes an occasional tipple, to flirt with other women, who wouldn't do the same in his shoes? Who wouldn't – she knows it, knows that she's letting them down, but the darkness fills her, colours her internal organs, shoves its way into every thought, even into her memories; everything goes dark. She can barely get up, lies in bed for two or three days at a time, just lies on her back, stares into space, absolutely motionless, as if sleeping, or even dead, says little, often nothing, the children are almost afraid to come close to her, and Oddur sleeps in the front room. These periods most frequently end abruptly, so abruptly that it's as if death itself is torn from her and replaced with life, glorious life. Her blood fills with sunshine, laughter, birdsong, ticklish joy, and she can't sit still, she's got to move, celebrate life, dance! She starts baking, puts all her energy into it, and dances about the house, hugging her children, who are happy, frightened and embarrassed all at once. She embraces life because it's so good, such fun, it's so important to be alive that it must be a betrayal of everyone, of the universe itself, of God himself, not to let oneself go. This is why she runs outside, wanting to change the world into a cry of joy, into a dance, runs outside and embraces the first person she meets, a farmer from up the valley, she knows his name but nothing more, yet that doesn't matter, because she loves all of life, wants to embrace all of life, embrace him, shouts, Isn't life beautiful, isn't it wonderful to be alive! In fact the farmer has to agree, he's making an ordinary trip to town and is unexpectedly embraced by such a beautiful woman, wearing only a nightdress, he can feel her breasts and presses her tighter against him, Everything's beautiful when you're in a woman's arms, he says, and kisses her. Afterwards, perhaps half an hour later, when her joy isn't quite as unchecked, or is tempered, and she's made hot chocolate for the children, filled their plates with sweet-smelling biscuits, she feels slightly ashamed. It was perhaps unnecessary to rush out like that, to embrace that man, let alone allow him to kiss her, and now she recalls that he ran his hands over her bottom, why did he need to do that, can you never show a man a bit of happiness without him taking advantage? She's slightly ashamed, and the older children are furious at her, especially Hulda, who has to endure the teasing of her peers in the days that follow, while little Gunnar, on the other hand, is peeved about not being allowed to run out into the street behind his mother and hop around with her there; Hulda stopped him from doing so, he squirmed and fought and wailed in her arms, to no end. Maybe no-one saw me, says Margrét in an attempt to calm them down, and in any case, what's wrong with rejoicing in life sometimes?

What's wrong, nothing, of course, shouldn't we all rush outside occasionally and shout in support of life, or is life so self-evident, so taken for granted? How often have we run out into the street to celebrate life, that tired beast, that windswept flower, that base note?

But no-one saw her. Apart from the farmer, of course, and he didn't see any need to keep quiet about it, which is why the news is waiting for Oddur at the pier when he sails into shore, many hours later, with a full load, as so often happens, his boat the most productive of them all in the last two years, that she had run out into the street, hugged a stranger, screaming hysterically. I didn't scream, she protests, That's not what I heard, he hisses, having just returned home, he paces the kitchen floor, she sits at the kitchen table, rosy-cheeked and so beautiful after the events of the day, free from the heavy darkness, having baked biscuits for hours, and though the smell makes Oddur even hungrier, it doesn't appease his anger; quite the contrary. Why did she have to do that, run out like that, shouting, half-dressed, and then, to add insult to injury, hug that damned Sigmundur of Kirkjuból, of all people! I didn't know you knew him, she says softly, her eyes lowered, as if speaking to the table. Know him, I don't know anyone who wants to know that rotten fucking lout, that goddamned lush, he's lucky he was back at home by the time I landed, I would have reduced him to a bit of saltfish; what the hell is all this supposed to mean?

What can she say?

How can she describe the happiness that overtook her when the darkness left her so abruptly, was wiped out in an instant, turning her despair into a celebration of life, how can she explain it unless she tells him about the night she blocked death's path, after which so many bad things happened? He'll never understand. She looks up from the kitchen table, at Oddur, he's handsome in the light from the window, and she still sees what she admires in him, what she fell for, which never left her even when she was in Canada and there was an entire ocean between them, she sees it and feels, at the same time, that something has put distance between them, distance that's impossible to measure, impossible to bridge with words, caresses, kisses, what is it that's come between them, what is its name, who created it, why does life have to be so difficult, and unfair, why does she have to be so unlucky, a shame to her family, why can't he make an effort to understand her, why can't he stop being angry with her and come to her instead, across the kitchen floor, step over the ocean on those strong legs of his, with his protective embrace, within which she could find comfort and sleep off the darkness?

She looks back down at the kitchen table, so that's how it looks, she lays her hands on it, they were once whiter, softer, not so cracked and chapped. She closes her eyes. And cries.

We cry because language is imperfect and fails to reach all the way down to the bottom-most depths of life, not even halfway down into the deepest chasms, our tears begin where our words stop, are they messages from the abyss, the unspoiled depths?

Oddur notices her shoulders beginning to tremble from the effort involved in keeping her tears in check, which at first makes him even angrier, because when you're angry you just want to stay angry, want to find an outlet, he wanted most to race up the valley, drag that bloody haybag, that pest Sigmundur, out into his farmyard and give him a good thrashing, beat his rotten teeth and rotten spirit out of him, he's always been unbearable, there's something about him that's seriously annoying, even enraging, and Margrét had to go and hug the man, and then he went around the village, bragging about it, pulling no punches in his description, saying that she'd come running up to him half-dressed and rubbed her breasts against him, all excited and eager to hook up with a real man. Mulling this over, Oddur becomes so infuriated that he clenches his fists, but then she starts crying, unable to hold back the tears any longer, cries, and his anger vanishes in a flash, so abruptly that it almost hurts, suddenly he feels utterly empty, doesn't know what to do, it isn't easy to be seething with anger and energy and abruptly find them gone, leaving you empty and numb, arms just hanging there; if only he were at sea, preferably in a storm, then at least his arms would have a purpose. She cries. If only he could turn these dangling arms of his into oars, himself

307

into a boat.

Margrét, he says finally, but his voice is so hoarse that the word, the name, can't be understood; it sounds more like a growl.

He clears his throat, tries again, says, Margrét dear – and the years pass.

# Keflavík

— 1980 —

*Stagnation is the sister of death –*
*but* Revolver *is on the turntable and we have*
*the album cover in front of us*

Ari and I carry the stereo system into the little single-family residence at the end of February, when there is nobody at home, neither his stepmother nor his father; Ari is careful about this, had mentioned cautiously, hesitantly, that he was saving up for equipment, a stereo, but the idea hadn't been taken very well; in fact, it had been taken very badly. That doesn't matter now, because soon we'll be able to listen to music through real speakers, we'll finally get to hear the full depth of the music, its unadulterated power. We hastily connect the Kenwood amplifier, the cassette player, the turntable and the AR speakers, our fingers trembling with excitement; we sit down on the sofa bed in his room, which accommodates little more than that, his desk with bookshelves, a chair and the stereo, put *Wish You Were Here* on the turntable and crank up the volume, crank it up loud enough for it to carry to Heaven, we want the residents of Heaven to hear it too, particularly she who died far too soon, whom death came to take from Vífilsstaðir Hospital in the late '60s, she was so emaciated that death had to lift her very carefully so as not to cut itself on her bones, very gently so as not to break her – we don't know where death took her. Everyone dies alone, and it hurts to know that our

311

presence and our consolation probably don't plumb the darkness. So instead, we try to play the music loud enough for it to be heard within the darkness, for it to carry all the way to Heaven, or wherever we go when everything ends, when the trees stop growing, words stop being heard, the rain to fall, the sun to shine, the soil to smell so sweet. When it all ends in such a way that we can't understand, don't want to understand, daren't understand, but that we ought to try always to understand, ceaselessly, without hesitation, because if we give up on the impossible, to capture what's out of life's reach, we'll fail, fail so completely that no power will be able to amend it.

This is why Ari and I play music so loudly that Heaven simply has to hear it, play Pink Floyd, the band that wanted to change the world, as we sit there on his sofa bed, listening to the music we know so well, having played it so often on the mono cassette player that Ari had bought three years before with money he earned from delivering the *Morgunblaðið*, but Lord help us, there's such a giant difference between a mono system and a stereo system with AR speakers, it adds an entirely new dimension to the music, we can hear everything more intensely, hear all the instruments better and more precisely, the voices are fuller, it's almost as if we've come closer, as if we understand life better. Listening to good music is like setting a direct course for happiness. We turn it up louder when David Gilmour sings, "How I wish, how I wish you were here," how we wished, how we wished; nothing can measure that desire, numbers are too limited, stupid, unimaginative, how we wished you were here. It's impossible to measure longing, nor is it possible to understand it, describe it, explain it, those who miss someone always have something dark in their hearts, a string of sorrow that time plays, strums, plucks; Ari and I hear this same sorrow in the album's title song, "Wish You Were Here", and we play it over and over again, repeatedly, can't get enough of it, lose ourselves in it, forget to watch the clock, Ari's father, Jakob, and stepmother are at work, but since it's Saturday it's unlikely that they'll come home very late. We forget to remain alert and keep an eye on the clock, which turns 4.00, turns 5.00, but if you play music for Heaven, you're likely to forget time, likely to vanish without a trace into the music. The room shakes. The whole house shakes. "How I wish!" The music floods the world, fills every corner, rushes to meet the stepmother who comes home tired from work, dead tired, greets her like thunder when she opens the door, like a heavy cloud bank from which longing strikes like lightning. She goes straight to the fuse box and shuts off the power.

The silence hits me and Ari like a blow between the eyes.

Ari, who buys good headphones the next time he's paid, less than a week later, having withstood a stream of scolding from both his stepmother and his father, for throwing away his money on such a bloody ridiculous, utterly useless thing, a stereo, what a load of bollocks, you can't eat a stereo, and don't they already have a high-quality unit in the living room, he could listen to it every now and then, when no-one was home, provided that he listened like a civilised person, not like a madman, blaring that screaming savagery that his stepmother was forced to hear when she came home exhausted, yes, they could come to an agreement about letting him use the unit in the living room sometimes, and he would have been much better off putting some of his precious money aside instead of squandering it on such unnecessary, foolish crap. Save his money so that he could move out sometime, so that he could become an adult sometime, though there was of course little likelihood that he would ever become an adult, that he would become something. Certainly not by cheating on his wife. Never. Not a chance.

They were in so much agreement on this point that it was very nearly beautiful.

But such is life: what for one person is a search for meaning is noise and waste to others. Clearly, it's hard to find balance in the human world, and we never seem to make any progress in understanding each other. So maybe it doesn't matter how many languages we learn, because disagreements, prejudice and misunderstandings seem to be inherent in language, lurking like weeds in the words; we probably never come together anywhere except in music. There we store our dreams, our desires for a better life, a more beautiful world, our dreams of being able to step up out of our faults, envy, faint-heartedness, vanity.

Maybe, says Ari after we've listened to the first classical-music record that he buys, *Best of Bach*, in the Hljómalind record shop, whose owner, once the singer in Hljómar, Rúnni Júll and Gunni Þórðar's band, stands watch along with his wife, who is so absent-minded that it's as if she's barely there, and is always dressed as if she's on her way to a dance in the '60s. Ari and I go to Hljómalind on Saturday mornings, after being paid the day before and looking forward to it all week; the owner soon starts greeting us like old acquaintances, this man over whom girls cried in the late '60s, throwing their scarves to him onstage, their tickets inscribed with declarations of love, their phone numbers, bras and even knickers, he treats us like equals, so happy that young men in Keflavík should take an interest in music and, to top it off, in musicians other than whoever's at the top of the hit parade, The usual stupid old soup, he says, and sells us, among other things, an album by

314

Oscar Peterson, an old bluesy Fleetwood Mac album from when Peter Green was still with them and played his guitar like it was made out of tears, and finally this one, *Best of Bach*, which he fished out of a dense row of white albums, *Best of Bach, Beethoven, Chopin, Grieg, Mozart*, a few fragments of eternity in white album covers, Try this, he said, handing us the album, with a peculiar smile, a bit as if he were holding a folded angel wing. We smiled back, smiled sincerely, but couldn't get the stories that Ásmundur told us about Hljómar out of our minds, about the dances that they played here on Suðurnes, when knickers and phone numbers and lustful messages rained down on the singer, who, a mere decade later, hands us a folded angel wing, to our eyes a middle-aged man, rather plump, the fat most apparent on his neck, shoulders and hips, which sway when he moves, making him appear almost feminine. Where are the girls who threw their knickers at him, the lustful tickets, phone numbers; did he call them, and would they be interested in getting a call from him today? Time changes everything, turning lustful messages into shopping lists, knickers into hoover bags; but Ari and I took *Best of Bach*, took the folded angel wing, went home, put the record on the turntable, hurrying before his stepmother and father came home from work, put on Bach and the angel wing unfolded, it spread itself overhead, and we understand why the former lead singer of Hljómar smiled so peculiarly at us. We listen and behold the blue sky, the blueness, we behold what must be eternity, see that it's beautiful, and see that there's a chance for considerably more beauty and harmony in the world and the human soul than we ever imagined. We listen to Bach, which makes us want to cry.

Maybe, says Ari after we've listened to the entire record once, some of it twice, maybe no meeting of the United Nations Security

Council should start until Bach has been played to the meeting's attendees for at least half an hour, because anyone who can think in a spiteful, unreasonable manner, anyone who desires something besides beauty, harmony and justice after half an hour with Bach, is mad as a hatter. Yes, I say, such a people are completely bonkers.

Music can dispel the darkness, rip us out of melancholy, anxiety, negativity, and swing us over to joy, exuberance at being alive, at existing here and now; without it, the human heart would be a lifeless planet. It's virtually impossible to own such a good stereo system without playing the Beatles' *Revolver*, without letting it spin on the turntable while you study the album cover, the photograph on the back, take a good look at those four people who changed the world, the friendship that bound them together and somehow made them invincible and amplified their creativity. Stare at them as the record spins. Stare and listen. Side A: "Taxman", "Eleanor Rigby", "I'm Only Sleeping". The fourth song is "Love You To" by George Harrison. Ari and I never skip it, show our loyalty, It's interesting of him, we say, interesting, this Indian connection, not the usual popular slop, damn finely done, George, may we call you George, great song, maybe not exactly entertaining, but you're searching, probably too seriously, otherwise wonderful stuff, as Ásmundur would say.

"Love You To" ends in a whirling Indian eddy. Yoga is practised seriously in India, and cows are seriously respected. India has majestic tigers, and elephants, we mustn't forget the elephants, What sort of person forgets elephants, mutter Ari and I, patter Ari and I, as "Love You To" ends in an eddy of sitars and the record spins, it spins into the silence between two songs. We're alone at home, it's evening, the stepmother and Jakob are playing bridge at Eiríkur and Elín's, Ásmundur's parents, it spins into the silence, or the pleasant buzz, the very slight crackle, we hold our breath, we open our palms, then close them, make them into fists.

Clenched fists were once Ari's grandfather's love poem.

On the beach at Neskaupstaður.

Of course, we don't have the slightest intimation of this, sitting there in that room in the winter of 1980, as Tito's heart trudges through the world like an old reptile, like a shattered hope, not the slightest glimmer, and Oddur and Margrét are both dead, terrible how time changes everything. Ari remembers her, but has only a very vague memory of his grandfather, who died when Ari was three, so vague that it's as if Oddur had never existed. Yet his certificate of recognition hangs in the living room, like an admonition that he'd really existed, and hadn't been just any old person. Unfortunately, however, we stop seeing what's steady and motionless right in front of us, it can even end up as nothing, and that's because it's always in the same place, doesn't move, never changes. Stagnation is the sister of death. You stagnate and many things begin to die, even love, which is, however, a primal element of the universe, the ancient gift of God, the only real answer to death. Oddur is dead, he's gone, vanished, and for me and Ari, there's nothing left of him in the world but the certificate of recognition hanging on the wall, motionless, invisible, except when Jakob, befuddled by alcohol, his composure lost, the shield that he holds up to life lying on the living-room floor, takes down the certificate and reads it to Ari.

In recognition of Oddur. Jakob's drinking. The stepmother's silence.

*Revolver* is still spinning on the turntable, we have the album

317

cover in front of us, and we study the large photograph on the back for so long that it's as if we become part of the quartet. The record spins silently between two songs. As if it's stuck in the groove between "Love You To" and "Here, There and Everywhere", not daring to start the next song, spinning in silence, spinning within the pause, giving us a chance to think all of this in the meantime. Surely the song must start; the world doesn't have the patience for a pause much longer than that. Ari clenches his fists. Clenched fists were Oddur's love poem. He clenched them on the shore a hundred years ago, and a few hours later, Margrét said, If I'm naked beneath my dress, then you'll know that I love you. Is it possible to receive a more beautiful declaration of love? For she was in fact naked; isn't the man blessed who receives such a declaration? Yet life would soon come to flash its knives at them, knives that would inflict deep wounds. I'm naked beneath my dress, said Ari's grandmother, who died six years ago, lived her final years in the big front bedroom at Elín and Eiríkur's place, old, with thin, wispy hair, unable to take off her dress without help, and was probably never naked beneath it, nor did anyone care to see her naked, far from it, we fear old nakedness, have no desire to see aged, wrinkled bodies, they remind us of prunes, they remind us uncomfortably of the destructive power that no-one escapes, remind us that we age, that we shrivel up, and that the day will come when no-one will want to see our naked-ness, and when we can no longer say, If I'm naked beneath my dress, then you'll know that I love you, because it would sound to the world's ears like a threat or a tragic joke. Nor would Margrét have managed to remove her dress without help; towards the end, she slept wearing a nappy, her teeth in a glass of water on the bed-side table, her swollen feet reminding Ari of dried-out old sausages, it had been so long since she was young in the night, charming, irresistibly naked beneath her American dress, and the mountains of the Eastfjords were hymns, that for me and Ari it no longer exists – for us, it has never existed.

Thus it happens – every single event of the past, small as well as big, awful as well as beautiful, laughter and the touch of a hand, all of it is sooner or later sent off the playing field, condemned to oblivion, condemned to death, elimination, yet solely because no-one remembers it, never thinks about it, doesn't keep it for later, and as a result, everything that we lived and experienced gradually turns to nothing, not even air, which is so painful, such an enormous waste, and edges us towards purposelessness. A human being's life becomes, at most, a few isolated notes without a melody, random sounds instead of music – which is why we've brought you this account of generations, this centennial history, or planet, comet, this pop song, this hit parade from the end of the world – because we want you to know that Margrét was once naked beneath an American dress, with her small, round breasts, her long, slender, yet strong legs, which shortly afterwards locked around Oddur, so that you know and hopefully never forget that everyone was once young, so you realise that sooner or later we all must burn, burn with passion, happiness, joy, justice, desire, because these are the fires that light up the darkness, that hold the wolves of oblivion at bay, the fires that heat up life, so that you don't forget to feel, so that you don't change into a picture on the wall, a chair in the living room, a piece of furniture in front of the T.V., into someone staring at a computer screen, into some-thing inert, so that you don't become something that hardly notices anything, so that you don't grow numb and become a plaything of the powers-that-be, economic interests, don't become insignificant, apathetic, at best the grease on a mysterious cog-wheel. Burn – so that the fire doesn't dwindle, subside, cool, so that the world doesn't become a cold place, the far side of the Moon.

If I'm naked beneath my dress, then you'll know that I love you.

Ari clenches his fists, I say something, and finally the turn-table's needle tears itself away from the groove and "Here, There and Everywhere" begins. Sigrún's right eye. She vomited against the Lada estate car, and shortly afterwards slipped out of her tight jeans and spread her legs in the Lada's back seat so that Kári, a thirty-something father of three with a black, bushy beard, could slip his stiff dick into her. Ari and I are sitting in his bedroom in Keflavík in the month of March, but at the same time in the front seat of the farmer's Land Rover on an October night outside the community centre, we see Kári's white buttocks going up and down, very fast, appearing rhythmically like two happy boys just above the back seat while BÓ sings, as if inspired, "I'll never forget you."

I want you everywhere, but above all in the back seat of a Lada estate car.

*Some songs are like giant redwoods in time,*
*towering angels*

Some events change everything. Someone dies and you begin to think differently about the planets in the solar system, how flowers droop their heads in a drizzle, someone kisses you or doesn't kiss you and the light shining on language seems different. The world is always in flux, there's no correct version of it, nor do we know how God views it, what shape the mountains have, whether they're violet herbs, old roses, God's eyes must see entirely differently than ours, perhaps the giant redwoods on the west coast of the United States resemble towering angels when viewed from Heaven. Some events change everything, the way we look, what we see, perceive – how we listen: Ari and I have to listen to "Here, There and Everywhere" many times this winter before we can enjoy it again, those two minutes and twenty-five seconds. Finally, we're fully, perfectly, able to enjoy merging, blending with the song, become a part of its 145 seconds, experience the bliss as well as the refreshment inherent in the music: some songs are like giant redwoods in time, towering angels. We can enjoy the song without seeing Kári's buttocks start shooting up above the seat backs of the Lada estate car like the Devil's spittle. "I want you everywhere," sings McCartney in an oddly melancholy way; we ran into her at the Co-op a bit less than a week later. Just before we left to return to the south, ran into her by the biscuits, not more than a metre between us, we could hear her breathe, she looked away, but we saw the corners of her mouth, saw that they had the same sadness from the beginning of time, saw every freckle, and saw that they were like kisses. She looked away, having clearly decided to ignore our existence, we who are nothing but a clumsily composed pop song, number 387 on the hit parade at the end of the world. We thought, O.K., so that's how she is, she just wants to let old fellows fuck her in the back seat, having just puked, O.K., good riddance, we'll forget you, *bye bye baby, baby blue, it's all over now, baby blue*. We walked off with a packet of biscuits, custard creams from Frón, expelled her from our lives, took the green bus south three days later, but it drove so slowly down Brattabrekka that we were unable to forget her freckles, her lips, let alone her eyes, composed by Lennon and McCartney, and

321

because of this, still find it difficult to put *Revolver,* or *Hard Day's Night,* on the stereo this winter. "If I fell in love with you," I would wipe the vomit off your face, tear off your tight jeans and fuck you in my fucking back seat, our white buttocks resembling two happy children's faces, resembling a devilish grin. We stubbornly persisted in listening to these two records, particularly *Revolver,* in the hope that the music would erase the memory; it's February, and then comes March, Tito's heart is an old lizard, a shattered hope, a bad conscience, we listen and listen to the songs, and wonder whether Kári wore a condom, or if he had to pull it out in time, whether he'd grunted, hoarsely, Fuck, man, I'm coming, but goddammit it's fun to fuck you, and she'd said, Oh Kári baby baby, you can take me whenever you want, you're a man, you're no lame-ass kid, you aren't number 387 on the North Pole's hit parade, cum on my breasts, get them all wet with your hot spunk, and she'd pulled up her blouse, unveiled her small breasts, which should have rested like a soft whisper in Ari's palms. Fuck, man, Sigrún's tits aren't much bigger than raisins, said some farmer's son, and it was the first time that we'd ever thought about undressing her, caressing her flesh, for several hours we longed to lay our hands on her small breasts, which are no doubt as beautiful as the dawn, as a tear, a falling star, and not too long afterwards, she pulled up her blouse, bared her breasts and urged Kári to shoot his semen over them. Still, the semen from such old fellows must be putrid and smell as bad as cured shark. We sat in the Land Rover, Bjöggi sang, "I'll never forget you," we drank straight from a bottle, took swigs from a bottle, and then snuck back into the community centre, the humiliation, the rejection like a pair of daggers in our backs, and the world was ugly, it was ugly, ugly, ugly, ugly.

"I want you everywhere."

Even in Keflavík. We desire you even there, miss you even there.

We listen and listen to "Here, There and Everywhere", to "If I Fell", and little by little it happens, little by little we begin to enjoy them again, are able to sing along with them, hum along, sigh along, immerse ourselves in the songs without seeing Kári's buttocks in our minds, without remembering how she'd looked away when we ran into her by the biscuits. We'd inadvertently grabbed four packets of custard creams instead of one in our eagerness to appear nonchalant, to show her that she'd never mattered, had not once been a comet in our lives, front-page news in the *New York Times*. Our eagerness to show her that to us, she meant exactly nothing.

*Fish have no feet, and*
*there's someone heading out to sea.*
*This most certainly won't go well*

In the oldest writings in the world, so old that they can no longer lie, it says that fate abides in the dawn, which is why you must take care, stroke hair, find nice words, side with life.

In fact, we sometimes awake like open wounds. Defenceless, vulnerable, and everything depends on our first word, our first sigh, on how you look at me when you awake, how you look at me when I open my eyes, when I emerge from sleep, that strange world in which we aren't always the same person, in which we betray people we could never conceive of betraying, in which we perform heroic deeds, fly, in which the dead live, the living die. Sometimes it's as if we're given a vision of another side of the world, behold a different version of it, as if you're being reminded that you aren't necessarily the person you're supposed to be, that life has a thousand sides, and that it's – unfortunately, or thank God – never too late to head in a new or unexpected direction. But then we wake and are so vulnerable, sensitive, fragile, that everything can depend on those first moments. The entire day, possibly our entire life. So take care how you look at me, say something beautiful, stroke my hair, because life isn't always fair, it's absolutely not always easy, we frequently need help, so come to me with your words, arms, presence, without you I'm lost, without you I will break in time. Be with me when I wake.

There's rarely a lot said in the little single-family residence in the mornings.

The stepmother has to be at work at 7.00 a.m. and is gone by the time Ari comes into the kitchen, where Jakob sits alone over his porridge, which he's sprinkled with sugar, perhaps because no-one looked at him affectionately that morning, yet neither did he look affectionately at anyone, he eats mechanically, stares into space, switches on the radio when Ari appears because the silence between them can be irritating, can be difficult. The announcer is talking about Mount Esja, how it looks, how the light hits it, as if that matters to us here in Keflavík, we can describe the colours of the sea to you, the black lava, that expletive of the soil, and the wind, for which we probably have more words than can be found in our language, but what does it matter to us whether Esja is violet this morning, as white as eternity the next, reddish-brown like an old Icelandic ghost the third – then the announcer plays jazz, or Beethoven's 112th symphony. Then comes the news, Ari and Jakob hear about Tito's heart, that it's an old moose staggering through the world. They say almost nothing, barely good morning, never goodbye, they just eat, read the paper, our image of the world, and then one goes to his job in the fishing industry, the other to his job as a mason. Jakob perhaps thinks of the mountains of the Eastfjords, of how he misses them, misses the mornings that can be so still it's possible to hear eternity, he thinks about his father, Oddur, honour and glory, one of the mountains towering over his life, perhaps the biggest, thinks about Margrét, his mother, thinks about his brothers, Þórður and Gunnar, they're also a bit like mountains; mountains influence the weather, the light, mountains are a benchmark, they stand closer to Heaven than the rest of us. He eats his sweetened porridge and goes to work, where the resin holds everything together.

Fortunately, Thursday mornings are often better, not to mention Friday mornings, when life is even good, when there are things like justice and eagerness, Jakob becomes positively cheerful and waggish, reacts to some article in the paper, or to the results of some sports match, and actually talks to Ari, as if nothing could be more natural, and Ari rocks in his seat, so anxious to finish his porridge that he burns his tongue on it, then rushes out, fleeing his father's chatter, his cheerfulness, flies out the door, leaving his father in peace to pour a shot of vodka into his coffee flask without worrying. He leaves so that his father doesn't have to come up with an excuse to go to the laundry room, the garage, the storeroom, or wherever it is that he's hidden his bottle this time. God help us, how brutish and unfair the world is, what a bloody bitch and bunch of bollocks if the stepmother finds the bottle before she leaves for work, pours out more than half of it and refills the bottle with water, making Jakob's first sip of coffee at work a horrible disappointment, the taste bland, like this bloody life tends to be, making him desperately want to

smash the coffee flask against the nearest wall. If she were in fact
to find the bottle; should she actually want to take the trouble to
find it. The stepmother walks through half-dozing Keflavík before
7.00 in the morning, whatever the weather, bright moonlight,
dark and heavy with snow, blizzards, the cold sometimes so harsh
and cutting that it saws thought in two and forces people to walk
with their heads bowed, as if in prayer, as if praying for mercy.
She presses on stubbornly, sometimes grateful for the foul weather,
for the hoarse wind, the whipping hailstorms, feels cheerful
even if the wind is like a herd of raging bulls, particularly if she
had difficulty waking up, when something related to pain awaited
her in the early morning.

The stepmother fights the wind, Jakob pours a shot of vodka
into his coffee, Ari puts on his coat, thinks about the wings he
had in his dream, they were red, he could soar on them between
worlds, and it was easier to enter the world of the dead than to
take the bus to Reykjavík. Stepping out into the wind, he misses
his wings. Trudges through the gusting wind, as his stepmother
had done just over half an hour ago, she'd walked bent forwards,
using her strength to push through the gusts, perhaps thinking,
I imagined that life would be different.

What happened to the Jakob she fell for towards the end of the
'60s, amusing, funny, an extremely hard worker, but a bit sensitive
too, why do I so rarely see his good side nowadays, are my eyes
betraying me, or has he changed so much for the worse? Can I
forgive a man who comes home smashed on Thursday night, or
Friday or Saturday night, yells at me, tells me I'm deranged, that
I could kill him with my silence? Why should I talk to him if he
starts drinking on Thursday and stays drunk until Sunday, when
he's squandered all of our money on alcohol and claimed that we

326

can't afford new furniture, better pots and pans? When twice in the last three years he's wasted an entire week's pay on one night of revelry, tossing down drinks with his bridge partners, gone to Glóðin, played the big man, bought a round for everyone, toasted the astronauts in the photograph, the heroes of the stars, and shouted something about flight, about mountains, about manhood, but comes home in the early morning, too drunk to walk straight, either whinging out of alcoholic self-pity or cursing, calling her horrible names, telling her that she's so much worse than his first wife, Ari's mother, the dead woman standing between her and the two men, Jakob and Ari. How can we compete with those who died young, those who repose in our memories, and become better and more beautiful with each passing year, while the rest of us grow older, put on weight, watch our breasts sag, our gait stiffen, the gleam in our eyes dim, our thoughts lose their sparkle, we make mistakes, say stupid or clumsy things, which hurt, injure, spoil; while the dead never make mistakes, they're never unbearable in the morning, never break wind at the breakfast table, never leave their dirty underwear on the edge of the bathtub, are never in a bad mood, unfair, selfish, grumpy, all the dead do is shine in our memories.

How can I compete with her, wonders the stepmother, cleaving the wind, the wet gusts, she has to cleave them alone, knows that no-one will toss her a life preserver, and that knowledge steels her, makes her stubborn, makes her mouth more resolute, perhaps a bit more inflexible, but that's the fault of life, not her own. Jakob returned home late last night, after playing cards, as he does every Thursday, at Keflavík's bridge club, You mean the drunk club, she says sometimes, knowing that she mustn't say it, knowing that it's annoying to hear her say it, and that saying such things just makes

327

everything harder, but she can't always restrain herself, keep herself under control, almost as if some unknown force were compelling her to say sarcastic, hurtful things. Jakob had played badly last night, had been dealt bad hands all fucking night, It wasn't normal, he said, emanating a strong odour of alcohol, his eyes swimming. Wasn't it just that you were so drunk you couldn't tell hearts from diamonds, she asked sarcastically, knowing that it was unwise to ask such a thing, and in such a tone, knowing that she was giving him the disdainful look he can't bear, that he finds infuriating in his worse moments. He who'd been so tender and sensitive, and if she'd been sweet in return, he would have even cried in her lap, maybe spoken a bit about his mother, said how much he missed her, and that it was hard to think about how he'd dreamed of a different, better life than the one she'd experienced, that she'd been unhappy, which was clear from her diaries, which Elín has, the diaries that Jakob, up until now, hasn't wanted, hasn't dared to read; and he might have spoken about Ari, that it felt as if they didn't know each other, were total strangers, couldn't communicate, "My son," he would have said, pronouncing "son" as if it were the most delicate word in the language – she might even have had to dissuade him from going to Ari's room, waking him with his sentimentality and reek of alcohol.

If only she'd shown a little sweetness in return.

If only.

But she couldn't, she just couldn't; she was too dissatisfied with life, angry at how he came home drunk like that, angry because it happened too often, which is why she crossed her arms and said what she did about his cards, that he probably hadn't recognised the difference between diamonds and hearts, giving him her disdainful look as she did so. It was enough. She was spared the whinging sentimentality, the alcoholic tears, instead found herself the target of anger, unreasonableness, ugly insults, to which she responded in kind, defended herself with sharp words, which are so tragically easy to find and to use as daggers. Everything would certainly be better, easier, if he learned to control himself, to keep himself in check. He hit her twice, not hard, didn't dare, or wasn't drunk enough to do so, and then continued with the insults, telling her she was frigid and ugly, a bird of ill omen, the worst thing in his life, he slung the heaviest words he could find at her, so heavy that he regretted them in the morning, Does he remember them, she thinks, trudging against the wind that seems to want to rip everything to bits today, blow everything away, cleanse the country of human vermin, yet is unable to lift her, unhappiness weighs her down, is two large stones in her pockets. She cuts through the wind, time, life, arrives at work, the Miðnes freezing plant, the biggest one in Keflavík, with huge processing operations, numerous ships at sea, 80 employees on land, the largest freezer rooms in all of Suðurnes, which the American military rents in part, to store food: turkey, beef, luncheon meat for the soldiers and their families – every Friday, just after noon, a truck drives down from the Base and loads up with food for the following week. The officer in charge of the Base's frozen stocks brings turkeys up to the office for its staff, a whole turkey per person, two for the boss, juicy turkey for dinner every Friday in some homes in Keflavík, an established tradition, what luxury! The officer is extremely handsome, tall, a hero of the Vietnam War, clearly of Italian origin, dark-skinned, sparkling eyes, black hair, a full, sturdy-looking chest, movements like a panther's. Some of the women at the processing section are diligent at taking their cigarette breaks when he's around, in bad weather as well as good, and why shouldn't they, why deny themselves the chance to admire what's downright beautiful? He joins them sometimes, smokes a cigarette with them, jokes with them, laughs, is devilishly handsome and clearly knows it, but what the hell, It wouldn't be so bad having him once or twice a year, you know, between my legs, say the women, laughing. The stepmother is never among them. Are you mad? She'd rather be shot than stand outside and preen herself for the American officer, fawn over him, act like a cow on heat. Every now and then, however, she takes a cigarette break like them, not very often, just on days when life has taken a turn for the worse, when it's a cactus, a fist, quicksand; on such days, it's nice to go for a smoke down below the building, where she can be alone, undisturbed, lean against the plant's bare wall, smoke, gaze at the sea, think about nothing, and do nothing except smoke and look at the sea, that old, ungainly friend from the north, her childhood friend. By the sea, all sorrows are soothed.

Nearly.

She inhales, fills her lungs with smoke, that sweet poison, why does something as good as tobacco have to be so harmful, filthy, filling your lungs with black tar?

The stepmother leans against the building, the grey concrete wall, shuts her eyes to savour the moment, savour hearing the sea, which speaks to her in a voice from the past, all she needs is to listen with her eyes closed to find herself back in the north, where she lingers, disappears behind more heaths and mountains than we can count at the moment, disappears into the north and the past. When she opens her eyes to check her watch, she sees one of the young girls picking her way over the slippery rocks at the shore, taking her time to avoid falling, taking her time to get somewhere, wherever it might be, because ahead of her there's nothing but more slippery rocks, some of them covered with seaweed, and then the sea, the ocean itself. The stepmother smokes her cigarette, is nearly finished, three or four puffs left, she wants to enjoy them in peace and curses the girl, who does she think she is, messing around like that instead of working, fumbling her way over the slippery rocks in her work boots, swaying and grimacing, trying to keep her balance. The stepmother recognises the girl, who's also from the north, knows her mother, and her stepfather. Dammit, she mutters, because the girl doesn't stop, despite having nothing but the sea and Reykjavík in front of her, across 30 kilometres of open ocean, or the Snæfellsnes Peninsula to the west, at a distance of at least a hundred kilometres, visible in good weather, clear skies, when the days are as joyous as children and the glacier is an ode to Heaven; one of Iceland's crowning glories. Today, however, the glacier can't be seen, far from it, and Reykjavík is barely visible. The silly girl neither stops nor hesitates but steps into the sea, despite no-one having been able to walk on water since Jesus walked on the Sea of Galilee two thousand years ago to charm a few fishermen. The girl from the north steps down from the rocks and one foot immediately enters the sea, as does the other a nano-second later. No-one, you see, can walk on water, and that's why fish have no feet.

What nonsense is this, wonders the stepmother, though she does nothing, just watches, which is unlike her, she can't abide idleness, nothing can be left lying on the floor or table or hanging on a chair without her picking it up, putting it back in its place, whether she's in her own home or someone else's; I always tidy up extra well before you come to visit, says Elín, Jakob's sister and Ásmundur's mother, she who would be thrown more than 3 metres on being hit by a black Mercedes-Benz in the capital of Germany, shortly after which her life would be extinguished, that good, gentle life, beautiful in its serenity, if only we had the words to describe her well enough for you to miss her too, then we would finally be of some use; I always tidy things up extra well before you come to visit, she always says, with her affectionate smile, to the stepmother, who smiles back, Elín likely being the only person on earth to whom she can display the same confidence as she displays to the sea.

The sea reaches halfway up the girl's thighs and she keeps going, slowly, perhaps, yet determinedly, as if she has a pressing appointment with someone out there, a drowned sailor, a merman. What in the hell is she doing, repeats the stepmother, yet does nothing, just watches, like the most abject coward, glances down at her cigarette, burning to no-one's advantage, raises it to her lips for one final drag, to savour the cigarette, and suddenly it's as if she awakes, the peculiar torpor falls away, and she realises that the silly girl probably intends to drown herself, she's gone so far out that the sea reaches up to her bottom, and she continues her advance. The stepmother tosses her cigarette away and dashes in the girl's direction.

She hasn't run in about twenty years. Ever since she was a teenager in the north, and, to tell the truth, has forgotten how to run, has forgotten how it feels, what happens inside the body, how the blood courses. She runs from the freezing plant down to the sea, the long-forgotten movements stirring up new memories of the north, so strong, so clear, that it's as if she's running in two places at once, and in two different times; here in Keflavík, in a cold, biting wind, and in the north, as a child, twelve years old, running down the green homefield on a bright and sunny day, sprinting over to frighten off sheep that had found a hole in the fence and slipped through to graze on the succulent homefield grass. She runs down the field, in sunshine, calm, the sky is a blue eternity, a blue smile, and her blood sings within her because it's such fun to be alive, because she's bursting with energy and eagerness for life, though this is the summer when many things change, and running's a bit different now, because her newly apparent breasts bump gently up and down or quiver on her chest, a little like intruders, she isn't entirely sure whether she should be proud of them or ashamed, but in this particular memory, she doesn't give that a thought, she just runs exuberantly down the homefield that summer day when eternity seemed to have come down to earth with its happiness and sunshine. She runs like a child, almost like a teenager, down the homefield in the past, lightly, playfully, like a filly, and runs simultaneously as a 30-something woman in Keflavík, wearing boots and a white apron that reaches just below her knees, which she quickly whips off, almost without realising, but then she gasps when she wades into the sea and the freezing Atlantic Ocean yanks her out of the past, out of her memories, and she senses, from the weight of her breasts, her stiff body, that she's no longer a filly, a playmate of eternity, it's gone, like any other silly illusion. The sea wakens her, sharpens her focus, she wades quickly towards the girl, the water deepens, after a few moments she has to start swimming, she moves quietly, doesn't scream or shout, feeling as if that would frighten the girl, like the sheep in her memory, and the girl would likely rush to swim further out instead of dawdling, floating on her back in the constricting waves, staring up at the grey sky, because someone who has decided to die has no need to rush, nothing awaits them but death. The girl lets herself float, and then starts to sink, because she intends to drown, intends to vanish from life. No, pants the stepmother, not if I can help it, and the girl cries out when the stepmother's arms grab her, cries out but then screams, pleading, ordering, Let me go, and then adds, as if to be sure, you bloody cunt! No-one's drowning herself on my watch, says the stepmother as she tries to dodge the girl's fists and fingernails, Sigga's, because it's her, the Sigga whom Ari and I met on a January morning in 1976, she whom GÓ pinned to the ground with his foot, who jumped onto the truck and said, The fuck if I'm missing out on this, but then intends, only four years later, to end her life, and would have done so if the stepmother hadn't taken a cigarette break because she wasn't feeling well, because life was hard, the stepmother who says, No-one's drowning if I can help it, but says it calmly, as if having a conversation out in the street, or with her neighbour over the fence on a fine Sunday, and there's something so absolute in the way she says it, something that resembles a mountain that's difficult to get past, that Sigga stops struggling, stops punching the stepmother, scratching her, calling her horrible names, goes limp and allows the stepmother to swim with her to shore, towards the slippery rocks, towards the life from which she was trying to escape.

# Norðfjörður

— PAST —

*The sea makes us men –*
*the longest day in human history*

Remember this with us: the sea is bigger than daily life.

You can find rest at sea. There you find vastness, incomprehensible dimensions that soothe, comfort and diminish life's difficulties. People's troubles on land, friction, frustration, interactions with others, obligations, you gaze into the waves and sense how existence is calmed within your chest. Then maybe the wind rises, the waves tower over the boat, higher, higher, the troughs so deep that you nearly behold the very bottom of the sea, as if it's on its way up to the surface to come and take you away. The cold and wet, the hardship, the toil, the work of hauling up the fish and gutting them in every sort of weather, sun and warmth, frost and snow. Seamanship is freedom. But freedom is also found in knowing that you can't rely on anyone, not a single soul, and absolutely not your prayers, because the benevolence of Heaven is left behind on shore. You can only rely on yourself.

That's why the sea makes us men.

This statement, the sea makes us men, penetrates like an exhortation to the depths of his sons, Þórður and Gunnar, as well as Jakob, later. An exhortation, a benchmark, the eleventh commandment.

337

Þórður becomes a fully fledged deckhand before he reaches the age of thirteen.

He'd joined fishing trips aboard *Sleipnir* since the age of seven, besides accompanying Tryggvi on his small boat just off the coast, but these things didn't make him a true sailor; he was still just a boy playing with the neighbourhood kids up on the mountain, down at the shore – but now he's approaching the age of thirteen, when things get serious, that's how it was with Oddur, and so it will be with Þórður, who, of course, isn't Oddur, not completely like him, far from it; Þórður has a bit of the dreaminess of his mother's side of the family, loves books and has written poetry, though secretly, without showing it to anyone. He was born in Norðfjörður, grew up in a village where human life measures itself against the sea, and Oddur's statement, the eleventh command-ment, that the sea makes us men, is like a symphony in his blood. He makes his first trip as a fully fledged deckhand in the spring, and can barely sleep from excitement. He's eager to have a chance to prove himself. Walk about the village as a sailor.

He's supposed to start among strangers. It's better that way, says Oddur to Margrét, being among strangers will steel him faster, make him more independent, stronger. It's invaluable to learn when you're young and immature that, when all is said and done, you're always on your own, that you can't rely on anyone but yourself.

Margrét doesn't see the same things as Oddur when she looks at the sea and thinks about Þórður; she doesn't see the blessing and the freedom, only the dangers, the hardship, a cold, wet world filled with profanities. How many worlds are there, in fact, in a person's life? More than anything else, she wanted Þórður to remain at home with her, always, but that was a naïve woman's

338

fantasy, she knows this, knows that no-one escapes life, knows that a life at sea is pretty much his destiny, despite his being something of a dreamer, able to vanish for hours within the world of books, as well as an outstanding student; he's always been drawn to the sea, dreamed of proving himself there. She knows that this is the cycle and rhythm of life; farmer's sons end up in sheep sheds, village boys at sea. All the same, it's terribly hard to watch him leave the house and head for the shore as a deckhand among strangers, she can barely watch, has to hold on to something, has to hold on as tightly as she can so as not to run after him and drag him back home, to safety, by force and tears. Which would, of course, be unforgivable. Þórður would have a very hard time forgiving her; Oddur never would. How can her heart bear to watch him leave, thirteen years old, with his dark blond, unruly hair, his sweet but determined character, with its underlying sensitivity, his eyes prone to smiling. Life has always seemed a bit easier when it came to Þórður, it's never a problem waking him in the morning, he's patient with his siblings, popular with his peers – though he still slips into bed beside her when Oddur is away, when he's at sea, comes to her like a sleepy puppy, and she hugs him, her arms feel how big he's grown, yet beneath her palm, a child's heart beats, calming her, they both fall asleep, and sleep just so; the most precious moments in life are rarely noisy.

How hard it is to watch him leave, so early in the morning that it's still night, the time of day when we're at our most sensitive, when we're almost completely defenceless, see him go down the slope, move further away, towards the sea where a boat awaits him, and seamanship, she clings to something, he puts distance between himself and his home, one moment he's an adult, the next, a child. The other children are asleep: the three girls, Elín, just one year old, Ólöf, nine, Hulda eleven, and then Gunnar, who is now four. He and Hulda wake up two hours later, furious with their mother for not having woken them, he wanted to watch his brother leave home and enter the world of adults, so incredibly exciting and menacing at the same time – he can hardly wait for him to come home. Gunnar is convinced that this first serious fishing trip will change Þórður so much that there will be almost no difference between him and their father, And then you, Mummy, he says, gnawing a piece of hardfish, his legs dangling from his chair, will have to marry Þórður too and live with him, and probably have Bjarni the Carpenter make you a bigger bed so you can all fit in it, but I'm still not going to call him Daddy. What if he gives you his pocketknife? asks Hulda, who is readying herself to go and make saltfish, short but always energetic, hard-working, with arms so strong that she has little trouble toppling boys her own age in fights. For me to keep, always? Yes, always; it would be yours. Then I would call him Daddy on Sundays and Wednesdays, replies Gunnar, who gets to go down to the drying lot with his sister, help her turn the fish over, so eager to grow bigger that it's hard for him to keep still, sometimes asking Þórður to pull his arms upwards in the hope that he'll stretch and grow faster.

This will be a long day for Margrét.

She's constantly looking out of the kitchen window, with or without binoculars, in the hope of spotting the boat carrying Þórður, so restless and worried that she can't bear to have the children around, all of her concentration and self-control are funnelled into dampening down her fear, into not crawling into bed and yielding to anguish, into not dashing down to the shore, taking the nearest rowboat and rowing out in search of her son, who's just a child, who has his painful, sensitive dreams, who's so sweet and so good and sometimes covers her face with kisses, childlike kisses, and says beautiful things, makes the world beautiful with his words, she stares at the sea, so terrified that it will damage him to be among rough, wild men, with their blather, their profanities, the things they say about women, harsh, vulgar, degrading things about their genitals and breasts – maybe Þórður will return with scorched ears and a damaged heart, and his soft eyes will look at her differently.

The longest day in human history?

At the very least, time crawls by so slowly that if Margrét had any dynamite, she would make a powerful bomb to urge it on. The longer that Þórður remains among the sailors, the more opportunity they have to change him, and take him from her. She tends to the girls, she does the laundry, she scrubs the kitchen floor, she carves a sword for Gunnar, who is on his way south, on a crusade to the Holy Land; hurry up, Mummy, he says, the army is waiting for me and I want to be home before Þórður returns from the sea.

Finally, evening approaches.

It draws near, with a hint of darkness and a few stars, and then the wind begins to blow and the clouds darken over the fjord, and the fjord itself turns cold, and Margrét's heart darkens and she feels her blood begin to freeze, the wind picks up and it starts raining and the children run inside, including Gunnar, who has to shorten the length of his crusade significantly and is both annoyed and hurt when he asks his mother to dress his wounds, which are deep and numerous, but she just says, Yes, yes, that's fine, and continues pacing, looking out of the window, pulling something out of a cupboard just to put it back again, and then stops looking out, can't bear it any longer, doesn't want to see how dark the sea has grown, that it's becoming almost as black as the eyes she'd looked into many years ago; as black and deep as two graves. She continues to reply to the children with absurdities, behaving so strangely that Gunnar is on the verge of bursting into tears, but then Hulda convinces her mother to make them some supper, her common sense tells her that it would do Margrét good to concentrate on something, Sing, Mum, she adds, sing some American songs, which Margrét does, she obeys, distractedly, prepares supper and sings verses she learned in Canada and has sung countless times to the children, and is still singing them when the door opens and they come in, father and son, Oddur had landed first but waited for his son, who enters to the sounds of his mother singing, tired, exhausted, but straight-backed, proud, and Margrét immediately stops singing, as if her voice had been cut in two, she looks at the two men standing there side by side, Oddur with clenched fists, just as long ago, to restrain himself, so that his pride isn't too obvious, Þórður stands straight as an arrow, not entirely the same person who'd left the house that morning, looks at his mother, who has to call on all her self-discipline and such a tremendous amount of strength not to cry out and run to Þórður, to hug and kiss him, that it almost hurts. Gunnar stands at the kitchen table, with his injuries from the day's battles, looking open-mouthed at his brother, so clearly filled with admiration that Hulda bursts out laughing, and then Margrét smiles and says, My men must be hungry. She looks at Oddur and their eyes meet, and their eyes want to meet.

So we do have our moments. In spite of everything.

# Keflavík

— PRESENT —

## Little America; the past in a live broadcast

December, it's winter, raining or snowing, nowhere has the sky been measured to be more distant from the earth than here, too far for the flight of angels, and the tourists who flock to Iceland all pass over the town on their way to or from Leifur Eiríksson Air Terminal, it doesn't occur to any of them to come here, they all give it a miss, it's as if Keflavík doesn't exist. Ari and I still remember the day the air terminal was opened, in the late '80s; the event was broadcast live on T.V., and we sat glued to the screen on the top floor of a four-storey house in Bergstaðastræti, bursting with pride. That this little nation could build such a splendid airport in place of the old one, which was located deep within the American military zone, in a dilapidated old building that looked like a worn-out, grimacing nag behind a fence displaying American insignia, like some sort of proof that we were too small to stand on our own two feet and couldn't even go abroad without driving through American power, American money. Before the days of Leifur Eiríksson Air Terminal, America was the first thing that foreign visitors saw after coming to this country, as if Iceland were a sort of "little America", a colony of the United States. It didn't do much for our pride, our self-esteem; it was already difficult enough to think of foreign visitors having to land on Miðnesheiði on a wasteland, surrounded by lava that sometimes resembles the

Devil's thoughts; as if Iceland were in fact little more than the American military base, jagged lava, inhospitable heaths and Keflavík, the blackest place, the wind's spoils. It wounded our national pride, which is why it was so wonderful to have this splendid air terminal, towering red and cement-grey over its surroundings like a stately assertion of Iceland's independence, as beautiful as a poem by Jónas Hallgrímsson,[18] with giant photos of the Icelandic landscape on its walls: waterfalls, mountains, hot springs, horses grazing on windless, sunny grass and beautiful girls in wool sweaters, with flowing blond hair. The photographs showed that Iceland is not Miðnesheiði or Keflavík, not at all, far from it, which is why it was important that the road from the airport lay well above the town, whose quota-less life depended on the Base. But then the military left; what can be said about Keflavík now, what words should we use – what can you possibly call a town that has lost everything?

Ari and I watched the official opening of Leifur Eiríksson Air Terminal.

Which was broadcast live. Ómar Ragnarsson hovered over-head in his Cessna,[19] giving us a view of the building from the air, from the perspective of gods and tourists. Hey, I said, look, there are Drangey's drying racks, and I pointed them out, a few kilometres from the terminal, and it wasn't bad at all that the racks on which we'd hung so many tons of fish, in all sorts of weather, during the toughest, most capricious winter months, dismantling them in the summer when the heath revealed its delicate gems,

18 Jónas Hallgrímsson (1807–1845), one of Iceland's most loved poets, is considered one of the founding fathers of Icelandic Romanticism.
19 Ómar Ragnarsson (b. 1940) is a popular Icelandic media personality and environmental activist.

secretly, timidly, hesitantly, as if afraid of being mocked; it wasn't bad, even if a bit strange, that our dull and isolated daily life was suddenly being shown on the T.V. screen, and in a live broadcast that the entire nation was watching! Our past, broadcast live! A distant past; something that we thought was entirely gone from our lives and would never return, but on the old desk next to the worn-out television lay a nearly complete manuscript of Ari's first book of poetry, with lines that were supposed to matter, supposed to illuminate the world:

> Dawnlight condenses to sunshine;
> Then ends up here / in this filthy hotel / the toilet paper expired;
> The day isn't ours, and she, she's so far away.

We were both convinced that the book's publication would shake society up, that it would be a big event; brothers and sisters, take note, words that will change the world are on their way! But these words turned out to change nothing, except our lives, of course. We had five hundred copies printed, which was supposed to be the first edition, expecting that we would need to reprint quickly, waited for phone calls from reporters, but the only tangible response was a call from Elín, Ari's paternal aunt, Ásmundur's mother, whom Ari hadn't seen for years. She rang early one morning, before 8.00 a.m., very enthusiastic, just having read the press release about the book's publication, and said that she wanted to order six copies. She chatted for a while with Ari, cheerful and sweet as ever, but suddenly burst into tears in the middle of the conversation, after mentioning her mother, Margrét, saying how much it would have pleased her to see one of her grandchildren publish a book of poetry; Margrét's brother Tryggvi would have been no less pleased, said Elín, let alone Þórður – and it was then that her voice cracked, when she spoke her brother's name. She stopped, and Ari thought he heard her sobbing. He thought, terrified, Dear God, she's crying, and his palm holding the receiver began to sweat. But it didn't last long, just a few difficult moments, and then she cleared her throat, twice, laughed gently, said something about how you become so oddly maudlin with age, unable to tolerate anything, Like a little bird, she said, just like a wren, and then laughed again, before adding that Jakob certainly had been tight-lipped about this news, that the family could claim another poet! No, thought Ari, feeling downright ill, his palm so sweaty that the receiver began slipping, of course his father hadn't told anyone about the publication of the poems – because he knew nothing about it.

Five hundred copies for the first edition, and we expected to have to print many more. A month later, we still had 452 copies; hardly any sold in bookshops, and we were absolutely useless at selling any ourselves. Poetry can undoubtedly save the world, but there are so few people who read it, in fact fewer and fewer with each passing year; a tribe in danger of extinction. It would be safer to protect them officially, put people who read poetry on UNESCO's World Heritage list.

But the day isn't ours, and she, she's so far away: the book didn't bloody sell at all. There was no need for a reprint – just a huge need for money to cover the printing costs, which is why Ari and I headed south, turned back, got jobs at Drangey and ended up, as you might recall, dismantling the drying racks. The same ones that the television presenter in charge of the live broadcast from the opening of Leifur Eiríksson Air Terminal spotted in Ómar Ragnarsson's aerial shots. I see drying racks there, he said, Yes, shouted Ómar, those are indeed drying racks, before breaking unexpectedly into song:

> Of sailing the seas the Suðurnes men seemed
> never to get their fill –
> and they eagerly sail them still![20]

Yes, ha ha, laughed the presenter, they're real sailors, that's for sure, but . . . Keflavík is like our Beatles' town, interjected Ómar, hyper from all the flying, the live broadcast, the celebratory mood, the thousands of people inside the terminal – it was jam-packed, and 70 per cent of the nation was gathered in front of their televisions. The presenter asked, "What's that?" – this was too abrupt a leap for him, from the fish racks to the Beatles. Beatles' town? Yes, shouted Ómar, on the verge of hysteria in his enthusiasm for this giant day, Rúnni Júll and Gunni Þórðar both grew up in Keflavík, for the most part, drinking in rock 'n' roll and the Beatles from American radio, man alive! And then Ómar burst into song once more, always pitch-perfect:

> So deep and clear
> your blue eyes shine
> two stars to light
> this path of mine.[21]

20  Lines 7–8 of the song "*Suðurnesjamenn*" ("The Men of Suðurnes"); melody by the Icelandic composer Sigvaldi Kaldalóns (1881–1946), text by the poet Ólína Andrésdóttir (1858–1935).
21  From Hljómar's song "Your Blue Eyes" (Icelandic: "*Bláu augun þín*"); music by Gunnar Þórðarson, lyrics by Ólafur Gaukur Þórhallsson (1930–2011).

Do you remember, I asked Ari, when Ómar mentioned, or rather shouted, Rúnni Júll and Gunni Þórðar's names; do you remember that morning in January 1976?!

Ari: Some things can't be forgotten.

I: Whatever happened to Ásmundur, anyway? I've heard almost nothing about him since he drove so memorably into the yard.

He went east, said Ari, raising a hand to silence me, then leaning forwards to hear the television better – east to Norðfjörður, joined a fishing boat, naturally wanted to take up his old grandfather's banner; but shhh, he said, because the presenter had started talking about the racks again, after managing to silence the overexcited Ómar, flying his Cessna above the air terminal, one hand on the stick, filming with the other, singing "Your Blue Eyes" by Gunnar Þórðarson, Keflavík's response to "Here, There and Everywhere"; Sigrún's right eye. We ran into her by the biscuits in the Co-op in Búðardalur, her left eye composed by Lennon, "If I Fell"; where were those eyes looking while Kári bounced up and down on her, baring his teeth in his frenzy, his white buttocks winking at Ari and me above the seat backs; where were they looking then?

Ari raised his hand to silence me, silence our memories, the questions about where her eyes were looking while Kári panted on top of her, she who isn't here, who'll never be here, we had to learn to live without her, which wasn't easy, and for the longest time we felt like birds who no longer feel the air, stars that have no sky to shine in. Shhh, said Ari, raising his hand, because the presenter had started talking about the racks again, saying that perhaps they weren't what one might call a source of pride, as near as they were to the magnificent new airport, and undeniably clashing with its terminal. Bloody hell, said Ari, did you hear that, our past clashes with elegant modernity; what should we do with it then, where should we put it? We probably have to forget it, I replied, as the scene on the television screen switched from Ómar's aerial shots to the terminal's interior, and to a reporter who stood trembling with joy and champagne in the throng. "This airport," he said, choosing his words carefully, staring resolutely into the camera, as if making a critical statement, "this airport is as modern as any other airport in the world. It is proof that we are a nation among nations, a modern nation, proof that we think big, and that the world of turf farmhouses is behind us, far, far behind us, that the cramped world inside those hovels belongs to the remote past. This airport is proof that we think big, probably bigger than most other nations, once we're given a real chance to show it and prove it to the whole world. Who has a fairer fatherland?"[22] concluded the reporter, inspired by his own speech, gazing deep into the camera, almost as if he wanted to see into the future, into the time when we were finally given an opportunity to show the world our true greatness; he gazed into the future, yet didn't see Ari and me in the month of December, walking down Hafnargata in sleet and a freezing wind.

We walk past the January 1976 bar, from which two middle-aged women emerge, lighting cigarettes before the door shuts behind them, shuts on Rod Stewart singing "Maggie May" inside. It's evening and we're a bit tipsy from the red wine and whisky we drank at the hotel, and we walk down Hafnargata, which is far

22 "Who has a fairer fatherland" (Icelandic: *"Hver á sér fegra föðurland"*): The title and first line of a patriotic poem by the Icelandic writer Hulda (Unnur Benediktsdóttir Bjarklind, 1881–1946), written on the occasion of the founding of the Icelandic Republic in 1944.

tidier now than in the past, when we first walked down it with Ásmundur; Mayor Sigurjón has done a good job of cleaning things up. We walk down Hafnargata, the sleet turns to snow, the sea is on our right, the evening is dark, like a quiet giant, it would be fun to go down to the shore and throw stones, listen to the waves die on the sand, but the residents of Keflavík can no longer go down to the sea, not to have fun, not without risk, the long shoreline was filled long ago with huge stones from Helguvík, two-hundred-thousand-year-old boulders; one or two people have tried to clamber over these giant rocks, wanting to reach the sea, let it calm them, fill them with peace, but broke their legs on the slippery rocks, their feet having slipped into a gap. Hundreds of tons separate the residents of Keflavík from the sea. Perhaps to emphasise that they no longer have any business with the sea, that the sea has been taken from them and they'd be better off accepting that fact, cutting the connections.

Ari and I listen to the sea, listen to the snowflakes falling, and speak in low voices about the American, the former military policeman, whom we noticed on our way out of the hotel. His wife was asleep and he was lonely, wanted to talk to someone, I've always felt lonely in this country, he said to the giant waiter; what the fuck, it's like fucking solitude is manufactured here, like it's spouted out in those volcanic eruptions of yours and poured over the whole world. Loneliness, he repeated, before stopping for a few seconds, as if lost in thought, and then starting up again with stories about the military, shifting from one foot to the other, as if to maintain his balance in this incomprehensible world. Ari and I managed to slip past them unseen, by a hair, fearing that the Yank would assail us with endless stories about the military, soldiering, saying "fucking" after every second word, we made it to the lobby door but hesitated for a second in the face of the dark night, which the sleet made almost hostile-looking. We hesitated, looked around, as if to find something that would give us the strength to step out into the darkness and sleet, and saw the photograph of the terminal. A recent photo, hanging in the place of honour in the lobby, taken when the sun was shining, beneath it an inscription in Icelandic, English and German, a detailed description of the terminal's grand opening and the importance of the airport. It quoted Hulda's line, "Who has a fairer fatherland?", and the reporter's statement about our greatness and ambition. Immediately following Hulda's line, there was detailed information about how much it cost to build Leifur Eiríksson Air Terminal and a statement that the Americans had footed a substantial portion of the bill, with the provision that they be allowed to take over the airport during "high-risk situations". "Might we therefore ask," concluded the inscription, Ari and I having realised that the text was likely written by the hotel manager herself, Sigga, "whether the Icelanders' image of themselves is, on closer inspection, based on illusion, and on our ability to forget what we prefer not to remember?"

Did you know this about the airport? I ask. No, says Ari, we've come as far as Duushús, in one of the oldest parts of Keflavík, between us and the sea are two-hundred-thousand-year-old rocks, boulders blasted from the cliffs of Helguvík when the American military built a harbour there for oil tankers. The wind blows over and around us, from the sea, from out in the darkness. The cliff of Bergið, which towers over the marina and extends far out into the sea, is illuminated by powerful floodlights, lit up

353

before our eyes, as if it's getting ready to depart, is ready to take flight, as if even Bergið, that ancient cliff, in some places a sheer precipice, wants to abandon Keflavík, the town without a fishing quota, the town without a military, where few things drift ashore but unemployment, shredded old fishing nets, memories of the Base, vanished income and two Norwegians who resemble long knives. No, he says, I didn't know, but should that come as a surprise, or isn't one of humanity's greatest misfortunes that it's quicker to forget than remember, undoubtedly because it's more convenient, life becomes less dramatic, daily life simpler and easier? This is why we suppress so much within us, set it aside, let the passing days bury it, relegate it to oblivion.

I: As you did?

Ari: As I did.

This is why we're standing here, looking out over the two-hundred-thousand-year-old boulders that the American military blasted out of the cliffs of Helguvík and that were later deposited between Keflavík and the sea, as if to emphasise that this town was no longer on the coast, that there were at least two hundred thousand years between it and the sea, we look at the cliff bathed in light, it's on its way to the sky, or some other place, for that matter, because it isn't allowed to repose in the darkness, because it's been sent off the playing field; from now on, nothing will happen here, and in fact nothing has happened here for decades, employment moved elsewhere, it wasn't possible to make big enough profits here, that's how human life is measured, by profits, not heartbeats, economic interests, not happiness, yet we're surprised at our unhappiness, stress, uncertainty. Is there someone out there who can bring us to our senses?

Here we stand, a little tipsy after the whisky at the hotel run by Sigga, she whom we first met on a January morning in 1976, and then worked with at Drangey for a few weeks in winter, when Ari needed to pay for the printing of his book of poetry, when we dismantled the racks with Þorlákur, who's shaking his fists in the window of the Suðurnes Estate Agency. Ari wrote a poem about Sigga's breasts, which are small, like Sigrún's, the vague melancholy at the corners of Sigrún's mouth was at least two hundred thousand years old, she joined Kári on the backseat of his Lada – which we considered the darkest night of our lives. We knew nothing, absolutely nothing, because later it turned out that the darkness was elsewhere, and there it was enormously heavy, heavier than the boulders separating Keflavík from the sea. Which is why we're standing here. Because Ari had forgotten, had let it happen, set aside what he didn't want to remember, didn't want to face; he let the passing days bury it, and lived that way until everything broke, until his arm swept across the kitchen table like a scream.

And: "From now on I can love other men than you."

Some lines of poetry are much heavier than ancient boulders, lying with unbearable weight on top of us, and the only way to lift them is to remember, look yourself in the eye, don't look away. Drag all that's lost and forgotten up from the depths. Remember Norðfjörður; remember Margrét and Oddur, when he clenched his fists, which were his love poem, and when, shortly afterwards, she took off her dress and the mountains were hymns sung to the sky. Haul every story up to the surface, about the Eastfjords and Keflavík, no matter how ugly, because if we don't dare to remember, to face things, if we hesitate in the face of what hurts, injures, humiliates, we're finished. Or rather, we never manage to become the people we were born to be. We become distortions. Shallower than we could have become. We betray.

So, where do we begin, I say, stamping my feet to try to keep warm; the wind blows in from the sea, blows through Keflavík, it can be hard to remember that in Iceland, the wind scatters all thoughts and sometimes blows too freezing cold for you to think deeply, all your energy goes into keeping warm, and perhaps into writing a verse of a poem, perhaps into telling a story. I've already begun, says Ari. I thought I'd begun in Copenhagen when I received the photograph from Dad, of him and Mum, but then I realised that that was no real beginning; because this didn't really begin until I was on my way out of the terminal. It was as if I needed to undress, bend naked over the lectern from the elementary school and feel Ásmundur's finger inside me, like a rebuke – it was only then that I began to remember. It was only then that I dared to remember. I'm going to visit Dad tomorrow, and I don't know how it will go. We've never been able to talk to each other; it's as if the language never had the right words for the two of us. I can quote lines from Shakespeare, describe distant galaxies, the trajectories of comets – but I can't talk to my dad. Not about essential things. We should probably have tried to learn an exotic language, Chinese or Swahili, some language that definitely wouldn't have held any of our common memories, in which words like *love*, *longing* and *betrayal* wouldn't be heavy enough to paralyse both of us, or make us irritated with each other, or force us to start talking about harmless topics within which you can hide: politics, football, the weather. First, I'm going to my hotel room to read the letter that my stepmother sent to me in Copenhagen – I mean, read it seriously, not glance over it as I did before, probably in order not to have to deal with the contents – and to read Sigga's article, which for some reason was enclosed with the letter. I knew immediately that the letter contained something unpleasant, that something difficult was awaiting me, which is why I pushed it away, intending, of course, to let the days bury it – but then I was forced to bend over the lectern.

Your stepmother, I say; I've always wanted to . . .

Ari: She came into my life through death.

*What sort of work do you do?*
*Well, I regret.*

The day is done. It began at a speed of more than a hundred kilometres per hour through the lava field surrounding Reykjanesbraut Highway, and ends in a hotel room in Keflavík. It's snowing. A white message sent from Heaven to us here in the blackest place, but the wind sweeps it aside and tears it to pieces as if to prevent us from reading what Heaven wants to say to us. Ari stands at the window of his hotel room and this evening will soon become night. He looks out but sees nothing apart from the snowflakes at the mercy of the wind, sees nothing but a jumbled message. The roundabout below is gone, as is the building opposite, which once housed Glóðin with its lamb and caramelised potatoes, chicken and chips, the photograph of the astronauts; what became of it, we wonder, and how far out into space did they manage to go, did they manage to get closer to the stars than we to our dreams, did they see something that might resemble God, something that could possibly comfort us, did they discover that the Northern Lights are music, a church organ of the sky? It's December, and is snowing so hard that even the Christmas lights are gone, despite being so plentiful in this town, countless, multicoloured and vivid, some blinking vigorously, as if with great impatience.

When he returned to his room, he found a smiley face made out of nine varicoloured sweets awaiting him. Someone had taken his luggage off the bed, put it on the luggage rack, smoothed the covers and arranged the nine sweets in the middle of the bed, transforming them into a grinning emoticon. Someone – maybe the hotel manager herself, Sigga? Ari was tickled no end; few things in this world are as precious, as important, as a smile. Even so, Brezhnev and Jimmy Carter didn't have smiles on their list of topics to discuss in the winter of 1980, when Tito's heart drew nearer to its final beat, drew nearer to the great silence, yet everyone was certain that they would be discussing the most crucial issues facing the inhabitants of this planet.

Ari sits down at the small desk, opens his laptop, intending to have a look at the BBC's website, check the world news, escape there, but sees that several unread e-mails are waiting for him. The only one that matters is from his eldest daughter, Hekla, sent half an hour ago, and Ari's heart beats faster, tears well up in his eyes, of longing, happiness, sorrow: "Dear old Dad! Are you coming home for Christmas?! Sturla is determined to remain in Spain, says he wants to experience Christmas away from Iceland. He thinks it'll help him grow up. He'll be crazy with homesickness on Christmas Eve! Aw, it would be much nicer if that idiot came home! But I'll be with Gréta and Mum. Have you and Mum spoken? It would be a whole lot nicer if you'd stop this nonsense and get back together – I'm not allowed to talk to Mum about it; it just makes her grouchy. Then Gréta starts crying. You two are unbelievable! How are you, Dad? Aren't you definitely coming home for Christmas?

You can stay with me, you can even sleep in my bed, I can sleep on the sofa. Your bones are far too old for you to sleep on the sofa (ha ha)! Write back, Jack – don't give me no slack! Here's a little song for you, Alabama Shakes, 'Always Alright' No-one can feel bad listening to it. We've gotta get dancing! Kisses!"

He listens to the song, listens with a smile, to the power, the exuberance, it reminds him of Hekla. He longs desperately to ring her, hear her voice bright with underlying joy, her refreshing voice, but first he has to read a letter, and he has to read an article. He puts his reading glasses back on, intending to start with the article, but then his phone, lying on the table, vibrates; it's a text message from his seatmates on the plane, Helena and Adam, a few words along with a photo of the two of them in Austurvöllur Square, both of them smiling widely: "Hi, we're here at the place where the Icelandic nation finally had enough of incompetent politicians and corruption and overthrew its useless government by beating pots and pans, brilliant! Europe saw you as the standard-bearers of a new and better time! We really like this charming little capital of yours. We had a wonderful dinner at a wonderful restaurant and drank fantastic amounts of excellent wine. We're drunk and we're going back to our hotel room where I'm going to make love with my big, beautiful man. Remember to be grateful for your tears, Icelander!"

Ari sees a sliver of the parliament building behind the couple. They'd probably posed in front of the statue of Jón Sigurðsson. Poor Jón Sigurðsson, forced to look day and night at the Icelandic parliament building; we've treated the hero of our independence badly – and what's more, he's wearing such a serious expression,

359

his hands tucked under his lapels, as if he's about to rummage in his jacket pocket for an egg to throw at the building, prepared to pull an egg out of his pocket if the President of Iceland happens to walk by. What can be done with this nation, which, in such a short time, became a role model, a hero of Europe, yet turned out, as so often in the past, to be a champion sprinter but a total failure at marathons?

Ari presses the middle button on his phone once more to access the list of text messages. At the top is Helena's foreign phone number, then "Hi, here we are . . .," but below that are Þóra's name and phone number, along with her profile photo, smiling at Ari, taken in the days when his presence brought a smile to her lips – and he threw it all away. Champion sprinter, lacking stamina? "Your father told me that . . ." She'd entered these words at 15.47, a little under nine hours ago, at a distance of only 50 kilometres. Her fingers, hands, shoulders, neck, dark hair, the tone of her voice, her grey-blue eyes. How she smiled at him sometimes!

Be grateful for your tears, Icelander.

He wipes his eyes. What shall we say; that it all started with death? When death walked down the long corridor of the hospital at Vífilsstaðir, lifted her gently with its big hands, its bones made of moonlight, and carried her away, carefully, in order not to cut itself, carefully so that she would be less frightened. Deprived her of her life, her hope for happiness, the songs that she dreamed of singing, the poems that she was going to write, the cities that she wanted to visit, lifted her gently. Took life from her and liberated her from the unbearable pain. We die when the pain has become greater than life itself.

Ari looks at the photograph of Þóra, taken at the time when

she looked at him as if he were something priceless. "If I let down my hair, then you'll know that I'm naked beneath my dress." Why isn't it enough to be loved, what more do we really need, why doesn't it heal our wounds, or at least make them treatable, how can we destroy what's most important, you'll know that I'm naked beneath my dress, the mountains were hymns sung to the sky – why does the light that shines at such magical moments fade? Aren't we strong enough, steadfast enough; are we too prone to choosing simple paths, short-term solutions – ten tips? There she's smiling. There she's pulling faces. Why does she have to be so beautiful? God help us, how beautiful she is! Yet the human body is just elements, mostly water. Approximately 18.5 per cent of our body weight is, for example, carbon; nitrogen approximately 3.9 per cent. Þóra normally weighs about 65 kilograms, which means slightly more than 2 kilograms of nitrogen. Does Ari love slightly more than 2 kilograms of nitrogen?

He loves her. And misses her! He's missed her endlessly since waking for the first time in the flat he rented two weeks after his trip to Hólmavík. Until then, he'd spent his nights on the sofa at the publishing company, buried himself in work, took pains never to stop, sped onwards, moved into the furnished flat, where he fell asleep exhausted, awoke twelve hours later to the sound of bitter weeping, and it took him several moments to realise that the weeping was his own. Since then he'd felt almost nothing but regret, as if reality had stopped there, was spinning its wheels there. He regretted, as if it were a full-time job.

What sort of work do you do?

Well, I regret.

She refused to speak to him, didn't respond to his messages, stuck to the vow she'd made in the e-mail she'd sent him during his stay at Hotel Hólmavík: 'From now on, you can expect nothing but coldness from me. That will be my revenge."

Weeks passed. Slowly. So slowly that it was as if time itself were dying. Finally, there came a glitter of hope. One of Þóra's favourite works was going to be performed at the Harpa concert hall: Mahler's Ninth Symphony; she would undoubtedly attend. Then Ari could see her, and who knew?, maybe something would happen, because music is so extraordinary that it can change lives, change fists into bouquets of flowers, bitterness into understanding. He bought a pair of opera glasses, reserved a seat in a side balcony, knowing that she would select a seat in the middle of the hall; he planned to watch her the entire time, watch as the music made her face even more beautiful. He arrived early. Sat down on the soft seat and kept his eye on the row where he was convinced that she would sit, his hands trembling so much to start with that he could hardly look through his opera glasses. Then she arrived – and took her seat precisely where he'd guessed she would! There was such a short distance between them. Hardly anything could cut that cord, neither life nor death, certainly not a stupid commotion at the breakfast table. He could hardly wait to see her during the intermission. See her smile light up her face, fairer than any music. He would kiss her hair, smell its perfume, sense her warmth and whisper, Forgive me, please forgive me, I can be so stupid, and she would rub one of his ears between her fingers and say, with a half-concealed smile, You're so silly.

He had to take the opera glasses away from his eyes and dry his tears. Taking a deep breath, he raised the glasses to his eyes again and saw that a man was speaking to her. The person sitting next to her. Might they have come together? The man had rather long, well-kept hair, and a dark, full but slightly scruffy beard. He was slim, dressed in a casual suit. An artist. Or something along those lines. Probably a contact from her job at the Art College. They were laughing. Then the concert began, that great symphony, which begins as if hope itself has descended to earth. Ari could barely take the glasses away from his eyes. The bearded man leaned towards her twice before the interval, said something that made her smile. His lips close to her ear, even touching it. He's probably a foreign lecturer, thought Ari, to whom she has to display professional courtesy.

Ari didn't go to her during the interval but watched them from behind a column, like a thief. The bearded man was dressed impeccably, held himself well, his shoes bang on trend – Not her type at all, thought Ari, feeling relieved. Thankful. Immensely lighter. Then it happened. They were standing close together, far too close, conversing, when the man lifted his right arm slightly, shifted to place the palm of his hand in the small of her back – oh, so elegant in the green dress that she and Ari had chosen together in Italy two years ago – before resting it there. Without excuse, hesitation or prudence but rather out of the nonchalance that came from knowing that it was permitted to do so. Rested there. She raised her face slightly, smiling gently. Then the palm moved lower, moved even lower, before it ran quite firmly over her backside. Over her ass.

After the interval, Ari was unable to make any connection with the music.

He sat in his seat, sweating with hatred, despair and astonishment in turn.

There was nothing Þóra hated more than having her backside caressed in public; such a thing made it seem as if a woman were a mare whom a man might stroke or pat at will, for all to see. She would have been furious if Ari had done the same thing a few months earlier; in any case, to do so would never have crossed his mind. But the bearded man in the stylish shoes fondled her ass as if nothing were more natural; and she smiled at him. Ari just sat there, and the line of Polish poetry, shaped like a saw, filled his consciousness, and sawed apart life's meaning: "From now on, I can love other men than you."

Three weeks later he was on a plane to Copenhagen.

Three weeks in Hell. At work, he managed to keep his thoughts fairly well in check, only to have them assault him even more frenziedly when he lay down to sleep, the image of the man's palm on her ass, on her green dress; what did they do later that night? Did Þóra allow him to accompany her home, into her house; into the bed where she and Ari had slept together all those years, had held each other, had woken together; and what did they do there??? She whom Ari thought he knew so well, better than anyone else, down to her very cells, but who then allows this man to caress her ass in a crowd, in plain sight; how, then, must she be in bed with him? What do they do? Does she turn into a completely different person than she was with Ari? Were there sides to her that Ari never knew, had never encountered, that were never given free play until after their separation? He tossed and turned in bed. He shouted into his pillow, shouted to erase the images in his head, the two of them in bed, the two of them doing – he shouted his lungs out. Sometimes polished off half a bottle of whisky just to be able to sleep. As if he were twenty-five years old again, composing late-night poetry, listening to Tom Waits, "It takes a whole lot of whisky to make these nightmares go away." To cut to the chase: he fled to Copenhagen. Has been unable to tolerate Mahler ever since.

The letter from Ari's stepmother is dated 2 October, just over two months ago, and Ari still hasn't read it. He started to but then set it aside, though he can't remember why; maybe the phone rang, maybe an idea hit him that he had to develop straightaway, and then forgot to continue reading it. Dated 2 October, a fairly long letter. Neatly written, as might have been expected, but at the same time a bit clumsily, in the handwriting of someone unaccustomed to writing; the stepmother had never really been one for writing. Enclosed with the letter was the article by Sigga, the hotel manager who arranged colourful sweets into a smiley face, who once said, The fuck if I'm missing out on this, before jumping onto a moving lorry on a January morning thirty-seven years ago, but who then tried, just fifteen years old, to wade into the sea, drown, die, end her life, and would have managed to do it if the stepmother hadn't been standing by a wall nearby, taking a cigarette break as a momentary escape from the knives of life, its disappointments, difficulties. A note is attached to the article with a paper clip, a piece of yellow, ruled paper, carefully cut, and on which the step-mother had written, or rather, scribbled, not having taken as much care with it as the letter, as if she'd been in a hurry, the post office in Sandgerði – where she lived in her final years – perhaps about to close, it's only open until 4.00 p.m., sometimes 3.00 if the clerk has to go to the hairdresser's, pick up her child from primary school or has made plans to meet her husband at home before the children return from school, share a moment of passion in the midst of daily life – we should try to make life stretch as much as we can. The yellow note, or paper trimmed down to make a note, is still attached to the unread article, lines scribbled in haste, on both sides: "Do you remember Sigga, who once tried to drown herself? I'm sure you remember it. I certainly can't forget it! I was a bit shocked, because at the same time, her stepfather was dying. It was that damned cancer, and he was suffering horribly. The next day, when Sigga showed up at work acting as if nothing had happened, someone asked her what the big idea was of killing herself, so young. I think it was Rósa who asked, that chatterbox Rósa, who could never stand Sigga. Was it because of a boy, maybe? she asked. I remember her asking this as a gibe, or at least not very nicely, which I found rather awful, because no-one tries killing herself just for fun, there must be something serious behind it, even some-one so young, and it's awful to belittle such a thing. Could have been, replied Sigga, rather curtly, putting on airs. A lot of people found it a rather cold and selfish gesture, attempting to kill herself because of a boy when her father – or the man who may as well have been her father, having raised her since she was two – was at death's door, suffering horribly, and everyone suffering along with him. But what do we know? In any case, I thought I'd send you this article, because you knew Sigga quite well for a time."

The article, "The Male World", is long, an entire spread, with a photograph of a large group of women. "The Male World", with the subtitle "Those who have the power can take". Take what?, thinks Ari, as he begins to read the article, before finding a reply in its fifth line, where it's specified that the verb *to take* in this context means: take a woman, abuse her, rape her. A rational, dense, aggressive, striking article about men's power over women, about the power that a man assumes, the attitude that seems to be innate to him, that is rooted in history, lurks in language, in pop songs, films, the media and now video games. We see it everywhere we look, writes Sigga, we stumble across it, run into it continually, in things big and small. "Language is masculine and constantly opposes itself to women, often without us noticing, tries to subdue her, keep a tight rein on her. If a woman displays great determination and resolution, she's called pushy. If a man displays determination and resolution, he's called strong, persistent. Language has many epithets for a woman when she strives to break loose from her shackles, from the role relegated to her by male authority. A woman who has strong ambition in the workplace is often accused of being cold towards her children, of having weak maternal instincts, whereas if a man gives top priority to his family instead of his job, he is considered womanly, a poor worker, a sissy."

A firebrand of an article. By its fifteenth line, Ari has almost started to hate men, yet the heaviest blow was yet to come: the violence, the brutality, the unforgivable. "This attitude, rooted in language, culture, the media, in pop songs, grants men a position of supremacy. A supremacy that is granted pretty much right from the start, because males are born holding almost all the trump cards. In addition, their certainty regarding this supremacy and, along with it, the image of the woman as a receiver, as compliant, results far too often in the madness, the violence and the unforgivable crime inherent in abuse and rape."

There are 365 women in the photo, as many as the days in a year. They have all been abused or raped, some of them more than once. "Abused by their fathers, relatives, friends, priests, raped at home, in clubs, in back yards, at festivals, in the back seat of a Lada estate car."

*

Ari's heart skips a beat.

Or it crashes.

And his reading glasses fog up. He takes them off, stands up, sits back down, grabs the article, scrutinises the photo of the women who number as many as the days of the year – reflecting the fact that every day, women are abused, raped, subjected to gross sexual harassment. Scrutinises the photo, but all the faces are blurred, rubs his eyes to try to sharpen the images and realises that he's not wearing his glasses. He puts them on again. All of the women in the photo look serious, not gloomy, sad but serious. Three hundred and sixty-five women, the youngest sixteen years old, the oldest ninety-two. They all have their own story to tell. "Unfortunately I don't have the space to tell all their stories here," writes Sigga, but she provides a link to a website created in conjunction with the article, 365.lif.is: "There you will find their stories, under their own names." Ari reaches for his laptop, opens it, finds the website, with pounding heart, fumbling fingers, laboured breathing. Sigrún is number 137. There's a photo of her, she's smiling, thirty-three years older. There she is. Ari recognises her immediately, despite the years. Her freckles are in their places. Her eyes are in their places. "If I Fell". "Here, There and Everywhere".

## It'll be O.K., baby

"It was the autumn of 1980. I was just a sixteen-year-old country girl who went to a dance. I'd been working in a slaughterhouse that autumn, the work was finished, it ended on a Wednesday and the dance was held that Saturday. On the first day of winter. I've often found this to be absurdly symbolic, because on that day, the summer of my life ended and the long winter began. How I looked forward to that dance! I had a bit of a crush on a guy I'd met at the slaughterhouse, and had the feeling that he liked me as well. He'd often given me such incredibly nice looks. I got my mother to do my hair, and my feet hardly touched the ground in anticipation. I don't remember much about the dance itself, however; I was just a kid and didn't know how to drink, lots of guys offered me drinks and I drank whatever they handed me. Which was a mistake. I do remember that I kept waiting for the guy I liked to come and ask me to dance, but he never did. He was probably too shy. I'd thought about dragging him onto the dance floor myself. Oh, how I longed to kiss him! But of course, mixing all those different drinks did me in. I vaguely remember leaning on one of the tables, struggling not to throw up. I noticed the guy I liked standing just off the dance floor and could only think that he absolutely mustn't see that I needed to vomit; I could never bear that – it would ruin everything! Then a man came over to me. He wasn't from the area but had relatives living there. He was in his thirties, married, with children. He'd worked near me in the slaughterhouse, but I'd never been interested in him, of course; he was too old for me. He teased me sometimes, and made the others laugh. I never found him funny and once complained about him to my mother. Told her that I didn't like how he teased me, saying that it sure would be fun to dance with me and that maybe I should marry him, and once he said, If sheep had as cute an ass as yours, it would be fun to be a farmer. My mother said that I shouldn't let it bother me, some men were just like that, always joking, which could be a lot of fun actually. In fact, she scolded me for being too uptight. Said that I was like some of my relatives on my father's side, too big for my britches. And that the man was a decent fellow, and a hard worker. I found him unbearable. But then he comes over to me as I'm standing there struggling, it was the first time I'd ever drunk so much and I felt so sick, besides being paralysed with stress, because everything would be ruined if the guy I liked saw me vomit. This man comes over to me and asks, "Are you feeling ill, dear?" It was as if he cared about me, asking in such a fatherly way, and I think I just nodded, and almost started bawling. He led me outside. I was so embarrassed that I kept my eyes lowered the whole time, but saw the guy I liked out of the corner of my eye and remember thinking, "When I feel better, I'm coming back inside and dragging him onto the dance floor!" Then I threw up by the man's car, which I remember was a yellow Lada estate. Puked my guts out. I remember the thought racing through my head that I'd better not get it on my shoes – just think, finally dancing with the guy you like, maybe even a slow dance, with puke on your shoes! The man was nice to me, rubbed my back, said that I was doing a good job, that it would be alright, and then he handed me a bottle, and I thought it was water and chugged it, but it turned out to be a mix of vodka and low-alcohol beer. I almost choked, but he laughed, rubbed my back some more and then started kissing me. I was petrified. He kissed me as if I belonged to him. Kissed me hard, and tried sticking his tongue in my mouth. I was still half dazed from vomiting, and from accidentally drinking that vodka drink of his. I was also grateful to him for having helped me and felt it would be rude to push him away immediately – nor did I want to appear snobby or cocky, as my mother had sometimes scolded me for being. In short, I was just a girl, hardly more than a kid, way too drunk and in shock. It all happened so quickly, but at the same time almost in slow motion.

I suddenly found myself in his back seat; he'd pulled off my knickers and I asked, like an idiot, "What are you going to do to me?" And he answered, rather short of breath, "It'll be O.K., baby." But it wasn't O.K. with me, and I asked him to stop, felt sick again and tried to get away, wriggle out from under him, but it just made him more aggressive and he held me down, so very much stronger than me, and then raped me. Afterwards, he asked, "Was that so bad?" and handed me the bottle again. Take a big swig, he said, patting me on the shoulder. I felt like I was somewhere beyond the world, looking at myself from the outside, saw that my thighs were bloody, while thinking, I hope that that guy didn't see us, because then he'll probably never want to dance with me. Then I saw myself taking the bottle and taking a big swig.

I went to the dance as a sixteen-year-old girl with a crush on a boy, dreaming of the slow dance, dreaming childish dreams, but sweet and beautiful in their own way, dreaming that we would move in together and later take over the farm from Dad and Mum. When I awoke the next day, without knowing how I got home but reeking of puke and having it on my shoes – for which I received a tongue-lashing – everything had changed. The girl who had gone to the dance the night before, dreaming of a boy, was dead; she'd been killed in the back seat of a car by a nearly forty-year-old man. I've often wondered how my life would have been if I hadn't been raped. Who I would have become. Sometimes I think, 'Will I ever again get to meet the girl I was, or is she really dead? Killed in the back seat of that fucking Lada?'"

*Dear God, how hard my little bird's heart*
*was beating!*

We'd run into her at the Co-op a little less than a week later, by the biscuits, when she'd looked away, as if she couldn't be bothered to look at us, who were nothing more than a clumsily composed pop song, number 387 on the hit parade at the end of the world.

Couldn't be bothered to look at us.

When do we tell what really happened, and what's the correct version of the world?

I became a different person, writes Sigrún on the website, before describing how her self-esteem crumbled. How she felt dirty, filthy, like a whore, that she was the one to blame, that it was her fault. For a few days, she lived in the hope that no-one knew about it, which would have made it easier to forget. "Then I ran into the guy I'd liked. It was in the Co-op. I saw him in one of the aisles and decided to head down it, towards him. Somehow, I felt that if he gave me one of those nice looks of his, everything would be fine again. Dear God, how hard my little bird's heart was beating as I drew closer! He definitely saw me coming but pretended to be busy looking at the biscuits, clearly not wanting to acknowledge me, and I thought, Oh God, he knows about it, knows how filthy I am! I looked away, looked down, hurried past and outside so that he wouldn't see me cry. I moved to Akranes just after Christmas, couldn't find peace at home, got a job at a freezing plant and was with so many men over the following years that I lost count and don't want to know. They were often older men. I just felt dirty. Word got around that I was easy and up for grabs by anyone, no matter what I said. Of course some of them abused me, did awful things to me. But I never tried to get help until after one weekend, when I spent two nights at a summer cottage with a man I called my boyfriend. He'd invited two of his friends along, and they seemed to regard me as some sort of object that could be used at will. When I drunkenly asked one of them to let me be, he answered, as if in surprise, that I'd been with so many men that it shouldn't make any bloody difference to me."

### Where were they looking?

The left eye composed by Lennon, the right by McCartney.

Ari is standing at the window of his hotel room, and it's snowing. The world outside is filled with messages sent from Heaven. Once we went to get our I.Q.'s tested, and Ari's result was 130. Not bad, we said, proudly, as if we'd been awarded medals, or certificates confirming that we weren't just any everyday, ordinary Tuesday, boring nobodies. It's easy to measure I.Q., which is probably why most things are evaluated according to it. Evaluated according to intelligence, marks; the obvious things. It's more difficult to measure what matters, what's more valuable: understanding, sensitivity, morality. An I.Q. of 130, but about a 12 in understanding. What use is intelligence if it isn't accompanied by understanding? We'd watched Kári get her into his Lada but understood nothing. Not until it was spelled out for us, more than thirty years later. Ari stands at the window but sees only his own reflection in the nearly black glass. Guilt can also gnaw at a person who hasn't done anything wrong. A person who doesn't understand anything.

Her eyes.

"Where were those eyes looking while Kári bounced up and down on top of her, baring his teeth in his frenzy?"

Where were they looking?

They weren't looking anywhere. They were fixed.

Or simply shedding tears.

*How heavenly it is to exist*

It's midnight, and Keflavík has vanished in swirling snow. I open my third beer with my and Ari's cousin-once-removed, as eighteen American fighter jets fly silently above us. This cousin is happy that I'm here, considerably happier than the cats lying on the floor, their yellow eyes fixed on me, staring as if trying to change me into a parakeet, making it easier to frighten me to death. Our cousin is drinking coffee, quite a lot of it, munching marble cake and telling me about his life, his years at the Base, with the Yanks, when everyone was prospering in Keflavík and capital rained down from above. A new collection of Hljómar's hits is spinning in the C.D. player, harmonious, energetic and poetic music: "Lie here with me / all is quiet / how heavenly it is to exist."[23] Occasionally our cousin stops what he's saying when an enchanting verse grabs him, spirits him away, carries him into the past, Where would we be without Hljómar, he sighs, before putting "Blissful Love" on again and continuing to recount the time when his family was still alive, when all those who have died were still alive and helped the earth to keep turning; he tells about Norðfjörður, the place that Ari and I barely know, yet that's in our blood, and perhaps it's Hljómar that makes him melancholy, gets him to say things that must have come from Margrét:

23 Lines from Hljómar's song "Bliss of Love" ("*Ástarsæla*"); music by Gunnar Þórðarson, lyrics by Þorsteinn Eggertsson (b. 1942).

Love, he says, is the galaxy that shines brightest and will never be destroyed! But most painful of all must be never to have loved enough, which I'm certain is unforgivable.

Hljómar sings, and our cousin is lost in his stories, loses his hold on himself, is so enthused, this tranquil man, that it's almost as if he's imagined calling those who are gone, dead, back to life, as if his words are a bridge between worlds, as if they're able to bring us the depths of the earth, the sky itself. As if they're able to bring us what we don't understand. I shove my fatigue aside, the longing to sleep, it's been a long day, feels like it's been more than a century, but what are our lives worth if no-one wants to hear about them?

Night. The cats are sleeping, everything is sleeping except my cousin and I, Hljómar, and Ari in his hotel room, having begun to read the letter from his stepmother – and tomorrow something will happen that's beyond our control.

My cousin is silent, his eyelids droop as he relishes the music, I mutter, "most painful of all must be never to have loved enough", and I look out of the living-room window but see nothing apart from the swirling snow. Keflavík is so utterly hidden that it's as if this black place never existed.

## A GUIDE TO THE PRONUNCIATION OF ICELANDIC CONSONANTS, VOWELS AND VOWEL COMBINATIONS

ð, like the voiced *th* in *mother*

þ, like the unvoiced *th* in *thin*

æ, like the *i* in *time*

á, like the *ow* in *town*

é, like the *ye* in *yes*

í, like the *ee* in *green*

ó, like the *o* in *tote*

ö, like the *u* in *but*

ú, like the *oo* in *loon*

ý, like the *ee* in *green*

ei and ey, like the *ay* in *fray*

au, no English equivalent; but a little like the *oay* sound in *sway*. Closer is the *œ* sound in the French *œil*

JÓN KALMAN STEFÁNSSON was born in Reykjavík in 1963. He is the 2011 winner of the P. O. Enquist Award and his novels have been nominated three times for the Nordic Council Prize for Literature. His novel *Summer Light, and then Comes the Night* received the Icelandic Prize for Literature. Spellbound Productions are making a film of his trilogy of novels, *Heaven and Hell* (2010), *The Sorrow of Angels* (2013) and *The Heart of Man* (2015).

PHILIP ROUGHTON is a scholar of Old Norse and medieval literature and an award-winning translator of modern Icelandic literature, having translated works by numerous Icelandic writers, including the Nobel prize-winning author Halldór Laxness. His translation of *The Islander*, a biography of Laxness by Halldór Guðmundsson, was published by MacLehose Press in 2008.

ALSO AVAILABLE

Jón Kalman Stefánsson

# HEAVEN AND HELL

*Translated from the Icelandic by Philip Roughton*

"A riveting novel . . . the action unfolds vividly and dramatically"

ALANNAH HOPKIN, *Irish Examiner*

*It's not possible to thread the tears together and then let them sink like a glittering rope down into the dark deep and pull up those who died but ought to have lived.*

In a remote part of Iceland, a young man joins a boat to fish for cod, but when a tragedy occurs at sea he is appalled by his fellow fishermen's cruel indifference. Lost and broken, he leaves the settlement in secret, his only purpose to return a book to a blind old sea captain beyond the mountains. Once in the town he finds that he is not alone in his solitude: welcomed into a warm circle of outcasts, he begins to see the world with new eyes.

*Heaven and Hell* – the first in a trilogy – navigates the depths of despair to celebrate the redemptive power of friendship. Set at the turn of the twentieth century, it is a reading experience as intense as the forces of the Icelandic landscape themselves.

"Jón Kalman Stefánsson is a wonderful, exceptional writer. Whenever I read him I remember what writing – and the deceptively simple business of living – are all about. He is a timeless storyteller"

CARSTEN JENSEN

MACLEHOSE PRESS
QUERCUS · LONDON

www.maclehosepress.com     *Subscribe to our newsletter*

ALSO AVAILABLE

Jón Kalman Stefánsson

# THE SORROW OF ANGELS

*Translated from the Icelandic by Philip Roughton*

"Recalls a Nordic version of one of Cormac McCarthy's journeys . . .
Devour this book with a hot drink in a warm room"

BOYD TONKIN, *Independent*

*The winter nights are dark and still, you can almost hear
the fish breathe on the sea bed. Snow falls so heavily
that it binds heaven and earth together.*

As the villagers gather in the inn to drink schnapps and coffee while
the boy reads to them, Jens the postman stumbles in half dead, having
almost frozen to his horse. On his next journey to the wide, open
fjords he is accompanied by the boy. Both will risk their lives for
each other, and for an unusual delivery.

*The Sorrow of Angels* – the second in the trilogy that began with
*Heaven and Hell* – tells the story of a tragicomic, epic journey; in
extraordinarily powerful language it brings the struggle between
man and nature vividly to life.

"Stefánson brilliantly conjures up the men's constant struggle against
the relentless wind and cold, capturing their shifting emotional and
physical states"     LUCY DALLAS, *Times Literary Supplement*

MACLEHOSE PRESS
QUERCUS · LONDON

www.maclehosepress.com     *Subscribe to our newsletter*

ALSO AVAILABLE

Jón Kalman Stefánsson

# THE HEART OF MAN

*Translated from the Icelandic by Philip Roughton*

"The trilogy overlays the colours of Dylan Thomas or Thomas Hardy onto spiritual scenery worthy of J. R. R. Tolkien"
                                   BOYD TONKIN, *Independent*

After coming through the blizzard that almost cost them everything, Jens and the boy are far from home, in a fishing community at the edge of the world.

Taken in by the village doctor, the boy once again has the sense of being brought back from the grave. But this is a strange place, with otherworldly inhabitants, including flame-haired Álfheiður, who makes him wonder whether it is possible to love two women at once; he had believed his heart was lost to Ragnheiður, the daughter of the wealthy merchant in the village to which he must now inexorably return.

Set in the awe-inspiring wilderness of the extreme north, *The Heart of Man* is a profound exploration of life, love and desire, written with a sublime simplicity. In this conclusion to his audacious trilogy, Stefánsson brings a poet's eye and a philosopher's insight to a tale worthy of the sagasmiths of old.

"Suspended between history and myth, this novel is peopled by uncanny characters roaming vast expanses. At heart this tale of tangled desire speaks lucidly of love, life and loss"          *Monocle*

MACLEHOSE PRESS
QUERCUS · LONDON

www.maclehosepress.com          *Subscribe to our newsletter*